The Mountain Town Series

Books 1 - 3

The Mountain Town Series

Books 1 - 3

Lesbian Spanking Romance

Leandra Summers

Design and Layout: Books by Bella
Cover Design: Debbie Boettcher
www.indiebookcovers.weebly.com

ISBN: 9798462719752

The author believes on the strength of due diligence exercised that this work does not contain any material that is the subject of copyright held by another person.

This book is best suited to lesbians who enjoy their romance with a handful of vanilla spankings and an underlying tone of domestic discipline

The Mountain Town Series

Book 1

'Emma and Melissa'

Lesbian Spanking Romance

By
Leandra Summers

PART 1

Dreaming of Wildflowers

CHAPTER 1

Emma stood looking out of the lounge window. It was the start of spring and still slightly chilly. The garden was beginning to show some splashes of color and it reminded her of the recurring dream she had been having the past few nights. The dream never varied.

In it Tess was saying, "See how beautiful the flowers are, babe." She and Tess were standing hip to hip looking out over a meadow filled with flowers. The bright green of the waving grass and deep colors of the wildflowers seemed almost unearthly. Emma would turn to Tess, certain to see the joy in her eyes at the flowers she so loved, but when she turned Tess was gone and only the faint scent of the perfume she used to wear lingered. She'd jerk awake with tears on her cheeks and a sense of impending change surrounding her.

Five years had passed since Tess had left her and although the pain had dulled into acceptance, it still cast a shadow in and over her. As Emma gazed out of the window she noticed the little yellow shoots pushing up out of the dark earth in the garden, and

1

she remembered Tess's desire to see wildflowers in their natural environment.

Tess had been a floral designer and had arranged the lavish bouquets used so frequently in her mother's fashion shows. People had often been surprised to learn that Tess was a florist. She had not fit the stereotypical image of a woman who worked with flowers. Her frame had been tall and muscular, her hair cut boyishly short and her figure had generally been clad in checked shirts and jeans. Emma had loved her individuality and the slightly butch manner that she exuded. She also appreciated that Tess had not been overwhelmed by Emma's family wealth as many of her previous lovers had been.

It had taken Emma's parents some time to accept Tess but when they saw how happy their daughter was, they welcomed her with open arms. They were overjoyed when Emma and Tess told them they planned to start a family.

Tess had suggested that they take an extended summer break to Switzerland or Austria for hiking before starting a family. She maintained that once they had a child their lifestyle would have to change and their child would need to be their first priority.

Within one month of their plan Tess had begun to feel an unusual tiredness and complained of pain in her lower back and legs. Numerous trips to specialists, physicians, surgeons and oncologists had taken over and once the diagnosis of advanced ovarian cancer had been made, the summer trip had become a once hoped for dream.

After Tess had died, Emma had thrown herself wholly into work much to the consternation of her friends and family. Although Emma and Tess had both worked for Emma's family business, Tess had always planned to set up her own florist shop. The 'wildflower trip' as they had called it, and starting a family were to be the precursors to their own hopefully successful business. After losing

Tess, Emma worked hard for five years, ignoring any outward show of pain, hugging to herself any feelings about losing her beloved Tess. At thirty- four she had felt too young to have lost her life's love and partner.

Emma had allowed herself to be ferried to and from work with her mother where she worked as the senior business manager for her parents' fashion design business. Her parents were proud of their daughter's business skills but had become concerned about how work consumed her. Left to her own devices, Emma would have turned up in jeans and a peasant style top covering her feminine figure and a pair of trainers or flat sandals. Whilst the look was pretty it did not fit with the image of the highly successful fashion business that her parents had started together. Her mother despaired of her fashion sense and made sure that as a representative of the company, Emma was impeccably turned out.

Seeing new life starting in the spring garden, Emma realized just how tired she felt. Her face was attractive, surrounded by wavy blonde hair but her green eyes that had sparkled like polished jade when Tess had been alive now looked dull. She looked at herself in the lounge mirror, aware of how fashionable she seemed with her tailored white pants, crisp blouse and high heeled, caramel colored boots that made her look taller than her 5'5". She had lost weight in the last five years, but retained her feminine figure with its curvy hips, which she used to despair of but which Tess had loved. Looking at her sophisticated reflection, she realized that although her blonde hair was sleekly shiny and her skin shone from all the pampering with her mother's insistence on spa days, she felt lifeless inside. Seeing the daffodils pushing their way up to new life out of dark earth in the garden somehow lifted her spirits. It was as if a voice was saying, it's time for a change.

That evening, Emma spoke to her parents. When she told them that she would be going to Switzerland for the summer they were taken aback at this sudden plan. They expressed concern at the idea, but at the same time felt a sense of relief that Emma had shown initiative and an interest in something other than work.

In part they were also concerned for her safety. Although Emma was an adult, she was their only child and since they had cocooned her with love when Tess had died, they were worried about her going away alone. Her father became slightly over protective and suggested that they accompany her or if not them, at least a friend. When Emma firmly refused, he then suggested that he organize a hiking guide so she could see the best that Switzerland had to offer. Looking at their anxious faces, she relented, thinking it would get them off her back. Besides, she thought, a paid guide would probably be only too happy to get time off once she got there.

That being agreed, her mother insisted on doing the hotel booking. Emma sighed, knowing that her mother would book one of the prestigious five star hotels. However, she reckoned, the lack of choice was a small price to pay to be able to follow her instinct without causing further concern for those who loved her.

The trip was booked for two months from mid-June to mid-August. It was peak season which meant lots of tourists. Her mother was pleased, stating that she felt happier knowing Emma would be safe among a lot of people.

"I don't think tourists would keep me safe. Mother, I need to be able to do something without you worrying. I know I have not been doing much other than working, but I need to try and move on," Emma said.

"Darling..." her mother started.

"Now, now," her father said, putting his arm around his wife, "she has to carry on her own life sometime." He smiled but Emma could see the worry in his eyes. She understood their concern for her and reminded them that she would have the guide her father would hire for company.

4

She spent some time researching the area she was going to. Seeing the pictures of the scenery, Emma cheered up. She needed to get out of the slump she had got herself into and say goodbye to Tess, she reasoned. She was thirty- nine years old and needed to move on.

Emma looked up the guide that her father had hired on the internet. There was no photo but a brief resume, headed with the words: Melissa Rustin, Senior Alpine Trekking Guide.

Her father entered the lounge and seeing Melissa's profile listed, started trotting out a long list of statistical data about the guide: Melissa Rustin, Australian, age 41, Alpine Trekking Guide. Height 5'8". Weight 65kg. When he started listing her educational qualifications and various previous jobs and experience, including a military background, Emma let the words flow over her head. She did not intend to use any of the guide's services.

The last few weeks seemed to fly past. Emma was not sure if this was because of the impending change or because she threw herself even deeper into work to ensure all business matters were up to date. The family chauffeur picked her up on the allotted travel day. Looking through the car window she waved goodbye to her parents. Her mother wiped a tear from her impeccably made-up face; her father stood up straight, his arm round his wife, and she felt an immense fondness for them. She loved them but felt suffocated. Emma was well aware that she had fostered this feeling by moving back into the family home and not remaining in the separate cottage that she and Tess had bought together. At the time she had found the memories of Tess in the cottage too painful.

She knew she needed a change and perhaps this holiday would be the start of a new phase of her life.

CHAPTER 2

Landing at Zurich airport Emma was met by the hotel limousine service. Noticing other travelers catching taxis, buses and trains, Emma wished she had thought to do the same. Her mood seemed to be lifting and she had a strange feeling that she was on the edge of a life changing experience.

The hotel her mother had booked was exquisite. It was built in the old wooden chalet style with quaint features and flower boxes hanging from the windows. The inside belied the charming, rustic exterior. It was modern and elegant. Emma could see the sign leading to the spa area. From the photos she remembered that it boasted warm and cold outdoor and indoor pools, along with its famous spa treatments and beauty regimens. She knew piped soft music would float through the massage and beauty rooms. It felt too familiar to Emma and she was determined to only use the pools for exercise. Her plan was to walk in the mountains and do the activities that she and Tess might have done together.

The hotel concierge informed her that she had one of the two suites on the top floor and that her hiking guide occupied the suite next door to hers. Chatting, oblivious to her coolness about the guide, he told her that Melissa Rustin had arrived the day before. She nodded politely, but refrained from commenting. She planned to let the guide know as soon as possible that she did not require her services and that she could enjoy a paid holiday and leave Emma to get on with hers.

A smartly clad porter loaded her cases and bags onto a trolley and led her up to the suite. The room and view were exquisite and the porter seemed to take personal pride when Emma gasped in delight. He told her he would send a maid up to unpack for her. When Emma said she would prefer to unpack herself, he did not seem as impressed with her new found independence as she did. He sniffed slightly, as if she was letting the five-star hotel down. To get rid of him she tipped him handsomely and his deferential smile reappeared.

Emma unpacked her new hiking boots and trainers plus the numerous pretty and stylish tops her mother had obviously thought suitable for hiking. Smiling fondly, she noted that her mother had also included a pair of high heeled sandals and an evening dress along with two sparkling evening wear tops. She was proud of her mother's fashion sense but did not think she would be needing it here.

She looked out the window. The view was breathtaking. The Swiss town lay immediately below the hotel, the lake beyond it and on every side one turned mountains rose up clad in brilliant sharply defined greens and browns. On one side a small yellow train was chugging up a mountain, making Emma think of 'The Sound of Music' film and the children going up into the mountains with their governess. The sky was blue with thin wispy clouds. *My flowers*. The sudden thought entered her head. It floated away on the breeze and Emma felt a sense of happiness and a sharp pain at the same time. "I will look at the wildflowers for both of us," she whispered.

Having unpacked and feeling tired from the flight, she lay down on the soft, large bed and stared out the wide, open windows. The air was soothing and she soon drifted off into a pleasant doze. She thought she smelled a light floral scent and trying to struggle out of a hazy sleep she again had a thought enter her head: *Follow your heart*. She jumped up from the bed. The scent was the same scent that Tess used to wear. Tears pricked her eyes, yet she felt oddly relaxed. *My mind is playing tricks on me*, she thought. It was bound to happen as this was where she and Tess had planned to come together.

She shook herself fully awake, looked at the beautiful view again and, noting the time, decided to shower and go for a walk before dinner. Hearing movement next door she froze. She did not feel like dealing with the guide now. Quiet, measured footsteps sounded down the outside corridor. A confident knock to her door followed. Holding her breath she tiptoed to the bathroom and started running the shower. Feeling slightly guilty she slipped into the shower and let the water wash away the remnants of her journey. She changed into jeans, grey and silver trainers, and a pale pink top. She tiptoed over to the door of the suite and placed her ear to it. Not hearing any sound, she grabbed her bag, slung it over her shoulder and quietly slipped out. The doorman opened the hotel door once she reached the lobby and she escaped onto the cobbled street outside.

Breathing a sigh of relief and trying to convince herself she was not being immature but merely asserting her independence, she headed toward what seemed to be the center of the small town. The center was beautiful with wide green park lawns, a fountain and statues surrounded by tourist shops and coffee shops and restaurants with outside tables. The shop fronts were typically Swiss in design. The wooden chalets that lined one side of the nearby lake were mostly local houses with some being listed as holiday homes. The mountains loomed high and green around them and she felt the tension leaving her shoulders. She passed the local arts shops and stopped briefly at a shop that sold all types of flower bulbs, their packets making a colorful display. She had to get some before she went home, she thought. Maybe she could get the gardener to plant them in the lower garden section or perhaps even move back into the cottage and plant them herself.

Spotting the tourist information services, she walked over. The hotel had plenty of guided tours and leisure activities on offer, plus numerous beauty packages. She knew she could also spend days lying at the pool, looking out onto the mountains, but for now she wanted to feel like an independent tourist. She thought about what Tess would have liked to do and asked the friendly Swiss tourist agent about hiking trails in the mountains and adventure type sports activities. She decided to ignore the memory that Tess had only allowed her to do the activities for which she had the ability and training and when Tess was present. The tourist agent explained the numerous activities, handing over lots of brochures. There was paragliding and mountain climbing, cliff zip lining, sailing and so many other activities that she could not take it all in at once. A popular sight to see seemed to be the local Swiss cheese making factory. She decided to give that a miss but noted with interest the local church with its history, a walking wildflower tour, and the steeper climbs where one might perhaps see edelweiss in the rock limescale parts of the upper mountains. She also took a few of the brochures on paragliding and zip lining.

Feeling that her walk had been quite productive, she sat down at a quaint pastry shop. Taking out her phone whilst waiting for service she realized that in her haste to avoid the guide, she had not let her parents know that she had arrived safely. There were three missed calls from her mother and two texts from her friend Anna. After giving her order for a glass of crisp white wine and a fresh pastry she phoned home. Her mother's voice was weepy with relief and although Emma felt bad for worrying her, she also felt irritated with having to check in. Her mother handed the phone over to her father who said the guide, Melissa Rustin, had phoned him to say that she had not yet been able to connect with her.

"I will see her when I get back," Emma said, a bit more sharply than she intended. "I am not a child, Dad," she added, softening her voice.

"No," her father agreed gravely, "but it seems like you are behaving like one, not letting anyone know you arrived safely." Emma's conscience pricked her. Her father was right. She agreed to meet up with the guide. Her father said if she connected with Melissa then he would ensure that her mother did not call her every day and that they would be fine as long as they knew she would contact them if she needed to. Emma agreed.

"Thanks Dad," she said, knowing that they were only concerned for her. She had, she supposed, put herself in this position by not taking charge of her life when Tess passed away. Her father hesitated, and then said as if confessing to something he knew she might not like,

"Emma, I hired Ms. Rustin not just as a guide but also to protect you."

"What?!" Emma exploded. "Dad ..."

"Just to protect you. It made your mother feel better. This is the first time you are traveling alone and we always used to feel that you were safe with Tess." He paused, then said, "Remember our deal," and quickly rang off before Emma had a chance to remonstrate with him further. Inwardly she fumed. Deciding not to let it spoil her day and that she could deal with the guide later, she called her friend Anna. Anna was chatty and just what Emma needed right then. Anna expressed friendly jealousy and told her she wished she was there. When Emma told her about her father hiring the guide as a protector, Anna laughed.

"Good," she said. "You need to be kept in line." She was an old school friend of Emma's and remembered Emma's tricks that were the bane of the teachers' lives. Anna also expressed concern for Emma's safety which had Emma realizing just how helpless she must seem to others. When she had been with Tess, they had been outgoing and social, but it seemed her hiding away for the past five years had not been good for her image. Anna also knew that Tess had set boundaries for Emma which she had flourished under.

Emma knew that she had had a life of privilege and had always been surrounded by people who loved her. Despite having had many girlfriends, it was Tess who had claimed her heart and it was Tess who had helped her see that she was a beautiful woman deserving of love. Tess also had not stood for any nonsense and had made sure that Emma, who had an inclination to be slightly spoiled, kept herself on track. Emma was known for her slightly stubborn streak and getting her own way. Tess had shown her that getting one's own way in life was not always realistic. She had blossomed with Tess and had ended up putting her expensive education to good use.

She had been employed at two external companies, gaining valuable experience outside the world of the family business. This had stood her in good stead when she had rejoined her parents' fashion business. She had been previously seen as the boss's daughter but she was now respected for her business skills and abilities. Smiling at the thought of Tess and how she had made sure Emma lived her life to her potential, professionally as well as within their relationship, she paid the bill and walked back along the pretty cobbled streets.

Reaching the hotel, she smiled at the doorman and turned to go upstairs. The hotel concierge came running over.

"Madam," he said, "I have a message for you." In his hand lay a white envelope. *'I will be at your room at 4 p.m. to introduce myself and discuss the next two months' agenda. Be there. Melissa Rustin.'*

Emma fumed inwardly. What a cheek. Who did the woman think she was? However, she smiled graciously at the concierge and caught the lift to her room. It was 3.45 p.m. now and if Ms. Melissa Rustin thought she would be waiting like a good little girl at 4 p.m. she'd have to think again. She decided to freshen up and make a cup of tea and sit by the window, read the brochures and plan a hike for the next day. Shortly, she heard an authoritative rap on her door. She felt annoyed. The knocking continued and became louder when she did not answer the door. Emma realized she was being immature; in addition, the sooner she had a heart-to-heart chat with the guide the better.

Getting up and smoothing her clothes, she opened the door intending to say hullo and invite the guide in using the most authoritative tone she could. "Hello..." she started. The next words froze on her lips.

Standing at the door, looking mildly amused yet with a slightly steely glint in her eyes, was one of the most attractive women Emma had ever seen. Her dark, brown hair that shone with vitality was pulled back in a loose ponytail. The pulled back hair accentuated her high cheekbones and slightly square jaw. Her skin was clear and her eyes were a deep brown. She stood taller than Emma and her frame was muscular and solid, yet definitely feminine. Emma was aware that she was staring and flushed, but was unable to tear her eyes away. The woman was so sexy. A chunky, silver link bracelet adorned her wrist which was still in midair as she had obviously been about to knock again. "Hello," the woman said. Her voice had a slight Australian accent to it and the tone was deep and pleasant yet firm. "I am Melissa Rustin." The woman extended her hand with the silver link bracelet.

"Em-Emma," Emma stammered, taking the outstretched hand. The hand was firm, yet soft and a heat radiated from it that sent a tingling sensation of desire down Emma's spine. Emma blushed; *what on earth is wrong with me,* she wondered. She felt an undeniable sense of attraction to this woman. As if sensing her emotions, Melissa gave an easy laugh and said,

"Shall I come in instead of standing in the doorway?"

"Yes, yes, of course, sorry," Emma said. The guide walked into the room, easy confidence and a sensual appeal radiating from her. Emma noticed the black shorts that hugged her muscular thighs and the tight white T-shirt that emphasized her form, showing off her small, firm breasts and toned abdomen. Ms. Rustin sat in one of the pink chintz armchairs and waited for Emma to close the door. She closed it slowly, giving herself time to collect her thoughts. Emma decided the best way forward was to stick to her original plan of letting the guide know that her services were not needed and to ignore the strange and unsettling feeling of desire that had coursed through her.

"Ms. Rustin," she began formally. "So, Emma..." Melissa said at the same time. "You first," Melissa said politely.

"Okay, well..." Emma said, suddenly feeling a bit uncomfortable in front of the calm, confident woman sitting easily in the chintz chair. "I don't want you to get the wrong impression about the need for your services," she carried on. "My parents are somewhat overly protective so I agreed to let them hire a guide. However, as you can see, I am an adult and your services will not be needed. I will be making my own plans for the next two months and you will

13

be free to carry on with plans of your own. This way we will all benefit and my parents will have peace of mind thinking that you are with me. Consider it a paid holiday." She smiled uneasily. She had wanted to sound mature and gracious, yet she found that the words seemed to ring a bit haughtily and that the guide's eyes had narrowed slightly.

Melissa had listened patiently whilst Emma talked. She paused for a few seconds when Emma stopped, looking directly at her. Feeling a bit nervous, Emma wondered what the guide was thinking. Certainly Ms. Rustin did not look like she appreciated what she had just heard. She was about to speak again to break the silence when the guide leaned forward, arms on her knees, fixed Emma with a clear gaze and said in a pleasant yet totally no nonsense voice,

"Thank you for seeing me at the time I requested, Emma. That is not how it is going to work. I was hired by your father to be your guide in this area and also to make sure you are safe and look after yourself." She held up a hand as Emma started to protest. "I will do my job as I have been hired and paid to do. I can see that your father was right about you being slightly spoiled. I certainly will not break my contract as set out just because you feel you can control others around you or feel sorry for yourself. I am sorry about the loss of your partner..." Emma gasped. *How much had her father told this woman?* "But if you refuse to let me carry out my job, I will escort you to the airport and put you on the next plane home. That will be all," she said. Rising whilst Emma sat open mouthed, she strode toward the door and turning said,

"I will see you for supper this evening and you can tell me whether you have decided to go home or to let me do my job." Leaving Emma speechless, she walked out, closing the door firmly behind her. Emma sat in the chintz chair stunned to her core. No one spoke to her like that; well, unless one counted Tess or a rather

14

strict home nanny she had once had as a child. The nanny had been hired by her loving yet despairing parents when at age thirteen she had been expelled from school.

Emma did not know what to do. She wanted to phone her father and berate him for treating her like a child. She also pondered the feasibility of checking into another hotel. A thought stopped her. It was almost as if she heard Tess's voice saying firmly, *you need this my love, you can't always have your own way and at some stage you need to move on from this depressed mood you've got into*. Couldn't have her own way?! Emma talked back to her own thoughts. *Well, Ms. Melissa, we will see about that*!

CHAPTER 3

For the rest of the afternoon Emma felt unsettled and uneasy. Part of her was fuming when she recalled Melissa's words, part of her felt annoyed with her father and yet there was a small part that wondered if Melissa and her father were right. *Was she spoiled?* She thought she had just been grieving. Well that was true, she was grieving, but she knew Tess would not have let her stay in a funk for this long. She also felt very physically attracted to Ms. Rustin. *It's just hormones,* she told herself. *Try and ignore that.* The woman was obnoxious. One could clearly see she had a military background, expecting Emma to obey her like a soldier. Well, she shook her head, she was not a soldier and she would let Ms. Melissa know that at dinner, when they were amongst people and she would not be able to give orders and then march out like today. For some strange reason she could not fathom, Emma felt quite energized and decided to dress for dinner in the evening gown her mother had packed and show Ms. Rustin just how confident she was.

She slipped into the midnight blue figure-hugging gown, hoping it was not too -over the top- for the hotel restaurant, paired it with the high heeled black sandals and styled her hair with two crystal studded barrette clips. Okay, so that was a bit over the top but she wanted to feel as in control as she could, she reasoned. Looking one's best always helped. The dress showed off her cleavage and hugged her small waist, flaring out over her fuller hips. Feeling in control she strode down to the restaurant, determined not to knock on Melissa's door. The head waiter came running over to greet her and escort her in. She made quite a sensation as she noticed people at other tables looking at her. She felt confident and sure of herself, up until the waiter led her to a table where a familiar figure was already sitting. Melissa stood up as she arrived. She was simply dressed in a black, knee length cocktail dress and her dark brown hair lay loose just above her shoulders. Her face was, as earlier, mostly bare of makeup except for her lips which were moistly outlined in a sexy shade of red. Emma swallowed, *oh she was so sexy*. Melissa sat when she sat, her eyes amused as if she realized what game Emma was playing. Emma felt a bit like a child instead of the mature, sexy woman she had aimed for. She started to talk but Melissa cut her off by asking what she would like to drink. After ordering two glasses of white wine and sparkling water from the waiter she looked back to Emma.

"Good evening, Emma," Melissa began. "You look lovely tonight." Having been ready to lay down her conditions again, Emma felt the wind taken from her sails. She felt oddly pleased at the compliment.

"You look beautiful in your dress," Emma replied. She blushed. *What a stupid thing to say.* They were not playing a game of who could compliment the other best. The waiter brought the drinks and menus over and Emma spent some time pretending to study the cream colored menu. She was still thinking when Melissa's cool voice asked, "Have you decided...what you want to eat?" Emma's head snapped up; was Melissa teasing her?

"Um, um'" she said, "yes, no, well..."

"Five more minutes, please," Melissa said smoothly to the waiter. Emma bristled. She was so bossy; *I would have told the waiter that,* she thought. She scanned the menu and decided on the first starter she saw and then the veal schnitzel with honey glazed, grilled aubergine. Melissa ordered steak medium rare.

Once the waiter had gone Melissa leaned forward and said in a direct manner, "Well Emma, what you have decided? Are we taking you back to the airport tomorrow or are we going to plan a pleasant two months?" Emma gaped at her; she had wanted to take control of this conversation and remind Melissa that she could be 'unhired'. Strictly speaking, though, it was her father who had hired Melissa so she could not fire her. Emma did not want to go home but she also did not want to be chaperoned.

"Listen, Melissa," she said, leaning forward and trying to regain some control, "I am sure you are excellent at your job, but I..." She did not even get to finish when Melissa also leaned forward and said pleasantly but firmly,

"No buts, Emma. I asked you a question; are you going to the airport tomorrow or are we planning your time here?"

Emma felt enraged and embarrassed. She wanted to throw her glass of sparkling water in Melissa's calm, controlled face. Her eyes must have flickered to her glass as Melissa said quietly but with a hint of steel in her voice,

"I wouldn't do that if I were you." Emma colored; how did Melissa know what had flitted through her mind?

"I'm waiting for an answer, Emma," Melissa said. Trapped in the dining room with other people all around, Emma fumed. She knew she did not want to go home but Melissa looked totally capable of forcing her onto a plane. She wondered if she could pretend to get on a plane but actually leave the airport without Melissa seeing her. *No, that definitely would not work.* Emma took a deep breath and said,

"I will not be going home, because I choose not to go home, not because of anything you have said." She added hastily, "I will be planning my two months here and you…"

"… will be right by your side. Good girl, that's settled then," Melissa said leaning back. Emma almost choked. This woman was infuriating. Melissa smiled at her.

"Shall I pour you some more water? You sound like you have something stuck in your throat." she said, her eyes laughing and knowing. Emma bit back a sarcastic reply and said in as dignified a manner as she could,

"No thank you. I am quite fine." Melissa laughed and started talking about all there was to see and do in the area. "I was thinking that we might be able to hike up to see some edelweiss in the higher part of the mountains, but that will depend on how fit you are," she added. "If you are planning on any serious hikes, I will be scheduling a fitness test with you in the gym."

A fitness test? Emma stared at her. *What was this; boot camp?* She felt pulled in different directions; she badly wanted to see the edelweiss in their natural environment in memory of Tess, but she also felt resentful that Melissa seemed to already be controlling her every move. On the other hand, *it felt quite nice having some activities planned.* Emma blinked; where did that thought come from? She wanted to take charge of her own activities here. Melissa laughed softly. "Edelweiss hike it is then. That is what we will aim for. I believe your late partner was a floral designer?" she asked in a gentle tone. "Um, yes, yes she was," Emma said, her voice softening. "She designed all the floral arrangements for my mother's fashion business. It was a dream of hers to visit the Swiss Alps and see the wild flowers in bloom."

"Well," Melissa said, leaning forward again and lightly touching Emma's hand, "we'll do that on her behalf." Emma felt part of herself melting when Melissa said that. Her hand tingled where Melissa touched her and she snatched it back. She wondered if Melissa felt any of the feelings she was. The woman was obviously gay, but did she feel any of the physical attraction that Emma did? Looking at her, Emma decided that she did not. She was so cool and composed, although that mask had slipped slightly, compassion in her eyes, when mentioning Tess. She lowered her head. "Thank you," she said, "Tess would have loved that." The soft words seemed to ease the tension that was between them and Melissa smiled a genuine smile at her. Emma responded with her own smile before she could stop herself. "You're very pretty when you smile naturally, Emma," Melissa said unexpectedly. Emma blushed. She now felt a bit silly dressing up as if going to a ball and acting as if she controlled things. She thought that perhaps a fitness test and preparing to take a hike might be quite enjoyable. After all, there would be many other things she could do alone.

Her shoulders relaxed and noticing this Melissa started making small talk, asking Emma about her work.

Melissa felt annoyed with herself wondering why she had the comment about Emma looking pretty when she smiled. Emma was more than pretty, she was stunning and it was inappropriate for her to feel any attraction to her: she had been hired by this woman's father. She forced herself to concentrate on what Emma was saying.

After explaining that she worked with her parents in their company as a business manager, Emma, intrigued by Melissa, asked her what had made her decide to be a guide.

"I was born in Australia," Melissa replied easily. "Growing up in nature and not the city I suppose ultimately led me to this career. After leaving school I joined the army but after an injury to my knee and having rehabilitation for two years, I felt I should move into something else. I moved to Europe and trained as a guide and then an alpine trekking guide." She smiled. Emma wanted to ask if she had a partner but felt that was a bit too personal. Mind you, she thought suddenly, her father had obviously told Melissa all about Emma's business. "Are you…I mean, do you have a family?" she asked awkwardly.

Melissa looked amused. Emma was so transparent.

"I don't currently have a partner," she said. "I broke up with Debbie two years ago. I don't have any children but I am close to my father and sister who live in Australia. And most people call me Mel," she finished up with.

Emma blushed. It was as if Melissa, well, Mel read her thoughts. She decided to order dessert. Mel ordered Irish coffee. It was a relaxing way to end the evening and when they left to go upstairs Emma was surprised to find that she felt quite content. Mel said good night and Emma stepped through the door to her suite. She heard Mel waiting for her to lock it and then her footsteps moved on to her own suite. She was not a teenager, she did not need anyone to see her safely to her room, she thought, but realized she did not feel as cross about it as she would have earlier. In fact, it felt quite nice to feel someone was looking out for her. The night was too dark to see the view so she pampered herself in the foaming jet bath before climbing into bed and falling into a deep, dreamless sleep.

CHAPTER 4

———————

The next morning Emma woke feeling disorientated. It took her a while to remember where she was. She had left the curtains open and the sun was shining behind the mountains, bringing back the splendid view from the day before. The meeting and dinner with Mel flooded back and she blushed. *Enough of the blushing and illicit thoughts of attraction,* she told herself sternly. She was here to spend the next two months regaining her independence and life. Deciding that Mel was way too bossy and had only been hired, she determined to start her list of activities as she saw fit.

Energized after the massage shower head had sprayed her body, she dressed in light brown shorts, grey trainers and spent some time wondering which of the numerous tops her mother had chosen would best suit her. Given that in the last five years her choice of outfit had not concerned her and she had simply put on whatever outfit had been chosen that day, she found herself surprised that she even cared about which top she was going to wear. *This has nothing to do with Mel,* she told herself. Selecting a pale maroon loose vest top with a lace cream panel down the front, she added a touch of makeup, tucked her blond hair behind her ears and decided to head down for breakfast. Thinking that coming back to the room after breakfast might mean she would bump into Mel, she packed a pale brown canvas handbag with her phone, camera, lipstick and money, and headed out the door.

"Good morning." A deep feminine voice made Emma jump in surprise. Leaning against the wall opposite her room was Mel, who had obviously been waiting for her. She was dressed in shorts, hiking boots and a black vest top. Her hair was once again pulled into a ponytail. She smelled of a woodsy scent that Emma could not identify but found pleasant. "What are you doing here?" she asked almost rudely. Mel's gaze did not alter but her eyebrows arched slightly. "Last night you had decided not to go back home and agreed that we'd work out a plan of activities, starting with a fitness test today," Mel said evenly. "Perhaps you have changed you mind?" Emma could be quite rude, she realized and yet it did not seem deliberate, more spontaneous as if she were fighting against something.

Emma stared at her.

"No, no, I have not changed my mind." she said. Darn, this woman was not going to leave her alone.

"Great. Let's go down to breakfast and we can hit the gym after that," Mel said. Emma stopped suddenly en-route to the lift.

"Listen, Melissa," she said, "I don't mean to be rude, but perhaps I gave you the wrong impression last night. I don't intend to have someone accompany me all the time. I have been thinking, what about if I paid you double the rate my father has given you and you can..."

She did not get much further as Mel turned to her, grabbed her arm and said firmly as if she had finally had enough,

"I have been paid to do my job. Do not insult me by thinking you can pay me off with money." Her eyes glittered dangerously. "Now, either we will go ahead as agreed last night or you will be on the next plane home. Got it?" She shook Emma's arm slightly as she said that and Emma's tummy tingled at the same time that she felt outraged. It was clear that Mel was serious and would not hesitate to carry out her threat. Under Mel's direct gaze she felt slightly ashamed that she had just tried to buy her off. *Come on Emma,* she told herself, *that was a thoughtless and insulting thing to do. No wonder people think you are spoiled.*

She pulled her arm from Mel's grasp and looking at her said quietly, "I am sorry Mel, that was rude and insensitive of me to offer you money. I just…well, I wanted some time alone, I suppose."

Mel's eyes cleared. She felt impressed with Emma for apologizing.

"You can definitely have time alone, Emma," she said. "I just need to know what you are doing and where you are. If you are doing any potentially risky activities or hiking then I will come with you. Okay?"

Emma nodded. The lift arrived and they caught it down to the hotel breakfast room. Breakfast was ordered a la carte. Although Emma had always liked the more tourist buffet breakfast she had had when she and Tess had travelled, the breakfast was delicious and well cooked.

"So," Mel said when breakfast was finished and they both had cappuccinos in front of them, "would you like to do some sightseeing or shall we go to the gym to see how fit you are and what training you will need to hike up one of the mountains?" Feeling a lot less prickly than before, Emma opted for the gym. The gym was a luxurious affair and although it had a beautiful view there were not many clients using it, most of them preferring outdoor activities in such good weather. Emma knew she was a bit unfit. She had not done much exercise in the last five years. Her exercise consisted of walking at work between various meetings and three times weekly treadmill sessions at their home gym.

Mel started her off on the treadmill at a walking pace, then a gentle jog, then at running pace. Within ten minutes she was huffing and puffing. Next came the weights and after twenty minutes Emma felt her arms and legs shaking. "Um...I'm a bit unfit," she said to Mel in a tone that hoped Mel might say the opposite.

"You are," Mel said directly. "However, I believe we can manage to increase your fitness soon, if you agree to fifteen-minute sessions building up to thirty-minute sessions each morning five days a week. We can also add in some weights to increase your muscle fitness. You won't be ready for alpine trekking this holiday," she said, "but definitely some of the more moderate hikes that reach the rocky areas where the edelweiss grow will be okay." Emma smiled. She must have some potential. Mel had worked out alongside her and Emma was conscious of her fit body and the way the muscles in her arms and legs rippled as she lifted weights. Emma's body was slender and curvy, but not toned and she was determined to try and get herself fitter in the next two months. She lay down on the bench to lift the bar which Mel was setting to a much lower weight for her. Mel stood behind her, spotting the bar as she lifted it. It was only 10kgs so she would not have dropped it, but she was highly aware of Mel so close to her. Finishing, she put the bar down and turned to look at Mel. She was surprised to see Mel's pupils slightly dilated in arousal as she felt her own were and she blushed furiously. *Maybe I am imagining it,* she thought and when she looked up again Mel had moved to the water dispenser and seemed totally at ease. *Yup, definitely imagined!*

The gym session energized her and she told Mel she would like to do the gym session every morning excluding weekends.

Mel nodded her approval. Perhaps Emma was not such a brat after all she thought. Emma was definitely sexy, but also had a vulnerable air about her. Not to mention that her attitude could do with some sorting, Mel mused. She reminded herself that Emma was off bounds. She was a client, a paying client; well her father was the client, technically speaking. She was impressed that Emma seemed to want to make the effort for the hike. As they left the gym, she decided that their time needed to be a bit more structured and asked Emma to sit down with her in the lounge.

Together they agreed on a gym session in the morning and Emma having her own time to wander the town in the afternoons, except for the days she wanted to walk in the lower parts of the mountains or do any activities or further out sightseeing, in which case Mel would accompany her. Emma balked at having her activities supervised but when she remembered Tess doing exactly the same, her eyes softened and she agreed. Without thinking she said, "Tess would have said the same." She bit her lip. *Why did I say that,* she thought.

Mel took the words in her stride and said, "Your Tess sounds like she was a good partner." Inside she was thinking, *aha, so the brat did have someone who had taken her under control.*

"Yes, yes, she...she loved me and cared for me and I for her," Emma said, softly. "I can't...Well, sometimes I still can't believe she is gone."

"Losing the love of your life is hard," Mel said compassionately. "I am sure Tess would have wanted you to grieve for her but not to give your whole life over to it."

Emma lowered her eyes. "Yes, no...I mean, yes, you are right. She would not have been pleased at the state I have put myself into. I have thrown myself into work for the past five years." she stopped suddenly. She was telling Mel too much. She jumped up and said haughtily, "Thank you for the gym session. I am going into town this afternoon, so there is no need for you to be around." Flinging her towel over her shoulder, she flounced off, feeling a bit ashamed of how she was acting, but talking about Tess had made her feel vulnerable.

Mel watched her go, deciding to let her have her little tantrum for now. Discussing Tess had obviously been something Emma needed to do and it was understandable that Emma might feel unsettled. Given what Emma's father had told her about Emma and her state of mind, it did seem that she was regaining some zest for her life; she had not missed Emma's attraction to her. She felt equally attracted to Emma. She was attractive with her blonde hair and green eyes and soft, feminine body. Her manner called out for discipline and Mel felt instinctively that Emma needed firm boundaries in her life. Yet at the same time she did not want to take advantage of her when she was stepping out of her self-imposed grief. She decided to watch Emma from a distance to make sure she really was going to the town and if so, she would let her have her space.

Up in her room Emma showered. Tears ran down her face from the aching she felt inside her. She missed Tess. As the steam from the hot water enveloped her, she remembered how Tess used to shower with her and how close they had been. *Darling,* a thought came to her, *I am always here, always, but you need to let yourself live again.* Emma wondered if she was going crazy or if it was Tess talking to her. Most likely it was her subconscious mind telling her to move on, she decided; certainly that is what her mother's psychologist would have told her. Her mother had begged Emma to see him and she had done so for three sessions and then stopped. Emma thought back to the compassion in Mel's eyes and voice. Unbidden, an image of Mel's strong and sexy body came to mind and she felt a throbbing between her legs. She dressed hastily and, grabbing her bag, almost ran down into the old town to try and forget the feelings and urges she had around Mel or while thinking of her.

She spent a pleasant afternoon in the town center again, browsing and trying different coffees at the quaint cafes.

Mel watched unseen from a distance and felt pleased that Emma was indeed doing only what she had said she was.

That evening they met again for dinner. This time Emma dressed simply yet elegantly. The air between them was free of tension and Emma seemed a lot more relaxed. Mel was pleased.

"Same again tomorrow?" she said to Emma as they went up the lift.

"Yes," Emma said, feeling pleasure when she thought about another gym session with Mel. In the next few days she would do something a bit more adventurous than just browsing around the town with its old buildings and beautiful churches, but no need for Mel to know that. Mel stood back for her to exit the lift and Emma accidentally brushed up close against her, her breast touching Mel's arm. They both froze. Emma blushed and licked her lips. *Good gracious what is wrong with me,* she thought, her breast felt on fire. She swallowed. "I'm sorry," she said. Mel laughed.

"No problem," she said, walking out behind Emma, breaking eye contact with her, but not before Emma saw the flare of arousal in her brown eyes.

She almost fled into her room and Mel laughed softly as Emma closed the door behind her.

Emma was so transparent...and so in need of someone to take her in hand and make her feel alive again.

CHAPTER 5

The next few days settled into a regular pattern. They met for a light breakfast, did a gym session, which got a bit longer each day as Emma's tolerance increased and then sat chatting over a cappuccino. It was during one of these sessions that Mel found out about Emma and Tess's relationship and how Tess was the one woman who had tamed Emma. She had set her on the path to becoming the respected business manager she was today and not the spoiled rich woman she had sometimes been seen as. Emma felt quite embarrassed telling her but seeing that Mel remained open and understanding, she felt more at ease with her. In the afternoons, Emma set off for the town, getting into the tourist way of life, browsing and sightseeing. Mel generally caught up on messages from home and did some shorter hikes in the mountains. In the evenings they'd meet up for dinner, sometimes in the hotel or occasionally trying different restaurants in town.

After a week Emma decided she had settled down enough and wanted to try her hand at some of the activities and sightseeing she had planned. Causally she mentioned to Mel at the gym session that she'd planned to do some cliff zip lining that afternoon.

"Fine," Mel said, smiling. "I'll come with you and check it out first." Emma, feeling annoyed, stood up and said coolly,

"No need, Mel. I am fully capable of doing this alone." Mel also stood up.

"Sit down Emma," she said.

"No," Emma said. "I need to get ready. There is a small train that leaves at 2 p.m. to the jumping site and-"

"I said, sit down," Mel said firmly, standing in front of her with her arms folded. There was a glint in her eyes and Emma hesitated. She wanted to flounce past but Mel looked capable of making her sit down. She sat down with a sigh. "Fine," she snapped. "I won't go. I will sit here, tucked up in a cozy cocoon, never doing anything more than sitting in coffee shops."

"Are you finished?" Mel asked calmly, looking down at her. Emma kept silent. She felt like a child. "You are free to do cliff ziplining, Emma, as long as I accompany you and check any risks first. We agreed on this and I also signed a contract with your father. If I do not come with you, you will not be doing it." Mel sat back down clearly feeling that her word was the last one. Emma was about to shout at her, "I am not a child" but realized how immature that was and that there were other ways to achieve what she wanted without having to have an argument with Mel. "Fine," she said. "In that case I will spend the afternoon safely at the hotel spa." She got up and walked off.

Mel sighed. Her palm itched to teach Emma a lesson but she restrained herself. If the brat wanted to sulk for the afternoon then she could.

She decided to make sure that Emma did indeed go to the spa and not somewhere else. Mel felt a bit like a detective as opposed to a guide and guard, but she had been happy to sign the contract with Emma's father, having previously had one such assignment. She was also well used to maintaining order and control on the treks that she led. At 1.30 p.m. she heard Emma's door open and she followed her at a discreet distance to the spa. Seeing Emma enter she sighed with relief. Mel tried to make sense of her feelings. Emma was a bit spoiled; true, she had been grieving but five years was a bit too long to act like a spoiled child. It sounded like her partner Tess would not have allowed Emma to wallow in her misery nor would have put up with any attitude. She also felt attracted to Emma and she longed to care for the vulnerability she saw in her. There was the added responsibility in the form of ensuring Emma's safety in the contract she had signed. She decided that whilst Emma was using the spa facilities she'd do some browsing in town herself. It might clear her head. The town was familiar to her and she settled down at one of her favorite tucked away local bars and ordered a beer. One of the hotel waiters, who was obviously on his lunch break, waved and came up to her. He made small talk and asked her if she was enjoying the holiday. Wanting time alone, Mel replied affirmatively, without explaining that she was not on holiday, but in a tone that discouraged any further conversation. He did not seem to take the hint and asked why she was down in the town when her girlfriend was up the mountain.

"My girlfriend?" Mel said in surprise.

"You know...the pretty blonde one...You're always together," he said, smiling. "Up the mountain?" Mel repeated, feeling a bit dazed.

"Yes," he said, "she came to reception just before I left for lunch break and asked the way to the mountain train for the cliff zip line jumping." Startling him, Mel jumped up, threw some money down on the table for her beer and hurried out. Anger filled her at

Emma's deliberate deception but she also felt a fear for her safety.

She made it to the small train stop in record time and found that it ran every half hour. She boarded the next one and got to the top of the stop which was half way up a mountain. There was a flat land that had created a natural cliff. Up ahead she could see a line of about eight people and the platform where people started the jump from. Her eyes scanned the line as she strode over. She spied a familiar figure-blonde head of hair, slender body, curvy hips-and felt a rush of relief. Emma was putting a helmet on and a guide was helping her into a harness. Mel excused herself to the people in the line and grabbing Emma by the arm, causing her to squeal, she told the guide,

"This one is not jumping today." Emma gasped when she saw Mel. She looked furious. She tried to pull her arm from her grip and hissed out,

"Stop it! Stop it, Melissa. People are looking."

"Well they will have a lot more to look at if you do not come with me now," Mel said calmly whilst pulling the harness off her hips, forcing Emma to step out of it.

"Let go of me," Emma hissed, mortification making her cheeks flush bright pink.

"No, and I suggest that if you don't want a scene you come with me now... voluntarily," Mel warned. Releasing Emma's arm, she undid the helmet and plunked it back in the surprised guide's hands. She pulled Emma away from the line and walked her forcibly back to the now deserted little station. Dragged behind Mel, Emma fumed and spluttered,

"How dare you? How dare you?" she almost shouted. Reaching a secluded spot near the station Mel turned around, grabbing her by the tops of her arms and said,

"You deliberately lied to me, Emma. That is not acceptable. Nor is putting yourself at risk and not letting me come with you."

She shook Emma slightly as she continued with, "I should spank you for this!"

Emma gasped in outrage and disbelief, yet her tummy lurched and tingled. It was a strange, yet familiar sensation from long ago; she felt angry yet cared for. She had forgotten this feeling she had had with Tess.

"Come back to the hotel immediately," Mel said. "You will not be going anywhere alone until I know I can trust you."

Emma folded her arms.

"I will not!" she said fiercely. "You are not the boss of me-" Before she could get out any more outraged words, Mel had turned her around and landed five stinging swats on her bottom. Emma could not believe it. She shrieked at the unexpected pain and gasped out,

"How dare you!"

A couple walked past and stared curiously at them. Emma tried to smile and act naturally but she was bright red with embarrassment and the fear that Mel might spank her again. Mel glared at her.

"Will you be behaving or will I be taking you over my knee?" she asked with a firm set to her eyes. She looked so capable and determined that Emma kept silent. She sat on the station bench and stayed quiet. Her bottom smarted; Mel's hand had felt like it was made of hairbrush wood and not the soft flesh she had felt on shaking it when meeting her. Emma had a sudden image of Tess. Not long after they had met Tess had spanked her when Emma had been a real brat. It had been such a shock to the spoiled Emma, but strangely enough after she had calmed down, she had felt cared for and cherished. Determined to not let the reminder of Tess diminish her outrage, she turned to Mel to tell her again that she had no right to stop her doing what she wanted.

As if reading her mind again, Mel pinned her with a steely stare and said, "We will discuss this back at the hotel," forestalling any further talk. Emma seemed to respond to being taken in hand and if Mel needed to spank her bottom with a hairbrush she would do just that to keep her safe and within the agreed boundaries. The small train arrived and Mel pushed Emma in front of her into the first section and they headed back down.

Emma felt miserable. The twenty minute trip gave her time to reflect. She had been scared of jumping. Tess had never allowed her to do it, due to an old shoulder injury she had had from one of her horse jumping shows and she did not know what had possessed her to do something that had scared her so much. She felt as if she had been trying to push some boundary, but what boundary and why she could not identify.

By the time they got to the hotel she felt quite tearful. Mel ushered her in and up to her suite. She unlocked her door and as they entered Emma's sitting area, Emma turned and tried to say something angrily but tears welled up in her eyes. Mel sighed.

"Come here, honey," she said. She gently pulled Emma toward her and Emma found herself embraced by arms that were both strong and soft. It had been a long time since she had felt anyone other than her parents embrace her and without knowing why she leaned her head on Mel's strong shoulder and let the tears flow.

"It's okay, honey," Mel said, her hand rubbing Emma's back. It was not a sexual touch but comforting and safe. Emma pulled back slightly, feeling embarrassed. She could not believe she had just cried all over a woman whom she had known for just a week. She had never cried with any of her friends in the last five years, not even when Tess had died. Mel led her to one of the chintz chairs and set about making some tea.

"I'm sorry," Emma said. "Acting like a moron and then crying all over you," Mel smiled, handed over a cup of tea, and gazing directly at her said, "Not a moron, just a hurt woman who is finally letting go of the pain she has felt these past five years. And perhaps looking for some boundaries in her life that disappeared when her partner left."

Emma sat silently. She sipped her tea. Was it true? Was she letting go of Tess? Surely letting go of the hurt would mean she was letting go of Tess? As if knowing what Emma was mulling over, Mel leaned forward and said softly, "Just because you are moving on and allowing yourself to feel again, does not mean that you will forget Tess or that it lessens the love you had with her." Emma nodded. She thought about Mel's earlier words of testing boundaries. Was she missing the security that being with Tess had given her? She had also been feeling slightly guilty about her attraction to Mel, yet that feeling and the town surroundings had made her feel energized and more alive than she could remember since Tess passed away.

"From what you say about Tess, I don't think she would have liked you to have hidden yourself away from life," Mel said.

"No, no, she would not have," Emma said. She took a deep breath but before she could say anything further Mel said,

"I think you need a good sleep and then we'll meet up for supper." Taking the now empty tea cup from Emma and setting it down, she led Emma over to her bed. She helped the now unresisting Emma to lie down and pulled the plush blanket over her. Mel brushed her hand lightly over Emma's forehead and suddenly Emma realized that she felt completely tired out as if her emotions had drained her of all energy. She felt oddly at peace and like a weight that she had been unaware that she was carrying had been lifted from her. Closing her eyes, she did not see Mel looking at her tenderly, nor did she hear her quietly leave the room and gently close the door behind her.

CHAPTER 6

On waking Emma found that she had slept not only the entire afternoon but right through the night. Bright morning sun filled the room. She sat up, feeling a bit disorientated but totally at peace and with a clearer mind. It was as if she had not known how heavy the weight of grief was that she had allowed to settle in her. Showering, she hummed a song. It had been a favorite of Tess's and yet this time it was not accompanied by the pain it usually was. She dressed in light cargo trousers with a grey and white lace top and light hiking boots. She knocked at Mel's door and was greeted by Mel looking attractive and rested, her hair pulled back as usual. Emma smiled at her.

"Just wanted to see if you are ready for breakfast," Emma said almost shyly. Mel nodded.

"Yes I am," she replied. "You slept a long time. How do you feel?"

"I feel rested...I mean, I feel good," Emma said. It was hard to put what she was feeling into words. Mel smiled and turned to get her bag. *Gosh she is so hot*, Emma thought. She could not help staring at Mel's strong, toned back and her lightly tanned long, muscular legs. She blushed and was trying to cover her embarrassment at gawking like a teenager when Mel turned back and said,

"I'll wait by the lift."

Mel smiled at her, thinking how Emma looked so sexy; clear eyes, plump lips, her lace top accentuating her femininity. She had been worried that Emma would still be reacting to the mild spanking she had given her, but if anything she seemed happier and relaxed.

After breakfast Emma said she was thinking about taking a short hike in the lower part of the mountains after their gym session. Mel nodded and said that was a good idea and she would join her as walking alone was not always safe. Emma nodded and felt oddly happy at the idea of walking through the beautiful surroundings with Mel.

Her easy agreement pleased Mel. It seemed that Emma just needed a firm hand and some time to completely get over her grief.

The hike was graded as easy in intensity and was four hours in length. They loaded one backpack with water and some snack bars, then set off. Emma felt oddly shy walking next to Mel. Her body senses were heightened. They came to a slightly steep part and Mel turned to offer Emma her hand. Grasping it, Emma almost gasped out loud. Her hand tingled in Mel's, sending a shiver down her arm. Mel pulled her up and standing in close proximity to her, Emma felt her body throbbing with sensation. Her arm brushed against Mel's and she bit her lip. She wanted to lean into Mel, she wanted... She caught Mel looking at her; her lips were full and sensuous and her pupils were slightly dilated. Unable to help herself, she leaned toward those lips, heart beating.

"Excuse us," a brisk voice said. They broke apart and stood

aside to let a couple pass them on the narrow path. The first man strode past without glancing at them; the second one grinned cheekily and Emma blushed. She looked at Mel and they both laughed, the hypnotic spell broken. "Come on," Mel said. "Just over that little rise is a sight that you will want to see." Emma followed her. Rounding the rise, she almost bumped into Mel, not realizing she had stopped. "Look," Mel said. Emma's breath was taken away. In front of her, on the lower foothills of the mountain, was a long stretch of meadow; the grasses were tall and green, still in the hot summer late morning air. Interspersed colors of various wildflowers caught her eye; violet asters, yellow ranunculus and pale purple alpine thistles showed their heads among the stems of grass. To their right on a rocky outcrop was a patch of the lovely flaming pink alpine rose. The beauty of the scene mesmerized her. She understood Tess's desire to see flowers not just in the artistic designs she had created them into, but in their natural landscape in their own perfect wild pattern.

"It's beautiful, Mel," she said, "so beautiful. Thank you for showing me." She flung her arms wide and lifted her head, feeling like one of the flowers growing under the warmth of the sun.

Mel watched her. Emma's face was open and relaxed, her eyes sparkled, her body moved freely and the sun silhouetted through her lace T-shirt, outlining her small waist and curved hips. She looked innocent and sensual at the same time and she felt desire course through her.

"Come," Mel said and gently took Emma's hand to help her down the rocky outcrop. They wandered down among the grass and flowers.

At the end of the meadow grassland was a line of trees. Just below was a large dirt path big enough for cars. It was an alternative route that many tourists took instead of climbing the part of the mountain that they had. They stopped just above the trees and looked out across the view the mountain opposite them offered. It was capped with snow. Emma thought how strange it was that they could stand there in the warm sun and yet further up it was so cold that the snow had not even melted. It was a surreal landscape. She turned to tell Mel her thoughts and found Mel looking at her. This time her arousal was plain to see and Emma knew she had not imagined it earlier. When Mel bent her head towards hers, she hypnotically leaned toward Mel, tilting her head up and slightly parting her lips. Her heart beat faster. Then those lips were touching hers, at first softly and then when she responded, with more intensity. She opened her mouth to Mel's searching tongue. The warmth of Mel's mouth sent a current running through Emma's body and she brought her one hand up to cup the back of Mel's head and moaned softly. The sudden sound of voices pulled them apart. Emma realized that she was panting slightly.

Mel looked at her, eyes half drugged with desire and her lips plump and moist, and tried to control the throbbing that seemed to fill her entire body. *This was her client for goodness sake.* She forced her lips into an easy smile and said, "Shall we go down to one of the restaurants?"

Emma nodded; she felt she could not trust herself to speak in a normal tone of voice. She wanted Mel to pull her down into the long grass, to cover her body with her own, to.... *What was she thinking?* Mel had been hired by her father. The kiss was probably nothing more than a moment of madness. Telling herself that the mountain air had both affected them both, she followed Mel as she led them down to the path below now filled with tourists who had come up with the cable car.

They chose one of the restaurants that populated the small village that was situated on the edge of a cliff. The entire village was surrounded on three other sides by towering mountains. Tourists filled the many small bars and eateries. They were lucky enough to get a table at a small Swiss restaurant that had outside seating. Emma busied herself with reading the menu and ordered a basket of fried chicken and potato wedges-not exactly good for someone training to get fit but totally delicious paired with a local beer in the summer air. She was relaxed and happy. Looking at her, Mel felt oddly pleased to see her so well and, like Emma had the day before, wondered about her strong feelings for this woman.

They decided to take the easier path back and then get the cable car for the rest of the way. The cable car gave them a different view from their walk. It was tightly crammed with tourists and Emma found her back pressed up against Mel's front as she faced the front window of the cable car in the standing area. It was hard to concentrate on the view when she could feel Mel's firm breasts at the top of her back and she was highly conscious of the fact that her bottom was pushing into the cup of Mel's top thighs. She swallowed and tried to focus.

"It's beautiful, isn't it?" she tried to say in a normal tone of voice. Her tongue felt thick though and the words came out slightly slurred.

"It is," Mel replied, her voice sounding softly at Emma's left ear. Her breath made Emma shiver and she felt her nipples tighten and her breasts swell. *Oh goodness, get me out of here*, Emma thought desperately. She felt wet between her legs and was finding it difficult to breathe through a closed mouth. Mel laughed softly as if she knew exactly how Emma was feeling. The cable car gave a shudder and Emma lurched slightly. Mel's arm slipped around her waist.

"Okay?" she asked.

"Er, yes... yes," Emma stuttered. The touch of Mel's arm was like an electric current searing her skin. She placed her hand on Mel's arm; it was smooth and cool and firm. Unable to help herself, she ran her hand along her forearm. Behind her she heard Mel breathe in sharply. "Emma..." Mel said at the same time Emma said, "Mel..."

Mel moved her arm and the cable car started moving smoothly again.

"Yes?" Mel said.

"Nothing," Emma said. The cable car slid to a smooth halt and Emma felt a sense of loss as tourists started getting off and the pressure of Mel's firm body eased from hers. Plastering a smile on her face which she hoped hid the lust she felt, she turned and followed Mel off the cable car.

They walked back to the hotel in silence. The town was as pretty as ever and the late afternoon sun was moving its way to early evening as they neared the exquisite chalet facade of the hotel.

"Thank you for the lovely hike," Emma said almost primly as they entered the lift. Mel laughed.

"It was my pleasure," she said softly. Mel stopped to see Emma safely to her room. She leaned forward to push the door open just as Emma turned back to say goodbye. Their bodies brushed against each other. They stood still for a moment, the air crackling with tension. Mel moved first, she backed away to her own suite entrance door. Emma swallowed.

"Mel..." she said, her eyes having darkened to a deep green and her words sounding thick and forced. She walked over to Mel at her door. Mel lowered her head, placing one hand on Emma's hip. Emma sighed as Mel's lips captured hers and in a feverish passion she put one hand on the back of Mel's head and the other on the nape of her neck trying to bring her closer, trying to drown herself in that kiss. Mel broke away, gasping but controlling herself.

"Please," Emma said softly. "Please Mel."

"Are you sure this is what you want?" Mel said. She was on fire with desire but did not want to take advantage of Emma no matter how willing she seemed. "Yes, yes, I want this. I am totally sure," Emma said. Mel pushed the door open and led Emma inside. Her suite was a twin image of Emma's but decorated in cream and muted gold as opposed to the cream and brighter pink of Emma's. The evening sun mellowed the light and sun rays fell across the king size bed. Emma felt sweaty and thought about showering but that thought left her mind as Mel pulled her lace t-shirt over her head and deftly undid the pretty bra beneath it. Emma cried out. The feelings Mel was creating in her before she even touched her were almost unbearable. Mel pulled off her own T-shirt and sports bra in one swift movement. She pulled Emma toward her and kissed her, her tongue plundering Emma's open mouth. Emma kissed her back feverishly, moaning as her full swollen breasts grazed Mel's. Mel lowered her head and trailed her lips over Emma's collar bone, then down her shoulder. She pushed Emma back toward the bed and as Emma sat on the edge she knelt in front of her. Her lips ran over Emma's right breast and Emma almost screamed when the searching tongue swirled across her nipple, teasing it. Mel's other hand caressed her left breast and Emma felt she might faint. Mel gently pushed her back, at the same time removing her trainers and socks. Emma felt a bit shy; it was so intimate. Her hands were then at the waistband of her cargo pants and they were pulled off.

"Take your shorts off," she whispered to Mel. Mel pulled them off, her Brazilian style panties following. Emma laid back and stared at Mel. Her body was magnificent; so toned and strong, yet still possessing the softness of femininity. A light sheen of sweat enhanced the sensuality of her figure. Her head was thrown back as she loosened her dark hair from its confines and her muscles contrasted with her curves. Climbing onto the bed, Mel moved up Emma's body, placing her lips first on one inner thigh and then the other. Her teasing tongue made its way to Emma's center covered by her desire-soaked panties. When Mel placed her nuzzling lips over her mons Emma could not help herself, she bucked her hips upward and grasped Mel's head, trying to bring her up away from that unbearably pleasurable sense of torture. Mel laughed.

"Babe, you are so sexy, so wet." she said huskily.

"I...I,oh, oh...I..." Emma tried to say something coherent but desire was robbing her of logical thought and speech. She felt Mel peeling her wet panties down her hips and then her legs were free of them. Her legs opened wide of their own volition and she felt stunned at her wantonness. Mel's eyes were fixed on her slick, wet center and Emma wondered why she did not feel embarrassed in such an exposed position. Mel moved upwards and when her firm body covered Emma's, it felt like coming home, it felt so right. Emma grabbed Mel's back and held on as intense sensations poured through her. Their bodies moved in feverish haste, their mons' pushing and thrusting against each other. She tried to get her hand between Mel's legs but their thrusting prevented her and she found herself clutching Mel's smooth buttocks.

"Please take me...take me," she panted. She felt she could not wait any longer. Mel silenced her by covering her mouth with her own. She thrust her tongue inside Emma's mouth at the same time that she lifted her hips away from Emma and thrust two fingers into Emma's open, waiting center. Emma screamed, the sound muffled in Mel's mouth. Her hips thrust upwards, impaling herself on Mel's fingers that were rhythmically plunging in and out. Suddenly Mel withdrew and tore her mouth from Emma's. She turned Emma over onto her front and Emma briefly felt Mel's open, wet intimate parts on her buttocks. It was incredibly sensual and erotic. She lifted her buttocks to try and rub against those velvety, slippery inner lips. Mel moved, robbing her of that wet, warm, slick feeling and grasped Emma's buttocks, lifting them upward. Positioning herself behind Emma, she used one hand between her shoulder blades to keep Emma's shoulders down on the bed. The position opened Emma's center even wider and she gasped as the sheer sensuality of it made her throb heavily. She felt Mel leaning over her back, the apex of her thighs against her spread buttocks; her breasts hung down and Mel's hands were cupping and fondling them from behind and above. She bucked and screamed and moaned, pushing back against the strong thighs. Her breasts swelled into those firm caressing hands. One hand left her breast and made its way over her stomach to dip down between her legs. It firmly circled her clitoris and when Emma moaned loudly it started to rub her clitoris harder and faster. Just when Emma thought she was about to come, the hand stopped and she cried out, "Babe, please...please..."

"Shh, shh, my love..." Mel murmured. Mel pulled back and slightly shifted her position. She pulled Emma's hips higher and again pushed her shoulders onto the bed. Moving slightly to the left of Emma she found Emma's wet opening and gently inserted three fingers into her center. Emma gasped at the sensation of fullness. Mel began to plunge in and out; at the same time she leant her body back onto Emma so that Emma had to push back to keep her balance. The thrusting and plunging became a torment, an incredible sense of slick fullness as Mel continued the pumping. Mel moved harder, testing Emma's tolerance. Her other hand slipped back around the front of Emma's body and found her thickly coated clitoris. Emma screamed. Adding a fourth finger, Mel pumping faster; wet, slapping sounds of the slickness that coated Mel's hand reached Emma's ears. Sensing Emma's need, Mel's hand thrust on and on, her other hand working the swollen clitoris until Emma felt herself falling and gasping and calling out as an orgasm shook her body in a force of pleasure and sensation. She collapsed forward onto the bed with Mel's hand still inside her. Mel waited until her body stopped shuddering and then gently removed her hand. She moved to Emma's side, her lips touching her neck.

"You okay babe?" she asked softly.

"Yes, yes," Emma sobbed. "I never...never...that was incredible." She turned on her side and gently kissed Mel. Her one hand sought out Mel's smaller breasts. The nipples were as hard as pebbles and she rolled each one between her fingers, loving hearing the sound of this strong woman crying out. She turned and Mel lay on her back, her legs open. Emma slid her hand between Mel's legs and lowered her head to lay her lips on Mel's throbbing center. Mel jumped when she kissed her and pulled her upward. She laid Emma on her back and opening her legs, straddling Emma's hips. Emma realized what Mel needed and inserted three fingers into Mel's opening. Mel gasped and grabbing Emma's wrist, rode her fingers fiercely until with a shout she came, collapsing forward over Emma's body. Emma held onto her back feeling both their hearts beating in tandem and then slowing as their breathing returned to normal.

They lay side by side, holding hands, utterly spent. Emma felt relaxed and lazy. A sated exhaustion entered her body and she wondered if she should go back to her room.

"Stay here," Mel instructed as she felt Emma move. Emma turned on her side, spooned into Mel and fell into a dreamless sleep. Beside her, Mel looked at her tenderly. She could have easily carried on coaxing Emma to another orgasm but she realized that Emma was worn out with emotion, the mountain walk and the unaccustomed energy that their lovemaking had just exercised on her body.

CHAPTER 7

Waking the next morning, Emma felt a long-ago familiar contentment of closeness that came from another feminine body curled into her own. She felt a bit stiff and her thigh muscles trembled when she moved. Turning, she looked at Mel's sleeping face. It was as attractive as when awake, except that her features were slightly softened. She was still admiring her when Mel's eyes opened.

"Morning, sweetheart," Mel said. She searched Emma's face as if looking for any signs of regret or discomfort. Finding none she wrapped her arms around her.

"Morning," Emma said shyly. She was embarrassed at her almost wanton display of passion the evening before. Mel laughed softly.

"You must be quite hungry," she stated. Emma blushed.

"I am," she said, suddenly laughing.

"Well, how about you have a shower and we'll go down for breakfast. I think we have a lot to talk about," Mel said. Emma pouted. She would have liked to have showered with Mel, but her commonsense knew that if they did that, they probably would not make it to breakfast.

"There is an adjoining door, you know," Mel told her.

"Really?" Emma asked, surprised.

"Yes," Mel replied, pointing to a door which to Emma looked like a cupboard. "But it will be locked on my side," Emma said.

"No. I unlocked it the day you arrived," Mel said, unperturbed, "in case I needed to get in. Your father had told me you were a bit spoiled, so not knowing what you would be like I took the precaution of having an entry point to your suite." Emma wanted to be outraged but was too full of a sense of contentment to feel much of anything other than pleasure. Pulling on her top and panties that had been discarded the night before, she tried the door. It opened into the sitting room of her suite and she wondered why she had not noticed it before. She showered and once again found herself humming.

Dressed in a bright yellow top to reflect her mood and cream-colored shorts, she grabbed her bag on her way to the door. She stopped short when she saw Mel sitting in one of the chintz chairs in her sitting area.

"Ready?" Mel said, holding out her hand.

"Yes," Emma said, feeling a bit shy as took Mel's hand. They walked down to the dining room and the waiter greeted them with a broader smile than usual when he noticed their clasped hands. Mel waited until they had breakfast in front of them before asking,

"Emma, are you still okay with last night?"

"Yes," Emma said, "I am. Why are you asking?"

"I don't want you regretting anything. I am also not the type of woman who sleeps with someone and runs," Mel said directly. Emma's heart beat a little faster.

"Neither am I," she said. "Mel, I have not felt this alive since...

since, well since Tess passed away," she said, lowering her head. Mel lifted her chin up with one finger,

"And are you okay with that feeling?" she asked. Emma paused; was she okay with it? She knew deep in her heart that she was and that this felt right to her. She did not want to think beyond the holiday, though. What if Mel only wanted her for the next few weeks? Her eyes clouded over.

"What is it?" Mel asked, noticing the change in her.

"I am okay with it, with you...With us," Emma said, smiling.

"Good," Mel said. She was still concerned about the worried look she had seen in Emma's eyes. "I hope your father will not be annoyed that his carefully chosen guide turned into his daughter's lover," she said, trying to probe if this had caused the clouding over in Emma's eyes. Emma laughed.

"No, no," she said, "they will both be pleased to see me so happy. They have been trying to set me up with someone for the past few years." Mel felt relieved but still wondered why Emma had seemed concerned. She decided to let it drop for the time being. If she saw it again, she would persist.

"Shall we do our gym session this morning?" she said. "You seemed quite fit on the hike yesterday...and afterwards..." she teased, trailing off. Emma blushed. "I thought we might be able to do the seven-hour hike and see some edelweiss in a few days, if you like," Mel added.

"I'd love to," Emma said, smiling. The thought of the edelweiss reminded her of Tess. She knew in her heart Tess would approve of her and Mel. She still felt tenderness and sadness when she thought of Tess but it did not hurt like it had before. Mel smiled at her and Emma felt her heart melt.

CHAPTER 8

The next two days passed in a pattern of breakfast, gym, holding hands and wandering around the old town with nights of wild and tender love making. Emma could not believe how her passion had returned and felt embarrassed of what she felt was an insatiable desire to hold, caress and be caressed by Mel.

The morning of the hike arrived and Emma felt excited. *This is for Tess,* she thought, *I am going to see the edelweiss that I know she would have loved.* It was odd that Mel was not beside her in the bed. Looking around she saw a note on her bedside table that read: 'Did not want to wake you. Have to attend to an issue. Will see you at breakfast at 9.30 a.m'

Emma stretched out, relaxing; she had a bit of time then. She showered at leisure and dressed in shorts, sturdy hiking boots and a pale blue T-shirt that covered her shoulders so as to prevent sunburn. Mel had said she would pack a backpack, not that they needed much more than water and snacks and some basic first aid things as it was not a serious climb.

She went down to breakfast at 9.30 a.m. Mel was not there.

Feeling a touch of unease, she nevertheless told herself to be patient. Half an hour later, Mel had still not arrived. Emma took her cappuccino out onto the wide terrace. She wandered over to the railing to look at the view. Her eyes were caught by two figures below. They were hugging and she smiled indulgently. The figures broke apart and she gasped. One was Mel and the other was a very attractive woman of the same height and build as Mel. She almost dropped her coffee cup. Her heart raced. Backing away, she put the cup down safely on an outdoor table. Emma fled back through the dining room and up to her room. Mel was with another woman. She did not want to believe it but she had seen it with her own eyes. How stupid she had been. What had she been thinking? Mel was a gorgeous, attractive woman. What was she; a spoiled brat! Mel had said so herself; well, she did not exactly say brat but she did say spoiled. Emma stared at herself in the mirror. She could not compete with the sexy woman outside; her hair was mousy blonde, she was slender with curved hips and looked totally nondescript compared to the raven-haired beauty Mel had embraced. She suddenly felt a surge of anger, which was more empowering than the self-pity she was talking herself into. *Mel was leading me on when she already had someone else. Well, I won't be waiting around here to be deceived and used any longer,* she fumed. Pursing her lips determinedly she squared her shoulders, grabbed her canvas bag, put two small bottles of water and some fruit in it and marched out the door. She felt tears in her eyes, but blinked them away and hurried down the stairs so as not to bump into anyone. She exited at the back of the hotel and followed the signs that pointed to the direction of the edelweiss path. She tried to keep upbeat but she felt heaviness in her heart. *I was so stupid,* she kept thinking as she marched along, totally missing the beauty of the scenery around her.

Emma walked on determinedly for one hour before stopping. She sat on a rock and whilst telling herself to feel nothing but anger at being deceived, she found tears dripping off the end of her nose.

"Tess," she wailed. "Tess, I've been so silly." The silence that answered her was just as depressing. She hoisted her bag up and went on again, hardly looking at where she was going. The path climbed upward and all around her the wildflowers nodded their heads; butterflies and bees hummed and lived their busy lives, but she noticed none of it. Her heart was too wounded and she continued to berate herself which made her even more miserable.

After another hour she decided to stop again. Seating herself on a flattish rock she looked around properly for the first time. Far below she could see the town. It was quaint and looked like a chocolate box painting. The view soothed her slightly and she decided to ignore the last three weeks with their ups and downs and concentrate on seeing the edelweiss for Tess. She would forget Mel and every other woman, and tomorrow she would fly home. At least she was appreciated at work, she thought. She stood up and moved on.

If she had looked behind her she would have seen a very determined, fast moving figure gaining on her. But Emma was engrossed in building the shell that she was wrapping around herself again, and she noticed nothing. After fifteen minutes of walking, she thought she heard a voice call her name; turning around, she could not see anyone and decided that her ears were playing a trick on her due to voices that carried in the mountain echoes. She started walking and heard her name being called again. The voice sounded closer and the tone was sharp and quite familiar. She turned and saw Mel rounding the corner of the rocky outcrop she had just been sitting at. Emma felt her temper flare. How dare this woman come after her after what she had just witnessed? She tossed her head and turned, trying to walk as fast as she could. Given that she was going slightly uphill this was not very easy and she was aware of Mel's footsteps sounding louder and nearer.

"Emma, stop right now!" she heard Mel ordering her. "What the hell do you think you are doing running off like this?!" Realizing she could not outpace Mel, Emma turned sharply and got a shock to find Mel almost on top of her. "What am I doing? What am I doing?" she shouted angrily. She felt almost out of control. "I am going on the hike that we said we would-" She did not complete her sentence as Mel reached out and grabbing her, pulled her over to a flat lying expanse of rock, sat down and pulled Emma over her lap. She began paddling Emma's backside hard with her hand.

"I told you not to hike alone. It can be dangerous up here alone. You could slip and injure yourself. What on earth possessed you to disobey me?" she said, punctuating her words with slaps. Emma gasped and cried out in pain, but her outrage still won out.

"How dare you spank me? How dare you ask what I am doing? I am an adult and if I want to hike out here alone I will!"

"No, you won't!" Mel said. "Not whilst you are with me." She felt a sense of anger and frustration surge through her; this woman was so stubborn. She pulled her shorts down with one hand and started paddling the barely covered panty clad bottom even harder.

"Ow," Emma screamed, gasping in disbelief at the quick turn of events.

"With you?!" Emma managed to shout, her temper taking over. "With you?! Yes, I am with you... just like you are with your lover at the hotel! Yes...I saw you!"

Mel stopped spanking her, confused. She pulled Emma up and sat her none too gently next to her on the flat rock. Emma winced.

"What did you see, Emma?" Mel asked. Emma glared at her.

"I saw you," she said defiantly. "you and your...your...your...

woman!" She stumbled over the words, pain making it difficult to speak coherently.

"My woman?" Mel said, surprised, her brow furrowing then suddenly clearing. "Emma," she said sternly, "tell me what you saw."

"You know what I saw," Emma said, looking down at the ground, tears blurring her vision.

"Honey, tell me," Mel said softly. "Tell me!" she said a bit more firmly when Emma kept silent. She lifted her chin and noticed the tears in Emma's eyes. "You...hugging... hugging another woman...a sexy woman...at breakfast time...out below the terrace," Emma said, her voice caught on a sob. Mel laughed and pulled Emma into her.

"Listen carefully, Emma," she said gently, "you did see me hugging another woman," Emma gave another sob. "And yes, she is sexy-" Emma gasped and tried to pull herself from Mel's grasp, but Mel tightened her grip. "But that sexy woman you saw me hugging is my sister."

"Your sister?" Emma said, her mouth open with shock. "Your sister...your sister?" No wonder the woman had a similar figure and height as Mel with the same dark hair.

"Yes, my sister. If you had not taken off in a huff and waited like an adult for me to arrive at breakfast, I would have told you," Mel said sternly. "The reason I was late was because I had a message from the hotel front desk telling me my sister had arrived. I went down after leaving a note to you. I was worried something was wrong. She was supposed to be in Austria. Turns out she finished her tour early and was just stopping over for one day before heading home for Australia. I did not get her message last night as I was caught up in bed...with some lovely lady." Mel looked at her directly and lifting Emma's chin forced her to make eye contact. "I was saying goodbye to her, Emma."

Emma looked at her. She did not know what to say; she felt embarrassed at her childish assumptions and behavior.

"I'm sorry, Mel," she said, lowering her head.

"You should be," Mel said, "I told you I was serious about us, Emma. It hurts and annoys me that you did not trust me." Emma kept her head down; she felt relief and shame.

"You almost can't help your reactions, can you?" Mel said, almost to herself.

"I knew I could not compete with someone like that," Emma burst out.

"Like what?" Mel asked curiously.

"Well...gorgeous and toned and fit and attractive," Emma said quietly. Mel looked at her.

"Emma," she said, "you are sexy and gorgeous and utterly adorable... well, except when you are acting like a brat." They sat in silence, whilst Emma absorbed Mel's words and the situation she had misinterpreted. Mel pulled her to her and Emma leant into her embrace.

"I was silly Mel," she said, not making eye contact. "I'm sorry."

"It's okay," Mel said, "but Emma, I will not tolerate such behavior from you. Else I will have to take you firmly in hand." Emma wanted to feel outraged, but the words made her feel cherished and loved. She decided that at a later date she would chat with Mel about the spanking. But for now she would enjoy the relief she felt and the love she had for this woman.

Mel kissed the top of her head.

"Well, my love," she said, "do you still want to see the edelweiss? Although if it weren't for the sake of Tess, I'd march you straight back to the hotel and cancel this hike." Emma pouted.

"Yes, I want to see the edelweiss," she said. "Thanks, Mel."

"It's not far now," Mel said, "just another hour. The hike is a seven-hour round trip and you already did two and a half of those." They continued and this time Emma's heart felt light; how stupid she had been. She noticed the various flowers and the warmth of the sun and felt alive and happy.

One hour later Mel extended her hand to help Emma up the last section of the steep path, and Emma was looking up at pockets of edelweiss: white and pretty against the rocky lime scale of the mountains. From this distance their white velvety leaves contrasted sharply with the brown of the rock and the natural picture of beauty they created made Emma's heart swell with pleasure. Tess would have loved this. She would have captured the image in a photograph and enlarged it to put in her flower studio. Mel looked at Emma tenderly, noticing the various emotions chasing across her face. To help her manage any pain she might be feeling Mel factually and calmly described the edelweiss to her; the small florets in their centers, the velvety white leaves around the centers and how the edelweiss was not strictly considered a flower. She explained that the edelweiss had originated in the Himalayas.

Emma leaned into her, loving to hear her gorgeous guide telling her facts about the edelweiss and although she felt sad that Tess was not there with her, she felt deep contentment and love coursing through her. Mel held her tightly. She gently turned Emma toward her and lowered her head. Emma lifted her lips to Mel's and melted into Mel's embrace.

A couple of hikers below looked up and saw an image of two figures outlined in front of a towering mountain, white edelweiss framing them. It made a striking photo and one hiker raised her camera to capture the loving beauty of the human forms silhouetted against the wild setting.

Emma looked up at Mel and the mountain behind her. She could have sworn she heard a voice saying, '*I love you my sweet one. Be happy.*' Tears filled her eyes but she felt so content and knew that she was right where she belonged: in Mel's arms. "Mel...," she began.

"Emma...," Mel said simultaneously.

"You first," Emma said. Mel looked at her, love shining from her deep brown eyes.

"Emma, will you be mine?" she asked tenderly. Emma smiled and with tears of happiness, threw her arms around her lover's neck.

"Yes, oh yes, Mel. I'll be yours...always," she replied softly. "Always."

The End

(For Now)

PART 2

Finding Home

CHAPTER 1

Emma looked out at the garden through the cottage lounge window. Once again the spring bulbs were pushing their way up through the dark soil, some with tips just showing and others racing ahead with their yellow petals starting to unfurl. She smiled, remembering one year ago looking out her parents' lounge window, seeing the new spring bulbs pushing their way up out of the cracked earth and feeling that her life was about to change.

Change it did that summer when she set off to Switzerland to see the wildflowers her beloved Tess had longed to see. She had hoped it would finally enable her to lose the self-induced melancholic state that had worsened over the years since Tess had died.

Meeting Melissa Rustin, the Alpine trekking guide her over protective father had hired, had certainly spurred her out of her depressed state. She had found herself inexplicably drawn to the attractive hiking guide and protector who had calmly and firmly taken no nonsense from her. Her heart beat a bit faster remembering the first time she had seen her: her toned and sexy body, deep brown eyes and smooth, dark brown hair. Emma had meant to set the rules with the guide or send her packing: instead, she had found herself firmly pulled into line as well as falling head over heels in love when she had least expected it.

After the summer they had travelled back to her home. Her parents, whilst slightly taken aback, were delighted to see the spirited daughter they remembered from her days with Tess, back in their arms. They welcomed Melissa as warmly as they had welcomed Tess. Taking a further step in her emotional healing, Emma suggested she and Mel move into the cottage she had owned with Tess not far from her parents' large home.

The first three months had been a whirlwind of settling in, with Melissa starting work at the nearby sports center and Emma settling back into her role at her parents' fashion company. Added to this was the more important aspect of Emma learning once again to live within the boundaries her caring, yet stern partner set for her. The next six months had seen them settle into a comfortable if busy routine.

The sound of the front door opening interrupted her reverie and the voice of that caring, stern partner floated down the hallway.

"Honey, are you home?" Emma smiled. She was not often home before Melissa in the afternoons due to her set hours at the family business and Mel's more flexible hours at the sports center.

"Hi babe," she said. "How was your day?" She had noticed that Melissa, whilst always upbeat and caring, had seemed a bit preoccupied lately and she wanted to find out if anything was wrong. She was aware that her American home was far away from Melissa's general European and Australian life. They had briefly broached the subject at the end of their summer romance and it had not seemed to be an issue at the time. Mel had settled as well in her hometown as Emma had with her new boundaries and Mel was one of the more popular and highly in demand instructors as the sport's center.

"Hi, darling." Mel's eyes widened in pleasure. "I saw your car. It's unusual to see you home this early. Everything okay?" She walked over and kissed Emma. "Everything's fine." Emma laughed. "Can't a woman surprise her partner?" she teased.

"Hmm...Of course she can." Mel swept her into a hug and jokingly bent her backwards as if they were dancing.

"Seriously though," she said, tipping Emma back upright and holding her steady whilst Emma rebalanced her stance, "you almost never get home before six most nights."

"I know," Emma said. "It's spring though, and when I saw those bulbs pushing their way up through the earth this morning, it reminded me of when I decided to go to Switzerland. So I decided to come home early and prepare a picnic for us. I was waiting for your arrival to surprise you at the door. Guess I got caught up in my thoughts." Mel smiled affectionately.

"Luckily I have no evening clients." she said. "I'll shower first, babe. I'm feeling very sweaty right now."

Mel strode off taking the small staircase that led upstairs two steps at a time, her toned legs and arms flashing through her thin gym wear. *I wonder what's up with Emma,* she mused. It was unlike her to be so spontaneous. Wondering if the time of year reminded Emma of her partner Tess who had died years back of advanced ovarian cancer, she had a hasty shower and went back down to find out if that was what was really bothering her.

As she reached the lounge door Mel paused. Emma was sitting in the chair and the sunlight glinted off the top of her blonde hair. Her heart melted at the sight and she fondly remembered seeing Emma the first time. After opening her hotel bedroom door, she had taken a seat in a comfy chair near the open window that looked out over the Swiss lake. She had not been in reverie like now however, her mouth had had a determined set to it and her green eyes had

61

glinted with passion as she told Mel she would not be needing her services. Mel could not help laughing softly as she remembered the shocked expression on Emma's face when she told her firmly that that was not how it was going to be.

Now, still smiling, she walked over to her.

"Daydreaming, my love?" She said gently.

"Yup. Mel, I..." She paused.

"What is it?" Mel asked.

"Nothing really. I just-well-"

"Yes?" Mel said patiently, wondering what on earth was making Emma so hesitant. It had been at least a month since she had needed any type of reinforcement to keep to the boundaries they had both decided on. She had enjoyed being back in a domestic discipline relationship although it was not the major focus in their relationship. Emma was someone who needed occasional boundaries in her life and Mel was well able and willing to provide those to the person she loved.

Feeling slightly alarmed, she tilted Emma's head up, one finger under her chin and looked at her sternly.

"I just wondered if you were happy, truly happy I mean... here...with me...away from all you know," Emma blurted out.

Mel let go of her chin and sat down opposite Emma. That was not what she had expected to hear. Emma had obviously noticed that she had not been as upbeat as she usually was and she realized just how much Emma cared for and loved her.

"I think it's time for that picnic," she said in response finally. "We can chat whilst eating."

"But..."

"No buts. We have lots of time to talk it all through," Mel said. "Don't worry," she added, seeing Emma's eyes cloud over. "Everything is fine. I'm touched that you think about me and worry about my needs."

Emma nodded and went off to the kitchen to fetch the hamper she had prepared. The various cheeses and rye breads with the flask of hot barley soup and bottle of red wine no longer seemed as appetizing and romantic as it had when she had prepared it earlier. The spring weather was still chilly so she put on her coat and after loading up a picnic blanket, walked back to the hall with the basket.

Mel took the basket from her and hand in hand they walked out, heading for the nearby park.

Emma felt her heart beating; *did Mel want to leave*, she worried silently. She had found love again and did not think she could bear to lose her Alpine hiking guide.

CHAPTER 2

They reached the slight hill that was just starting to shed its winter coat of dry grass and cracked earth. The trees' green buds were a stark contrast to the brown earth below. Walking up still hand in hand, Emma could not help a sense of unease uncurl inside of her. She had wanted to show that she cared for Mel and her needs but now she regretted it. *What if Mel wants to leave,* she thought again in a slight panic.

Cresting the hill, they saw the small park lake, quiet and still below them. The last sun rays turned part of the water silver and gold. It was pretty and Emma relaxed slightly.

Mel, for her part, was smiling. She remembered coming to the park for the first time after Emma had strode out of the cottage in a huff over Mel's admonishment about her long work hours and constantly going to bed so late that she'd wake up grumpy. Her eyes flashing, as they had on the first day she had met her back in the Swiss hotel, she had told Mel to mind her own business and that she was a grown woman. She had flounced out of the house. Mel had smiled grimly to herself. She had realized it was tiredness talking but decided that Emma needed some guidance in getting back on track. Following her had led her to the park where Emma had strode up the very hill they had just walked. She had jumped when Mel touched her arm and told her firmly to go back home. Unable to help herself, Emma had crossed her arms over her chest and told her to stop following her. Mel had grabbed her arm and marched her back to the house. Emma protested all the way whilst at the same time glancing around in embarrassment to make sure no one was watching them. Once back inside Mel had pulled her over lap and begun spanking her backside hard and fast until Emma had suddenly started crying and gone limp. It never took long for Emma to regain her control once Mel took her in hand.

Mel grinned; Emma was so stubborn. However, that was not why they were here today. Clearly Emma was worried about her and it was a good time to chat about their mutual needs and how to meet them in a way that satisfied both of them. She was touched that Emma had noticed that, whilst content, she was not as happy as she had been when they had first come back to Emma's home town.

In silence Emma laid the blanket down and they sat leaning against each other looking out over the water.

"Honey, what made you think I'm unhappy here?" Mel asked once they had both mellowed in the evening light.

"I'm not entirely sure," Emma said. "I just feel like you are not as upbeat as you usually are. Mel..." she said, getting up on her knees and looking at her directly. "I love you, but if you are unhappy here, I don't want to keep you away from what you know and love." She averted her eyes, worried that Mel would see the upset in them. She wanted Mel to have the life that best suited her: but what if Mel wanted to go? Could she leave her home, her parents-she was their only child. Still, she was forty and should not be this attached to them, she reasoned. Mel pulled her down beside her.

"Babe," she said, "I love you too and I am happy with you. I am so touched that you have thought about me and what I might need. It's true I feel a bit...well...separated from..." she paused as she noticed Emma breathe in as if in anticipation of bad news, " the type of life I led. It was far more adventurous than working at a fitness center."

"Oh," Emma bit her lip. "I thought perhaps you missed Australia or Switzerland and your family."

"No, I miss what I used to do: guiding for hikes, the mountains and the more adventurous sports. I can go anytime I like to see my dad," she said. Emma felt lighter in heart but then suddenly depressed. How could she ensure Mel's needs for her career were met? She was happy as a business manager in parents' business although she was quite stressed at times due to the long hours and the pressure of being the owners' daughter.

"Do you-I mean, do you want to leave me?" Emma asked hesitantly.

"Leave you?" Mel asked, in surprise, "No, I never want to leave you. But perhaps we could talk about moving elsewhere where we could both be happy in what we do." Mel spoke gently: she did not want Emma to panic. She knew Emma had an issue about losing people close to her, having lost her partner to cancer when she was only thirty-four and being very close to her loving parents.

"You are asking me to leave all I know!" Emma burst out. She bit her lip. That sounded so immature and she knew it was not what Mel was asking. "I'm sorry," she said. Mel laughed.

"You are a little spit fire, Emma. I am not asking you to leave your country nor me. I just need to do the career that I love." She loved Emma which is why she had moved to be with her and spent a year here. If Emma refused any type of change, she would accept that, but Mel did not know if she could accept that forever.

Emma felt torn. She loved Mel and was afraid of losing her yet she was anxious. *What about my parents?* she thought miserably. Being such a close knit family and being the only child would make it hard for her to leave. "Honey, if it upsets you, we don't need to discuss it now, but you need to think about it over the next few months. You asked me, and that is my honest answer. I love you and I am content, but I do miss the people I knew and most especially the career I loved. However, I love you and will stay here if this is what you want."

Emma took a deep breath.

"What would you want in an ideal world?" she asked. Mel smiled, and pulled her into an embrace.

"You-of course. I can have my sister and father visit here anytime. Wendy loved it when she visited us before. But what about if we moved nearer to mountain ranges? They are always looking for experienced guides over the summer and autumn months."

"You mean you'd still be happy here...in this country?" Emma asked. Mel nodded. As Mel continued talking it was obvious she had researched a lot about it. She knew the areas where the best hiking was and which areas needed experienced hiking guides.

"Well," Emma said, her heart breaking a little as she realized just how much Mel needed her working life back, "you need to go and do that then. I will see you after summer time." Mel held her close.

"Would you not come with me, my little spit fire?" she asked. Emma started; why had she not thought of that? Six months of hiking and six months back home in a year did not sound bad at all. She had a deputy at work who was very competent and it was her parents' business after all. She did not want to let them down, though, so she knew she'd have to talk to them. Nothing was impossible, she suddenly realized. She must not let her past and sadness over losing Tess make her see the gloomy side of things. Instead she needed to see the possibilities.

"Yes," she said smiling. "Yes, this spit fire will come with you."

CHAPTER 3

The next few months were a flurry of activity. Conversations had been held with Emma's parents. They would miss seeing their daughter daily but were supportive of Emma and Mel's decision to live six months of the year in a mountainous hiking area. The hardest part turned out to be convincing Emma's parents they did not need to buy them a house in the new area as they had immediately suggested.

Mel had found a company that provided not just her employment but also a cabin in one of the small towns that bordered the mountains popular with hikers. Emma's mother immediately wanted to see photos and have the cabin decorated for them. Not wanting her to feel left out they agreed that as the cabin was already basically furnished, she could arrange the soft furnishings decor. This was a good idea as it gave Emma's mother focus and she was able to pour her love into her designs and the arrangement of getting it done as opposed to worrying over missing her daughter.

Emma found herself getting excited. They had discussed what she would do whilst Mel was working. She might look for part-time employment in the small town or start her own writing for self-publishing; writing had been a hobby she had always meant to get around to, but never had. Mel's hours would have to be flexible to manage various hikers needs and the hiking packages offered by the company. There were hikes that lasted a few hours to a few days. Some were for casual hikers whilst others were more suited for high fitness individuals involving high altitudes and the scaling of sheer mountain rock walls.

Mel had to go for training in the area earlier for a month to learn about the area and Emma had missed her. The month break had been good for her, though, as it had affirmed that she needed and wanted to move wherever Mel went in life.

The day arrived for their departure and Emma rolled her eyes as Mel, looking directly at her, reiterated the facts of where they would be living. Although they were on the outskirts of the small town still within its border, their cabin nestled into the mountain foothills so Emma would need to be careful, she stated again, and not go wandering off unless it were into the town or with someone else. Mel was well aware of the eye rolling and her palm itched. It was perhaps time for Emma to learn that she might need a bit more than just an occasional spanking.

Emma was saved from making any exasperated reply and any resultant consequences by the arrival of her parents to say goodbye. It was reminiscent of when she'd left for Switzerland on holiday a year earlier and again she found herself smiling with deep tenderness and affection for her loving parents. She noticed that as Mel hugged them tightly, her eyes had a slightly bright sheen to them. Emma was filled with gratitude that her partner and parents got on so well and loved each other.

"Now you two need to look after yourselves..." her mother said, her eyes tearing slightly.

"They'll be fine, my love," her father soothed, putting his arm around her shoulder reassuringly just as he had when they had watched their daughter leave for the airport on her way to Switzerland.

Mel started up their 4 x 4 and they drove slowly out of the small driveway, Emma waving until she could no longer see her parents.

The area they were moving to was only four hours away and yet the landscape looked so different it felt as if they were in a totally different country. The small town ahead of them was postcard pretty. As it was an area popular with tourists, the town had grown to include quite a few restaurants and cafes as well as two supermarkets, some clothing outlets and numerous arts and crafts shops. The greenness of the mountains stood around the town in a semi-circle and at the far end was a large lake.

"It's so beautiful," Emma enthused. "Pull up and let's look around." Mel grinned, pleased that Emma liked it as much as she had in the photos.

"Let me show you the cabin first and then perhaps we can come in for an early supper." she suggested. Emma agreed. They drove on passing through the main shopping area which gave way to some houses and cabins. Tourist cabins and a hotel were on the opposite side of the lake. Mel drove up a dirt driveway that led to a medium sized log cabin. The porch with two low steps faced toward the town, the view of which was mostly blocked by trees, with the lake over to the right. The water could be seen shimmering through the trees. To the left were more trees and shrubs and the back of the cabin was framed by mountains.

They got out and stretched. Emma laughed as a sense of lightness filled her. Mel grinned, and acting on impulse, she swept Emma up and carried her up the two porch stairs setting her down just outside the front door.

They smiled at each other. Turning the key in the door, they entered. The cabin was light and bright due to the large windows that ran the length of the porch. The lounge with its warm wood walls had been decorated in creams with rosy hues provided by cushions and paintings as designed by Emma's mother and decorated by two of her trusted staff she had sent over. The layout was open plan: the kitchen sat to the left of the lounge and at the back were two doors each leading to a room with an attached bathroom. It was not large but it was perfect for them. They unpacked their cases and put out the few knick knacks they had brought with them.

"Shall we hit the town, babe?" Mel asked. Emma grinned and they headed back out. It seemed very 'holidayish' out there, she thought. Life was going to be very different for the next six months with no routine of the office.

The town center was only a ten-minute walk away.

"Let's try the small restaurant with the flowers outside; the first one we saw driving in," Emma suggested. Mel nodded assent and they walked past the various stores and shops. Emma felt tempted to pop into some of the art shops but she knew there would be lots of time for that. The residents of the town were an older crowd and there were numerous tourists of all ages still browsing even though it was late afternoon. Some young men passed by in an open van and hooted loudly at the two women walking hand in hand. Mel stiffened and pulled Emma closer.

"I don't think I want you coming into town alone," she said. Emma looked at her.

"Relax babe," she said, "I can't be cocooned up in the cabin. They were just young lads being silly." She hoped silently that was true and that they had been hooting just as fun and not in protest at them walking hand in hand. They reached the small restaurant which turned out to be as inviting on the inside as it looked from the outside. Small tables with late spring flowers on white cloths stood waiting and as it was late afternoon, lamps and lanterns had already been lit. They twinkled in the dim interior and provided a comforting, relaxing and rustic atmosphere.

"Ladies, what can I do for you?" a tall attractive woman with black hair styled into a Cleopatra bob asked.

"Table for two please," Emma said, facing the woman who smiled at them, her deep blue eyes assessing.

"Sure, this way. I am sorry; our waitress has just popped out to see her baby. In the meantime I'll help you." They sat at their shown table as the woman who seemed to be the manager or owner went to fetch menus. She returned with two brown and white menus and said,

"You can look at the menu but I can recommend the burgers; fresh made burgers from a secret recipe courtesy of my wife." She smiled at them and they smiled back. Emma was relieved; it might be easier making friends here than she had thought.

"By the way, I am Maria and that lovely lady over there…," she said gesturing toward the counter and the kitchen beyond which a sturdily built woman in a blue checked shirt with short cropped blonde hair was peering, "is my wife and our chef, Marty."

"I thought I heard voices," Marty said in a deep voice walking out from the kitchen. "We are normally quiet until 6 p.m when it's not the full tourist season."

"Hi," Mel said, politely extending her hand to Maria. "I am Mel and this is my partner, Emma."

"Are you just passing through?" Maria asked, as they all shook hands.

"No. We are staying here; well, for six months at least. I am starting at the adventure sports center."

"Oh, the new hiking guide; Melissa?" Maria said. "You are the

73

talk of the town. When someone told us you were coming we were pleased to think of new additions to our small town and lesbian community. We did not get to see you when you were here last month. Steve and Andrea kept you busy at the center it seems."

Emma raised her eyebrows. How had they known Mel was lesbian? What had she been doing when she was here training? Mel saw her raised eyebrow and smiled inwardly, knowing exactly what Emma was thinking.

"Yes. I was busy," she said. "I was completing the week-long hikes and showing off my fitness levels. I had heard however, that there were two lovely ladies we needed to meet."

Maria laughed and Marty snorted.

"Lovely-hmm-I'd love to know who said that! Anyway, will you try the burgers?"

"Sounds good," Mel said, looking at Emma to see if she agreed. Emma kept quiet. She felt a bit put out. As soon as Maria and Marty retreated, she looked at Mel but before she could open her mouth, Mel said,

"Relax babe, I did not mention there were other lesbians here as I had not met Maria and Marty."

"Did you...well, are there others-I mean, did you go out with any others?" she asked, hating how jealous and insecure she sounded.

"Yes and no. Meaning yes, I met a fellow hiking guide who is a lesbian and is here alone and no, I did not go out with her."

"Why didn't you tell me?" Emma said.

"What...?" Mel asked in surprise. "Tell you that one of the guides was a lesbian? Why would I focus on someone's sexuality? What is wrong with you?" she asked.

"Well..." Emma said lamely, not quite sure herself why she felt so worked up about it. "You could have just said. I might as well go

74

home if you have been gadding about with other women, without me." She stood up in a huff and Mel caught her wrist.

"Sit down!" she commanded quietly. Emma hesitated. "Sit down, before I make you sit down." Mel said. Emma sat. She did not want a scene, especially not in front of the two women they had just met. It bypassed her at that moment that she was the one who had started to create a scene.

"What is wrong with you? Spit it out," Mel said. "Now!" Emma looked at her. Goodness, she was behaving like a teenager, she scolded herself and not a mature woman.

"Sorry," she said. "I just suddenly felt left out. You will be gadding about with another woman who does all the things you enjoy doing and I'll be left at home isolated."

"Is that what you really think?" Mel asked, smiling. "We will be taking separate hikes and won't see much of each other but even if we did it does not mean I would be 'gadding' around with her as you put it. I love you and will be 'gadding' around with you. Hopefully she will become a friend to both of us." Emma knew was being foolish but had an uneasy feeling that she could not compete with an athletic lesbian who was able to hike up mountains and do all the sorts of activities Mel did and loved. Perhaps, she thought, she was stressed from the move and so this brought her insecurities to the front. "Sorry," she said again, smiling now.

"It's okay babe. It is a big change from what you are used to. I get that," Mel said. She stored the information in her head. This was something similar to what Emma had felt back in Switzerland when she had said she could not compete against other strong women who enjoyed the athletic side of life like Mel did. Could Emma not see she did not want an athletic woman, but the beautiful, softer yet independent woman that she was?

The burgers were as good as Maria had said they were.

"Wow. That was delicious." Mel said when Maria came up, after asking if they wanted dessert. "I think we are too full for dessert." At that moment, a young woman ran in.

"Sorry, Maria," she panted, "I just got Johnnie to sleep."

"No problem, honey." Maria said. "This is Mel and Emma. Hopefully they will be frequent customers." She winked at them both. "This is our waitress Ann."

"Hi," Ann said, her mind clearly elsewhere, as she rushed off looking for an apron and began setting out cutlery.

"Forgive her," Maria smiled. "She has a small baby and life seems to be one big rush to her."

"I bet it is," Emma said, laughing. Her heart ached slightly. She and Tess had planned to start a family just before Tess had died.

"Thanks," Mel said as she took the change from Maria when she returned with the check. "Perhaps you would visit us for a drink one eve?"

"We'd love that," sounded the deep voice of Marty from the back of the kitchen. They all laughed.

"Eavesdropper!" Maria teased.

"Well...anything for a break from this kitchen," Marty teased back.

They walked back hand in hand. The late afternoon had given way to early evening and the sun had just lowered. The sky was a pale blue and grey.

"I have a good feeling about this place." Mel said.

"Me too." Emma smiled at her.

They stopped at the nearest grocery store to get some essential items, then went to their cabin. Too tired out to explore further or make love, they drifted off to sleep tightly spooned into each other.

CHAPTER 4

"Morning, sleepyhead." Emma whispered in Mel's ear. She had one arm round Mel's waist and, hearing the various bird calls, felt a sense of gratitude for all she had. Mel's eyes opened. She was one of those people who generally woke early and had energy from the minute the sun rose. It was odd that Emma had woken first.

"Morning babe," she said, turning on her side, her left arm running down Emma's smooth back. "Hmm...you feel so good." She breathed in the scent of Emma's hair. She trailed kisses down the side of her cheek. Emma laughed, her hand briefly cupping Mel's firm breast and lingering over her taut abs.

"I won't smell so good if you try and kiss me," she teased. "...Haven't brushed my teeth yet." Mel groaned as Emma rolled out of her touch. Emma giggled. She knew her brief caresses had teased Mel, but Mel needed to get to work on time especially on her first day.

"Up you get," she said. "I'll get breakfast on."

"I'll get you for this later," Mel said, getting out of bed and grinning as she watched Emma's bare legs flashing under her short night dress. The rim of her buttocks peeped out enticingly as she walked. *Best make my shower a cold one,* Mel thought.

After Mel had left for her first day Emma wandered back to their room. *Right,* she told herself, *I best make a plan. Tidy up and then walk into town or walk around the lake, perhaps even explore the surrounding lower mountains and meadows.* She would also have to make an effort about writing everyday if she planned to put her idea of self-publishing into action. During the week she would find out if any part-time work was available in town. She did not need the money but working part-time would occupy her and help her to become part of the local community and meet other people. She knew many people would envy her current situation and felt she should not laze it away as tempting as that would be after years of hard work.

Two hours later, dressed in fitted grey ski pants, green and grey trainers and a pale green sports top that accentuated the color of her blonde hair, she headed out. She had decided on exploring the lake and perhaps going back via town.

The lake was shimmering blue and silver in the day light sun. There were a few sail boats out and even some people swimming in one part of it. The water looked quite cold still and Emma admired their bravery. The lake was large: bordered on one side by tourist cabins and a quaint hotel, and on the other sides by mountains and trees. It reminded her slightly of Switzerland.

There were a few tourist shops and eateries near the tourist cabins which were about ten-minute walk away from the town center which was further left. On the shore opposite she could see the trees thickly grouped with the mountains rising behind them further in the distance.

She thought it would be an adventure to see if she could get around the lake on the side opposite to the tourist cabins. Emma turned and started walking, keeping nearer the shore side than the trees. It was beautiful and she felt alive in such scenery. She heard church bells ringing. The sound was behind her and looking back she could just make out the white spire of a small church. It added to the charm and peace of the area.

She rounded to the right, noticing the lake seemed to continue for miles. She started sweating slightly and wished she had brought some water with her. An hour later she decided that the lake was too long and wide for her to walk that day without proper preparation. It was colder than when she had set off and she realized that the sky was grey. Emma turned back but when she did, the terrain looked all the same. Feeling slightly panicked she told herself to remain calm and to keep the shore line to her right as it had been to her left when she walked up. As she turned, she heard voices and the sounds of footsteps. A small group of hikers was coming through the trees heading in the direction of the lake shoreline. The woman in the front was obviously a guide. She wore a light weight jacket with an adventure center logo on the front and held a walking pole. She was taller than Emma's 5'5" with dark hair and an athletic figure. Emma wondered if this was the guide Mel had mentioned that she worked with. Hurrying off as she did not want to appear lost in front of anyone, she tripped over a stone and stumbled.

"Can I help you? Are you okay?" the guide called out. Her voice was deep and confident.

"No, no, I'm fine thanks," Emma called back. She carried on walking.

"Are you lost?" the voice said again.

"No," Emma said loudly starting to feel annoyed. How dare this woman assume she was lost! The guide was walking over, her eyes appraising Emma's slightly sweaty state and the goose bumps on her arms.

"The town is that way," the guide said.

"I know," Emma said haughtily.

"It's not wise to walk without a jacket or water. If you do not know the area it can be dangerous walking alone," the guide said, eyeing Emma speculatively.

"I know," Emma said, gritting her teeth. This woman sounded just like Mel when she got into one of her 'lecture moods' as Emma called it.

"Thank you," she said, trying to smile politely and turning away.

"We are walking back. Walk with us." the guide said. The way she said it made it sound a lot like an order as opposed to a suggestion. Emma opened her mouth to refuse, but the guide was already calling the group over, and had walked up next to her. She had no option but to tag along with them unless she wanted to look like a total idiot and run off. She was being silly anyway, she told herself. Why did she feel antipathy toward this woman just because perhaps she and Mel worked together? She was not even sure they did. "Thank you for letting me walk with you," she said. "I'm Emma."

"Pleased to meet you, Emma. I'm Charlie." The small group was happy bunch of tourists, low level hikers on a a few hours guided walk around the lower foot hills and lake area. They talked among themselves about the elk they had seen and two who were obviously avid bird watchers compared detailed notes about the various species they had seen. Emma was not a bird watcher but she envied their obvious enjoyment of the hike.

"Thank you for your help," she said to the quiet guide as they got to the start of the lake.

"Pleasure," Charlie said. "For future, if you don't know your way around, you need a guide or at least a map and supplies. The weather changes easily and the terrain is not easy for inexperienced walkers." Emma colored, her annoyance flooding back.

"I have a guide" she said curtly. "She's...she's...just at work at present." Awareness sharpened Charlie's gaze.

"Are you Emma," she asked, "Mel's partner?"

"Um...yes," she said reluctantly. Charlie laughed.

"I'll tell her I met you when I'm back at the office."

"Oh, no need...no need. I'll tell her I bumped into you when she's home." Emma said her heart sinking. She did not need Mel to over react about her going off for a simple walk. This smirking woman would probably tell her that Emma had looked helpless.

"Thanks once again," Emma said and virtually ran off. Forgetting her idea of wondering through some of the art stores, she walked back home feeling irate and defensive.

Once back home, she showered, dressed in a warmer outfit and went to sit out on the porch and relax with a beer. She needed to calm herself and perhaps think about downloading a map of the area.

The tension flowed out of her. Small birds were hopping on the ground among the pine needles and the chatter of gentle chirrups and whistles filled the air. The lake shimmered in the distance.

"Emma!" Mel's voice shook her out of her relaxed state. "Are you okay? Why aren't you answering your phone?" Mel was coming up the two steps of the porch toward her.

"Home already?" Emma asked calmly, ignoring the phone question as she had totally forgotten about it out here in nature. "Yes, I'm allright. How your first day?" Mel took a deep breath.

"My first day was fine until I was informed you were wondering around alone seeming lost way down by the lake." Emma blinked in annoyance.

"Oh," she said. "I see Charlie could not wait to tell tales. I was not lost. I merely went for a walk along the shore side of the lake. It was sunny and beautiful when I set off. There's no need to talk to me like I'm five!" she finished off. Mel ran a hand through her hair and lowered her voice. Worry over Emma had made her sound a bit sharp and Emma was a grown woman. Still, she was not used to nature settings.

"Emma, I understand you have to occupy yourself and be out and about but remember we spoke about this at length; what you can and can't do. I even gave you a map before we left that clearly marked safe areas for you." Emma remembered zoning out during Mel's last talk and had not even taken notice of the map. She had just stuffed whatever pieces of paper Mel had handed her into her bag.

"Oh, relax babe," she said. "Tell me about your day."

"My day is not finished yet. I came to see if you are okay... And if you plan to act like this perhaps you need a reminder of the facts I told you about regarding the area." Her voice had sharpened again and instead of it being a warning to Emma, it irritated her even more.

"Mel," she said, standing up, "I am not a teenager or a weak woman who needs your protection to walk around. You have your job to do,...so go and do it and leave me to enjoy my days though they might not be as busy as yours." Mel tried kept her temper. They both needed to adjust and it was only day one after all. However, the stubborn Emma seemed to be out in full force and needed a reminder of the boundaries set for her. She would not be able to work effectively if she had to constantly worry about her.

"Sit down!" she said. Not waiting to see if Emma obeyed, she pulled her down beside her on the porch bench. "Listen, love," she said, looking at her, "I need to know that you are safe whilst I am working, so I don't want you going out for the rest of the day." She held up a hand as Emma started protesting. "I want you to find the map of the area I gave you and look at it. I have marked out the safe areas for you...well, safe areas for inexperienced walkers and hikers. There are many dangers here. And even if the area is fine for you to go, you need to take water with you as well as a snack, torch and a jersey. The weather changes quickly."

Emma felt guilty and annoyed at the same time. She should have read the map and details Mel had given her but had not bothered. She had been too busy finishing up the projects from her job and handing everything over to her deputy, leaving her feeling tired when she got home. It annoyed her though that Mel felt she needed to be looked after.

"Mel," she said, firmly, "I am quite sensible and yes I will look at the map and yes, I do remember the talks you gave-" She closed her eyes briefly knowing she had zoned out during those talks. "but I am grown woman and can easily handle looking after myself." Mel looked at her.

"Well, you best mean that," she said, "because if this happens again, I won't be talking to you,-my hand will."

"You will not touch me," Emma said haughtily, her cheeks flushing.

"I will...and painfully too," Mel said firmly. "Now..." she pulled Emma up with her and landed a swat on Emma's backside just hard enough to sting as a warning, "I'll see you later. No going out until I know you know where it's safe to go."

"Fine," Emma said, trying to sound dignified and cursing her complexion that flushed so easily. She hated it when Mel spanked her even though it created a sense of security in her.

"And you look after yourself at work," she came back with.

Mel grinned; Emma could be such a brat at times.

Once Mel had left, Emma did feel a bit silly. Even a child might have a taken a jersey and some water. She went to her bag and fished out the papers Mel had given her. One was indeed a map and easily readable. Mel had clearly marked areas that were safe and accessible and made good short hikes. The second page, which obviously came from the adventure center listed facts about the area and precautionary tips of what to wear and take and what to do in the unlikely event of coming across of bear or cougar. She noticed with interest the meadow elk hikes which the group that day had been enthusing about. She might try that some day; after all, it was right on the edge of a -safe- area.

She had supper cooking when Mel returned. They did not mention the earlier incident and settled outside with a glass of white wine each.

"It was a good day babe," Mel enthused when Emma asked her about it. Mel lit up and Emma was happy that she was able to do what she loved in an environment that she loved. "Maybe I could show you around the center and you might even want to join one of the hikes." Mel said.

"I'd love to," Emma said. "As long as it's with you and not that Charlie!" she added.

"Charlie's alright." Mel laughed. "You're just annoyed because she called you out for not thinking. If you had gotten into trouble the rescue services would get involved." Emma knew she was right but could not bring herself to admit it. She felt a bit jealous about Charlie. "Are we clear about today?" Mel asked.

"Did you read the map and brochure?"

"I did," Emma said stiffly. "Thank you for giving it to me."

"Show me the areas you can go on the map." Mel said.

"Mel," Emma said. "I am not going to be treated-"

"Go and get the map and show me.," Mel repeated in an even tone.

"No," Emily put her foot down. "No. I have read it and

understand it." Before she could get further the wine glass was whipped from her hand and she was pulled up none too gently. With one hand firmly gripping Emma's arm, Mel spanked her bottom hard ten times before Emma could even draw breath. "Ow...ow... ow!" she finally managed to shriek. Her jogging bottoms were fairly thin and the slaps had stung.

"If you don't want to go over my knee, I suggest you get the map," Mel said calmly, looking at her. Emma hesitated. She hated it when Mel was like this; so totally calm and not budging an inch. Mel's one eye brow lifted and not daring to push the issue further Emma went in. They sat together. The discussion did help as it made the walks and town area much clearer.

Mel pulled her close and she leant her head on her shoulder, their hands intertwined. Emma's heart calmed; she so loved this woman. Lifting her head, she found Mel's brown eyes looking down at her with tenderness and desire. Mel put one finger under her chin and titled her head up. Emma gave way to a lingering deep kiss, her hands automatically reaching for Mel's breasts. Mel groaned.

They stumbled through to the bedroom together. Emma turned to Mel and taking the lead, pulled her sports fitted t-shirt over her head. She ran her hands over Mel's firm skin and pushed her hands away when Mel moved to remove her T-shirt. Her hands ran over Mel's firm breasts and Mel groaned her nipples hardening like pebbles. Emma felt a surge of intense desire run through her, wetness flooding her center. She lowered her head to those breasts and in turn licked and sucked each one, pushing Mel back against the bedroom wall as she did so. She lowered herself down slowly, her mouth and tongue trailing over the firm abs, her tongue going over each ridge of muscle and lower to the rim of Mel's ski pants. Her one hand ran up the inside of Mel's leg and squeezed her inner thigh. She nuzzled her face over Mel's center, reveling in the sounds of desire her partner produced. Mel pulled her up when she started to remove her jogging pants and led her over to the bed. She pulled off Emma's T-shirt and bra, freeing her full breasts, her jogging bottoms and panties swiftly following. Emma found herself being turned and pushed face down onto the bed. The feel of the fabric on her stiffened nipples and smooth stomach was torture. She felt Mel lift her hips and bring her bottom back into Mel's apex. She gasped.

"Please," she said hoarsely. Mel had obviously removed the rest of her clothing; her skin was warm and naked against her backside. Mel's smooth body pulled back and Emma felt her strong hands running down over her buttocks, caressing them. One hand found its way between her legs, and she moaned and opened her knees further inviting access. The hand was removed and replaced by smooth skin as two hands found her breasts from beneath caressing them and tweaking the hard nipples. She screamed and bucked. Oh, what this woman made her feel was unimaginable sometimes. She tried to turn on her back but felt a gentle swat on her buttocks.

"Mmm," she moaned. The body was withdrawn.

"Stay where you are," Mel said. Not daring to move, and biting her lip longing for the release she already wanted, she waited. A few minutes later the pressure was back and she felt the strap on touch her from behind. She gasped and looked back.

"Mel," she said.

"Shh, shh," Mel said, "turn to me now." She gave her a tube of lubricant and said, "Oil it."

Emma licked her lips and felt a bit shy. She took the lube and oiled her hands and then grasped the strap-on. She loved it but preferred the natural feel of her partner.

"Can we rather-"

"Later," Mel answered hoarsely and commandingly. Emma rubbed the oil on the strap- on. Watching her from above, Mel felt wetness run down the inside of her legs. She grasped Emma's hips and turning her again, tilted her pelvis up. Her center gaped open and was slick with wetness; she was so ready. Mel entered the dildo slowly and began to thrust as Emma moaned, slowly and then faster and harder. Emma's body thrust forward with each motion.

"Oh, oh," she gasped, "please...please..." Mel dipped one hand between Emma's legs, bending her over even further and finding her clitoris swollen and taut, she rubbed it gently and then harder as Emma screamed. Once she felt Emma come, she stopped thrusting and held her fingers cupped over her swollen bud as she felt it pulsing and ebbing. She withdrew gently so as not to hurt her.

Emma, once freed, turned immediately, and pulled Mel down, forcing her onto her back. She trailed her lips down that taut stomach inching lower whilst her hands remained on the small firm breasts. Lowering her mouth her lips captured the swollen clitoris. She tasted Mel deeply and groaned. Mel thrashed her head.

"Come up here," she said, dragging her up. Emma lay over her and plunged four fingers into Mel's vagina and started thrusting. Mel's hips met her thrusts as she rode Emma's hand, holding onto her back. Reaching her apex, she shouted her release and pulled Emma down to lie on her shoulder.

"You are amazing darling," she whispered.

"So are you," Emma said, her body sated. They lay breathing in each other's scents and let the closeness of their bodies bond them.

An hour later they made a light supper and afterwards, like the night before, feel asleep early spooning each other.

CHAPTER 5

Over the next few weeks, they developed a routine. Mel settled very quickly at her work place as she was doing what she was familiar with and had passion for. She had a weekend hike for experienced hikers coming up and did some training sessions for her own fitness level when not working, and Emma joined her in, although at half the pace and with less weights.

Emma had developed a routine after finally setting up a work station for her writing and Googling how to self-publish. She also tended to venture into town and visit the art shops daily. She had stopped by to see Maria and Marty at times when the restaurant was quieter. They were a loving couple and Emma felt at ease with them during those brief visits. It amused her to see the banter between the two of them although one could see that Marty was the more dominant of two. They had been invited to their house for dinner and she was looking forward to it. She stuck to the town and the area around their cabin and felt relaxation steal into her bones. Once or twice they had ventured into town to eat supper. Now that Mel had settled, Emma planned to look in earnest for any part-time work. She chatted to her mother every second day. All seemed well and they both felt they had made the right decision.

That evening they prepared for supper at Maria and Marty's. They lived at the back of the restaurant in pretty house bordered by flowers that gave it a look similar to the external part of the restaurant. It was a week day night so they assumed the restaurant was not as busy and that the staff they hired were obviously well trusted.

"Welcome," Maria said, opening the door as they walked up. Their house was inviting decorated in various shades of pale yellows and browns. From the lounge with the sliding windows wide open one could see the lake. It was a stunning setting. A table had been set outside on their terrace area.

"Hi," Marty's deeper voice sounded, as she came forward and hugged them both. They had drinks to start and the conversation moved to the small-town life and how Maria and Marty came to be there. Marty's family had always lived in the area and she had come back after her chef training and experience. "As exciting as the cities were, I always felt something was missing. I knew I had to come back home to the mountains and lakes I loved," she said. Maria had turned up in the small town as a tourist five years earlier.

"She created havoc," Marty said drily. Maria blushed.

"I did not! I was just-well-finding myself," she said a bit lamely. Marty snorted, "Finding yourself! You found the palm of my hand first before you found yourself." Maria blushed to her roots and quickly changed the topic.

"There is an amateur photography club here," Maria said. "I belong to it. The club was started by a new resident who arrived almost a year ago." Mel and Emma had taken in the interplay and words between Marty and Maria. Mel grinned to herself. She thought she had detected some brattiness in Maria when they met her at the restaurant. It was a surprise though; after all one would not really expect to meet lesbians who practiced some form of domestic discipline in a small tourist town. She knew that as they got to know them better the couple would open up more to them.

"They get up to a lot of mischief," Marty grinned.

"Not true," Maria protested and laughed. "Unless you count taking wine with us and ending up with some very unusual looking photos." Marty looked at her and Maria's cheeks flushed again slightly. Feeling a bit sorry for her Emma said, "I see there is an art shop that sells photos of the area here. Is that the photography club then?"

"Yes, all the club members display photos there and we use the funds from tourists' sales to keep the club going." Maria replied.

"That's brilliant," Emma said. "I might join." Marty rolled her eyes.

"Welcome to the world of high jinks," she said to Mel. They laughed together.

Emma felt a tinge of dismay at the seeming ease with which Mel and Marty seemed to be bonding. Mel did not need another dominant woman encouraging that side of her. Her thoughts seemed to be a premonition when Marty casually said,

"Well, I can watch out for them in town and you can look for stopping any antics up in the hills." Mel laughed loudly. Emma seethed inside. She certainly would not need a friend who was a top; having a partner as a top was enough. Maria was light-hearted about it and laughed politely, steering the dangerous conversation to the others' hobbies. Emma explained her love of writing and that she planned to try and get down to self-publishing, but in the last few weeks had not actually written anything yet. Maria laughed.

"You need to get out and find a place that inspires you; just as a painter is inspired by the dramatic scenery in front of him or her," she said. "Climb a mountain or something…" she added, waving her hand. Marty coughed.

"She might not be mountain climbing material. You don't want her getting lost-like a certain person I know!" Maria grimaced.

"That was years ago, and I know the area well now." Mel looked at Emma.

"Don't go getting crazy ideas. I don't want to be worrying about what you're doing," she said. Emma smiled politely but felt humiliated. Mel should be supportive of her, not imply that she was an unfit idiot who could not find a pleasant, quiet place to write. The idea was very tempting though. Being higher up, totally away from any tourists or other signs of human life would certainly stimulate her creative thoughts, she mused. The remainder of the evening was pleasant and they walked home feeling relaxed and mellow.

That night whilst reading before sleeping, Mel put her Kindle down and putting out her light said,

"Babe, please don't wander far alone. I know Maria's idea was intriguing but I do worry about you." Emma bristled silently and kept her facial expression neutral. The way Mel spoke made her want to run out and do something outrageous like find a bear and photograph it as evidence that she knew to care for herself. There was no need to start an argument before bed though she thought,- and mentioning such a thought to Mel might lead to unpleasant consequences. Back in her natural habitat Mel seemed much sterner than at home. She said patiently,

"I have settled into a nice routine and managed well so far. You seem happy at work and settled so I think my next step is to look for some part time work in town." Mel breathed a gentle sigh of relief. She had seen Emma's eyes light up when Maria had mentioned finding *'a place that inspires you, just as a painter is inspired by the dramatic scenery in front of him or her.'* She had a worrying thought that Maria, lovely as she was, might not be a good influence on Emma, even if it would be unintentional.

She closed her eyes and felt Emma's arms encircle her from behind. Pushing back into the embrace she fell asleep.

CHAPTER 6

The next morning dawned bright and clear. Mel had a full twelve-hour day ahead with a six-hour hike booked in the early morning to one of the waterfalls. For the later afternoon she had a two-hour elk meadow walk scheduled with a group of young teenage tourists. She was looking forward to both although she hoped the teenagers would not be too boisterous.

She patted Emma's back gently through the duvet she was still curled up in and kissed the nape of her neck.

"Hmm..." Emma said groggily turning. "I have got to get up earlier."

"Sleep in, babe," Mel urged. "You don't have to rush for anything." The words were meant to be reassuring but Emma felt a pang of concern. She did enjoy lying in and organizing her own day, although the best days were when Mel had her time off. As some of her shifts were twelve hours, it meant that her days off were quite generous. Still she felt that she should be getting up herself, doing a job, contributing to the world and doing all the usual things that one normally does in city life. She supposed it would take more time for her to adjust completely. After all, there were many ways one could contribute to the world, she reasoned.

She dozed for another hour; all the while the hazy thought from last night was transforming itself into reality. She'd pack her small lap top as it was fully charged and be more prepared this time. Take a jersey and some water-well, a small picnic perhaps and-what else, she mused-a first aid kit. There was a small one in the kitchen.

Her mind having run over it all, she felt energized and, sure that creative thoughts would result from an inspiring writing place, she showered and dressed in hiking boots, long jogging pants and a black fitted vest top. The hiking boots were a bit stiff so she took them off and replaced them with her trainers. She filled a back pack with the thought upon items, adding pen and paper in case her lap top battery ran out of charge. She left out the map Mel had supplied, as her guilt would not allow her to look at the areas Mel had marked as safe in case her desired inspirational spot was outside the bounds.

This time she headed straight from the back of cabin, away from the lake, town and the direction of the adventure centre. The tall mountain behind beckoned her with its green and blue majesty. A path led through the floor of pine or fir tree needles. She wondered absently if fir trees were the same as pine trees and determined to learn more about the flora and fauna of the area. There might even be some volunteer program she could help with, with regards to wildlife preservation, she mused. The path narrowed and all the while had been leading upward; at first gently and after half an hour more steeply. She turned and was surprised to see that the town looked so far away even though she had only walked a short time. She could see their cabin below. The terrain grew rockier as she climbed and there were lots of small flowers and shrubs. The trees were slightly less thick. The narrow path led down again and she gasped in delight as stretched before her was a flat meadow. It was unexpected; she had always thought meadows could only be lower on the grounds below mountains, not hidden between them. Stopping to have a drink, she looked from various angles to see if she felt any creative ideas for writing.

When none presented she decided to move on. She skirted the right of the meadow to go higher up the mountain. When she turned around to look she could no longer see the small town or their cabin, or any cabin for that matter. There was a silence around her that was intensely calming. The sun warmed her gently and she felt it was a perfect day. The path curved and still climbed. She had to use two hands to pull herself up in certain places. Emma slipped at one part but was quick thinking enough to grab the branch of a bush along the path. After an hour she stopped again. The mountain top seemed as far away as ever. Looking around she could see the mountain was not a straight up and down walk as she had thought. It had small hills and valleys. The meadows inbetween were havens of shrubs with purple and black berries dotted among their green leaves. Way above her she could see granite towers of the mountains and the white lines of waterfalls.

"I don't think I'll be able to make it up there but perhaps I can go just a bit further," she said out loud. The sound of her voice seemed puny in the immense space. The 'bit further' was harder than expected but worth it as she came to a small crest. Way below her was a river fed by a waterfall far in the distance. She collapsed in a heap, took out the towel and laid it down. It was awe inspiring scenery and a humbling experience to be in this setting, she thought. The sun shone upon her and she drank some water and ate a sandwich. Emma lay down and decided to let the beauty and immensity of the surroundings stimulate her creative thoughts.

She woke up feeling chilly. The sun had drugged her and she

had slept for at least an hour. Grateful that she had brought a jersey with her, she pulled it on, noting with dismay that the sky was grey and a bit windy. She also realized her phone was ringing. *Well at least I know there is a signal here so I can't be far away,* she thought. Hesitantly she looked at the caller ID. '-Mel-' Her heart sank. She decided not to answer. The phone rang twice more. She noticed Maria's number. Damn, she thought, that meant Mel must be looking for her, not just calling to say hi. It could not be that late...she had just got here...surely the sleep could not have made much difference, she thought.

A glance at her watch showed it was much later in the afternoon than she had thought. Her bottom was tingling as if in anticipation of what would follow and her heart beat fast. She knew Mel would not take any disobedience the second time lightly. The thought made her angry. Good grief she was not a prisoner, she told herself fiercely. She blinked back the tears and headed in the direction she thought she had come. She cheered herself up by reminding herself this area might have been on one of the map's safer areas to walk. As she had not looked at it this was entirely possible. Also, there was a slight chance that both Mel and Maria calling was pure coincidence and both had phoned just to say hello.

Feeling more spirited, she walked back. After two and half hours of solid walking and her phone ringing twice more, she saw the white spire of the town church. Feeling totally wiped out, she sighed in relief as she saw the main road that led past the top part of the drive to their cabin. How on earth had she managed come back this way? She was convinced she had taken the same path back. The sun was almost setting. A figure was walking purposefully along the path above the road.

"Emma!" Mel's voice thundered as she walked wearily toward the road. The tone of that voice was a mix of relief and anger.

Emma glanced up and bit her lip. She wanted to fall into Mel's arms and run away at the same time.

Mel had obviously run her hands through her hair as parts of it looked in complete disarray.

"Where were you? Are you okay?" she asked as she ran up her eyes searching Emma from head to foot for any signs of injury.

"I-yes, I'm fine-" Emma said.

"Where were you? Did you not see I had called? Why have you have come down this way-?" The barrage of questions left Emma stammering, trying to answer. She took a breath and said,

"I went up to find an inspiring-" she did not get any further when Mel seemed to boil over.

"Were you up there?" she asked, pointing to the mountain now to their right that was behind their cabin.

"Yes, I, no-well, yes," Emma tried. "I was trying to find a place to write."

Mel did not wait a second longer. With one hand she undid the belt at her waist and with the other grabbed Emma's arm, pulling her around in one swift motion so fast that Emma had no chance to move away. She brought the belt down against Emma's bottom and upper back thighs ten times, whilst at the same time lecturing her. Emma felt paralysed with the shock of it. Mel had never hit her with a belt before.

"No, no-Mel-stop," she shrieked. The pain from the leather belt was intense. Mel ignored the crying, grabbed her by the top of her arms and shook her.

"I will not accept you disobeying me in this issue. Do you understand me? Do you?" She gave Emma another shake as she said it. Without waiting for her answer, Mel turned and pulled her along by her arm. With bottom and thighs on fire Emma tried to stop her by pulling backwards. Mel turned and, pulling her forward swiftly, landed the belt across the top of her thighs again three times.

"I suggest you get inside now," she said sternly. Emma choked back a sob. She could not believe that she was being spanked with a belt out in the open. It did not matter that it was a more isolated area; anyone could pass by and see. She walked on, trying to maintain her composure and dignity. Inside the cabin, Mel let go of her arm. She knew she needed to calm down. When she had not been able to find Emma after leaving work and with no answer to her phone she guessed that Emma had gone off to find a place to write. She thought she could have been lost or injured and the feeling was unbearable to her. She looked at Emma who was biting her lip and trying not cry. She blamed herself. She should have been sterner the first time this happened. She should have followed up weekly to see that Emma was adhering to the rules.

"Sit down," she said sternly. Emma sat immediately on one of the kitchen chairs and her head drooped. Mel came and stood near her.

"Look at me," she said. Emma looked up. She felt angry and yet guilty. She knew she had been wrong but Mel should first ask her about things and not assume she had strayed.

"Where did you go?" Mel asked. She pulled up a chair and sat straight opposite Emma. "Just...just up the mountain behind us."

"Fetch the map." Mel said. Emma hesitated. "Now," Mel said her voice calm but steely. Emma got up and took it off the pin up board. "Is the mountain behind us marked as a safe walk?" Mel asked. Emma felt like a child. She threw the map on the floor.

"I won't be treated like this!" she shouted and stalked off, indignation and outrage set in her posture. For the second time that day she found herself being grabbed at lightning speed. Her jogging bottoms were pulled down along with her panties.

"No-no!" She shouted. Mel sat on one of the wooden chairs

and pulled her unceremoniously across her strong toned thighs and her hand cracked down with hard, punishing slaps.

"I will not," ...slap...slap... "tolerate this,"...slap, slap... "behaviour,"...slap... "do you,"...slap, slap... "understand me?"... slap...slap. "Do you...do you?" slap...slap! Emma shrieked in pain and tried to pull herself off Mel's lap. Her bottom was throbbing and felt hot and red. This resulted in an even harder and faster spanking and she burst into noisy sobs her body slumping down. Mel felt the tension leave her body and she hauled Emma upright plonking her down none too gently on the chair.

"Ow," Emma said softly. She sobbed her hands over her face. Feeling very exposed she stood and pulled up her panties and jogging bottoms and sat back down quietly. "I'm sorry," she said. "I'm sorry. I was just trying to say I'm not a kid who needs supervising."

"No, you are not, so I don't expect you to act like one." Mel said. Mel's phone was ringing. She answered after looking at who it was.

"Yes, she's here. I found her. Thanks for your concern." Mel said. "Don't worry I have." Emma's cheeks flushed bright red; she wanted to know who it was but was nervous to ask.

"That was Marty. She wanted to know if I had found you or if we needed call out rescue services." Emma cringed. She had been selfish. It had all seemed so innocent. With tears in her eyes she finally dared to look at Mel directly.

"I'm sorry," she said. "It did not seem...I mean...it was so... well...easy." Mel sighed. "I know," she said the anger and some of the worry finally leaving her. "That is the nature of things here and that is also why I have a map for you. Go and have a bath. We are not finished this discussion. I need to clear my mind." Emma bit her lip but did not push it. She hated it when Mel was in this mood, as it made her feel small and helpless like a child even though she had been in the wrong. She also knew that her previous partner Tess would have done exactly the same as Mel had done.

Mel sat outside on the small patio breathing deeply. She was overwhelmed by her feelings. What if she lost Emma, what if Emma had been injured or worse? Perhaps she should send her home, nearer to her parents; after all she would join her after the six months was finished. Maybe this was a mistake, and they should both leave. The thoughts raced around her head. As the sounds of the evening gradually calmed her, she realized she was over reacting. They had agreed to come here and they were enjoying their life. Neither of them needed to leave. She needed to be firmer in ensuring adherence to the boundaries set for Emma and see through to the end any consequences.

By the time Emma came back through she had regained her calm.

"Sit here," she said using the same, level firm tone of voice she had used the year before in Switzerland. "We are going to make this work. If you cannot keep to the safety rules then you are going to face the consequences until you do. If need be we will move into the town and I will find someone to make sure that you do not go out unchaperoned." Emma's mouth gaped.

"A chaperone!" Emma could hardly get the word out. This was the 21st century not Victorian England.

"That's the way it is," Mel said, her tone brooking no argument. Emma knew how much she loved her; she also knew that she was headstrong and that it was only with Mel that she felt as loved and secure as she had with Tess.

"Well, it works both ways then," she said a bit haughtily. "If there is something you do that I find unsafe or not good for you I will also expect you to listen to me." Mel laughed tenderly and kissed her head. She hugged her close.

"Deal!" she said knowing that Emma was regaining some dignity. It was not easy to go over someone lap or receive a spanking even if one needed it and she knew Emma found it embarrassing.

"Right," she said, deciding still to not let up. "Supper for you and bed."

"But it's…" Emma protested. "Bed," Mel said firmly. "Today has been a long day for both of us and there has been a lot of emotions. Tomorrow we will go through all the rules again."

Emma nodded, dreading the next day but secretly pleased she could finally fall into bed, forgetting the trouble she had caused. She fell asleep before Mel came to bed. Mel leaned on one arm watching her. She loved this woman so much; she wanted to hold her, make love to her and protect her. Knowing Emma's needs and personality structure, she knew she had to be firm for her own good. She could not reward behavior which could lead to possible danger, with a night of passionate love making.

CHAPTER 7

Mel remained firm in the morning. She felt a bit tired as this was one of her days off and she had been hoping to take Emma to one of the elk meadows. However, she did not want this issue to escalate so she decided to continue with managing any boundary issues straight after breakfast.

Emma for her part felt annoyed with this. She did not want to feel like a child. Mel brooked no arguments. Emma found herself sitting at the kitchen table opposite Mel whilst she went through all the safety rules and what she expected again.

Emma felt bad as she knew that Mel also needed rest and did not constantly need to be looking out for her no matter how much she loved her and no matter how naturally dominant and 'toppy' she was. Her bottom and thighs felt tender, but she wisely apologized and agreed to stick to the safety rules. She could not resist reminding Mel that she was a grown woman who was well educated and who had held down a responsible position. Mel smiled, nodded, and agreed that she was but kept her gaze firm and voice steady as she told her that she expected her to stick to their agreements. If she did not then the spanking she had had the day before would be nothing compared to what she would get. Emma gulped and nodded, not daring to speak. She blushed and her tummy tingled. She felt an odd mixture of excitement, dread, anger and anticipation. Could any spanking be worse than the one she had received yesterday? She did not think so.

Mel smiled. She had grown to know Emma well over the past year and knew that a hard and fast punishment was best for her. Emma might well be surprised at the type of spanking she might be getting in the future though.

Feeling better now that the incident was behind them, they went into town together to explore the art shops and have lunch.

The art shops were quaint. The small town attracted quite a few creative people. As they walked around, Maria came out of a door. "I thought it was you," she said. "We are in the middle of our photography club meeting. Come and join us." Mel laughed. "Not for me thanks, but you go Emma and I'll meet you at the brown café near the lake when you're finished."

Emma nodded. It would be good for Mel to have some time alone and she did want to see if she wanted to join the photography club.

The club members were an unusual bunch of people ranging from a teenager to an older man in his eighties. There were five other women as well as the photographer club leader who had arrived in town earlier that year. He was a flamboyantly dressed man who had numerous photos published by nature and fashion magazines.

"It was all too much for me, darling," he said a bit dramatically when Maria was introducing him and explaining his background. The members obviously loved him. That week they were learning a new technique on focusing. Emma loved it; the idea of capturing an image forever appealed to her. The members were unusual and lively and she felt welcomed and accepted. She offered to help by managing their small financial side of things due to her business management background. The members were delighted as managing finance was not a strong point in their creative natures.

Emma and Maria walked down together to the café.

"Don't you have to be at work?" Emma asked Maria.

"No, we have a surfeit of waitresses. Some have been working for us a long time and some are teenagers earning a bit of cash during the summer holidays. Plus, it's pretty quiet until the later lunch rush," Maria said. "It still feels dreadfully decadent sometimes when I compare it to my previous life before moving here."

They met up with Mel who was sitting at the café, people watching, with a beer in one hand. She hugged Maria and inquired how the club meeting had gone. Emma explained that Maria had been telling her about her previous life and encouraged her to continue.

Maria launched into the story of arriving in the small town which enlarged on the brief part they'd heard at dinner. Apparently she had been an assistant to a high flying executive and feeling burnt out with constant demands she had come to the small town trying to find some peace. She mistook trying to find peace through drinking and partying with the tourists and creating havoc.

One evening she found herself in the restaurant owned by Marty. Her reputation for dancing on tables and breaking glasses preceded her. That evening she drank too much again and ended up smashing some glasses and dancing on a table much to the horror of the older patrons and the delight of the younger teenage customers. Her friends egged her on. Marty, who heard about the woman's wild ways, had unceremoniously hauled her off the table and for the first time in her life Maria had found herself receiving a spanking which she undoubtedly deserved. The crowd had roared with approval and Maria had screamed and cried, threatening to sue Marty. Marty had snorted and said she would be suing her for disturbing the peace and breaking up her restaurant. She had then carted her off and deposited the very tipsy Maria on a spare bed at the back of her restaurant house. Upon waking the next morning, Maria had found herself strangely repentant. Their relationship had blossomed from there. She told them both easily and Emma wondered why she was open about it.

"I can see you are the same way," she said, finishing off her story. Mel raised an eyebrow, "Really?"

"Yes. You have Ms. Toppy pants written all over you," Maria giggled. "I best run before the late lunch crowd comes in." She walked off with a cheeky grin and Emma and Mel looked at each other and laughed.

"Well, that was interesting."

"Very," Emma agreed. "I'm sort of pleased I'm not the only one getting tanned around here." Mel laughed, "Well you know you need it and you also know the way to avoid it." she added. Emma felt a warm glow. It was amazing to be so loved and accepted by someone. It did not stop her squirming in her seat a bit however.

The tourist café was a good place to 'people watch' along with having the beautiful backdrop of the lake and the various activities on it. Emma reflected on how at home they felt within this one month.

"You should invite your parents," Mel said.

"Yes," Emma smiled. "I will but let's have another month to ourselves before that." Mel laughed and leaned forward kissing her lightly on the lips. "Hmm...so you want me all for yourself?"

"Get a room," a teasing voice said. They looked round to see Charlie the guide sitting there watching them in amusement.

"Join us," Mel said. Emma stiffened. This was the guide who had scolded her. Mel tapped her leg under the table.

"Behave," she whispered.

"It's nice to meet you-in a more relaxed setting," Charlie said, her eyes glinting with fun.

"Likewise," Emma said, relaxing.

Without her 'official guide' hat on Charlie seemed a genuine and pleasant person. Emma still wondered how much she and Mel worked together though. "You two settled and enjoying it here?" Charlie asked.

"Yes," they replied, simultaneously.

"It is a different life for me so I'm surprised by how much I love it." Emma confessed. "For Mel though, this was her life before she met me."

"I sense a story in your meeting then," Charlie said, leaning forward slightly and downing some of her beer at the same time.

"Oh no, no story," Emma said, whilst Mel said at the same time,

"Yes, a most interesting story." They all laughed. Emma felt relaxed despite her annoyance at how she felt Mel treated her. She knew that their relationship flourished under the dynamics of Mel's top and her bottom roles but that did not stop her from feeling irate about it at times. She did however decide to address the issue of Mel spanking her with a belt and publicly. *What if someone had seen?* She also knew that Mel understood that she was not the type of person to respond to the soft approach and once Mel had meted out the discipline she felt relaxed and once again in control. However, she did not want Charlie knowing this. She could sense that Mel was stepping up to her top role and she respected this.

Charlie was that rare mix of a woman who was both feminine and butch and thus quite alluring. Emma felt a natural attraction toward her and saw that Mel had an easy going joking manner with her. Charlie had moved on to talking about an upcoming party Marty and Maria would host. There would be a good mix of artistic people, older people and the whole population of seven lesbians now that Mel and Emma had arrived.

"Yes, we'll be going," Mel said.

"Good," Charlie said. She got up and briefly touching Mel's shoulder, strode off. Emma felt jealousy flare through her. How dare that woman touch Mel's shoulder so intimately!

"I'm going to the shop," she announced and flounced off leaving Mel still with her beer in her hand. Mel watched her stride off and tried to go through her head of what had happened. Emma was definitely going through a patch lately. She decided to nip it in the bud; no more leaving issues halfheartedly. Putting down money for the drinks, she strode off after her partner. She caught up with her just at the turn off to the town center and taking her arm none to gently she pulled her close and said,

"What was all that about?" Emma looked at her, shook off her hand and said. "Well, you know, allowing that woman to paw at you!" Mel was surprised.

"Charlie?" she said. A light went on in her eyes. This was an issue that Emma had struggled with before. It was time to make Emma take responsibility for her feelings.

"...Because she touched my shoulder? She has become a friend and you need to trust me...and my love and loyalty to you," she said. "If you can't, there will be no future for us. This is something I cannot spank into you-as much as I'd like to." She said the words firmly and calmly, although her heart was hurting at Emma thinking she would betray her. "I am going to give you some time to calm down and then we can talk. I will be at home when you are ready."

She left for home and Emma walked around miserably. She was not by nature a jealous person; certainly with Tess she had never felt this way. But Charlie was so athletic and toned and well-adventurous. She could never be like that. Surely Mel would prefer someone like that? Logically she knew that was not true and her heart also told her that Mel loved her. Knowing that she had hurt her partner, she set off home after an hour. Mel was outside on the porch. She had set up her easel as she painted when the mood took her. Emma came up and slipped her arms around her.

"I'm sorry," she said. Mel looked at her.

"Let's talk about it," she said. "Why would you feel I would not be loyal to you?"

"I don't know…Well, I mean…I can't compete."

"Compete with what?"

"Charlie…people like her…like you…you know all athletic and 'adventurous'."

"I don't want you to. When will you understand that I don't want someone like that? I want someone like you." She said it so simply and sincerely and her gaze was so clear that Emma melted at her words. She knew as sure as anything that Mel meant those words.

"I would like us to stay here-longer term-forever!" she blurted out. As she said it she felt it was what she had been looking for. Perhaps it was also that their natural top and bottom roles flourished better here.

"Forever?" Mel kissed the top of her head, as surprised as Emma was when she blurted it out. "Forever is a long time to say we'll live somewhere. We've only been here one month and we have another five months to make our minds up. How about -we have found our home for now-?'"

"Perfect," Emma said, holding her tighter. How she loved this woman. "We have found our home for now then," she agreed, smiling. *I only hope my butt survives here,* she thought ruefully. There seemed to be many temptations to get her into trouble. Mel was meanwhile thinking along the same lines. They had found their home for now, she thought, where she felt relaxed and fully happy. She would probably have to do some online shopping though…a nice wooden hairbrush, a paddle possibly, and a nice hook to hang them from. She might even have Emma fetch her one when she needed her spanking. She smiled and hugged Emma.

"Go and stand in the corner of the lounge. Now!" she added, when Emma hesitated. She had never been made to stand in a corner before. This was crazy. Mel stood up, calm but with a determined look in her eyes and, losing her nerve, Emma fled off to the lounge. She stood in the corner, her head resting against the wood of the cabin wall. A feeling of resentment filled her but it was soon swept away by a strange tenderness stealing into her heart. This woman really loved her, all the way, in all ways and she hoped, for always.

Mel stood at the door looking at the shapely figure of her partner, her blonde head resting on the wood, not resisting but trusting her. She crossed over the room and her heart filled with a deep, intense love.

"I think we can continue this over my lap," she said. It was time for Emma to learn what being home with her truly meant.

The End
(For Now)

The Mountain Town Series

Book 2

'Ava and Gemma'

Lesbian Spanking Romance

By
Leandra Summers

CHAPTER 1

A va looked at the familiar paramedic team in front of her. The group of professionals was diverse in age and gender and she knew each of them was fully dedicated to their job. It was hard to leave the team that she had been in charge of for so many years and felt such respect and fondness for.

The team, ranging from the mobile intensive care ambulance and air paramedics to, the clinical instructors and basic and intermediate EMTs looked somberly back at her, their eyes mirroring the same respect and fondness.

Ava had agonized over resigning from her position as director of the highly competent regional team. It had been a few years since she had worked at the front line and she had become an expert in her executive role, never losing sight of the fact that being an excellent senior manager meant being seen and available to the team.

Over the past year however, a nagging feeling that she wanted something different had grown in insistence. As work got busier and health care budgets grew smaller, she had abandoned her love of hiking and outdoor activities, burying herself in the challenging work. This year she would turn forty-seven and it was this birthday, she felt, that had intensified the feeling of wanting, or perhaps needing, a different path in her life.

She had given up on love a few years back when her last partner turned out to be manipulative and unfaithful and had thrown herself with determined dedication into her work. It was not easy to find a partner who wanted to be an independent woman yet submissive to her natural dominant self. Ava was not into BDSM but thrived best in a more top-oriented role in her romantic relationships. Lately she had missed more and more the feel of a soft body beneath hers, the lowering of submissive eyes when she disciplined her loved one and the feel of a rounded, yielding bottom beneath her hand. The top/bottom dynamic relationship was not easily understood nor even desired by many but Ava was determined not to settle for anything less than a match for her needs.

Knowing that she had made the right decision, she drew herself to her 5'8", smoothed her caramel brown, shoulder length hair and cleared her throat. "It has been my pleasure to work alongside you," she said, her voice breaking slightly but unable to help the smile that curved her lips upwards. The weight lifting from her shoulders made her light of heart.

The team started clapping before she got any further and she waited until they had quieted down before continuing. This was her last day and the office organized party had a poignant feel to it.

After her farewell words, John greeted her.

"I hope you have made the right decision," he said, his tone of voice implying that he thought she had not.

"I know I have," Ava said, smiling. Her warm brown eyes lit up from within as she looked at him. She shook his hand firmly, hoping to convey to her trusted colleague as well as dear friend

114

that he need not worry about her. The staff crowded around asking questions and hugging her, stopping any further voiced concerns from him.

There was no surprise when she said she was moving stateside and going to live and work in a mountain town. Ava was naturally athletic, and her love of outdoor hobbies was well known.

"Not as a paramedic, surely?" one of the younger paramedics said. "I mean…" The young woman blushed as she stammered to explain. "I mean it's just that you…well…being management and not in the field…" Ava laughed.

"You're right. No, I am not taking up a paramedic position. I am going to work as an outdoor activities and hiking guide part time. However," she continued fixing the artless young paramedic with an affectionate stare, "even though I've been out of the field for a few years, my continuous training and experience are a bonus as a hiking and outdoor activities guide in the event of any injuries."

John eyed her, noticing her sparkling eyes and an energy in her stance and tone of voice that had been lacking in the last few months. He nodded slowly. She had made the right choice. Ava had lost her family in her early twenties to a car accident in the mountains. He knew that she had run away from the area she had grown up in. As the years had passed and her emotional wounds had healed she had longed to return to a more natural setting. It was time for her.

As the work afternoon ended, and the staff started drifting off, leaving her surrounded by cards and gifts, Shanine drifted over.

"I bet you'll find the love of your life there," she teased. Ava rolled her eyes. Her colleague could be so irritating at times.

"I don't think there will be any lesbians of my type in a small tourist town," she said. Shanine looked at her, her eyes deep and thoughtful.

"You never know. I think there might just be." Ava snorted.

"Don't scoff," Shanine said indignantly. "My Gran had the sight you know. I predict-" she did not finish as Ava laughed and said,

"Enough, off you go now. You'll be late for the night shift briefing." Shanine gave her a hug.

"You have been the best boss this team has ever had!" Ava laughed again and lightly tapped her bottom.

"Off with you, you flatterer."

Shanine sauntered off, calling back over her shoulder,

"I'll be right; you'll see...the woman of your dreams is waiting for you." She decided not to tell Ava that she had done some in-depth Googling and found out that one of restaurants was owned by a lesbian couple. She liked the look of the couple on their web page and the restaurant seemed very successful. It would make sense that there were other lesbians in that area, even if the town was small. She knew Ava would have researched the nature area and the work to be had in and around the town, but would not have bothered to research about the inhabitants or social scene.

Ava shouldered her bag. Her other personal work items had been packed and removed the preceding week. All she had to do was walk out the door and toward her new life. Taking a deep breath, she stepped out the glass door into the late afternoon sunshine. It felt so right, she mused. Time for a new phase of life or perhaps an old one reinvented; mountains, like those of her childhood, swimming and sailing, small shops, quaint houses. Her smile broadened.

The town she was going to was situated in a mountain setting that she was familiar with from her childhood. Ava had left the area when her family had died, fleeing to the city not only to escape the pain she had felt, but also to train as a paramedic. It was her way

116

of helping others who would be victims of accidents such as her parents and her sibling had been.

Twenty-five years had seen her work her way through years of field work, which she had loved. In the last five years she had moved into education and then senior management. It had been good and worthwhile, but she knew instinctively that her current course of action was right. She felt it in her bones and laughed. She was thinking like Shanine.

Head held high, hair catching the light from the sun as she stepped outside, Ava felt a delicious shiver down her spine, almost like the caress of a lover. Her life was changing.

CHAPTER 2

Gemma looked up at the rolling hills and towering mountains that stood majestically in front of her. The ocean lay behind the mountains and could not be seen from the town. She had been in the small town for three months and loved it. The area would not have appealed to everyone, but that was one of the reasons she had chosen to apply for the part time job as receptionist at the town's small museum.

She had longed for quiet, yet not isolation, the relaxation and tranquility of nature, but still to have the benefits of town living like shops and restaurants. She wanted to be around people who noticed each other, not walked past each other as if cloaked in invisibility as in the city.

The salary was small, but it came with accommodation and she had accumulated a modest investment sum which she could access. Over time if she withdrew the recommended 4% per annum, those investments would still see her capital grow. Her father also insisted on providing a modest trust fund to which she had tried to object. He had hugged her and said he wanted her to be happy and well cared for and had assured her that he would visit as soon as she had settled in.

She had thought carefully before making the move. Her love life was nonexistent. Her ex-lover had told her she was mousy and uninteresting. Gemma had flared with hurt at the cutting words, but internally believed her ex-partner's comments. Her hair was a mousy brown and her blue eyes were a common feature. She failed to notice, though, how her hour-glass figure was shapely and envied by many women. She was unaware of how the depth of her eyes and the sweep of her cheeks had men and women turning their heads. She felt stifled in the perception she had of herself, she realized one day. She also felt dwarfed in her older sister's shadow, and the dreams that she had held dear to heart in her twenties seemed to have slipped away from her as she approached forty.

One evening she had courageously decided to discuss her plans with her father and sister. Falteringly she had explained how she longed for the quiet of a mountain town, near a lake. She might even take up a new hobby, she had added. Hiking or sailing and failing that, well, she'd learn to knit. Her sister had snorted.

"Honestly Gemma, one would think you were eighty not about to turn forty." The words were sarcastic and Gemma had slumped forward, unconsciously accepting her self-induced status as being plain and uninteresting.

Later that evening, sitting silently on her bed thinking, she reflected on how her sister's comments reinforced her feeling that, as much as she admired her, she would be relieved to not be living in the same city as her flamboyant sister.

She loved her sister, but being known as the talented one in the family had fueled her natural drive and ambition to succeed in areas where Gemma was more content to coast along. She loved painting quietly in her room, whilst her sister was CEO of a chain of private financial companies. She had an outgoing personality and even whilst in secondary school had won a coveted prize establishing her as a young and upcoming entrepreneur. Her parents had loved both their daughters equally, but naturally gravitated toward the educational, financial and emotional support that their oldest daughter had required to establish her business skills.

Gemma had felt like the dowdy, average, dutiful daughter beside her. She had coasted along, content to work as a receptionist in one of the local businesses, gaining pleasure from the oil and pastel painting she did over weekends. Occasionally she accepted a date and her one serious relationship had proved disastrous. Gemma longed for something deeper, something different. She longed to feel independent yet controlled, safe yet free. It had been difficult to put into words and the relationship had fizzled out with her lover becoming frustrated with her. When they goaded each other with their words, they had both agreed it was time to end it. Gemma still remembered the words, taking them to heart even though she knew they had been voiced out of hurt and frustration.

When she came across an article about the benefits of small-town living, she was intrigued. She had taken to researching small towns in her region on the internet and had been intrigued by one tourist town that had an amateur photography club and a string of art shops. It was surrounded by mountains and bordered a lake. The locals were mixed in age and gender, and creativity seemed to be the norm. No chain stores for this area, she had noted. Arts and crafts flourished alongside trendy bistros and bars. Numerous bed and breakfast establishments and boutique hotels bordered the lake and outdoor activities were widely advertised. The location was ideal for painting and it piqued her interest further when she saw there was a local club for amateur painters. Gemma had not missed the discreetly placed rainbow flags over various businesses.

It seemed to be a sign that everyone was welcome without needing to be overt or pushy. She applied for the part-time receptionist position at the small museum that detailed the history of the town. When she had received an invite to interview via Skype she had been surprised and excited and then had wondered if she dared to allow herself the chance she felt she needed to live as she wanted to.

She could follow her passion, she had thought, allowing herself a small dream that maybe-just maybe- she could even display some of her paintings for sale. Tourists might purchase a souvenir of an oil or pastel painting of the area where they vacationed.

An even deeper dream lingered on her mind. She might find someone who loved her for the person she was, someone who might even want to take charge of the relationship. Gemma blushed at that thought. To be cared for, scolded, punished was a secret desire of hers and one she held very tightly to her chest.

The evening she had spoken to her sister and father had cemented her idea. Her sister continued her outspoken ideas about Gemma. Listening to her, Gemma realized that she had always been her foil, there to make her shine all the brighter.

"You are getting old before your time," her sister said bluntly, after the comment about her age. She had looked at her sister. Certainly, Lee-Anne did not look her forty-six years of age. Her brow was perfectly smooth, her cheeks and lips full and her hair a glossy chestnut brown. Yes, she had had fillers and Botox, but she also followed a set skin care regimen and strict diet. Gemma also made sure to cleanse her skin and use a moisturizer, but her beauty routine went no further. Lee-Anne had the perfect husband, provided the standard two grandchildren and held down her empire without any effort it seemed. Her shoulders slumped. If only she was as...together.

Her father looked at her, wondered why his youngest daughter could not see that her smooth shoulder length hair her suited her heart shaped face, that her blue eyes were as deep a shade of blue as her sister's, and her body, whilst not toned or razor thin, like many city women, was soft, feminine and appealing with its curves. She was creative and held a silent courage of which she seemed unaware. When she said good night to leave for her own flat that night, he once again urged her to follow her heart.

Gemma sighed contently. She was heading up to the restaurant at the entrance to the town. It had brightly colored flower pots lining the outside wall and a small discreet rainbow flag that showed it welcomed all clientele. The restaurant was rustic and the two women who owned it, Marty and Maria, were friendly and good company. They served hearty food at lunchtime and a more bistro type menu in the evenings.

The dark-haired Maria had soon got Gemma chatting when she first shyly tried out the restaurant and now she enjoyed going over for a glass of wine. She had met Marty, Maria's wife, who was also the chef of the restaurant. Marty was lovely and down to earth, though Gemma was careful to note that she tolerated very little unruliness with customers if they had had a bit too much to drink. She was the perfect partner for Maria's more flamboyant and chatty manner. Gemma had not missed the slight firmness with which Marty also kept Maria in check. The day that Maria had invited her to join the photography class and introduced her to a friend, Emma, who had lived there one year was etched in her mind.

It had ended with them all imbibing a bit too much wine. Marty had come down to fetch her errant wife. Gemma had at first giggled when she saw Marty ask Maria to come home and tell her that they'd "talk tomorrow".

She had slightly emphasized the word 'talk' and Gemma had

noticed Maria swallow and nod. Her own tummy had somersaulted.

Marty had then turned her attention to Gemma and Emma. With her arms folded and one eyebrow slightly arched, she asked how they were getting home. The tummy tingling feeling intensified and she was grateful when Gerry, the club leader, had come through from the back when he had. He had been working on a new layout for the town magazine on local photography. As usual he had been flamboyantly dressed. Sensing some tension, he said he would be taking them home and both women immediately fled off to get their bags. Gemma wondered what dynamic was happening between Maria and Marty and then between Marty, Emma and herself. She had felt a tingle through her midpoint that was not unwelcome. It felt as if Marty had cared. Perhaps she was annoyed they were tipsy and disturbing neighbors, but she had wanted to be sure they got home safely.

Remembering the small incident she grinned, and walked past the flower pots. She had her easel and paint bag with her and planned to go down after lunch to the lake to try and capture the clear sky with the mountain framed dark green in it.

Entering, she saw the usual lunch crowd of locals. The outside was crowded with tourists enjoying lunch in the sun. She entered and sat at a table near the door, placing her bag and easel out of the way. Maria grinned.

"Hey girl," she said. "How are you?" Gemma smiled.

"You look so busy today. I'm great-Going down to the lake to paint later."

"Will you have the lunch special?" Maria asked. Gemma smiled.

"If Marty cooked it, sure." Maria eyed her. Gemma was so pretty when she smiled and the faint distrust and hurt at the back of her eyes disappeared. Maria was a natural busy body, as her wife never hesitated to tell her. When Gemma first arrived, she thought about Charlie who had recently been in for lunch and worked at the Adventure Sports Centre. Maria had decided that they might be a good match. Charlie was that rare mix of a lesbian who managed to look both butch and feminine simultaneously. Her hair was cropped short, and she had recently dyed it blonde on the top from her natural dark color. The resultant dark roots with blond top was strangely attractive against her light coffee-colored skin and she wore one side shaved with the longer top flopping over it. Her muscles were taut, and one shoulder sported a tattoo of a motorbike. Women flocked to her charm and she flirted shamelessly with female tourists, but seemed determined to never settle down with a committed partner.

Marty was always cautioning her to be careful about meddling in other people's love lives but from the minute she had seen Gemma hesitantly entering the restaurant with her shy manner, she felt she needed to give her a hand. She had made sure to engage Gemma in conversation and take note of when she came to the restaurant. A few weeks ago she had arranged that Charlie attended lunch at the same time Gemma was there. Nothing had happened as Charlie had seemed way more interested in chatting up a tourist who was walking around in shorts and a bikini top. Maria had been going to point out their dress code but decided as it was lunch time, she would let it go. And it might spoil Charlie's fun. Afterwards Charlie had sauntered up to her and casually said in a voice loud enough for Marty her wife to hear,

"Best not meddle too much in people's lives darling. Marty might have to tan your hide again." Maria had the grace to look embarrassed. Was she really that overt in her matchmaking? Her flush had deepened when Marty came out wiping her hands on a tea towel.

"Meddling again, babe?" she had asked half sternly, and yet she had winked at Charlie so Maria felt she was fairly safe.

"No, yes...well, Charlie needs...Gemma looks so...alone..." she trailed off.

"Honey," Marty had said affectionately, leaning forward and landing a playful warning slap on her bottom, "lay off the meddling. Remember your last attempt?" How could she forget that? She had tried to set up the new local sport center owner, John, with one of their regular customers who had always said she was looking for a man. It turned out that John had a wife and was waiting for a few months before he brought her to the town to be sure it was something that would suit them. The whole sport center staff knew about it, which meant that Charlie and Mel knew about it as they trained there.

Charlie had winked, put her cap back on and sauntered out, hands in her pockets.

"And don't you be too cocky," Marty called out to her. "Bit more of this constant flirting might bring you some hot water." Charlie laughed and flipped a hand gesture. Maria grinned ruefully. It was hard to be cross with the upbeat Charlie. She had squared her shoulders. Charlie was not the only fish in the sea. She'd try again, she vowed. Perhaps she could get Gemma to meet Melissa and Emma. She giggled as thought of the rhyming names. She might meet some friends through them. Melissa and Emma had arrived over a year ago to the town and were well settled and good friends of Maria and Marty. Melissa and Charlie worked together. Charlie tended to rub Emma up the wrong way with her sometimes-toppy manner. As if Melissa were not top enough, Maria grinned. Life could get very interesting.

Gemma had indeed met up with Emma and the two of them seemed to enjoy each other's friendship.

As Maria took her order over to the kitchen, the door opened and a young girl entered with a dog. The exuberant dog bounced around and knocked the easel over from behind the chair where Gemma had safely leant it.

"Honey, please take your dog outside," Maria called over. "He is welcome to be on the outside patio." The door opened again, and a tall, attractive and toned woman strode in. She tripped over the easel the dog had bumped into and hopped around, releasing an expletive before grimacing. Gemma scrambled forward.

"Oh, I'm sorry," she started, lifting her eyes. Speech deserted her. She looked into the most intense brown eyes she had ever seen.

"It's okay, but you should be more careful," the voice belonging to the intense eyes said, slightly scolding. Gemma continued to stare at her. Her body had come alive as the brown eyes surveyed her head to toe and she flushed. Those eyes seemed to be almost undressing her. She fought to get a grip on her body and control of her tongue.

"I never..." she said starting out indignantly then trailing off. Maria came running over.

"Sorry," she said, "the dog knocked the easel over. Ma'am, how can I help?" She noted the way the warm brown eyes had roved over Gemma and her antenna pinged. "Um...we are quite full. Do you want a table? You can share with Gemma if you like?" Gemma's heart leapt into her throat. Share a table with this tall attractive creature!

"I-um-no, no, I'm going. You have the table. Sorry again," she stammered and grabbing the easel and bag, fled out the door. As she got to the door she cursed and turned back.

"Maria! Sorry, I need to pay you." Maria waved her off.

"Pay next time," she said, easily taking pity on Gemma's flushed cheeks and embarrassment. She did not point out that Gemma had not even eaten yet. The poor woman was too flustered.

Ava looked at the scene in front of her. Her shin hurt but her interest was piqued by the woman who was now fleeing through the door. Her back side was shapely in her jeans and her small waist and rounded breasts were highly defined by a clinging white T-shirt.

"So...can I help you-with a table?" Maria said, turning back expectantly to Ava. Ava looked at her, amused. If she did not know better, she would have thought Maria was trying to set her, a total stranger, up with another total stranger.

"No, thanks. I just came in for directions."

"Where to?" Maria asked.

"The Pruddis Adventure Sports Center," the tall woman said.

"Yes. I can direct you," Maria said. "Will you be going on a hike?" she probed. This woman was certainly attractive, Maria thought. If she was not as confident as she was she would have been as flustered as Gemma.

"No," Ava said, "I am working there." Maria almost glowed at the words. The attractive woman seemed gay although she should not judge on looks and now she would be working at the sports center along with Charlie and Mel.

"Maria," Marty's deep-toned voice called from the back of the restaurant. "Table 10 food is ready."

"Excuse me one second. I'll be back," Maria said.

Ava looked around. Locals on the inside, she guessed, and tourists mostly outside. Maria looked cute with her long page boy styled black hair. She wondered who the woman was who had hurried out the door and why she had apologized for the easel when it was clearly not her fault. Had she seen a spark of interest flicker in her eyes? The blue eyes looked like two small pools that held a promise of deep longing and she had cast her eyes over the rest of the form, her own body betraying the physical attraction she had felt to her. Shanine's prediction briefly entered her mind and she smiled inwardly, dismissing it.

Maria reappeared, this time with a sturdily built, short blonde-haired woman at her side. She looked slightly harassed, but her eyes were kind if stern. Ava recognized a fellow top instantly.

"This is my wife, Marty," she said. "I am Maria and we own the restaurant. We want to welcome you."

"I'm Ava," she said.

"Ava will be working at Pruddis," Maria continued, turning to Marty. Marty held out her hand.

"Nice to meet you. I hope we'll see a lot of you here. You will enjoy the center and be in good company."

Ava nodded. They seemed very likeable and she felt herself relaxing. A town- where the first people she met turned out to be a shapely attractive, accident prone woman and a lesbian couple? It seemed too good to be true.

Maria gave her directions and she set off in her 4 x 4 along the narrow roads. She had an inexplicable feeling that her life had really taken a turn for the better. She put the attractive, stammering woman out of her mind and looked for the turn off sign Maria had warned her was slightly hidden by an overhanging tree.

Back in the restaurant Maria was gazing straight ahead, her thoughts whirling and scheming. Life was going to get interesting.

CHAPTER 3

Charlie saw the 4x4 draw up and neatly park in an empty bay at the back of the Adventure Centre where employee parking was located. She recognized the tall woman from her Skype interview. Attractive, sexy for sure, she thought, looking her up and down from the window.

Ava looked at the small buildings in front of her displaying the words 'Information and Reception' and 'Administrative staff'.

As she pushed her dark glasses back the door of Reception opened, and an athletic woman strode out. Her blonde hair with dark roots was cut boyishly short and her muscles rippled through her gym wear.

"Hi," she greeted Ava easily. "Ava Green? I was asked to look out for you." She grasped her hand and gave it a firm shake. "I'll take you to our HR staff member-just one-." She laughed easily. "We are a small operation. Then I'll come and collect you in about 30 minutes and show you around." She had glanced away mid way through talking and Ava looked to see what had caught her attention. Two women, obviously tourists, had rounded the

129

building and were looking for the entrance. She laughed to herself. The woman in front of her was a player for sure. Charlie's gaze had sharpened as she eyed the women and, smiling at Ava, she hived over to help them.

The atmosphere was definitely not as formal as her city job and Ava relaxed. Her paperwork took a short time as it was a matter of receiving the keys and directions to her cabin and signing various paperwork.

"Brad will meet you later," the HR coordinator told her. "The owner," he added, unnecessarily as Ava had been interviewed by him. "Charlie has been allocated to show you around and take you through all the safety training. I can see you are up to date, but we'd like to make sure you are comfortable with our procedures. We've started your work schedule from Tuesday." She appreciated the thoroughness shown and was pleased to have a few days to settle in.

Charlie was waiting once she exited and without preamble, she started showing her the buildings and various activities available. Ava went with the flow easily. The drive had not been long, and she felt ready to start seeing how things worked. She had been given a detailed job description prior to arrival and figured she would be allocated personal training and swimming lessons for tourists whilst she got used to hiking routes. Her schedule confirmed this and she noted that sailing and zip lining had been added. Charlie said that she would have this week to familiarize herself.

Her fitness tests had been completed before she arrived, and she had sent off her sailing and swimming certificates to HR. Charlie explained she would be showing her the hiking routes and she would be paired with two of the other guides for a month before she took serious hiking groups alone. This suited her fine. She noticed that the tension that seemed to have plagued her shoulder muscles had dissipated and she felt alive in a way that she had not felt for many years.

After the tour and safety demonstration with regards to fire safety and various equipment checks, which were familiar to her, Charlie deemed that was enough for the day and offered to show her the way to her allocated cabin.

Ava nodded briefly and followed Charlie slightly out of the town and to a small wooden cabin that stood below a hill facing out toward the sparkling blue lake that dominated almost two entire sides of the town.

"I'll leave you to get settled," Charlie said in her no nonsense manner. "Pick you up for dinner?" Ava decided the best way to learn about her new environment was to dive straight in, so she agreed and started unpacking her car as Charlie drove away, the wheels of her Jeep slightly kicking up the dust.

Lifting a box she had brought despite knowing the house would be fully furnished she turned slightly hearing a noise. The woman from the restaurant was walking up the steps of a similar small cabin not that far away. She recognized her by her hair and the large easel which she had dropped on the stairs causing the noise. "Darn!" she heard the woman swear as she rubbed her thigh where it had caught the wooden railing along the steps. Darn…darn? How many people said that, Ava thought. Sexy woman, but obviously quite accident prone. The thought endeared her to the unknown woman.

She watched as the woman bent over to retrieve the easel, her shapely buttocks showing through the Lycra joggers.

A familiar sensation jolted her lower abdomen and she looked away fighting the sense of lust and equal desire to tan that shapely behind. Noticing that the woman had picked up the easel and moved off to her front door, she decided that she did not need any help and walked into her own cabin.

The house smelt deliciously of wood and pine cones. The light pouring through the large lounge windows caught the wooden walls and furniture making it gleam as if everything had just been highly polished. The sofa was pale brown and the curtains were cool beige.

The effect was calming and serene. She knew it would need just a few personal items to make it more homely. Three hours later, all small items were unpacked and, freshly showered and dressed in black jeans and T-shirt, she waited on the small porch for Charlie to pick her up. Unable to help herself, she looked over to the cabin she had seen before. The lights were on as the dusk set in and she could see a figure in the lounge. Her stomach lurched and her pupils widened.

She forced herself to turn and look at the other side. All she could see were trees but through them some lights twinkled. There were obviously other small cabins nearby. In front of her was the lake. It looked to be about a ten minute walk across a road further down. To the left lay the town and she could see the solid street lights and the small twinkling one that adorned the hotel and restaurant buildings. The town was easily walked to within about twenty minutes she guessed.

Charlie's car drew up and she jumped out, wearing the same clothes as before. "Just gotta fetch someone," she said. "Maria asked me to pick her up." Ava watched as Charlie strode over to her nearest neighboring cabin. Ava watched as Charlie spoke to the figure that seemed quite reluctant to be '-picked up-.'

"Come on, Gemma," she heard Charlie say. "You don't want to disappoint Maria, do you? No...what...you look fine." Ava smiled. It seemed her neighbor really did not want to join them. Her stomach growled. She felt hungry and realized she had not eaten since breakfast. Charlie leaned closer to the figure and whispered something. It seemed to work because the figure retreated and then reappeared clutching a handbag. They walked back to the car together. The neighbour got in the back.

"Hi," Ava said easily, turning to greet her. "I'm Ava. I think we bumped into each other earlier." Gemma stared back, again mesmerized by the deep brown eyes that almost seemed to see right through her clothes.

"Hi-Gem-Gemma," she said, hating the way her voice sounded squeaky. She could hardly believe it. Her new neighbor was the sexy woman from the restaurant. She should have brushed her hair or at least put some more mascara and lipstick on, she thought. She promptly squashed the thought and wondered why she felt the need to do that. Unconsciously she lifted her chin. Ava noted and grinned; sexy, nerdish and spirited. It was a good combination.

"So-are you here on holiday?" Gemma asked, determined to appear calm and suave.

"No. I'm working at the adventure sports center," Ava said. Gemma's heart did a double leap. This gorgeous woman was not only living next door to her, but she was also not a tourist and not going to leave in a week or two.

"Welcome," she said. "It's a quiet area where we stay. There is someone on the other side of you, but the trees block the views. I can see two other houses on my side." *Shut up,* she told herself. *You're babbling like an idiot.*

"It seems like a lovely area," Ava said sincerely. She felt a need to put the nervous, attractive woman at ease even though she was the newcomer.

"What do you do here, Gemma?" Before she could answer, Charlie cut in. "She's the local museum's sexy nerd administrator." Gemma could not help laughing at Charlie's outrageous comment.

"I am the receptionist, sort of a 'Jill of all trades" for the local museum," she said. "It's small and the work is part-time, so it suits me well. There's a part- time curator as well."

"That must be interesting; meeting so many people," Ava said quickly before Charlie could jump in and start teasing again.

"She has some of her paintings in the local art gallery shop," Charlie added seriously and almost admiringly.

"Oh-they're nothing, really," Gemma said. "I'm just an amateur." Charlie laughed. "Hey! How did you know that?" Gemma suddenly said. She had only met Charlie twice and once had been a non-conspicuous attempt at a set up by Maria.

"The tourists talk about it," Charlie said. "One even asked if they could take a photo and was going to ask the art gallery if the artist Gemma who painted all the others could capture it."

Gemma remembered the incident. Two weeks ago, a tourist had turned up with a photo and asked if she could paint it. Still, it did not necessarily mean that she was good, she reflected. A small town only had a few artists.

Ava was impressed, although she noted how Gemma down played her skill.

The talking quieted as they reached the restaurant on the edge of town.

Maria peeked out one of the front windows as she heard the distinctive sound of Charlie's enhanced engine draw up. She turned back to a nearby table who had called for assistance after scanning the quaint wooden menus. The two waiters were busy and even though she had match making plans on her mind, she was ever attentive to the needs of the customers. Her earlier thought of asking Charlie to pick up Gemma for dinner when she heard Charlie was bringing the newcomer, Ava, had her quick mind on the ball. She knew Melissa and Emma would be in as well.

CHAPTER 4

Ava was pleased that Charlie was taking her to the small restaurant she had stopped at for directions. It had seemed welcoming and the atmosphere was trendy. The food seemed delicious if the smell and full occupancy was anything to go by. She also liked Maria and Marty, who had welcomed her and given her directions.

Charlie was looking forward to an evening where she could chat with her work colleague Melissa and her partner Emma. She enjoyed teasing Emma and looked out for her just as Melissa did. Marty would be supervising the kitchen staff but as it was later in the evening, she'd probably join them toward closing time. Charlie had timed the meal as Maria requested, knowing that the break with friends was good for Maria and Marty as well. She instinctively felt that Ava would fit in but was worried about the shyer Gemma who seemed a bit uneasy in a group.

Gemma was sitting quietly in the back seat, her mouth dry, wondering if she looked okay. She could not understand her reaction to Ava. She felt like a gauche schoolgirl next to the confident, attractive, athletic woman. The invite had been last minute. She had decided to turn it down, but when Charlie had whispered to her that Maria had specifically asked for her to come and that Melissa and Emma would be there, she relented. She preferred to forget that Charlie had also said she was prepared to carry her to the car if Gemma felt too lazy to walk to it. She had said it with a wink, but there was a slight warning tone that made her realize Charlie would probably do that. She liked Emma, with her creative flair although she was a bit nervous of the dominant looking Melissa. She got on well with Emma and felt they were becoming good friends. She also planned to ask her more about the photography club she had mentioned that she and Maria attended. She had spent more time perfecting her art, but photography was a good complement to her portraits.

"Come on, no one's going to bite you." Charlie's voice broke into her reverie and she looked to find Charlie had opened her door and was grinning at her. Her black eyes sparkled with humor, and she lightly flicked the tip of her tongue over her lips. Pursing her lips in irritation as she saw Ava smiling next to her, unable to see Charlie's teasing face; she jumped out of the car. Just as Charlie shut the door, she leant back to reach her bag she had left on the seat. Ava shouted out a warning, grabbing her arm at the same time with lightning reflexes and pulling her away from the door as it slammed shut hard.

"What the--I could have hurt you badly!" Charlie cried out. Gemma was so clumsy. She paled as she thought of the damage that she could have caused to Gemma's arm.

"Sorry," Gemma mumbled, her face pale. "I...er...just wanted my bag." Charlie opened the door, got it out and passed it to her, one eyebrow slightly raised. It was a pink Gucci; a leaving gift from her father. She felt her cheeks flush. If only she had not had to hurry, she could have chosen a less ornate bag.

Ava's hand was still on her arm, and Gemma was acutely aware of the strong, slim fingers on her skin. Tingling warmth was spreading through starting at the point where those fingers touched her.

"Sure you're okay?" Ava asked quietly, looking at her.

"Yes, yes of course," Gemma said, pulling her arm away. The quiet, serious tone irked her. Did Ava think she was drunk or something? "I am perfectly fine and in control of my faculties!"

"I meant; is your arm okay? It did not get hit by the door?" Ava asked calmly. She itched to show this prickly, shapely woman some manners, but restrained herself. Gemma's upper arm where she had instinctively grabbed her had felt soft and feminine and she had wanted to stroke it and draw her closer. She stood back. It was inappropriate. She had just met this woman.

Charlie tapped her shoulder lightly.

"Come on, ladies," she said, smiling, wondering whether the undercurrent she was sensing between the two was tension or attraction. "Gemma's well known for being clumsy." Gemma smiled back stiffly. She was a bit clumsy, but she did not want Ava thinking she was a total idiot.

Charlie gently put a hand on Gemma's back and pushed her forward slightly, so Gemma had no option but to walk in front of them. The restaurant door opened as they approached.

"Welcome," Maria said, all smiles. She was prettily dressed, and but for the name tag one would not have realized she was the co-owner of the restaurant. Her white peasant style blouse was long and covered the top of black slim jeans. Her black hair was held back with a silver ribbon.

"This way, girls. I have your table ready. Mel and Em are already here."

Ava's eyes took in the rustic décor and candle lighting. It was lovely at night. Not all the tables were full as had been at the lunch hour.

"Marty and I will join you in a short while," Maria said as they approached a table nearer to the back and next to a low stand obviously used for live music events. Two women rose as they neared.

"This is Mel, and this is Emma-well, we call her Em," Maria said doing the introductions. "You've probably met Mel at the center today."

"Not yet," Ava said, shaking the woman's strong hand.

"No," Mel said simultaneously. "I was off work today. I heard that you were coming though. Charlie told me about your interview." Like Charlie, she was well toned and athletic. Her hair though, was brown and shoulder length, lending a feminine air to her strong looks.

Emma shook Ava's hand. Ava took in her attractive long blonde hair, green eyes and fair skin that glowed in an understated way that spoke of having been pampered by expensive products. Ava sensed a lively and challenging air in her. She instinctively guessed Melissa had her hands full with her.

"Gem! How lovely to see you," Emma said, hugging Gemma. The two women were building a friendship, connected by their love for art. Em felt for the quiet woman who seemed unaware of her natural beauty and seemed to melt into the crowds. She exuded a vulnerable air despite hiding it under a prickly layer. Gemma relaxed. Emma was sweet.

"Em told me about your paintings," Melissa said, trying to put Gemma at ease. "Seems like your paintings are becoming quite famous."

"Oh, oh-thanks...they're nothing special really," Gemma said,

138

brushing the compliment aside. She sat down next to Emma hastily pulling the chair forward before Charlie could do it for her. Charlie laughed easily.

Ava frowned slightly. Gemma certainly did not have a good opinion of herself. She wondered what made her feel so unsure of herself when she was obviously a highly attractive and talented woman.

The women chatted easily, getting to know each other. When Marty and Maria joined them, Ava felt a kinship to Marty. She recognized the same natural top tendencies in her as she had and carefully noted the close relationship between her and her wife Maria. When she asked about how they came to the town Marty explained how her family had always lived there and after doing her chef training and experience she had come back to start the restaurant. She noticed Maria squirming a bit as Marty continued the story and suppressed a smile as she heard the story of Maria's antics in the town as a tourist five years ago and how Marty had taken her in hand when she had gotten drunk again, danced on her tables and smashed glasses. It seemed Marty had shown no mercy and delivered a thorough spanking in front of the crowd of restaurant regulars and tourists. It had been a turning point for Maria, who seemed to have found her inner brat neatly curtailed. Marty was solid, short haired and fair in complexion; a perfect opposite for Maria's tall slenderness, olive colored skin and black hair that hinted at her Latin ancestry.

The evening passed all too quickly and Ava found she had not had enough time to chat in depth with Gemma, Mel or Em.

Gemma, though, she noticed, had seemed comfortable around Emma and Maria. She chatted animatedly and was relaxed when she was not the center of attention. Even though she had not dressed up, she was highly attractive, her rounded breasts straining against the almost see-through white material of her T-shirt. This did not seem to be a conscious effort to attract attention rather that she had thrown on her clothes without much thought.

Gemma happened to glance up as Ava was looking at her and, noticing the appreciation in Ava's eyes, she colored. She averted her eyes, her heart beating faster, and continued her discussion with Emma and Mel that seemed to involve painting, photos and mountains as far as Ava could tell.

She wanted to get to know the shy, brown haired Gemma better she decided.

CHAPTER 5

The week after dinner was a bit of a blur for Ava as she settled into her new life. She attended further safety training, caught up with the owner and manager, who explained the mission and values to her and what he expected of all staff. He acknowledged her experience in paramedics, outdoors activities and personal training as well as noting her previous managerial position. He spoke about advancement in his company as this was one of many he operated. Ava listened carefully. She had to first settle in and decide if this was for her.

She took personal training sessions once she was familiar with the gym and boot camp. She ran classes with Charlie and did sailing and kayaking with Oliver. A few days later she went through the maps of the area and walked the shorter hiking routes. The week after she would start classes by herself and was set up to navigate the longer hikes with Charlie and another guide.

At home she rearranged her small cabin, familiarized herself with the area and met Charlie for a drink after work on a few of the evenings. She had not had time to meet Gemma, but as the days drew into the end of the week, she decided she would make an effort to stop over and officially meet her closest neighbor.

Gemma continued her daily routine after the restaurant dinner. Her thoughts kept straying to the tall, athletic woman with caramel colored hair. She'd get up in the mornings and studiously avoid looking at the house not too far from hers. She told herself such an attractive and obviously well put together woman would not be interested in her.

One evening, she joined Em and Maria at the photography club and diffidently asked how Ava was settling in at the outdoors activity center. Em and Maria exchanged knowing glances.

"Mel says she's getting on well," Em said. "She's even suggested offering classes in basic life support to teenage tourists." Gemma was impressed. Ava sounded energetic as well as socially conscious.

"So," Em said, changing topics. "I saw you out with Charlie a few weeks ago."

"Oh, oh, yes," Gemma said. She liked Charlie, despite her flirtatious and teasing manner.

"She is sexy," Emma commented. Gemma reddened.

"I'm not...we're not...."

"Relax," Maria laughed. "We're just teasing you. I don't think Charlie will ever settle down."

"Not for your lack of trying," Em said, laughing. "You best not get into more mischief matchmaking or Marty will have your backside." Gemma's ears pricked up at this. She wondered if it was a joke.

"Now Ava...she looks like 'settle down' material," Maria continued with what seemed to be her favorite topic, totally ignoring Em's comments on her backside. Gemma smiled. Maria was a born matchmaker and meddler.

"Ladies! What do you think?" Gerry's voice interrupted their small talk. He waved a leaflet in front of them. Maria grabbed it.

"Scenery of talent," she read aloud. "Open to all members of the photography club, including short term members. 'The most memorable scene of the town.' Winner gets their photograph displayed in the local newspaper and for one month in the gallery. Sounds great," she said enthusiastically. Gemma nodded. She was not a good photographer, but the concept was appealing and searching out different scenes and lighting around and in town would afford her greater scope for her paintings.

Em agreed. She had recently released her first self-published novel and was taking a break from writing. Something fun, yet with purpose, was just what she needed. Gemma readily agreed when Em asked if she wanted to join her in taking some local shots.

"I'm not working for the next two days," she said, "so that will be great." Maria was mostly occupied with the restaurant but said she'd try and join them the following week if they needed more shots.

Gemma started the two kilometer walk back to her house feeling content. She thought about her life four months ago and realized she had been existing as opposed to living.

A horn sounded, making her jump off the road in fright. She tripped over the grass edge of the verge. A 4x4 drew to a stop and a familiar tall figure jumped out of the driver's seat. Gemma's heart skipped a beat, and she was sure it was not just due to tripping in fright. "Sorry," Ava called out. "You were walking in the middle of the road, and I wanted to warn you." She leant down, extending her hand to Gemma. It would be churlish to refuse it, Gemma thought, even though this woman had almost knocked her down. She knew that was an exaggeration. She had been lost in her own thoughts and maybe, just maybe had wandered a little bit into the road. She took the hand, drawing her breath sharply in at the contact of her palm against the smooth, firm feel of Ava's hand.

"You okay?" Ava said. This was the second time she had asked Gemma that. "Yes," Gemma said. "You were driving quite fast." Ava arched an eyebrow. Nothing could be further from the truth. Gemma certainly was a defensive little madam.

"I was driving within the speed limits," she said calmly. "You need to be more aware of your surroundings if you are walking on the roads." Gemma stared at the road. She wanted to poke her tongue out like a child, but it was true that she had been daydreaming about her life and might easily have wandered into the road. "Come along. I'll give you a lift home...not far to go," Ava continued. She noticed the mutinous look on Gemma's face and grinned inwardly. This woman needed some discipline.

Gemma told herself to refuse. She warred between wanting to be close to this gorgeous creature and run and hide. Her sister's words of her acting old before her time came back to her. She squared her shoulders and flung her light brown hair back, unaware of how alluring this looked.

"Thanks," she said. Ava swallowed. This woman was so femininely attractive. She felt relieved. She had thought Gemma might turn her offer down.

Holding the passenger door open for her, her eyes were drawn to Gemma's shapely bottom as she climbed in. Ava relished the quick desire that flooded her. Her whole body was coming alive again.

"So, you've been here a couple months?" Ava tried to make conversation. "Yes, well, almost four now," Gemma said. "I love it."

"I can see how attractive it is. I also like it." Ava said. "What drew you here?"

"I don't know," Gemma said slowly, "a desire..." She blushed

144

and changed her words, "A need to get away…change something." She stopped abruptly as if she had said too much. It felt odd to be talking so easily to another person.

"I felt the same," Ava said.

"What did you do before here?" Gemma asked. Ava told her about her background and how she knew she had to come back and do something different from her city life. Gemma's gaze softened when Ava told her she had grown up in an area like this. It seemed Ava might be planning to stay.

"You suit being here," she said. Her eyes shone a deep blue, and she unconsciously licked her lower lip as she said it. It was an innocent gesture, but Ava's stomach contracted with desire.

"So," she said, "what were you doing in town-finished work for the day?"

"No. I am off work this afternoon and the next two days. I was at the photography club with Em and Maria. There is going to be a competition and Em is going to enter."

Ava smiled. It was good to see Gemma so at ease.

"What's it about?"

"Local scenery. Em and I are going to photograph some local spots…something unusual."

"Such as?" Ava asked, her voice lowering slightly.

"I was thinking about sunrise or sunset over one of the mountains. I'd try to obtain an angle from above the town," Gemma said. "Em is thinking of some shots from the middle of the lake."

"An angle above the town? As in from the mountain tops?" Ava asked. "Have you been up the mountains before?" Gemma might be sexy and attractive, but she did not seem like a hiker or a very sporty person.

"Yes and no," Gemma said. "I've mostly kept to the town and lake. But I don't mean the very top. I mean as high up as I could to get the perfect shot. I'm really more interested in the colors and how I could use this in my paintings."

"You should be careful," Ava said. "Keep to the lower hills. It is tricky out there. The slopes can be treacherous, and it is easy to get lost." Gemma listened to her with growing indignation. Did she think Gemma was an idiot?

"I am quite sure I am able to walk around without any harm," she said.

"Besides, I'll be with Em."

Ava noticed the attitude.

"I am concerned for you is all," she said. "Please be careful. There are notices about not hiking alone and if one chooses to, they are advised to leave their name at the center."

"Thank you," Gemma said. Honestly, she fumed, had Charlie led everyone to believe she was brainless? She jumped out of the car as it drew up to Ava's house before she had fully stopped.

"Gemma! Wait!" Ava called out. She drew to a stop and leapt out, walking around to the passenger side where the door was still open. She grabbed Gemma's arm. "That was crazy! I would have driven you to your cabin. You could have gotten injured!" Gemma blushed and pulled her arm away.

"For goodness sake, Ava," she said. "I am an adult."

"Yeah- one that could do with some discipline, I think. I could have injured you Gemma!" Ava said. They stared at each other. Gemma backed down first.

"I'm sorry," she said, lowering her eyes. Ava noticed the slight submission and felt her heart soar. Not only was she attracted to Gemma, but Gemma certainly seemed to respond to measures to curtail her bratty side. She softened.

"Just be careful, honey. That's all I'm saying. Keep to the lake and low-lying walks. Follow the advice on the posts all around."

Gemma nodded. She had hardly heard anything Ava had said after the words 'discipline' and 'honey.'

Conflicting emotions swirled in her; outrage at being scolded, warmth at feeling cared for, a squirmy feeling of being taken in hand. Taken in hand? She blinked. She was thinking of some maiden-like scene from a Georgette Heyers or Mills and Boons novel. Adding to the myriad emotions was the intense sexual attraction she felt toward Ava.

"Um...thanks. Yeah, you're right," she said. "Well... I...thanks for the ride home. I'll, um...see you." The last words came out slightly breathlessly and she looked up hoping Ava had not noticed. Blue eyes met brown ones. Gemma saw Ava's dilated pupils. She was aware of her nipples straining tightly against her tight T-shirt and was grateful she had put on a black one that morning. Perhaps it would be less visible. She resisted the impulse to run off like a love-struck teenager and walked off slowly. Unbeknownst to her, this had the effect of making her almost seem to saunter and Ava enjoyed the view.

"Gemma? Want to come to dinner tomorrow evening?"

Gemma turned and impulsively said, "Yes, but why don't we make it at mine? You're probably still settling in and I should have invited you last week to make you feel welcome."

"Thank you," Ava said, accepting. She was surprised and pleased. It would be good to get to know the desirable looking Gemma better.

Gemma walked off, feeling elated and scared. She was not a great cook, she reasoned, but passable. It was a normal neighborly thing to do. She breathed deeply. Her heart beat faster than it should. Her very center ached with desire. What was wrong with her, she wondered. Maybe it was a cold, she decided. But in her heart, she knew she had at long last fallen prey to that longed for condition; '-lust at first sight-.'

The fact that she felt all warm and cared for at Ava's stern looks and tone was something she put temporarily out of her head. There would be time to think about how she felt about that later, she mused.

CHAPTER 6

"Mel," Ava called out, seeing her colleague exiting the back door of the gym area and heading toward the pool. "Do you have a minute?"

"Sure," Mel said. She liked Ava. She worked well, had good ideas and was a team player. The clients liked her and her manner exuded confidence without arrogance.

"It's a bit of an odd question but I have not yet done the hikes up to some of the higher mountains and I wondered if they are easy for people who are not hikers." Mel eyed her. She assumed Ava was concerned about any inexperienced hikers who might sign up when she took her hikes alone in the next month.

"The mountains around here can be dangerous," she said. "We have signs guiding people and we do caution people to leave their names at the center's reception, hike in a group and if they have signed up for a hike through us, we don't take them if they are too inexperienced. Don't worry," she laughed. "You won't be left alone with inexperienced hikers, although I think you will manage well enough."

Ava smiled. "I don't doubt it," she said. "I was thinking, rather..." she trailed off, wondering how to phrase her question.

"Yes," Mel encouraged, becoming more interested.

"It's just that Gemma..." Mel smiled inwardly; so Ava *was* interested in Gemma, as Em had suggested. "Do you know her well? She does not seem to be a very experienced hiker."

"No, she's not," Mel said. "She's been here almost four months and she's more into arts and crafts, not sports. Em said she was signing up for personal training sessions next month though."

"And Em? Is she an experienced hiker?" Ava asked.

"Em?" Mel's gaze sharpened. "She's okay. Not experienced but fit enough. She does not hike off alone. Why?" Mel asked bluntly. If Emma was planning to do something stupid, she needed to know. She would not tolerate a repeat of her being alone in those mountains. A few months after they had arrived Emma had gone off and ended up getting lost. Mel had wasted no time in taking a belt to her. She tolerated no flouting of their agreed rules when it came to Emma's safety.

Ava thought for a minute. It was clear that Mel was top in her and Em's relationship. She did not want to get Em into trouble, but she also felt that she needed to protect Gemma and Em if they planned to do something dangerous. "A few days ago, Gemma told me she and Em were planning to go up one of the mountains to get some shots for this photography competition that's on."

Mel nodded. She had heard of the competition and knew Em was entering. She had not realized she was planning to hike off to the top of a mountain though, to get some shots.

"I'll chat to her," she said evenly. "Thanks for the head's up. I don't suggest either of them go up the mountains alone. Gotta run. I have a client waiting."

Ava watched the athletic woman run off. She'd speak to Gemma later that evening when she saw her. Her clitoris throbbed as she envisioned Gemma's curved body and she took off at a slight run to try and rid herself of imagining the curvy body beneath hers. She noticed Charlie in the distance, arm around a giggling woman, and shook her head. That woman was incorrigible.

Gemma spent the morning lying in bed, gazing at the ceiling as if it would provide her with inspiration of what to cook for her meal with Ava that evening. When no images presented themselves, she got up.

Em rang to ask if she wanted to discuss photography shot plans and she told her to come around. That meant having to do a quick tidy up. Although she was a naturally tidy person, her lounge sported the half empty wine bottle and glass she had had the night before whilst thinking about Ava and dinner the next night.

Gemma's artistic flair showed in her décor with vivid pinks and purples offset by the cool creams. It should have been garish, but the effect was cozy and spacious, almost as if she had brought part of the untamed world of nature into her living room and naturalized it into a cozy and serene space.

Emma arrived and eyed the cookbooks Gemma had laid out.

"Are you cooking something special?" she asked.

"No, I'm just having…um…I asked Ava to dinner. She asked me first, but, I…she is a new neighbor after all, so I decided to have her over."

Emma nodded and smiled gently. It was a good development, she thought. It was great to see Gemma socializing more, not to mention that the interaction was with the gorgeous Ava. She wanted to tell Maria but felt Maria would become over involved and overly enthusiastic. Ava and Gemma needed space.

The two women talked about the shots they hoped to capture. Gemma appraised photography shots with an artist's eye and was aiming for colors that would keep viewers guessing whether the scene was sunrise or sunset. Emma longed to capture a fishing eagle landing on the lake but knew that would take ages. They discussed their various options and eventually decided that heading up to the nearest and smallest of the mountains in the range that encircled the town would be best. They would set off the next morning.

"You have hiked before Gemma, haven't you?" Em asked.

"Yes, well, I mean, I am not experienced but of course I have hiked before," Gemma said. "I even have brand new hiking boots," she added innocently.

Em smiled, not stating the obvious fact that an experienced hiker's boots would be well worn.

"Okay. We obviously won't be going right to the top but just high enough to get some good angled shots. I was also thinking of a creative shot from Peak's Pike."

Gemma did not know what that was, but it sounded good. She nodded.

"Good luck tonight," Emma said.

"It's just dinner." Gemma shrugged, but Em did not miss the way she flushed slightly, and the tip of her tongue instinctively peeked out just enough to touch her top lip. Emma suddenly missed those heady days of getting to know someone or falling for someone. She loved Mel, but there was a lot to be said for the first lustful attraction to another person. Probably one of the reasons their friend Charlie never settled down, she thought. Sometimes though, she wondered if Charlie was deep down a bit lonely. She laughed, thinking of the first time she met Charlie on the mountains, her slightly toppy and flirty manner managing to rub her up the wrong way.

Once Em left, Gemma sat at the table. Was Ava vegetarian? No, she had eaten lamb skewers the other night. Did she have a gluten intolerance or nut allergy? Realizing she was being ridiculous, she got the slow cooker ready and placed a roast beef surrounded by new potatoes in it. She was relieved that she had gone shopping a few days ago.

The day drew on and Gemma, being organized if a bit clumsy having knocked over the flour and broken one bowl, had the meat coming along well. The salad was made. A crisp chardonnay from South Africa was in the fridge and she had made the lemon sorbet, which had come out fluffy and light.

She put on some music and went off to bathe. Her thoughts and anxieties started as she got out of the bath. What if Ava thought the music was romantic? Should she wear makeup? Would Ava kiss her? Kiss her! What was she thinking? Gemma realized she had never been one to abandon her senses and had never even kissed anyone on a first date.

Sure, she had slept with her partners but only after they had committed to each other. She was being way too analytical and silly over having a neighbor for dinner, she decided eventually.

She took a white blouse out of the dresser, which, although she was unaware of it, showed off her cleavage, and a pair of long white shorts. She left her brown hair down and lightly brushed her lips with a pale tinted lipstick. A few sprays of perfume and she felt ready.

Gemma answered the door at the first light knock. Ava caught her breath. Gemma looked so sexy. She could think of nothing but wanting to taste the mounds of delicious creamy flesh she could see peeking through the lace part of Gemma's blouse.

"Come in," Gemma said, annoyed that her voice sounded breathy. Ava was so hot. She wore casual clothes; tight black joggers and a tight black T-shirt that enhanced every lithe toned curve. She was momentarily worried. She was much fleshier than

Ava although she was slender. She also lacked the obvious strength that Ava possessed. The sight of her curved upper arm sent a tight spasm through Gemma's center.

"How was your day?" she asked. She gestured to the kitchen table and listened as Ava told her a story about a tourist who had taken their first ever swimming lesson at the age of eighty. It was brilliant how Ava reached out to people. The whole center focused on helping people achieve an enjoyable holiday and Ava was obviously a good fit. She also described how a ten-year-old boy had slipped and she had iced his leg and taken him to the local hospital thirty minutes away just to be certain it was nothing more than a sprain.

"Wine?" Gemma asked. She poured two glasses and set the dinner out. The beef roast was tender and melted in the mouth, the salad was crisp.

Ava watched her eating and her obvious enjoyment of the delicious meal. Gemma was good company, a good listener, a good cook and utterly sexy and adorable, she thought. It had been a while since she had felt so relaxed and 'at home' in the company of another woman. She got up to help Gemma carry the plates to the sink.

"It's okay. You sit, I'll..." Gemma said, turning. Her breasts brushed up against Ava's strong arm and she gasped aloud. She longed to push her breasts harder against her.

"Sorry," she started. Ava leant her head down without even being aware she was doing it. The moist, plump lips slightly below hers were just too irresistible. The breasts against her arm begged to be held and molded and caressed. Gemma's pupils dilated.

"No need to say sorry, honey," she said. She lowered her head. The minute her lips met the full ones below hers, her senses wheeled.

Gemma opened her lips, gasping and eagerly taking in that tortuously erotic tongue.

Was this what it was like…lust…love…desire? Time seemed to disappear. She almost dragged Ava toward the bedroom. Ava followed with no hesitation. She had thought of Gemma as a shy, sexy woman but this wanton display was as equally desirable.

Shrugging out of her shorts whilst trying to pull off Ava's joggers, Gemma caught her breath. What was she doing?! She stopped short.

"I…" she started. Her words were lost as Ava's mouth covered her own. Hungrily she opened her mouth, kissing back with a passion that she usually reserved for her paintings. Their tongues met, hot and heavy. She drank Ava in, feeling as if no breathing was needed. Her hand, cupping the back of Ava's head, drew her closer. Breathing raggedly Ava finally pulled back.

"Hmm, babe…" she murmured. Her pupils were black with desire and she roughly grabbed Gemma's white blouse, pulling off the offending material that Gemma had been unable to remove. She looked at Gemma. Her eyes were equal dark pools of desire, virtually no trace of the surrounding sky blue. Removing Gemma's bra, Ava pulled off her own T-shirt and sports bra and drew Gemma toward her forcefully.

The feel of her soft, heavy breasts against her own taut and hardened ones with peaked nipples drew a husky cry from her. She traced her thumbs over the erect nipples and Gemma moaned, unable to help the guttural sounds coming from her mouth. Was this her, she wondered, did she really sound so brazen, so wanton?

"Please…" she managed to get out. Drawing her to the bed, Ava removed her shorts as she laid her down, her panties soon following.

Gemma watched as Ava removed her joggers. Without realizing it her legs had parted and her hand moved to cup that area of her that felt so wet and was longing for the feel of Ava's body over it.

Ava watched her, her eyes drawn to a slit. Gemma gasped and removed her hand.

"Don't stop," Ava said. She leant over her and lowered her naked body onto Gemma's. Gemma cried out as that taut, feminine body touched her mons and she bucked upward, thrusting wildly. Ava caught her hands and, clasping them above her head bent her lips to the heavy aching breasts, tracing her tongue over the swollen flesh and then capturing one of the nipples and suckling it hard. Gemma screamed, her hands breaking free and clasping Ava's head to her breasts. She felt she would come just from that exquisite feeling. Ava felt wetness against her leg and, consciousness briefly returning, she slipped one hand below and stroked the swollen clitoris. Gemma brazenly thrust three fingers inside Ava. Ava struggled to maintain composure, but the sensation had her riding Gemma's hand, thrusting back as she fought for control.

"Fuck...you are so beautiful," Gemma breathed. Her voice broke the lazy drugged desire and Ava pulled herself off and roughly pushed Gemma's thighs wide open.

She lowered her head, and cupping Gemma's buttocks in both hands, her lips and tongue nuzzled, suckled and teased Gemma's center until Gemma was screaming and begging Ava to enter her. Before Ava could oblige, she came, waves crashing over her and she breathed raggedly. Ava laughed.

"Your turn..." Gemma sighed softly. She pulled herself upright and pushed Ava down on her stomach, her hands pulling her hips back until Ava was positioned with her butt in the air. From behind she thrust four fingers into her and started pumping. Ava wanted to resist, this is what she should be doing to Gemma, but Gemma held her firm, thrusting and pumping until Ava could do nothing but go with the climax as it took her.

"You are wicked," she said a few minutes later. Ava lay her back and said softly, "Open your legs."

156

Gemma complied and felt her wetness seep out of her. Ava kissed her hard and as she plundered her mouth with her tongue, she thrust her fingers into Gemma pumping in and out hard. Gemma thrust upward, something she had never felt the need to do before. She tried to insert herself deeper onto those fingers and she could feel the slap of Ava's hand against her pelvis.

"Fuck," she screamed as she came again, her wetness pouring over that same hand that had brought her to this pinnacle. Her body slumped down. She felt Ava move and protested.

"Wait, babe," Ava said. She moved from the bed. When she returned Gemma gasped. Ava was wearing a dildo.

"But...I...I've come. I..." Gemma said. But Ava leant over and slickly fitted the dildo into her wetness. She began to move slowly, her hips bumping rhythmically against Gemma's clitoris. The sensation built like a slow fire and Gemma came again, her clitoris pulsating against the firm hips and the dildo slipping on her wetness. Ava pulled out and tucked Gemma into her.

"You are amazing, babe."

"I think it's the other way..." Gemma said. She felt a light slap on her exposed buttock.

"*You* are amazing," Ava said. Her gaze was intent. Gemma melted under its sternness and care.

"I must be," she said grinning. "Tiring you out like this." Ava laughed. She smacked the exposed backside again, a bit harder this time.

"Ow!" Gemma said. She felt sleepy and too drugged to protest much.

"Honey? Should I go?" Ava said. She wanted to check that Gemma was okay with her sleeping in her bed for the night. Gemma blinked. *What?!* They had just made love and Ava was talking about leaving. Ava caught her look. Gemma was obviously not someone who casually slept about.

"Gemma, honey, I was just..."

"Can't you stay until morning?"

"Of course, babe," Ava said, smiling. She decided to tease her a bit. "But what about the dishes?"

"Dishes?" Gemma reached up and gently pulled Ava down to her. "Dishes are for tomorrow," she said sleepily.

CHAPTER 7

A sliver of light played over Ava's face, waking her. For a minute she was disorientated. The bed felt different and the coloring of the room was not cream but pale blue. The feel of the soft, curvy body next to hers brought memory flooding back. She looked down at the sleeping Gemma and her heart contracted with deep conviction. She would end up loving this woman.

For now, the more immediate concern of having to get to work prevailed and she gently kissed the top of the head nuzzled close to her shoulder. Gemma's eyes opened. She immediately blushed. She was naked. The sexy body next to hers was naked. Memories of last night and her brazen, unusually forward behavior flooded back.

"Hey, sexy," Ava said, smiling. Gemma's heart melted at the words and look of desire in Ava's face.

"Hi," she said. She wondered uneasily if Ava thought she was an easy lay. It was not the type of relationship she wanted. She wanted love, commitment, care, and companionship, in addition to amazing sex. Ava would think Gemma slept around. She felt unable to say anything other than her brief greeting.

Ava's heart dropped. Perhaps she had misjudged Gemma and this was a once off for her. She needed to step back and evaluate.

"Okay," she said slowly. "I'll check in later and see how you are. Be careful today on your walk."

"I will," Gemma said.

"I mean it," Ava said firmly, unable to stop her natural dominant tendencies from issuing the gentle warning. Gemma might not want a relationship but she could not turn off her feeling of concern for her. "We can't spare guides from the center or the emergency services to look for you."

"I said okay!" Gemma snapped. Ava narrowed her eyes. Gemma was displaying some major brat behaviors.

"I mentioned to Mel that you and Em would be going out so perhaps put your name at the center and the route you are taking," Ava said, trying again to enforce on Gemma the seriousness of possible danger.

"Em and I are fine, and not your concern," Gemma said. "I'm sorry," she added immediately. "That was rude of me. Thank you for your concern."

Ava leaned down to kiss her and Gemma's nipples contracted in desire. She put her arm defensively across her chest and Ava chuckled. At least she knew Gemma desired her if nothing else. Gemma needed a spanking. She wondered if Gemma knew that about herself.

Ava left. Work first ,she thought. She was determined not to let herself get too heavily involved if Gemma was not up for a fully committed domestic discipline relationship and if they were to be only casually involved.

Gemma turned over and, putting her flaming face into her pillow, groaned. Ava must think she was someone who slept around.

She had mentioned seeing her again. She cursed her treacherous body. Her stomach lurched when she thought of Ava's eyes turning stern and telling her to be careful when she went out later. She was tempted to touch herself. Her body felt sated, used and relaxed. Her thighs trembled slightly as she got up.

Em was making her way over to Gemma's when she saw her door open and Ava emerge. She stopped, so that Ava would have privacy and grinned. Gemma was a dark horse. She waited ten minutes, figuring Gemma had perhaps forgotten she was arriving early. Gemma answered; she had a gown on and apologized for not being ready.

"It's okay," Em said.

She wondered how to tell Gemma that they would have to change their walk. Mel had said in no uncertain terms she expected Em to not go out alone with only Gemma. Mel was fine if she stuck to the low foot hills. Her bottom tingled, remembering the belt blistering Mel had given her the year before when she went off alone up the mountains.

Em was not one to need discipline very often and when she did, a quick hard spanking and a talk usually had her back on track. It had been awhile since her last correction and she did not welcome another. Em and Mel were in a domestic discipline relationship as she had been with her previous partner who had died. They were a stable and happy couple. She knew Maria and Marty practiced domestic discipline as well, but as Maria was a natural brat, she tended to have her backside warmed often.

Em had noticed similar traits in Gemma, combined with stubbornness, and she thought Gemma could benefit from some discipline in her life. Perhaps Ava would be the one to deliver it, she mused.

Gemma changed quickly, putting on some soft cargo trousers

and her new hiking boots. She went through to the kitchen where Em was waiting.

"Sorry for keeping you waiting. I'll make us some coffee and breakfast. Then we can get going."

"I saw Ava leaving. Did you have a good evening?" The question was said with a hint of teasing. Gemma blushed.

"Yes...well..." Em laughed and hugged her. "There is nothing to be ashamed of. Good for you." Gemma felt herself relaxing. She had had a great night, with a very sexy woman and she was spending the morning with a friend. What could be better?

As they sat over their coffee Em brought up the subject of their hike. She explained they'd not go too far. Gemma was surprised. She did want to take those shots. They would form the basis for her paintings.

"Mel would not like it," Em continued. Gemma decided not to protest. She must respect what Mel wanted.

She could not help thinking, though, about what Em wanted. Em laughed when she asked her about it.

"I make my own decisions for my own life and my life with Mel, but Mel keeps me on track." she said. Gemma listened intently, feeling conflicting emotions. The relationship sounded good. But spankings? She was not sure. The way her tummy lurched and somersaulted as Em spoke to her about it, the way she felt when Ava was stern and when Marty had eyeballed her and Em made her wonder, however.

She agreed to go only as far as Em suggested, but asked her to point out Pike's Peak to her. She'd try it alone another time. The two women set off. It was a beautiful morning. The sun was not yet high, although they had missed sunrise and the paths through the trees once they reached the start of the trails was cool. Em took plenty of scenery shots whilst Gemma focused on the various colors around her. They stopped for a drink which Em had packed and she pointed out Pike's Peak. One could see it overhanging about halfway up the nearest mountain side. It did not look that far away and Gemma suggested they try to make it. Em laughed. "No, It's way further than it seems," she said. "Another day perhaps if we bring someone with us."

They set back and Em hived off to the photography club where she could use the dark room. Gemma sat in her lounge going through her shots, looking at the various colors. Her full attention was not on them though, and she wondered whether she would see Ava that evening. She felt wet just thinking about her.

Her phone pinged, and heart beating fast, she saw a WhatsApp from Ava. 'Fancy a drink and chat this eve...my porch?' Gemma replied in the affirmative with no hesitation and her heart soared. Another WhatsApp pinged back with a smiley face and a question. 'How did the hike go? Were you careful?' She felt a simultaneous flash of annoyance and tenderness. She was not an idiot to have to account for her actions, yet the care and squirmy feeling the simple question brought to her excited her. Suddenly she was filled with self-doubt. Maybe it was just about sex. Perhaps Ava thought they'd have another passion filled eve. Well, she would not mind that of course, but she wanted more; a lot more.

CHAPTER 8

Ava had an energizing day at work. Her senses felt at attention as usually happened to her after a lust sated evening. Professional footballers and rugby players were told sex drained them, but for her it was the opposite. She frowned slightly. She did not only want sex, though. She wanted to date Gemma, get to know her, find her prickly defensive, bratty side and punish her bottom as needed. She felt instinctively that Gemma would respond well to this. She had been with too many partners not to know the signs.

Ava drove home at the end of her shift feeling inexplicably calm. Tonight, she was going to ask Gemma if she wanted to date her. There was no sense in prolonging it. It had been a long time since she had felt this way about someone. She was going to be upfront and ask her about a domestic discipline relationship. Gemma seemed inclined toward it but whether she allowed herself to follow her unconscious desire of being disciplined remained to be seen.

She smiled as she thought of having overheard Mel's conversation with Emma. Mel had called her from the office and despite keeping her voice low, Ava could hear her ask if Emma was home safely and where she had hiked to. Judging by Mel's response, suggesting that Emma might want to watch her tone, it seemed that Em was slightly annoyed. Ava felt a sense of longing and belonging listening to that one-sided conversation and easily imagined the response of the more submissive woman on the other side.

She parked her 4x4 outside her cabin and feeling light hearted entered her home, showered and got ready to meet Gemma.

Gemma arrived exactly at six p.m. bearing a bottle of chilled white wine and smiled shyly when Ava opened the door and hugged her. They breathed in each other's scent and Gemma lent into Ava. It felt so right and natural, as if she could stay securely tucked into those arms forever. Her one arm curved around Ava's back and she felt a surge of protectiveness toward the dominant, attractive woman. Ava felt Gemma relax into her and she held her tight. They pulled back and Gemma leaned in for a kiss. Ava kissed her immediately. Her lips were soft and warm. She moaned, feeling Gemma's nipples tighten against her own breasts. Gemma's one hand kneaded her left buttock and she fought to keep a lid on her physical desire.

Drawing back, she smiled tenderly. "Let me get some snacks to go with this wine. Take a seat." Gemma sank almost dreamily into the swing style patio chair with the pale cushions. The sun was starting its journey below the horizon and the rays twinkled in and out of the tree branches. It was beautiful and she drank it in. Every one of her senses tingled with anticipation, as if she was on the brink of something large, something important, something right.

Ava came out bearing a tray with wine glasses and two small dishes. Gemma did not even look at them.

"Ava-" she started.

"Gemma-" Ava said simultaneously. They both laughed.

"You first," Ava said. Gemma blushed.

"I just I mean...the other night...and I-" she stammered. "You are so...," She trailed off. Ava sat next to her and took her hands.

"Gemma," she said, relieving her of her awkward stammering. "I loved being with you. I loved our night together. I want to have a relationship with you." Gemma's eyes sparkled.

"I...that was what I was going to say as well," she said.

"Good," Ava said. She leaned back slightly, a more serious look in her eyes. Gemma's stomach lurched. Did she not want that as well? Ava turned fully to her. Confessing her preference in relationships made her feel vulnerable.

"In my romantic relationships I prefer to practice domestic discipline." Gemma dropped her head and blushed. Her tummy lurched and rolled. It felt exciting.

Ava smiled. A typical submissive response, she thought.

"That is what I would want in my relationship with you." The words were simple and honestly said. She kept quiet, waiting for Gemma to answer. When Gemma kept her head down, she asked, "Do you know what I mean by domestic discipline?" Gemma nodded, her hair obscuring her face. Ava tilted her chin up.

"Look at me," she said softly. "Tell me what you know."

"Well...like...like Mel and Em," she said. Ava nodded slowly.

"Explain it to me," she said. She needed to ensure Gemma understood. Gemma started talking and Ava listened carefully. She stumbled over words like spankings and bottom and rules. Ava encouraged her.

"Well," she said at the end, "what do you think?" Gemma nodded. "I...er...yes..." she said. "I think--yes," she said, half laughing out of nerves and embarrassment. It made her feel vulnerable admitting that being spanked was something she craved. Ava hugged her. She sensed Gemma's anxiety and knew that Gemma felt as vulnerable as she did.

"We can discuss this more before you decide," she said. "You might find you don't like it." In her heart she knew Gemma would like it and that the relationship would benefit them both.

Gemma looked at her seriously.

"This is right," she said. "Right for me and right for you." She looked so innocent and sexy with the low evening light making her eyes shine as if she was lit up from inside.

"Perhaps we should practice spanking now," she said teasingly. Ava looked at her. The little minx. Gemma probably had no idea what a real spanking felt like. She was looking at her, a challenge in her eyes. The brat was already testing her.

Ava grabbed her wrist and Gemma gave a squeal, finding herself up-ended over Ava's lap. Her bottom was in the air, the tips of her toes just touching the floor. A firm hand landed on her bottom. The slap was not hard but it made her gasp, myriad emotions swirling through her. She felt ungainly and awkward dangling over Ava's lap, her tummy somersaulting but wanting more.

"Was that it?" she said.

Ava smiled grimly and landed her hand on the skirt-clad bottom again, this time harder. Gemma could not help a little shriek escaping her lips.

"Had enough, my love?" Ava said. Gemma wiggled a little bit. Her bottom was tingling, but she could not help the sensation that was between her legs. It felt exciting, she thought. The center of her mons was tight against Ava's hard leg and she gasped, pushing herself experimentally harder against that smooth skin. Ava noticed and gave and smiled. There would be time for that later. Right now this little brat needed to learn that teasing would get her into trouble. She lifted the skirt, exposing pale pink legs and a nicely rounded bottom clad in a lacy Brazilian cut panty. Gemma cried out in embarrassment. "Ava..." she said.

"Well, this is what you wanted isn't it?" Ava said calmly. With one arm tightly around her waist she held her tight and proceeded to raise and bring her hand down twenty times in a row. It was satisfying to watch the bottom cheeks bouncing under her hand and the pale skin start to flush red. Gemma started to gasp and wail lightly. She felt embarrassed and her bottom hurt. She knew had been asking for it, though. She had wanted to feel what it was like. Not the playful spanks from her college days but to be disciplined properly if she needed it.

Ava stopped spanking, one hand resting on Gemma's back, the other on her bottom.

"What do you think? Is it what you wanted?" she asked lightly. Ava helped her to sit up and pulled her next to her. She put one finger under Gemma's chin, lifting her head and forcing her to look at her. "I asked you a question," she said firmly.

"Um..." Gemma lowered eyes.

"Look at me!" Ava said. Gemma looked into her brown eyes, noting the compassion, amusement and desire in them. She flushed. Ava took pity on her. "That was just a taste," she said. "I might have to spank you sometimes, not just with my hand, but a paddle-a hair brush-my belt..." she trailed off.

Gemma felt that the words should have shocked her, but they did not. She felt excited and turned on. She got up and paced the room so that Ava would not see the desire in her eyes. Ava smiled. She was well aware of what Gemma was feeling.

"Come here," she said calmly, yet firmly. Gemma hesitated. "I said come here." Ava took her wrist, bringing her closer. She guided her to a sitting position on her lap and, placing one hand behind the back of her head, brought her lips down to hers. Gemma groaned as the heat in her bottom and the intense heat in her center made her wiggle.

"Sit astride me," Ava commanded. Gemma readily complied. The position opened her legs, making the slit at her center ooze with moisture. They kissed hungrily, their mouths devouring each other. Gemma inched closer, so that her very center was touching Ava's stomach. Oh goodness, she thought, she wanted to grind herself against this woman, she wanted this woman to enter her, she wanted to be entered.

Ava pulled her top off. She released the clasp of her bra and Gemma's heavy breasts sprang free. Ava buried her lips between them. Gemma could not stop herself from bucking against Ava's firm stomach. Her panties were saturated.

She slipped off Ava's lap. Standing in front of her, she removed her skirt and panties. Before Ava could touch her, she knelt down between Ava's legs and lowered her mouth, nuzzling her over her shorts.

Ava leant back. She grasped Gemma's head with one hand and commanded her to wait. Lifting her hips slightly she slipped her shorts and panties off. Gemma greedily eyed the mons before her, the glistening open slit and swollen clitoris that issued an invitation to be suckled and licked.

"Suck me," Ava commanded. Gemma leant down, her breasts caressing the sides of Ava's thighs and lowered her mouth. Her tongue lapped the thick swollen bud as Ava's two hands grasped her head forcing her closer.

"Harder," she commanded. Gemma complied and thought how amazing it was that she was in control of this incredibly sexy woman at that very moment. The clitoris swelled beneath her tongue and she nipped at it gently. She wanted to enter her. Just as she put two fingers into the plump center she felt herself being moved away.

"Turn around," Ava said.

"Hey!" Gemma, said indignantly. "I was enjoying-" She felt a sharp slap to her already tender buttocks and gasping, immediately turned, still kneeling. Ava moved behind her, pushing her shoulders down and forcing her buttocks to be raised. She thrust three fingers into Gemma from behind and the unexpected sensation had Gemma cry out. It changed to gasps and pants as the thrusting continued. The feel of Ava behind her and the fullness in her center consumed her. She came, gushing out over Ava's hand. Ava turned her and, lying flat, pulled her on top of her.

"Enter me," she said, her voice thick with desire and need. Gemma slipped two fingers in, then four as Ava commanded, "More!" She thrust rhythmically until Ava shouted out with release.

Gemma collapsed next to her.

"You are amazing," she said.

"Hmm...and you are so sexy," Ava said.

"I liked the spanking," Gemma said cheekily. Ava laughed.

"My love, the day will come when you are begging me to stop spanking you," she promised. Gemma snuggled in. She doubted that. That spanking had been utterly amazing.

CHAPTER 9

The next few weeks saw Ava and Gemma settle into their new relationship. Part of this included establishing some rules for Gemma. Although they did this together Gemma had conflicting feelings. Part of her was settled and relieved to have help, whilst her 'brat like' part wanted to rebel. It was the smaller part and she had to admit she felt cherished and cared for.

"You seem very happy lately," Mel said one day as Ava walked into the office. "I am," Ava said easily. "I was happy, well more content I suppose, when I arrived but yes, I am happy."

"That's good," Mel said supportively. She was pleased to see her colleague so settled. "And Gemma…" Mel let the question trail off. They had spent many lunch hours discussing their partners and shared lifestyle choices, but Mel did not have as much chance to see Gemma as she did Ava.

"She seems very settled," Ava said. "She has even suggested we move in together."

Mel was pleased for Ava.

"I wonder what those two are getting up to this morning,"

Mel said. "Emma mentioned that they were going to go walking." Ava frowned. Gemma had not mentioned that to her. Mel seemed relaxed about it though. She knew that Em would have discussed their route with Mel and where it was safe for them to walk alone. They were probably aiming to take more shots for the competition, she reckoned.

Back at home, Em and Gemma were getting ready for a hike. They had decided to go out to Pike's Peak after seeing the photos they had taken for the competition. The photos were great but both wanted to capture something special and out of the ordinary. Emma had decided not to mention it to Mel in case she worried. She mentioned that they would once again be taking a walk like their last one. Mel had kissed her and left for work, knowing that Em was sensible and seldom flouted their safety rules.

Gemma did not even think of mentioning it to Ava despite the rules they had gone through, one of them being about safety and thinking before acting.

The two women packed water and their cameras. Gemma took a few pastels and light canvas paper in case she was inspired to capture the essence of a scene in front of her immediately as opposed to from a photograph. They both carried their mobile phones and Em had packed trail snacks. They set off, spirits high.

Em pushed away the niggling thought at the back of her mind that she should have let Mel know where she was going. She had let her think they were doing the same walk as her last one with Gemma. She was a bit bored lately. Her novel was completed and she felt at odds. She needed to establish a routine and think of her next project. Time enough for that after the photograph competition, she thought.

They talked as they walked, gradually trailing off as the incline steepened. They stopped to admire the view every half hour. Pike's

Peak came into view. It was wrong to call it a peak, Gemma thought. It was more of a large overhanging rock above a canyon. It was not on top of a mountain but only half way up.

On arrival they high-fived each other and sat down far from the edge. Em was aware of the clouds in the distance. Gemma also noticed them and suggested they hastily take photos before the lighting changed. She loved the more somber mood of pastel blues and grays that she could use to represent the clouds coming over, but knew that Em favored light and brightness.

The two women walked as far as they dared and then knelt on all fours, crawling toward the edge. Gemma laughed.

"We look silly," she said. She stood up and Em grabbed her.

"Careful," she warned. The wind was picking up and Em hastily got her tripod ready. A gust of wind blew one of Gemma's sheets from her hand that she had sketched a rough outline on and she gasped. How could the sky be so clear with clouds only in the distance and yet the wind be so strong, she wondered.

Em was slight in stature and Gemma held her steady, as took the shots. Once done she turned to her.

"We best go," she said. "I'm sorry about your drawing Gemma."

"It was only a rough sketch," she responded. Em's phone rang and she dared not look to see who it was.

"Come on," she urged. "Look at the clouds rolling in."

"I know," Gemma said, her eyes sparkling. "Please Em, take some shots for me...please. I can draw from them later." Em relented. The passion in Gemma's eyes could not be resisted. She stepped back toward safer ground and set up again, taking shots from angles Gemma directed. Truth be told, the change in weather was scaring her.

Once done, the two women turned back. The clouds had made the path less clear. They both tried not to upset the other. Em's phone rang again. She put her bag down and looked at it. Melissa! Her heart skipped a beat. Gemma noticed her face.

"What's wrong?"

"It's Mel," she said. At the somber words it was as if all the rules and guidelines she and Ava had discussed came to her consciousness.

"Oh shoot," Gemma said lightly, trying to push her thoughts away. "Let's carry on."

Em let the ring fade out and they continued. She hoped she could get home before the really bad weather started and wondered what she would tell Mel.

Half an hour later they seemed no further away from Pike's Peak.

"Darn, we've walked in a circle," Gemma said. "Look where we are." Her phone rang and without thinking she answered.

"Gemma! Where are you? Have you seen Em? Mel has been trying to phone her. I knew you were seeing her this morning." Gemma hesitated. This was her first time answering a question that she knew might get her into trouble with Ava.

"Um..." she started.

"Who is it?" Em hissed over her shoulder.

"Is that Em?" Ava's voice had sharpened?

"Um...I...er...."

"Gemma! What's going on?" Ava said. "Tell me this instant!" Gemma looked at Em. She cleared her throat. She was an adult and able to take a mountain walk if she wanted.

"I am almost home," she said breezily.

"Where are you exactly? Is Em with you?"

"Um--yes," Gemma said, whilst watching Em shake her head no. "I-we...we went on a walk," Gemma said.

"Where to?" Ava asked.

"Oh, just a short way. To take a few more photos for the competition."

"What!" Ava said. "Have you seen the weather?"

"I have," Gemma said snootily. "I am not blind. Now I have to get home." She ended the call. Em was staring at her openmouthed. Gemma was clearly new to domestic discipline and unaware of the trouble she was in.

"Let's go," she said. They pulled each other along and Em took the lead, being more familiar with the surroundings. They reached the lower slopes. Em was aware of her phone ringing but ignored it again. The wind buffeted them and it started to rain. Great crashes of thunder filled their ears and their eyes were almost blinded by a sudden flash of lightning.

A single figure appeared out of the misty rain. Gemma shrieked in alarm.

"Relax," Charlie said. "What have the two of you been up to? There's a mild panic down below. Luckily I remembered how you like the viewpoint from Pike Peak." She looked at Em as she said this. "I thought Mel might be too worried if I mentioned it, so I came on up instead." Em smiled wanly. She was relieved to see Charlie although not relieved at hearing the news about Mel. "And you-I don't think Ava is too happy either."

Gemma looked at her, her buttocks contracting involuntarily.

"Er..." she said awkwardly.

Charlie landed on swat on Em's back side. Gemma stepped neatly to one side before she could be swatted. Charlie grinned.

"Come on," she said. "Let's go down. Time to face the music." The two women followed Charlie's lead. It was comforting to see her red anorak just in front of them. The comfort did not last more than fifteen minutes though.

"Gemma!" Ava's strong voice called out. It was with relief that

Gemma saw her even though Ava did not look at all happy. She was clearly concerned but anger glinted in her eyes. Gemma's arm was firmly grasped.

"Are you okay?" Ava's taut expression did not bode well. Ava exhaled. A knot of tension left her. She was relieved that Gemma was okay. She did not know what she would do if something happened to her. The relief made her voice sharp.

"Go and get in the car," she said. She turned to make sure Em was okay. Mel was waiting with a clearly anxious Em standing next to her.

"You get Gemma home," Mel said. "Em is fine."

"I'm sorry," Em said sincerely to Ava. "I should have looked after Gemma a bit better. I'm sorry."

"You will be," Mel said ominously. Em winced at the words. Mel nodded to Ava. "I'll see you tomorrow. Will you be okay?" Ava nodded.

Hugging both women briefly, she turned toward the 4x4. Gemma, seeing her stride forward purposefully, felt her tummy lurch. This was not good. She leapt from the truck, not sure where she would go but anywhere from that look of disappointment and determination on Ava's face. Ava grabbed her arm.

"Get back in the car," she said. "Now!"

"I'm sorry," Gemma said desperately.

"I'm sure you are," Ava said, her voice softening slightly. "Honey, get in the car. Now!" Her hand moved to her belt and Gemma's eyes widened, her tummy cart wheeling, a feeling of panic and excitement flooding her. She got back into the car.

Ava leant in and did up her belt buckle. "Don't even think about getting out again until we are home," she said, her voice low and yet totally clear, near to her lover's ear. Gemma nodded. She had been silly. She had frightened Ava and she or Em could have been injured.

"I'm sorry," Gemma tried in the car, trying to ease the butterflies in her stomach.

"We will talk at home," Ava said curtly. She reached out and patted Gemma's knee. The tender gesture dispelled some of the panic, but completely increased the excitement she felt.

Ava drew up at her house.

"Inside!" Gemma felt a bit awkward. She followed Ava . The cabin looked cozy with the inside lights on.

"Go and dry off," Ava instructed. "Put on one of my dry T-shirts. Then come back to the lounge."

"Ava?"

Ava came to her, relenting slightly, understanding that Gemma was caught between wondering if Ava was angry or concerned.

"Honey, you scared me and broke our rules. Go and dry off, shower if you prefer. I'll be here waiting for you." She hardened her voice slightly.

"Um...are you...going to...?"

"Yes," Ava said. "Go shower now...don't make it worse." Gemma's stomach somersaulted. She should feel nervous, she thought, but she felt anticipation at being cared for in such a way that showed how much she meant to Ava.

When she got back to the lounge Ava had placed a single backed armless chair in the center of the room.

"Come here." The words were not angry but commanded attention. Gemma hastened to obey, standing in front of Ava.

"Gemma," she said, taking her hands, "what you did today was reckless. Why did you do that?"

"I--er...we..." Gemma trailed off. Her excuse sounded lame. "I wanted some more shots so I could paint a better scene for the competition". She tried to hold Ava's intense gaze but failed and lowered her eyes.

"I see. What about keeping safe, not going into the mountains alone?"

"I ...er...was not alone. Em was with me."

"Did you check with Em that she was experienced, comfortable going off alone? Did you check that she was allowed to wander off, without informing anyone, into the mountains at this time of year when the weather is unpredictable?" Gemma had thought carefully, not about the things Ava listed, but about what she had wanted to do. She had not thought about putting herself or Em in danger or how Ava and Mel might worry. She knew she had not thought about what might happen if a search party had to be sent out, about the time, energy and effort that that would have taken.

"No. I thought about getting the scenes I needed. I'm sorry," she said quietly.

Ava was pleased. Gemma was accepting responsibility for her actions that could have resulted in harm.

"I will be spanking you with my hand and then the hair brush," she said. Gemma gasped; Ava's hand was fine, *but a hair brush?!* She shuddered. Ignoring the gasp, Ava instructed her to go to the bedroom and bring back the wooden hairbrush in the top drawer. Gemma hesitated. She saw Ava's hand at her belt buckle and scarpered. Opening the drawer she took the brush out, testing the weight in the hand. It was not too heavy and actually quite beautiful with its ebony wood on the back.

"Gemma?" Ava's deep tone pulled her back to what was coming and she hurried back. Delay would only make it more painful. Ava stood with her hand stretched out. As if mesmerized, Gemma handed it to her, although part of her wanted to throw it across the room and run.

Ava placed it on the floor near the chair and sat down.

"Come here." Gemma's feet did not obey her mind. "It's okay, babe," Ava said. She stood and, taking Gemma's wrist, pulled her forward gently and drew her over her lap. The borrowed T-shirt rode up, displaying the rounded buttocks clad only in a thong.

"This is to remind you of our rules, not to put yourself or others in danger and at the minimum let someone know where you are going." Ava lifted her hand and brought it down on the plump buttocks. The resounding spank echoed along with a small shriek sounding up from the floor. Ava alternated buttock to buttock, the white globes turning red quickly from the unaccustomed hard spanking.

Gemma felt the heat burning in her bottom and tried to shift.

"Ava." she said. "I am sorry, please babe…"

"Quiet, honey," Ava said. "I will decide when you have had enough." She changed to the sit spots and further down the back of the thigh which had Gemma shifting her legs in agony.

"Ow…ow…sorry," she sobbed. Ava rested her hand on one soft buttock feeling the heat emanating from it. She picked up the hair brush.

"Twenty with the hair brush," she said.

"Oh no, Ava, please no," Gemma said. "It will be too sore." However she did not try and move off Ava's lap. She was starting to feel she deserved this. She had been silly, and worse, thoughtless.

"It's supposed to," Ava said, smiling grimly. She rubbed her one hand lightly over Gemma's back and the tender gesture calmed her. "Right, okay…ready." She lifted the brush and thwacked it down on the back of one thigh. Gemma shrieked, jumping upright.

"Ah…oh…it's too sore."

"Back down," Ava said, firmly holding onto Gemma's wrist so that she could not flee. Her voice and face were unyielding but not angry. Gemma gulped. Ava lifted one eyebrow. Gemma sank back down. The hairbrush landed another nineteen times. Gemma jumped up the minute it was finished, her hands rubbing her buttocks.

Ava looked at her. Gemma did not realize how sexy she was right then. Clad only in a T-shirt, riding high in her waist, her hands caressing her now flame red buttocks. She breathed in. She knew she had to stay in control. This was not a good time to reward the brat by turning her punishment into an enjoyable sex session.

She stood and held Gemma in her arms.

"You scared me," she murmured into her hair. "I thought something had happened to you when the weather change started and I could not get hold of you. Charlie set out immediately without telling us and called to say she had found you. Don't do that again." She suddenly pushed Gemma back a little, her hands grasping the tops of Gemma's arms. "Please," she said, her voice even and level although Gemma detected a slight crack in it. "You need to remember our rules. I want you to be safe. I don't know what I would do if…" Gemma melted. The look in Ava's eyes was intense. It was worth her sore bottom to feel so cared for, so loved. She felt sorry for the agony she had caused.

"I'll apologize to Mel. She would have been worried about Em," she said. Ava felt proud of her. Gemma showed insight into her behavior.

"Go and have a lie down. I'll make dinner," she said.

Gemma nodded. She felt unbearably tired.

"I wish you could lie with me." Ava wanted that as well but wanted Gemma to have time to reflect and not become amorous.

"Later tonight," she said. "For now, go and have a sleep." Gemma hesitated.

"-Or you could have another twenty with the hairbrush and then stand in the corner whilst I cook?" Ava said in a questioning tone. Gemma did not say another word but walked back to the bedroom and sank into the double bed, wrapping Ava's duvet around her torso. She fell into a soundless sleep.

Later she was awakened by Ava tickling her cheek.

"Come-on, sleepy head," she said, "Supper." The smell of curry wafted through the door and Gemma stretched for a minute, forgetting her punishment. Ava's hand touched her buttock ensuring she remembered the spanking with the ache it bought.

"Oh!" she said. Ava laughed.

"Come on. I've put a cushion on your chair for dinner time. I think it's time we also discussed moving in together, as you suggested." Gemma nodded. This felt so right.

Feeling happy and calm, if sore, she tucked into the fragrant curry and the wild jasmine rice. Life was good. No, better than good, it was wonderful.

CHAPTER 10

―――――――――

"Let's do it," Maria said enthusiastically. Her dark eyes shined. Em and Gemma groaned inwardly. They loved Maria but even though she had seemingly mostly been tamed by Marty, she was still a wild cap at heart.

Weeks had passed since their last escapade and Gemma and Ava had settled fully into their domestic discipline relationship. Gemma felt like a full part of the group and she had blossomed. The scenery competition had come and gone. Neither of the women had entered, not being sufficiently prepared. They planned to enter the upcoming Christmas competition however.

They both understood Maria's need for '-thrills-.' Marty and Maria owned their business which involved a lot of commitment, time and energy. When Maria had time off she wanted to spend it doing the things she loved. Still, they were not sure about this latest idea of hers. Heading off on a one-hour bus trip to surf seemed a bit reckless when none of them had ever surfed. The fine wining and dining she had suggested with it, though, seemed like fun. A resort had opened at the surfer's beach the year before and they all wanted to visit it.

"What does Marty say about it?" Em asked. Marty was not one to be taken lightly. She gave no chances and brooked no arguments. She was a perfect fit for the unruly Maria.

"Oh, she's all for it," Maria said, her eyes momentarily sliding sideways. Sure, Marty had been up for it. She had said it would be good for Maria to get away with her friends and try out the restaurants at the year old resort. The attempt at surfing, well, Maria saw no reason to mention that.

"You'd love to go wouldn't you, Gemma?" Maria said. Gemma nodded.

She did want to see the resort as it boasted a set of small upmarket art and photography studios and she wanted to see if she could use any ideas from there in their small town. She was not a sporty person, however, and had never surfed, nor had a desire to. In addition, the waves were large on the coast. Putting the thought of surfing out of her mind, Gemma had assented. Getting wet and maybe feeling a bit embarrassed at falling into the sea a few times was a small price to pay to see the resort.

Ava had been all for it.

"It will be good for you to get away for the day," she said. "Maria and Em are good friends to you. You'll have to take some photos of the area and the resort. We might even go for a romantic weekend if you like it." She smiled and landed a long kiss on Gemma's lips. As per Maria's gentle warning she did not mention surfing. Em had tried to point out most likely they would be on their faces most of the time but Maria waved off her concerns. Em's comments had pricked her conscience but she had pushed the thoughts away.

"Yes, I'll take photos. I might even ask to see one of their rooms," she had murmured through Ava's searching lips.

"You would tell me if anything was bothering you, wouldn't

you?" Ava said, standing close to her, one finger under her chin. The day of their trip had dawned and Gemma had been a bit quiet. The words were soft, but there was a subtle sternness beneath them. Gemma was an adult woman and if she wanted to go and surf at one of the roughest surf sea spots she would, she thought mutinously.

"Yes," she murmured, kissing Ava deeply so that she lost her train of thought.Out of the three tops Mel was the one who was most concerned. She knew Emma well and wondered at her silence around the upcoming trip.

"You okay, babe?" she asked.

"Yes!" Em snapped, lowering her head to a task so Mel would not see her faint blush. This deception made her feel like a schoolgirl.

"Watch your tone," Mel warned, her voice deepening.

"Sorry," Emma snapped the word out, which made her feel even guiltier. She kissed Mel lightly and told her to have a good day at work.

The three women set off in high spirits, boarding a local bus along with a group of excited and happy tourists making their way to the coast for the day. Maria assured them they could rent surf boards. But first she announced they would check out the small art and photography galleries. They also decided on coffee at one of the trendy coffee shops dotted around the resort. After surfing they would decide on the lunch venue.

"Maria, are you sure Marty was okay?" Em asked as they set off.

"Of course," Maria said. "She was happy we are going to check it out."

"As was Mel," Em said. "But, I meant about surfing. It's not like any of us know how to." Maria laughed.

"No need for anyone to know that," she laughed. "What the

eye doesn't see…"

"The buttocks don't feel!" Gemma finished, displaying an unusual flash of humor around their domestic discipline relationships. The three women laughed.

"Exactly," Maria said. She winked at Em who smiled back. Em could not shake the small sense of unease that had not left her since Maria had first suggested the trip. It seemed a bit immature to be running off to do something they did not know how to do even if it was Maria's dream. They could have planned it a bit better and brought along both Mel and Ava who were expert surfers or at least booked a lesson. Maria had a streak in her that tended toward involuntary self-harm.

The women spent a pleasant morning wandering around the resort, checking out shops and small local galleries. The clientele was a mixture of tourists who stayed in the resort and those who were visiting from surrounding small towns and villages.

They took coffee at one of the quieter coffee shops and discussed where they would have lunch. That decided, they headed off to the beach. Maria arranged the renting of the surf boards and they changed in one of the small huts that were for daily rent. The ocean beckoned them and it was a good sight to see all the surfers and swimmers. Em was a fair swimmer but neither she nor Gemma had surfed before.

"Nothing to it," Maria said breezily. "I've bodysurfed. So surfing is probably just a matter now of standing up and balancing when a wave comes."

"Well, let's just body surf," Gemma suggested.

"No way!" Maria said. "My dream sees me standing tall and proud…and sexy!" Gemma laughed. Maria was incorrigible. She did look sexy and toned though. Someone totally suited to surfing. The women carefully watched other surfers and tried to follow suit.

They fell off their boards constantly. Eventually Maria laughed and shrugged her shoulders.

"Alright, body surfing it is. Follow me," she said, lying on her board and taking off, arms paddling either side. Gemma admired her toned, sleek arms. She herself was not overweight but was not toned and muscular. Her curves were soft and rounded. She wore a two piece whilst Em had donned a one piece that showed off her small waist and balanced out her rounded thighs.

The waves were a bit rough and Gemma gasped and coughed as spray hit her. "I think I have to go back in," she shouted to Em. Em felt relieved. Nodding agreement to Gemma, she turned to find Maria.

"Maria," she said loudly. "We are out of our depths. We need to go back in. The waves are too strong!"

Maria pouted. "Come on, Em..." she started.

"No! We go back in now," Em said firmly. "Now, Maria! I won't have us in danger like this."

Surprised at her fellow brat's sharp tone she turned, helped Gemma to turn her board and arm paddle back in. Once the three women were at knee depth, Maria suddenly turned back.

"Wait for me!" she yelled. "This time I'm going to do it!" She tried to leap on her board as a medium sized, fast wave crested in. It was a wave totally unsuited for surfing and she over balanced and fell awkwardly, still in the shallows.

"Ow!" she screamed as her hand hit the sand, caught beneath the heavy board.

"Maria! Are you allright?" Gemma shouted. The two women dashed over to her as fast as the swirling water around their knees would allow, their faces pale with anxiety.

Gemma tripped in her haste and Em hauled her up. A tall lifeguard came running up.

"Are you okay?" she asked, whilst both her hands lifted Maria up.

"Yes, yes!" Maria said, wincing in pain.

"Your wrist looks broken," the lifeguard said.

"No, no, it's not," Maria said. "I'm fine. Let me go!"

"Maria," Gemma said, "Stop! You are not fine." The lifeguard called someone over and helped Maria to shore. Em and Gemma flanked her, Em trying to hold onto two surfboards. On shore the lifeguard gestured to someone.

"Paramedic on the way," the lifeguard told them briefly. "You ladies should not have been out there if you cannot surf. The currents are strong here." Em apologized and agreed with her. Maria kept her head down, in obvious pain. The lifeguard made her sit down and said she would wait with them.

A paramedic arrived within a few minutes from the resort. He looked at Maria's wrist.

"Best get you to the hospital," he said. "It's fifteen minutes away." Helping Maria onto a stretcher which she said was unnecessary, the paramedic pushed off to the ambulance. Gemma and Em followed behind. One of them was allowed to accompany Maria. Gemma said she'd stay behind, hand in the surf boards, collect their items, and catch a taxi to the hospital.

At the hospital the ED doctor confirmed that the wrist was broken after an x-ray was taken.

"Fortunately it is not a compound fracture and will heal in about six to eight weeks in a cast," he told them. "She needs to have the cast fitted and I will prescribe some analgesia tablets for her to take at home. Once that's done, you can take her home. The receptionist will give you a follow up appointment for her." She smiled at them and hurried off to see the next client in ED.

"I think we should phone Marty," Gemma, who had arrived not long after the ambulance had, said.

"No please," Maria pleaded, close to tears. "Let's just go home after the cast is on."

"No," Em said firmly. "Honestly Maria if you were not in pain I'd blister your backside myself." Maria blushed. Em hugged her. "Maria, listen-I love you and your spirit, but we were silly to do something that we were not prepared for. Now you are injured."

Whilst they were talking Gemma rifled through Maria's bag that she had collected from the rented day hut.

"I'll phone," Em said gently. She understood how Maria was feeling and felt guilty. She had encouraged this and now one of them was injured.

Gemma was worried. She felt bad for Maria. She pushed back the thought that she had been complicit along with her worry over what Ava would say. Right now they needed to take care of Maria.

Emma dialed Marty's number. The other two listened to her explain that they were at the hospital and Maria had a broken wrist. She put the phone down and turned to them.

"Marty is on her way," she said, putting a comforting arm around Maria.

"I wish you hadn't called her," Maria said. "We could have just gone back on the bus. With pain killers I'll be fine."

"You will be fine," Gemma said. "But it will be more comfortable for your arm if Marty picks you up." She heard her phone ring at the exact time Em's rang. This was not a time to ignore a call and both of the women answered. "Gemma, are you allright?" Ava's voice was concerned.

"Yes," Gemma replied, her heart sinking.

"Marty called the office to say she is on her way down to the hospital and that Maria had a broken arm."

"Wrist," Gemma corrected.

"What happened?" Ava's tone was even and level.

"She slipped," Gemma said lamely.

"I'll come to fetch you," Ava said.

"No, it's okay, we'll come back with Marty and Maria," Gemma said. She knew she sounded defensive. Ava did not argue. She knew the women would be safe with Marty. She informed Gemma that she and Mel would pick them up at the restaurant. She told Gemma to WhatsApp her the minute they left the hospital. Gemma's heart sank slightly when Ava informed her they'd be

'-having a talk'- when they got home.

She wished she could turn the clock back.

"Allright?" she said, turning to Em who had just clicked her phone off.

"Yes," Em said. "Melissa is picking me up at the restaurant." The three women stared at each other. Suddenly Maria burst out laughing.

"Oh...but it was worth it!" she said. The absurdity of the situation made the other two laugh and the tension was broken. The analgesia effects were kicking in and Maria's pain had decreased to a bearable throb. She was whisked off to have the plaster applied.

Gemma and Em sat side by side not talking. Without the incorrigible Maria present, both of them felt somber and guilty. The ED waiting room door opened and Marty walked in purposefully. She spied the two women and held up a hand to them. She walked over to the reception and inquired about Maria. Satisfied she was being cared for she strode over to the two women.

Her gaze was stern and both of them gulped. Marty was a top not to be trifled with.

"You ladies okay?" Marty asked, drawing up a chair and sitting facing them. Her eyes looked them up and down taking in their wet hair and bedraggled looks. There were no obvious injuries. "So what happened?" Her voice was even but dangerous.

"Er...we...I..."

"I have no hesitation taking you both out to the car park right now!" Marty said, rising.

"Um...we--well, we were surfing...no, attempting to surf--" Gemma stammered hastily. Marty's eyebrows rose as she sat back down.

"Surfing? As is in surfing on a board at the surfer's beach? I did not know either of you could surf?"

"Um-no, we can't..."

"Hm...and who decided this?" The two women were silent. "Who had this delightful scheme to surf when you can't surf? And who decided it would be better not to tell me nor, I assume Mel and Ava?" The women looked down. "We all did," Em said eventually when Marty cleared her throat. It sounded lame and immature as she said it.

"Well, you are lucky I don't march you outside right now," Marty said. Em gulped. She had once seen Marty disciplining Maria and she was thorough in her spankings. "You could have been seriously injured." They stayed silent. Gemma's cheeks flamed.

"Ava...won't...let-" she stammered.

"Ava has given me permission to discipline you, if needed," Marty continued evenly. "How is Maria?" Despite her obvious anger at their collective stupidity they could both see the anxiety behind her eyes.

"She is okay. Well, I mean in some pain because of the fracture. But it is a simple fracture."

"Tell me how it happened." Marty listened to their story. Both of the women decided it was best to tell the truth and take responsibility for their actions. Sifting through the words, it was clear to Marty that her minx had put the two women in front of her up to it but they had gone along.

She admired their loyalty to their friend by refusing to state that it was her idea and their willingness to share their part in it.

Her sexy minx would be sorry in a few days' time though.

"Excuse me, ladies," she said. "I need to let Ava and Mel know you are okay." Her direct gaze had softened slightly and the two women relaxed. There was no danger of any immediate chastisement. She walked away, taking out her phone. Em groaned.

"Oh no. This will set me back." Em did not need many spankings in her life but if she did, she responded well to a hard, intense spanking, which was not easy to take. She and Mel had a good understanding between them but she knew Mel would not let this go lightly.

Gemma felt her stomach lurch. She had a strong feeling Ava was also not going to approve of this latest adventure.

The sound of squeaky wheels brought them out of their rueful musing. Maria's voice could be heard coming from the direction of the squeaky wheels. She was complaining about being able to walk and that it was her wrist that was broken, not her ankle. Marty rose to her feet and headed toward the passage. Maria teared up upon seeing her wife. Marty's beautiful face was so full of concern and it touched her deeply, even after all their years together and even though she knew her butt would be on fire sometime in the week. She leapt out the chair, swaying slightly from the effects of the strong analgesia and fell into her arms.

"Babe, oh I'm sorry," she said. "It was so sore, but I'm okay." Marty held her tight, breathing in her scent and welcoming the feel of the slightly damp black hair tickling her nose.

"It's alright honey, you're okay." she soothed. She lowered Maria back into the chair and the aide took them back to the waiting room. The doctor came through and explained that it was a clean non compound fracture and that Maria needed to come back in six weeks for cast removal and check-up. Marty thanked the doctor and went to settle the account. Fortunately, she had brought their health insurance cards with her.

"Come along." she said, her voice half stern as she helped Maria into the front passenger seat. "Don't think you're getting away with this, honey. After a few days your butt is mine." Her voice was matter of fact and Maria could practically feel her butt on fire. She smiled sleepily. At this minute all she felt was cared for by her strong wife. Marty checked that the two women were safely in the back.

They sat silently, the enormity of what could have happened hitting them.

The car drew up to the restaurant and Ava and Mel came forward. Gemma was part way to opening the door when it was opened for her and Ava helped her out.

"Are you okay?" she said. Her eyes were concerned but there was a glint of steel in them.

"Yes," she said quietly.

"To the car please," Ava said. Gemma did not get a chance to say goodbye as her upper arm was firmly grasped and she was marched along to Ava's car. "Wait here," Ava said. "I need to check if Marty needs anything." Gemma seethed. She was not a dog to be told to wait in the car. Ava went back and spoke to Marty. She hugged Maria briefly and came back. Mel was busy chatting to Marty, Em tucked into her arm. Gemma gave a small wave.

"I'm sorry," she blurted out as they took off.

"You will be," was Ava's calm response.

"It was just a--whim," Gemma said. She felt desperately guilty.

"A whim that had been planned and not told to any of us," Ava said. She drew safely in on the side of the road, stopped the car and turned to her. "Gemma, what were you thinking? All of you could have been seriously injured." Gemma ignored the concern and worry in Ava's eyes.

"For goodness sake Ava...it was just a-"

"What? What was it? A thoughtless act? No regard for your, nor your friends safety? No concern about how I would feel if something happened to you? Or how your father or your sister would feel?"

Gemma fell silent, the anguished words pricking her.

"Not to mention the disregard for the rules we established." Ava added. She felt bad. Ava was right. It had been thoughtless.

"I would have taken you surfing. Taught you a beginner's session," Ava said. "Yeah well...I don't always need a babysitter." Gemma could not quite give in. Ava was right. Her guilt ate her up and made her defensive.

"Right! That's it!" Ava got out of the car and coming round to the front passenger side opened the door. In one swift movement she leaned over, released the seat belt and pulled Gemma out by her left arm, leaving Gemma no option but to get her legs out. Ava pulled her resisting form over the bonnet and leant her over. She landed a series of heavy wAllops to her backside before Gemma could even draw breath.

"Now," Ava said, "do you want to try that again?" Gemma felt miserable. "We'll continue at home but if I need to take my belt to you I will," she said. "This attitude of yours stops now or you face the consequences." Gemma felt that twisty feeling again. Part of her dreaded what was to come but the other part felt excited and loved. She nodded assent briefly. The sight of Ava's hand at her belt made her feel weak at the knees and wet with desire.

They carried on home in silence. Once they reached the cabin, Ava led her inside, releasing her only once they got to the lounge.

"Go and shower," she said, aware of how salt drenched and

uncomfortable Gemma must feel. "Then put on some pajamas." Gemma did as she was told. In truth she felt she deserved the punishment that Ava would mete out.

Once showered and dressed she went timidly to the lounge. Ava turned as she came in. She wanted nothing more than to hold and cuddle Gemma but that would be counterproductive and later Gemma would suffer for it; testing the boundaries and not being punished, until she pushed them further to test Ava.

"Honey, "she said carefully. "If you want this-us...-our relationship, then you will accept this spanking. If you have changed your mind about us that is fine, but I need to know now." Gemma teared up. This was not what she had expected. She loved Ava, she loved their relationship, there was not one part of it that she wanted to lose. She walked straight up to Ava and hugged her.

"No, you are right. I was thoughtless. I want this...I want you... us." Her voice was firm and Ava relaxed her shoulders not even aware until then of how tense and anxious she had been. Gemma meant the world to her, but if they were to be together Gemma had to accept her role and want it. Perhaps with the misadventures so close together Gemma was testing her, testing their relationship and boundaries, she mused. Gemma noticed the relaxation and realized how vulnerable Ava was in her role as top. She had to be more thoughtful in future.

"I want you to place your hands against the table," Ava said, "and lean forward. I will be spanking you with a paddle."

"No!" Gemma gasped. Her hands went automatically to her buttocks.

"Now," Ava said, "or I shall add my belt?" Her hands went to her buckle and Gemma's legs obeyed independently of her mind. She placed her hands against the cool table and leant forward.

She felt her pajamas and panties being pulled down, and

her cheeks flamed with the heat of embarrassment. She felt the smoothness of the paddle against her cheeks. It disappeared, and one second later, landed hard. She shrieked aloud, jumping up and turning to face Ava in shock.

"Ow! Fuck!"

Ava looked at her and, grabbing her wrist, pulled her over to the sofa. She pulled her over her lap.

"It seems I will have to hold you in place." With that she calmly and evenly brought the paddle down over and over again until Gemma was squirming, gasping and struggling to escape it. Ava thoroughly covered the round cheeks, the sits spots and back of the thighs.

"I'm sorry," Gemma wailed. She started sobbing. It was painful and she felt stupid and sorry. "I won't do it again," she pleaded.

"I hope not," Ava said. She landed twenty more spanks and watched Gemma go limp.

Laying the paddle down, she waited until Gemma had stopped crying and helped her up.

"You are so mean," Gemma said but her tone was soft and relieved, almost teasing. Ava hugged her.

"You scared me," she said. "When that call came through from Marty, I thought..." she trailed off and cleared her throat.

"I'm sorry," Gemma said again. "It was thoughtless." She stood in front of Ava, not daring to sit down. Her bottom and the backs of her thighs felt on fire. Ava turned her around. She leant down and Gemma shivered as she felt Ava lower her head. Soft lips kissed her one tender buttock and then the other. She moaned. Wetness gushed from her. Ava laughed gently. She stood up.

"No reward for naughty women," she said. Tipping a finger under Gemma's chin, she said, "Let's start clean. We'll go through the rules again tomorrow." Gemma sighed, but stopped when she saw Ava's raised eyebrow.

"Yes," she hastily agreed.

"Go to bed, honey. I'm going to have a glass of wine to calm down," Ava said, well aware that Gemma was feeling aroused. She needed to show her that breaking the rules did not get rewarded. Gemma was wise enough not to say she would also like a glass of wine.

"I'll be through in about half an hour," Ava said. She drank her wine, worrying about Gemma, worrying that she cared this much but so full in her heart that she had someone to care for in the way she needed.

When she went to the bedroom, she looked at the brown head, tenderness filling her. She slid into bed fully clothed, cradling the woman she loved. Gemma snuggled back into her, their two bodies fitting together like two pieces in a puzzle.

On the other side of the town, on the far side of the cabins, two other women lay spooned. Em tried not to press too hard against Mel. Her backside was aflame but her heart felt relieved. Mel cradled her tenderly. They lay quietly until sleep claimed them.

CHAPTER 11

Mel frowned. Looking through the window, she noticed Charlie flirting with one of the female clients again. Charlie seemed out of control lately. She was still popular, hardworking and well liked. Naturally athletic and with cropped blonde hair, her confident manner and obvious strength had women admiring her. Charlie played up to this and was no stranger to flirting, even with the straight ladies. Usually Mel laughed off Charlie's antics, but this particular lady was one Mel had seen hanging around a few times and was obviously smitten with her. Charlie appeared to be leading her on which was unlike her normal happy go lucky manner. She wondered if she should chat to Ava about it. She didn't want any negative feedback to the business and it would not be good for Charlie if the owner started hearing any complaints from scorned women. Ava had settled so well though in her job, the town and her relationship with Gemma. It might be unfair to burden her with this side of Charlie at the present time. Still, she might mention it to her to see if Ava had noticed anything unusual about Charlie recently. She could discuss a plan with Marty to help Charlie. Marty would stand no nonsense from their friend. Satisfied with her decision she scrutinized her schedule for the day.

Charlie wandered in, her hands in her pockets, whistling.

"What was that about?" Mel asked casually.

"Nothing," Charlie said.

"That woman seemed upset," Mel said.

"She was. Can't help it if I'm a babe magnet." She laughed, as she said it but her eyes betrayed her annoyance at being questioned.

"Charlie," Mel said. "I don't know what's going on, but you can't lead someone on and then have them hanging around the center."

"What's it got to do with you?" the normally calm and upbeat Charlie snapped.

"Everything," Mel said calmly, rising to her feet. She stood close to Charlie seeming almost to tower over her although they were the same height.

"I don't want your flirting to affect the business," she said. "And, you look unhappy." Charlie blushed. She was not used to anyone taking her up on her behavior. She was used to dealing it out to others and expected them to obey her orders.

"I'm sorry," she said, "I'll sort it out." She strode out, almost bumping into Ava who was on her way in.

"What's going on?" Ava asked, used to a smile from the confident Charlie. Mel sighed and discussed her concerns with Ava.

"We need to try and get to the bottom of it," Ava said thoughtfully.

"My palm was itching," Mel confessed.

"Maybe it's what she needs," Ava said. "Although I don't think she would take it easily." The two women continued their work, feeling vaguely uneasy that something seemed wrong with their friend.

That evening Mel and Em met with Marty and Maria for a drink. Maria was her usual chatty self and asked how they thought Ava and Gemma were getting on. "They seem happy." Emma replied.

"That's more than I can say for Charlie," Mel said. Marty agreed. She had also noticed a change in Charlie.

"Charlie came in here twice this week and ended up totally smashed. We had to take her home the last time," Marty said. Her eyes were thoughtful as she said this. "I think we need to help her."

"I tried," Maria said. "She said nothing was wrong."

"Hm," Marty grunted. Mel watched her. Marty knew Charlie well and she was glad she had alerted her. She'd see how things went this week.

Ava and Gemma walked in hand and hand. They looked happy and relaxed. A subtle change had occurred in the preceding weeks. Anyone seeing them together would have undoubtedly thought that the couple had been together years and not months.

Marty smiled. It seemed Ava had found a match and Gemma had found a lifestyle that suited her. She changed the subject not wanting any dynamic in the group to affect the status of their relationship. Gemma already seemed a bit jealous and unsure of herself when Charlie was around. She knew that Ava had not fully explored the limits of their domestic discipline yet and wanted to ensure their relationship flourished along with the discipline.

On Friday evening Charlie was in the bar of the restaurant again. She had dumped the tourist who sat miserably in a corner. Marty pursed her lips. Charlie was openly flirting with two pretty younger women. She was clearly well on her way to getting drunk. She called out for more beer and the two younger women giggled, as Charlie put her arms around both of them. Maria approached her.

"Charlie," she said firmly. "That's enough."

"I will say when I've had enough," Charlie said. She swung her arm around Maria's waist.

"Come on, lighten up, join us." Maria hugged her and then said "Charlie, cool it. You've had enough to drink."

"Damn it woman...!" Charlie said. She got no further. Marty marched out from behind the bar and Charlie found her muscled upper arm firmly gripped. Geez, she thought, who knew Marty was this strong.

"Hey!" she exclaimed. "Woman! Let me go!" Marty ignored her and pulled her through the back door to their quiet lounge area.

"Now listen to me Charlie-" she said, her tone of voice brooking no argument. "What is wrong with you?" Charlie looked at her friend, her firm stance, and her hands on her hips. Her eyes were soft and concerned despite her stern tone of voice.

"Nothing," she said sullenly. In truth though, she felt tired. Tired of flirting, tired of not committing to someone special, tired of getting drunk. She was being an ass but could not admit it.

"Besides," she flared up, "it's none of your business."

"Oh yes, it is," Marty said. "You are my friend and this is my bar and the town I love. I won't have you going around flirting, damaging town business, breaking things in the bar. You are not caring for yourself."

"Really, and who are you to make that judgment?" Charlie sneered. Without warning Charlie found herself turned around, her white cargo style shorts lowered. Her naturally dominant personality tried to assert itself but before she could react a hard paddle was lashing her backside, her one arm held hard and fast by Marty.

"Listen, little girl," Marty was saying. "I won't let you ruin yourself, my business or other people's lives." Charlie tried to answer, but the pain of the paddle prevented speech. She had only ever given someone a spanking, not received one. She tried to formulate words but only a growl emitted from her throat. "Hmm- still not listening, are we?" Marty said. She led her over to the desk area and placed Charlie's hands on either side of her desk. "Bottom out," she instructed. To Charlie's surprise she found herself obeying. "I am going to belt you for not listening, not taking care of yourself and letting it come to this," Marty said.

"Do not move. Do you understand me?" she said.

"Yes," Charlie muttered sullenly. Marty breathed a sigh of relief. She was getting through to her. She took off her belt and again instructed Charlie not to move an inch. She brought the belt down and Charlie leapt up in agony clutching her buttock.

"Damn it woman," she shouted. "What do you think you are doing?"

"Get back to the desk," Marty bellowed, raising her voice above Charlie's. Charlie needed someone else to take control right now. She pulled Charlie back, noticing that Charlie was not resisting. "Stay still!" She brought the belt down again and again until she saw Charlie's shoulders sag and the tension leave her, sobs coming from her. Marty immediately stopped and gathered the strong, sobbing woman into her arms. "It's okay, Charlie." After helping her to pull her shorts up, she led her over to the sofa, and pulled her down next to her. Maria popped her head around the door. Satisfied but somewhat stunned to see the scene in front of her, she backed out again.

Charlie leant back. She felt soothed and the tension that had been plaguing her had dissipated.

"Better now?" Marty said kindly.

"I should hit you." Charlie said, unable to look Marty fully in the eyes yet.

"Girl-you try it," Marty said, knowing that Charlie needed to save face. "You know I can whip you with one hand any day." Charlie laughed and sobbed. "What's wrong, honey?" Marty asked. "Everyone's noticing how different you've been from your usual happy self."

"I'm not sure," Charlie said. She slumped down, hands between her thighs and Marty's heart pained to see her upbeat friend this down. "Well, I...no... everyone seems so happy, so settled and here I am. Still fucking up...fucking up my life...and others." Marty let the swearing go. Charlie needed to express herself.

"How stupid is that? I am forty and love my life and yet I feel something is missing." She looked up at Marty as she said that. It was embarrassing to admit. She had always been so happy being the flirt, the 'never pinned down' type of woman, free and independent. In fact, she still wanted that, she just felt like the odd one out, she explained further. Marty nodded. She got it. "You've seen Ava and Gemma settled," she said. "You wish perhaps you had got to Gemma first. Honey, you know you weren't suited."

"I know. But it's not about Gemma. It's just about-someone-someone special. And then I think-I could not bear it...giving up my freedom." Charlie said honestly. "I've been working a lot with Ava recently and she seems so content in her life. I feel a bit jealous." The words were raw and honest and yet it was clear that Charlie was not yet ready to be tied to one person.

"There will be someone for you, even if you can't ever give up your philandering ways. Maybe you'll even meet someone who has the same ways as you." Marty understood Charlie's personality, but she was wiser in that she knew one could only truly be at peace if one lived the way that made one happy. However that did not mean that it was acceptable to hurt others who did not share that same lifestyle. Rather, it meant finding someone who shared your values.

"I want to," Charlie said, "give up my ways and then-and then I don't." The relief she felt at just being able to talk, to tell someone how she felt, was immense.

"I've had my eye on you," Marty said. "You know I won't hesitate to spank you again. You think you are a big shot? Well, sometimes, little girl, you need taking down-and I'll be here to do it." Charlie laughed. Marty was a good friend. She reflected on how Marty had been a constant for her since arriving. Maybe Marty was enough for now. She was not isolated; she had friends. Friends that were family to her. Marty put her arm around her and she relaxed briefly against her solid form.

Maria crept back in and came over tentatively.

"Is everything okay? Charlie, are you alright?"

"She's alright," Marty said, opening her arms to her wife and gathering her up. "She just needed to let off some steam and feelings."

"Charlie, we're here for you," Maria said in her sweet way, "and Mel and Emma. They're outside. Shall I tell them to come in? They can kiss your sore butt better." Charlie laughed good naturedly. She kissed the top of Maria's head affectionately.

"Nah. I got some things to think about," she said.

On the way out she bumped into Mel on her way to the table with two drinks. "Charlie! You okay?" Mel said. "I've been wanting to talk to you." She trailed off as she noticed the faint tear streaks and lessening of the tension she had seen in Charlie earlier. Only a top would recognize the signs. Marty knew what was needed, Mel realized.

"I'm good," Charlie said, the slight swagger already back in her voice. Mel put down the glasses and hugged her.

"You know that we are all here for you right?" she said. Charlie grinned.

"Yep, I know!" She strode out into the night. No more silliness, she thought. She saw an attractive blonde ahead of her. *Maybe seriousness was for later.* She hastened her step.

Ava and Gemma were heading in to the restaurant and smiled as they saw Charlie. Ava was pleased to see Charlie as she had first met her. She was grinning and her usual saunter was evident in her stride. Ava's sharp, toppy eyes noted a faint line on the back of Charlie's taut thighs and slight traces of tears on her cheeks, but she said nothing.

Ava hugged her warmly, guessing at what had happened. She did not notice Gemma's eyes cloud over. They entered the restaurant and Mel called out from the bar area, to alert them as to where they were sitting. Ava glanced back and grinned ruefully as she saw Charlie catch up to an attractive blonde woman. Gemma saw her turn and bit her lip, watching Ava's eyes follow Charlie.

CHAPTER 12

Melissa and Em walked along the path. They had just left the restaurant and it was too good an evening not to walk home.

"Do you think they'll be alright?" Em said.

"Yes," said Mel. She knew Ava and Gemma loved each other. Sometimes a brat just needed reminding that being a total brat does not mean dependency but rather that a domestic discipline relationship could guide them both to a fulfilled loving life.

The evening had been dramatic. First with Charlie being spanked by Marty and, then the incident with Gemma running out of the bar. Emma smiled.

"Does Gemma remind you of me?" she asked teasingly

Mel thought for a minute and answered seriously.

"No," she finally said. "You are totally different. More serious, mature in your work and what you want and know you need. Plus," she added, "you know what I needed. Our type of relationship was something you weren't new to."

Em smiled. She was fortunate in finding true love again in the way she needed. She hoped Ava and Gemma's love and lifestyle would always be as strong as hers and Mel's and that they were able to sort out tonight's upset.

Ava walked along the narrow straight path. She knew Gemma loved the serene walk by the river and often wandered down there if she wanted to think. The sound of the river lay ahead and she walked on, eyes scanning to each side. Ava was anxious and worried. Not so worried that she would not be tanning Gemma's hide, however. Gemma was not silly, despite her sometimes reckless side. Ava thought back to earlier that evening.

After meeting Charlie just outside the bar, Gemma had gone very quiet. They had been getting on so well in their life together. Sure, Gemma had seemed a bit jealous of the times Ava worked late with Charlie and Mel but she had not discussed it with her. Ava had assumed she was imagining Gemma's quietness whenever she mentioned Charlie. This evening, though, she realized she had not been imagining it. When the group had started talking about Charlie, Gemma had totally overreacted and stood up, snapping that she was sick of hearing about Charlie. She had then turned to Ava and in front of everyone had choked out that if Ava preferred Charlie to her that was fine, but she did not have to stand for it. Tears falling down her cheeks, she had run out of the bar.

Ava berated herself as she walked along the path to the river. Gemma was still fairly new to domestic discipline life. She should have pointed out Gemma's manner and found out what had been going on in her head. Then she should have spanked her soundly for having such a low opinion of herself and believing that Ava would cheat on her. Unfortunately, not doing that had led to Gemma totally overreacting to an innocent hug.

She reached the clearing by the edge of the river. To her relief, she saw a familiar brown-haired figure sitting on a large boulder mid-river that she had obviously got to by boulder hopping. Her hands were clasped around her knees. Ava hopped over the boulders, the sound of the water masking her footfalls.

"Gemma," she said, hoping not to startle her, yet at the same time wanting to spank her. Gemma looked up, almost overbalancing. Ava grabbed her arm steadying her.

"What the…" Ava bit her lip. This was not the time to let her anger overcome her words or actions.

"Honey," she said, "why did you run off?" Gemma looked at her.

"Let go of my arm! You know why I ran off!" she said stormily, her eyes glinting with unshed tears. Ava took a breath in.

"Right! Let's get back to the riverside and then we can chat." She expected some resistance from Gemma, so was pleased to see common sense prevailed when she allowed Ava to help her up. Together they made their way back to the side of the river. They reached the bank and they stood looking out to the river, hands in their pockets.

"Gemma…"

"Ava…"

"You first," Gemma said.

"What made you run off? We have been doing so well," Ava said.

"I…" Gemma gasped in her attempt to explain, "you…you…I saw you with Charlie two days ago…and the week before! I know you need someone different! I am just a mess; a mess you keep trying to fix. I heard you say how difficult it was picking up after me. And--and then-you hugged her this evening-and I…" Ava fixed her with a direct stare.

"When did I say that? That you were a mess" she asked patiently.

"This-this morning. I heard you on the phone. I know I'm not like Charlie. She is athletic, she likes the activities you do, you work together...she's clear headed and..."

Ava felt like shaking and spanking Gemma, but she needed to clearly understand what Gemma was thinking and feeling. She had been spending more time with Charlie the last two weeks, trying to complete the work needed before the new adventure section opened. She exhaled and pulled Gemma down onto the soft leaves beside her.

"I have been spending time with Charlie and I should have explained why. But instead of running off you need to speak to me directly. You had been doing so well, feeling much more sure of yourself. As to talking about you being a mess-I was referring to the new secretary. She is young and totally unsuited to the job."

Gemma was taken aback. She had expected Ava to immediately deny seeing Charlie or given an instant explanation that she loved Charlie. She squirmed. "What do you think Charlie and I have been doing?" Ava asked. Gemma sat silently thinking. What had she seen? Ava and Charlie talking during work hours and once out of work hours. They had not looked intimate and were not touching each other. She relaxed. A bit of her old insecurities had flared up. "Um...well nothing, I suppose," She felt a bit foolish. Charlie and Ava did not really make a match. She doubted Ava would like to be in a relationship with a switch.

"Honey," Ava looked at her. "I love you. I love us. I love our relationship. But our relationship cannot grow if you don't talk to me about your worries." She raised an eyebrow as she said that and Gemma's tummy lurched. "You are not a mess and if you do get into a self doubting phase I am here to help you out of it." She leaned closer as she spoke and her lips were warm and moist against Gemma's cheek. Her breath tickled and Gemma's center contracted sharply.

"I'm so…out of control," Gemma said, not exactly sure whether she meant emotionally or sexually. Ava had a way of making her feel like she could orgasm just by talking to her. Ava laughed.

"You will always have me to help you keep control. Perhaps you need some control right now!" Gemma grew wetter. Ava leant around her, her hand cupping one buttock.

"Perhaps this is the time for a proper spanking," she said, her voice low, raspy and totally sexy. Gemma melted into her, her legs parting as Ava slipped a hand under her skirt, the strong fingers cupping the sopping fabric of her panties.

"I think it might be," Gemma managed to croak out, although she really had no idea what Ava meant by the words 'proper spanking.' Ava had already spanked her many times.

Ava covered her lips with her own, claiming her. Gemma submitted willingly. This was her true home, her true life. She moaned slightly as Ava deepened the kiss. She pulled back.

"I am yours," Ava said, "as much as you are mine." The words echoed in Gemma's thoughts and throbbed in her clitoris. She submitted her heart and body as Ava leant her back on the bed of leaves. She was claimed forever. Ava's fingers entered her, thrusting and pounding until Gemma came, her screams of release washed away by the sound of the powerful river.

"Honey, your butt is mine later," Ava breathed in her ear. She leant forward and a key on a chain around her neck, fell forward just in front of Gemma's eyes.

"I think you need to learn a few more lessons."

Gemma shivered deliciously.

"Take the key, babe," Ava said. Her voice was soft and intimate but her eyes held a deeper warning. "Go home, open the bedroom cupboard. At the back, you will find another standing closet. Open it. Choose any implement and wait for me on the bed." Gemma's eyes widened. Her heart beat fast. She took the key slowly, slipping the chain off her lover's neck. "I think it's time you learnt to trust me, as you obviously doubt my love for you," Ava said.

Gemma's breath caught in her throat.

"Yes, my love," she whispered. She got up and headed home. She knew Ava would not be far behind. Her heart sang and her body throbbed in anticipation. She found it hard to swallow. She was caught between dread and anticipation. She craved what was coming, but her buttocks throbbed as if already caned. As the cabin came into view, any doubts she had faded and a smile curved her lips. Tonight she would totally give herself and her trust to Ava.

Not far behind her in the dark evening light, Ava's lips also curved into a smile. Tonight, Gemma was hers to claim fully.

The End
(For Now)

The Mountain Town Series

Book 3

'Marty and Maria'

Lesbian Spanking Romance

By
Leandra Summers

CHAPTER 1

Marty stood behind the bar, her eyes lovingly fixed on her wife, who was animatedly talking to some of their friends who had come in for evening drinks.

Maria, black hair styled into a sleek bob, olive colored skin hinting at Latin ancestry, laughed out loud at something one of the women said. It was a far cry from five years before when Marty had first laid eyes on her.

She looked around the bar and small restaurant beyond it. It was still the same in structure as all those years ago, but now twinkled with lights and displayed local artists' paintings, courtesy of Maria's flamboyant and artistic personality. The clientele was the same mix of tourists who flocked to the trendy mountain town and locals who lived in it. Their group of like-minded friends enjoying an evening together at the bar had become part of the local community. Hearing them laugh again she smiled with deep affection for the group of women who had become her family.

She relaxed and slipped into the memory of her first sight of Maria.

It had been peak tourist season. As it was early dinner time the restaurant section was packed with families and couples. Singles tended to hang out at the bar. It had been noisy but the hum of voices and background music had not managed to drown out the shrieks of laughter of a group of women. Marty had judged them to be ranging in ages from mid-twenties to late thirties; they were professional looking, letting off steam.

One in particular had seemed quite drunk. She was an attractive woman, one of the older ones in the group, tall, slender, dark hair hanging over her shoulders in waves. Her eyes were deep blue. She had risen unsteadily to her feet and swayed. Her friends had laughed and one had grabbed her arm. Marty had heard of this group. They had frequented another bar apparently causing quite a show with their dancing antics and drinking.

When the unsteady dark-haired woman stood on a chair, Marty had watched silently. The waitress had gone over and asked her to get down. The woman had sat down obediently. When the waitress turned away, the woman stuck her tongue out. Marty had laughed silently. Little brat. She needed to be taught some manners.

The group had left shortly after that and the evening had continued smoothly.

The next evening the same party had returned. They had arrived already drunk and within ten minutes of being served three of them had stood up on the tables, dancing. A few glasses had been smashed. Parents had grabbed their children out of harm's way. Marty had gone over and asked them to sit down. Good naturedly, the women had clambered down. The dark-haired woman danced on the table a bit longer than the others, her deep blue eyes catching Marty's brown ones, taunting her, offering a direct challenge. Marty had been struck by the brilliance of the blue shine in her eyes but also the vulnerability that hid behind the woman's cheeky demeanor.

After an intense stare from Marty, the woman had laughed and accepted her hand to climb down from the table. She lurched unsteadily against Marty, forcing her to use her strong arm to hold her up. The woman was slightly taller than her and more slender than Marty's sturdy strong build. She felt the woman melt into her arm as it encircled her waist to prevent her falling and Marty saw her pupils widen in desire.

"You're cute," the woman had said. She hiccupped and giggled. Marty had picked up her bag from the chair.

"Ladies," she had said courteously, but firmly. "We will be closing shortly."

"We'll be back tomorrow," the woman had said. "I'm Maria." The words were slightly slurred but her eyes were focused.

"Well, Maria," Marty had said, "…if you plan to come back, you had best be sober and not dance on the tables." She held the woman's eyes. The eyes had flashed in annoyance and challenge, but slid away first.

"Yeah…and who's gonna stop me?" she had said.

"Well, perhaps you'll find out tomorrow," Marty had replied. Her palm had tingled and she had been aware of the thrill of excitement of dominance that shot through her. The dark-haired woman had given a mock salute.

"See you tomorrow, cutes," she had quipped.

Marty had smiled inwardly. The woman interested her; a challenge for sure. She had not missed the heat in her own body corresponding to the desire in Maria's eyes.

"Hey--" the woman had shouted as her friends half dragged her away. "I did not get your name." Marty had smiled, her teeth showing in an almost wolfish grin.

"Marty," she said. "Owner of this restaurant." The group of women turned silent. They had not realized they were talking to the owner. Maria had then flipped a little wave which melted Marty's heart. That woman needed taking in hand, she had thought.

The next day Marty found out more about her. She could not help but feel intrigued by and concerned over the vulnerable looking woman. Some of her friends worked at the hotel the women had been staying at, and had eagerly given her some background information. They knew Marty had been alone for a few years after her last complicated relationship with two submissive women had ended. They enjoyed seeing her intrigued by someone again.

Maria was one of a group of women celebrating their PhD graduations at one of the mid-level hotels popular with professionals and academics. The behavior demonstrated by Maria, she had thought, was unusual for a well educated woman. More suited to a teenager on a parent free break. Perhaps, Marty had mused, she was just letting off steam, although the rest of her group was not as unruly. Steam or not, she would not allow her business to be damaged. She had also needed to keep her other customers feeling safe and comfortable.

She had shaken her head. Probably they would not be in again. Besides lately she had had enough on her hands with her booming restaurant and bar. Part of her wanted to retreat. The last love interests, she reminded herself, had taken a long time to detangle herself from. It had been a heady experience at the beginning, but the ending was best forgotten.

The next night the group of women had not appeared. Marty had felt a pang of disappointment. She had reflected that that was rather pathetic of her. She was a forty-five-year old woman wanting to see a half drunk, obviously troubled woman. Dismissing the thoughts she had concentrated on ensuring all the meals were efficiently served by her new waitress.

Unusually there was a long line at the door. More customers than the norm had turned up. She had hastened over to ensure seats were allocated appropriately. Listening to the customers' conversations it seemed that a group of women had caused havoc in a neighboring small restaurant. Apparently the owner had tossed them out after they had broken two tables. Marty tutted in annoyance. That was beyond acceptable. Their businesses were important to ensure the small tourist town flourished.

Not long after Marty had set up for the extra customers, she heard high pitched laughter.

She had turned to the door to see the same group of women entering. Noting that the tables were full they headed for the bar to order drinks. When they started to shout out their orders, Marty grit her teeth. She went over to the group and asked them to quiet down.

"Hey! Marty!" Maria had shouted. "Look. We're here to dance." She started to move her hips in time to the music, her friends joining her at a small open space near the bar. She had flung an arm out, knocking a bottle of beer off the counter.

"Watch it man," one of the regulars had growled. Marty had hastened over. Discreetly she signaled for the bartender to get another beer on the house for the customer.

"That's enough," Marty had said firmly, walking up to the group. The group of women, except for Maria, had quieted down immediately, reacting to the authority of the owner. They had the grace to look slightly ashamed. Maria had continued dancing, her movements enticing.

"Dance with me, Ms Marty," she had said. She grabbed a nearby chair and leapt unsteadily on to it.

"Come on, baby," she had said, "or am I too much for you?" She had taken a step up from the chair onto a low table. Her skirt was very short and in the elevated position she put herself into, her black panties were clearly visible above her enticing thighs and the plump curves of her buttocks.

"Um…Maria…" one of her friends had said seeing the owner's face. "I think you had best come down."

"Come down? We just got here." Maria had retorted, oblivious to the advancing Marty's thunderous expression. She kicked out to a beat and knocked over the glass candle holder on the table. It had fallen with a loud crash and shatter of glass. The restaurant and bar had turned completely silent except for the faint throb of the background music.

"Get down now," Marty had said in a quiet voice that still managed to sound like steel. The women with Maria had started to back away, apologizing on her behalf. Maria had laughed.

"Yeah, who's going to make me?" she had taunted. Marty had had enough. She marched up to the table, lifted the dancing woman off it in one swift movement, slung her over her shoulder in a fireman's lift and spanking the back of the upturned bottom with one hand she had turned and marched out of the bar.

Maria had shouted in shock. The bar and restaurant had broken out into thunderous applause which died down as Marty exited the bar into the kitchen. The usual hum of voices and music returned as the excitement disappeared from view.

The woman over Marty's shoulder had continued to curse and shriek and kick her legs, her hands batting at Marty's back. It was like swatting a wall. Marty was strong and fit. She walked through the kitchen of the restaurant and made her way to her own house at the back. Entering the lounge she set Maria down none too gently.

"How dare you…how dare you?" Maria shouted. Her protests, however, had started to seem weak. Her body appeared to have given way to Marty's natural dominance.

"I dare because you need me to," Marty said simply. "Now are you going to calm down? You are wrecking my bar and chasing away my customers." Maria's eyes had glittered. She inhaled raggedly.

"No," she said, "and I did not ruin your bar. I merely knocked over a stupid candle holder. I can pay for it!" She did not get to continue her next sentence.

"Pay for it you will," Marty said. Before the other woman could blink, she had pulled her over to the couch, placed her over her strong thighs and begun tanning Maria's backside. Her short skirt rode up exposing her thighs and the edge of her black panties.

It had been an alluring view but Marty had concentrated on landing her hand hard and fast over the firmly rounded buttocks. Maria had wailed and screamed. Her bottom had not been assailed in that manner for many years. Amid her shouts and wriggles and squirming, a long forgotten calmness entered her, along with a throbbing between her legs. Marty had smiled softly. Just as she had thought. The woman over her knee definitely had needed and wanted to be taken in hand.

Marty had kept the spanking up until the back of the woman's thighs glowed bronze against her olive colored skin and the hint of plump buttock just edged below the rim of the black panties shone in a rosy hue. Maria had gone limp over her lap.

Marty had hauled her up right.

"Right," she had said, standing facing her, her arms gripping the top of Maria's arms, as she noted the tired and exhausted look in Maria's arms.

"You're sleeping this off here. We'll talk in the morning." She had laid Maria on the couch, slipping off her shoes. Maria laid down quietly drifting into a deep sleep enhanced by alcohol and spanking. Marty had covered her with a blanket and when she had fallen soundly asleep, had slipped from the room back to the bar.

Later that night when the restaurant and bar had closed, she had checked back in on her. The woman had been lying curled up where she had been left, a contented look on her face. The scent of alcohol was strong and Marty had sighed. The brat might not even remember the spanking the next day, she had thought.

She had though of course. Her bottom had probably still been stinging when she had woken up. Marty grinned, remembering Maria waking up and blushing as she had taken her a coffee, a shy look in her eyes. It had touched Marty's heart. She had sat on the sofa next to Maria, torn between wanting to hug her comfortingly, scold her further and ravish her. Maria had looked at her sheepishly and apologized for the damage. She eyed Marty sideways taking in the short blonde hair that framed her beautiful strong face, her muscular body, sturdy in build and the depth of brown eyes. Her pupils had darkened in desire and Marty had smiled when Maria had averted her eyes.

It had been the start of a tumultuous yet loving relationship. Five years later there they were, happily married, owning the bar and restaurant together. Maria had enhanced the décor and atmosphere and the demand for Marty's excellent food had become very popular with locals and tourists. The restaurant was listed as a hot spot in the local tourist guide.

Life was good, Marty thought. Maria lifted her head mid laugh and caught her wife's eye. She grinned cheekily and blew her a kiss. Marty smiled at her. Life had changed so much for the better in the past five years and she hoped nothing would alter the balance she had achieved. A faint and fleeting shadow crossed her face as she thought that. Maria had seemed a bit unsettled lately, or was she imagining that? Probably just a natural concern as she, Marty, had hit the life changing and exciting milestone of fifty a few months back. It was natural to wonder if everything was still good in a relationship as one got older, wasn't it, she mused.

CHAPTER 2

Maria sighed with despair. A short while earlier she had been laughing with her friends. All that had changed within the blink of an eye. One minute Ava and Gemma were walking in for a happy evening and the next minute chaos had erupted as Gemma had lost her temper and ran out.

Maria had initially helped facilitate the meeting between Gemma and Ava. It seemed they were getting along so well. They had become a couple and the last few months had seen them cement their romantic relationship.

Maria loved seeing all her friends settled and happy. She never thought to wonder why she had this need or if it related to her own life and desires in some way.

The happy and relaxed planned evening had evaporated before it had even started. Gemma had run out of the bar, after mistakenly believing that Ava preferred Charlie. As if it had not been a dramatic enough evening with Marty spanking Charlie, Maria thought. Although realizing she was probably over dramatizing the situation, she sighed again, this time loudly enough for Marty to hear.

"What's up, my love?" Marty left her place behind the bar where she had been getting drinks for them all. She had been about to join their group of friends when she noticed Gemma run out, with Ava following some moments after. Em and Melissa had left after Mel had nodded slightly in Marty's direction. They understood each other. Charlie had been taken care of; now it was time for Ava and Gemma to sort out the misunderstandings between them.

"It's a mess," Maria said with a slightly dramatic flair. "Gemma has run off. She thinks Ava prefers Charlie; at least that is what she sort of shouted out at the table. I worked so hard to get them together." Marty laughed at her indignant words.

"Honey, relax. They'll be fine. You need to not get so worked up over other people's business." Maria snorted.

"I'm not worked up about 'other people' Marty, these are our people, our friends and--"

"--And our friends will sort it out," Marty said firmly. "Ava is well able to handle Gemma. If they have a misunderstanding, they have to be the ones to sort it out."

"You're right," Maria conceded, pouting slightly, which should have been inappropriate on a forty-two-year old woman but was endearing on Maria. She leant into Marty.

"I hope we don't ever argue like that," she said. Marty tilted her chin slightly. "If we do..." she said, placing her lips against Maria's, "we'll sort it out." Maria opened her lips to the soft touch of Marty's lips. Even after five years Marty's kiss electrified her senses. She closed her eyes.

"I love you," she murmured.

"Me too babe." Marty deepened the kiss. A gentle wolf whistle stopped their affectionate display. Maria giggled.

"Hey, get a room!" one of their regulars teased.

Marty grinned.

223

"Almost closing time boys," she said.

A couple of hours later they were both sitting in their cozy lounge, TV on, relaxing after the hard day.

"Marty, do you think I should…" Maria began.

"No babe. Leave them to it."

"Maybe I should go after Gemma…see if she's…"

"No," Marty said firmly. She pulled Maria to her. "Ava and Gemma will manage. Besides, you're too busy with me." Her hands slipped under Maria's blouse pulling the silky material over her head. Maria straddled her lap, her breath quickening. She could never resist Marty's passionate nature. Leaning down she tried to capture Marty's lips beneath hers.

"Take your trousers off first," Marty's instruction was firm. Maria stood and in one swift movement removed them along with her panties. Marty looked at her. Maria's body was slender but strong. Her abdomen was tight and her hips almost boyish. Her breasts, full and heavy, contrasted with this delicateness. Her nipples were peaked in anticipation and her dark pubic curls were already wet with desire.

"Please Marty, take your clothes off," Maria groaned. She loved the feel of her wife's bare skin against her own.

Marty grinned. "I make the rules," she said, but capitulated. She wanted to feel that curly, wet mons pressed against her abdomen. Marty's body was fleshier, her abdomen slightly larger but there was strength in her solidness and Maria loved the feel of Marty's skin against hers. She straddled Marty again, willingly surrendering her breasts to Marty's seeking mouth, her legs open and clasped around Marty's middle. Her mons pressed against Marty's lower stomach and both women groaned at the intimate touch. Maria ground her open center against the solid flesh gasping. She had to hold on, and fought for control.

Lowering her head, bringing Marty's searching lips up from her breasts she kissed her deeply, their tongues lashing each other's until Maria's mouth submitted under her stronger lover's lips. She slipped off Marty's lap and knelt down, opening her thighs. Trailing her mouth down the soft stomach she reached the muscled thighs, licking each one in turn as she neared the clean shaven center. She let her tongue bury itself in the slick folds and licked each side of the swollen clitoris. Uttering a guttural sound, Marty arched, her hands clasping Maria's head. Maria concentrated on capturing the thick bud and sucking it. Marty opened her legs wider, ensuring access to that open, hot mouth. Just as she felt she would come, she lowered herself and pulled Maria up.

"Fetch the strap-on," she said. Maria was disappointed. She wanted Marty to come first.

"Now!"

Maria recognized the tone. She got up, her rounded buttocks moving with each roll of her hips. Marty bit her lip. She wanted to come but even more she wanted to take her wife, hear her scream as she came. Maria returned and Marty stood.

"Put it on me." Maria obediently knelt down adjusting the straps. As much as she enjoyed the strap on she preferred the flesh and hands of her wife, but did not demur.

"Suck it," Marty said. Maria blinked. She had never been asked to do that before. Marty took her head guiding it to the dildo. She looked down at the ebony haired head and the mouth taking in the dildo and she smiled. She felt turned on. It was seldom that she experienced the desire for this scenario but right now it was what she wanted and needed.

"Come here," she said relenting, sitting back down and helping Maria onto her lap. She guided the head of the dildo into her wife's wet opening and grasping her hips, helped her gain a comfortable rhythm.

Her mouth captured a taut nipple whilst her hands squeezed Maria's buttocks. Maria gasped, sobbed and panted her way to an orgasm she tried to fight against. It was her wife's fingers she craved more, but the closeness of her seated position and the feel of both of Marty's hands on her buttocks left her body no choice. She called out with breathy sobs as she climaxed, her thighs trembling.

As her body eased down from the high, she felt slightly unsatisfied; she wanted to watch Marty writhe under her. Marty had other plans. As the dildo slipped out, she turned her wife to sit on the edge of the sofa. Opening her legs, she pushed her back, making her gasp. Marty's mouth descended on her clitoris which started swelling again. She nuzzled and sucked until Maria felt she would burst with desire.

"Oh, fuck," she screamed as a second orgasm tore through her. Although their love making was less frequent than the heady first years, their sex life was good. She loved this passionate side of Marty.

Once she relaxed and managed to catch her breath, she propped Marty's one leg on the coffee table. She wasted no time thrusting three fingers between the inviting opening on display, pumping her hand. Marty rode it, her breasts heaving. Maria reached up, her other hand lightly slapping at the pale breasts with the taut nipples. Marty came silently, her wetness coating Maria's hand, running down her forearm.

"That was naughty," she said.

Maria grinned. "But you liked it."

"I did." Marty laughed, color painting her cheeks from the sated sensation of giving and receiving pleasure.

They curled up together on the sofa, Maria's head cradled on Marty's defined shoulder. Marty reflected over the past few days. Yes, life was good, settled and sexy. In the back of her mind the thought of 'too settled' seemed to cast a warning or caution again. She tried to shake it off and concentrate on other thoughts.

Tomorrow she would encourage Maria to contact Gemma and make sure all was okay. The uneasy feeling returned, fighting against her conscious effort to ignore it. Maria was too edgy and had thrown herself into her match making with more zeal than usual or was warranted. She could not allow this concern to go unchecked. Adding to her mental list of things to do, she determined she would find out what was going in her wife's head.

CHAPTER 3

The day started like any other. Maria woke first, her usual 'I'm a day time person' energy filling the room as she dressed for a run.

"Wake up sleepy head," she said, tossing a pillow at Marty, who turned and grunted. "Are you going to come for a run?"

In reply Marty pulled the thrown pillow over her eyes. Even after all these years she could not get used to the energy her wife had. Her body suited the hours that owning the restaurant and bar demanded. She stretched.

"Come to back bed--"

"No way! I've got to work off some..." Maria stopped.

"Work off what?" Marty said half sitting up. The cut off sentence was unusual from Maria who was generally open and transparent in her feelings.

"Nothing," Maria grinned and turned around, cheekily waving her Lycra clad bottom at Marty.

"Babe...wait..." Marty said, trying to disentangle herself from the duvet.

"Later!" Maria blew a kiss at her and bounded out of the bedroom. The front door opened and closed before Marty could get up to stop her. If she had energy, Marty thought, she'd run after her. Still, it was good Maria had woken her. She wanted to plan the restaurant's '-daily specials-' for the coming week. Being up earlier would give her a chance to do that without becoming overloaded later once they opened for lunch.

She knew she could take more time off. Their staff had grown as their business's success had and they now had a part time manager, a full time chef in addition to herself, and four wait staff. She loved being there, living her passion and interests daily.

Unable to fall back to sleep now that the thought of the daily specials filled her mind, she got up, her firm, sturdy body aching for the shower. Stretching she remembered the night before and ached for Maria's touch again.

What was worrying her wife she mused as she stood under the warm spray, letting it cascade over her shoulders and back. She imagined Maria's hands soaping her body, trailing over her buttocks and sliding around to her front, reaching down between her legs. She groaned again. Time to get out and plan the meals over a cup of coffee. She would get to the bottom of what was troubling Maria when she returned.

Maria pounded along the outskirts of the small-town road. She generally ran through the town, heading down to the tourist populated section of the lake. It was a popular run and she loved meeting neighbors, friends and tourists who were out exercising. Today she needed to be away from all that. She ran faster than her usual jogging pace, her neon orange trainers pounding the tarmac and then the dirt road as she turned off the main road leading out of town. Marty did not like her running alone out of the town borders. She felt it was not safe. Not just from wildlife, which were really uncommon occurrences, but from hikers or campers who might think a lone female jogger or hiker was fair game for some unwelcomed harassment disguised as fun.

Hoping the run would clear her frustrated feelings, she focused on each stride. The feelings had been growing over the past few months and in the past week had seemed to intensify.

After a good hour-long run, she stopped and stretched her hamstrings, breathing hard. The sense of boredom had crept into her life so slowly she had barely recognized it, was inching its way to the middle of her forehead, causing a mild throbbing headache.

She hung her head and concentrated on breathing in and out. How could she feel bored? Guilt ate into her. What right did she have to feel unfulfilled? She had an amazing wife and life. Thinking back to her life before Marty, before this vibrant little town, before her like-minded friends, only enhanced her guilt. The city she came from had been full of color and busy activities and although she had danced nights away at trendy night clubs she had felt empty. Her PhD study had been dull, as was her Masters degree before it. She had continued studying only to fit in with the academic circle she had been part of. Working full time as assistant to the executive manager of the university ensured her work and academic life had been full. Yet it had been tense and she had felt overstretched.

Her photography and designing classes had been the highlights of her weeks. The customer's designs she created in her part time position had given her great pleasure. She had pursued photography albeit as an amateur and she had captured various city scenes that stirred her creative nature. Viewed through those photos, the city had seemed alive and alluring, yet when viewed through her eyes, the realism of her life had been depressing.

Here, in this small town-quiet and yet vibrant in the paradoxical way of tourist towns-where she had landed five years ago, was where she belonged. She knew that with a deep internal sense of '-rightness-'. She did not want to leave it. Certainly she never wanted to work as she had before with never ending demands and the pressure of academic study.

Here, she belonged to the amateur photography club, had great friends and her wife was a mostly perfect partner, stern yet loving. The scenery was amazing and the restaurant and bar were thriving. She would not swap her life for any other.

Maria sat on a log feeling despondent. She let her thoughts flow. In truth she felt stifled at the restaurant and bar which Marty had so willingly made her part of. She felt bored and as if she was not contributing to society.

True, she had redecorated the bar and restaurant. Marty had amazing cooking skills but her artistic flair was minimal, which had resulted in plain although cheerful décor. It had taken Maria two years to achieve the look she wanted for their business and was satisfied with the result.

The redecorating had helped improve their clientele base and Marty loved it. But that was three years back. Maria continued trying to engage with customers, taking a keen interest in their friends which was an innate part of her personality, but something was missing.

What did she want, she mused, her brow furrowing as she tried to form her feelings into thoughts. Marty's love and interest? Yeah, well she had that, she reflected. But lately Marty had seemed more wrapped up in her cooking and the love of the bar. Since they had become so successful she spent more time there. It had given her time needed to help their friend Charlie, although Maria was not sure what she felt about Marty spanking Charlie. She grinned; Charlie so deserved it though. Their single friend was a breaker of hearts and a total flirt. Her heart skipped a beat thinking of the attractive Charlie.

She looked up for a minute leaving her musings to gently slip back into the space where one can leave unsolved feelings and access them later. The backdrop was amazing. The mountains were high in places, foreboding where the peaks were sheer, inviting in others where the trees were sturdy and plateaus of fields and flowers could be seen. She turned. From her small vantage point she could see the massive lake which bordered the town on one side. It was a pearl-blue color in the early morning light. If only she had brought her camera, she thought.

She headed down through the trees and toward the water, away from the road she had come on. A line of trees guarded the water in front of her and to her right in the distance she could see the outskirts of the town. She walked along the water line toward it. The surroundings were still and devoid of human noise. The boats and skiers from the lake had not yet started for the day. No human sounds were heard from picnickers or hikers. The only sounds were the birds with their strangely soothing cacophony of calls and her own soft footfalls.

She inhaled deeply, holding the breath and then exhaling, absorbing the moment.

As she neared the town she passed a set of empty wooden cabins. The buildings were small and cozy in design and had been owned by a family who had lived in the area a decade ago. They had moved to one of the large cities, leaving their collection of cottages and art and snack shops. Maria stopped, wandering around the old wooden buildings. The last one nearest to the town, which lay only a ten-minute walk away, was made of weathered deep orange wood and had been a small store. The sign still hung above it. She trailed her hand over the external walls, tracing the weave of the grain showing in each log.

Maria had not been there when it was open but she had seen old photos of the area. She peered through the glass front door which was dusty and stained yet surprisingly not cracked. Hands on either side of her head she stared into the dusty interior. For a second she saw not the empty rooms, nor the dust on the floor but the echoing memories, long forgotten, of the hopes, dreams and lives of the people who once worked there and those who wandered through to buy items.

She blinked the image away and focused her eyes to see a large open space, the floor as richly colored in woody sandy orange as the walls were. The little building was as splendid and proud as the wooded trees it had come from. Her mind ran free. She visualized ornamental lighting in the shape of flowers and the sleek and simple lines of cream stands in the corners on which stood statues or paintings. Along the walls, she saw photographs, some in black and white and some in the jeweled colors of the mountains and lake and the quaint features of the town. She blinked again. The images had faded but remained clear in her mind: a photography studio or art boutique or art and souvenir shop. Her heart missed a beat. This little place felt like hers. Perhaps it could be. A smile curved her lips. Then reality sunk in. How could she afford something like this? Probably it was not even for sale.

She turned and started running again, back to the town and the little house behind the restaurant and bar that she loved.

CHAPTER 4

Marty sat at the bar. She had a pencil stuck behind one ear, although her lap top was in front of her. Maria often teased her about it. The pencil was her real guide. She would research and write her menus up on her laptop, but she kept a journal near her, to jot her thoughts and ideas down. Sometimes actually writing an idea in her own hand, made the flavors and set combinations come alive for her.

It was too early for the bar to be open but the restaurant had been opened earlier by her assistant manager and was humming with breakfast clientele. The area where she sat at the bar was quiet and dim. She would type up the week's special on the web site, she thought.

Maria poked her head around the door from the kitchen.

"Babe, do you want coffee?"

"I'd love a cup." Marty set her lap top and journal aside. She had not decided on the complete menus for the second week and would have liked to finish but there would be time enough for that later, she reckoned. This was an opportune time to find out what was bugging her wife. She needed to get to the bottom of it, before Maria became more frustrated. Experience had taught her it was best to deal with any issues as they arose. Maria would be anxious and being unable to express herself easily would allow her feelings to silently chip away at her until she erupted in unacceptable behavior.

Maria returned to the bar, pushing the swing door of the kitchen open with her hip. The smell of rich roasted coffee assailed Marty. She had had breakfast but normally waited to have coffee with Maria before they started work for the day.

"Did you have breakfast?" she asked Maria casually, knowing full well she had not. Maria had color in her cheeks and her mood was slightly lifted from the early morning's pensiveness. However, she knew that look in her eyes. Her mind was elsewhere.

"Yes-no, I think so," Maria said. "Babe, do you think I should find out how Gemma is today?"

Marty smiled. Okay, first things first.

"Yes," she said carefully. "Call her and invite her for a drink this afternoon. Tread carefully...you know what you are like. Don't be too direct. If either she or Ava needs our help they will ask."

Maria bristled slightly. Honestly, sometimes Marty annoyed her. As if she would just directly approach what had happened the night before. Okay, well, she probably would, she conceded. She smiled and leaned toward Marty, kissing her gently on the lips and smoothing her blonde fringe to the side.

"Get some breakfast and let's chat," Marty said. She added a slightly firm tone to her voice, hoping that her wife would get breakfast without too much fuss. Maria tended to become very irritable when she had not eaten. It was sometimes as if she thrived on the dramas around her and her care for others as opposed to actual sustenance.

Maria opened her mouth to say she had eaten, but seeing the glint in Marty's eyes she went off to get some breakfast. Marty knew her too well. She really just wanted to phone Gemma and after that get back to work.

Going back to the kitchen she filled a plate with some scrambled eggs and grabbed a small bowl of fresh fruit salad.

"Did you sleep well, babe?" Maria asked, a naughty glint in her eye. "I mean you fell asleep pretty quickly after you came!"

Marty rapped her wrist lightly. She knew Maria was teasing her.

"How are the menus coming?"

"Okay. I want to plan next week's menus as well. I was thinking about a different country's dishes represented each week for the next month. What do you think?"

She wanted Maria to keep calm and settled until after she had finished eating.

Maria loved the idea and whilst spooning down her eggs, planned the décor she wanted to represent each country.

When she had finished Marty leaned forward. "Okay, out with it. What is wrong with you?"

Maria looked at her.

"What do you mean?" She was taken aback, feeling that she had managed to keep her feelings well hidden. She felt Marty was too busy to be bothered with any of own small unhappiness.

"You know exactly what I mean. You have not been yourself the last few months."

Guilt flooded Maria. Her cheeks beneath her olive skin colored. Her life was so full and she hated seeing the concern that flooded Marty's warm eyes. She ducked her head, thoughts whirling whilst trying to find an excuse.

"Nothing is wrong," she said finally, looking up again. "I think you are imagining things. You do work a lot darling, perhaps you need a bit more rest." She stood up with her empty plate.

"Perhaps you need a spanking...a reminder not to lie to me." Marty's voice was even but firm, and she put one hand out as Maria passed her, effectively stopping her.

Maria immediately flared up. Really, did Marty suddenly think that any time she was unhappy she should spank her?! She had just spanked Charlie.

"I'm not Charlie!" she snapped. "If you need to spank someone, go and spank her." The words sounded rude and she winced. Why, oh why was she such a prickly person, she thought? But it was true. If Marty was going to spank Charlie she might as well spank the whole town. She could tolerate shared sexual attractions... possibly...but spanking belonged to them and them alone. Marty's eyes had narrowed. Maria swallowed slightly. She knew she was being silly. After all, Marty would never have hesitated to spank either Em or Gemma if needed. And that did not upset her.

She thought she had not minded seeing Marty spank Charlie but her emotions were definitely off kilter. She wanted something more in her life and at the same time felt jealous seeing Marty give more attention to one of their friends. The deepening of her attraction that she felt toward Charlie, seeing her bent over as Marty paddled her, had taken her by surprise.

"Maria, are you jealous of my attention to Charlie?" Marty was surprised. Maria was not generally a jealous person. She was confident and seemed content with and aware of Marty's dedication to her. Marty reflected quickly. She had only ever delivered one other spanking to a mutual friend whilst she and Maria had been together. That had been a few years back and there had been no issues. Maria certainly had not been jealous on the very few occasions she had scolded Em or Gemma during some of their schemes. She was fully aware of the spark of attraction between Maria and Charlie, but then most women fell for Charlie's overt sexuality. She herself was definitely not immune.

Pulling Maria gently toward her, she turned her so that her back leaned against Marty's front and put her arms around her middle. Maria leaned back against her. It felt soothing and comforting and she relaxed into her wife's body. She was aware that if she tried to pull away, Marty's arms would tighten and she would not release her.

"Honey-?" she waited patiently for a reply.

"Um...no of course not. Well, slightly..." Maria conceded.

"What do you mean by slightly?"

Maria thought. She had been taken aback when she realized Marty was spanking Charlie. Personally, she felt that Charlie had needed it. She also knew that Marty loved her but that she was immensely fond of Charlie and cared about her as she did all their friends. She had not felt any qualms when Marty fixed her same steely glint on her friends, if they got up to any mischief.

"I'm not...sure," she said slowly.

"Do you think I love you any less?"

"No," Maria said firmly. She felt annoyed and pushed herself away slightly. "I need to get started for today," she said.

The arms did not budge and Maria felt an urge to bat them away.

"Let me go."

"No," Marty's voice was calm and made of steel. "I need to understand what's going on in that head of yours. You know that you will only become more irritable as the day wears on."

"Well, you are already irritating me," Maria snapped. She grimaced and immediately regretted the words. Without time to take a breath she felt herself turned and a heavy hand landed across her bottom twice. She yelped.

"Sit down," Marty said. She hooked one of the chairs with her foot and brought it close, lowering Maria into it so that they sat knee to knee on the same level. Maria's cheeks colored. She wanted to shout with frustration and an indescribable feeling of sadness, but her bottom tingled as if in warning and she lowered her eyes. On one level she was aware she was being churlish.

"I'm sorry," she muttered. Marty surveyed the dark head, well aware that if she titled that chin she would see the deep blue eyes glinting with irritation.

She phrased her words carefully.

"Honey, I should have spoken to you first, before spanking Charlie. Unfortunately when I saw her disrespecting you and knowing how she has been lately, I felt I had to act. You know that I care for her and want the best for her, but that it's you I love." Now she did tilt the chin in front of her. To her surprise the blue eyes held not irritation, but a shimmer of tears.

"Babe-!" she exclaimed, bringing her in for a hug. Maria leant into it.

"Thank you for explaining," Maria said. She felt quite grateful for the excuse of Charlie's spanking. To think of telling Marty, this amazing generous lover, that she wanted something different than the business she had built up felt so very wrong.

Marty hugged her closely. She felt relieved hearing the words, but uneasy. It did seem an extreme reaction on Maria's side who took to a spanking disciplinary lifestyle as naturally as a duck to water. She had even once been on the receiving end of Mel's firm hand. Her hare-brained schemes tended to drag her friends into them and she had on that occasion tried Mel's patience too far.

"Honey, is anything else wrong?" she persisted.

"No..." The word was soft, almost hesitant.

"Time for the bar!" A loud voice pulled them apart. Marty

looked up at the clock. How had the last two hours flown like this? It was already midday and their lunch time regulars would want their pre-lunch drinks. Maria jumped up, grateful for the reprieve. She kissed Marty lightly and went back to the kitchen, plate in one hand. Marty stood and set about opening the bar, her mind working overtime. Something else was up with her wife, she was sure. A faint unease filled her. Was she enough for Maria?

The day was busy, filled with regulars and tourists. Marty reveled in it. She carefully stored the recent conversation with Maria in her mind. She would need to revisit it with her soon, she felt.

CHAPTER 5

Maria decided that she would not ask Gemma over for a drink. It would be best to phone her. The situation might still be too raw for her and she might feel embarrassed. She knew what it was like to lose one's temper or get upset when one did not totally understand what one was feeling.

Gemma answered on the third ring. That was a good sign. After inquiring how she was, she went on to ask if she was okay after the '-incident-'. She emphasized the word and Gemma gave a little laugh tinged with shame.

"Yes." Her voice was light. "I need to apologize to all of you for shouting like that and running out."

"No need, honey," Maria said immediately. She wanted to encourage her friend to talk to her. "Did you...well, did you...are you and Ava okay?" She stumbled over her words, not quite sure how to ask the normally shy Gemma. If she were talking to Em she would have been able to ask directly.

"Um...yes."

"Okay. Do you want to meet for coffee? Is there anything you need to chat about? If you and Ava--?" Before she could finish, Gemma hurried to reassure her.

"We're fine. Ava and I are good. I...it's...I mean..." Maria could almost hear Gemma blushing over the phone. "Come around. I think it's easier to talk face to face."

Maria's heart sank. Maybe it was not good news. Perhaps they had broken up. Gemma was a vulnerable person and very sensitive. Ava had seemed to settle into the town life so well. It would be awkward initially if they had broken up, as they both belonged to the same group.

She rushed through to the kitchen, kissed Marty and said she was going over to see her friend.

"Babe-" Marty was slightly alarmed by the tension in Maria. "Make sure to-" She did not get to utter anything further about treading carefully as Maria had already exited the kitchen door through the back. She followed her and caught up with her wife at the car. Maria had started the engine. She put her hand on the window, tapping on the glass, indicating for Maria to lower it. Temper flashed in Maria's eyes but she lowered the window.

"What is it now?" she said. Marty's eyes narrowed.

"I beg your pardon?! What is wrong with you? You seem like a tightly coiled spring. Whatever it is, it better end before you are back. I just wanted to say be gentle with Gemma; you know how sensitive she is."

Maria wanted to scream. What did Marty think of her? She swallowed back a sharp reply and felt tears prick her eyes. What was wrong with her? Her wife did not deserve her impatience or sharp words.

"I will," she said lightly. "Sorry, babe...just a bit tired."

"Okay. Drive safely, have a good time," Marty said. Her palm itched. She really wanted to take Maria back inside and sit her down to find out what was causing this strange mood of hers. However she knew Maria was stubborn and probably had not yet herself understood why she was acting the way she was. She knew Maria loved seeing their friends settled but this seemed over the top. It was as if she was pouring her energy into something else and pushing to the back of her life something she did not want to feel.

Marty leant down and kissed her through the window.

"I'll see you when you come back. Give my love to Gemma... and Ava if she is there." She stood back and watched, hands on her hips, as Maria pulled off and drove down the road far faster than was needed or the speed limit allowed.

Within a few minutes, she was pulling up outside her friend's cabin. She should have walked, she reflected. It might have worked off some of the restlessness she felt.

Gemma was shyly happy with a contented air emanating from her and all Maria's concern about her and Ava vanished.

"Are you okay? We were so worried when you ran out the bar," she asked politely. Gemma nodded. A faint blush was creeping over her cheeks. Maria laughed, for a minute forgetting her own inner unease.

"I was...overreacting," Gemma said. "I felt...insecure."

Maria hugged her briefly. Insecurity was a major personality feature in Gemma.

"All of you are so close and well...attractive and..." she trailed off.

"Honey," Maria exclaimed. "Do you feel insecure around us? Please don't. We totally adore you--as you are." Gemma smiled.

"Ava was..." she hesitated, cautiously choosing her words. "She... well, she let me know that as well...how...I mean...what I meant to her..."

Maria sat upright. For some reason her bottom was tingling.

She could guess quite clearly what Gemma was trying to say. When she first met Ava properly, she saw the same top tendencies in her as in Marty. Slightly more than the milder firmness found between Mel and Emma. She could almost guarantee Ava had a closet of implements-that had been put to good use for both discipline and sex that night.

It was good to see her shy friend so relaxed. Marty had been right when she said everything would be okay.

Gemma surprised her by leaning forward and gently touching her leg as if worried that what she might say would scare her off.

"Maria….Are you okay? I mean it's just that-" Gemma stuttered slightly. She did not want to upset Maria who had been her first friend here. Maria did tend to get worked up easily.

"Yes, of course I am! What's making you ask that?" Maria asked slightly indignantly.

"You seem-I don't really know how to describe it…As if something is bothering you." She noticed Maria inhale and continued hastily so that she could finish what she wanted to say.

"You are mostly always upbeat, but your need for adventure seems to be increasing. Sometimes I feel as if you are thinking of something completely other than what we are talking about. Em noticed it as well."

Maria sat silently. She was not sure what to say. If she confided in her friend would that be disloyal to Marty?

"Honey, if something is wrong, please tell me." Her friend's voice was soft and gentle and Maria almost opened up.

"I am perhaps a bit distracted," she said, "but it's nothing serious." She lightened her tone, and started teasing Gemma slightly about the other night. Gemma knew that Maria would not talk to her that day.

The two of them chatted about nothing serious and made lunch, taking it outside to enjoy on the small patio.

Maria mellowed after drinking two glasses of wine and enjoyed Gemma's new relaxed and happy state of being. A twinge pricked her conscious mind. If only she felt as happy as Gemma did right now. She polished off another two glasses of the crisp, fruity wine and felt quite tipsy by the time she stood up to leave.

"I don't think you should drive back," Gemma said. She was alarmed to see Maria slightly tipsy yet still getting her car keys out.

"I am quite capable of driving!" Maria flared. She saw the hurt in Gemma's eyes at the uncalled for, sharp tone of voice. "Oh, I'm sorry, honey…really, I'm okay."

"No," Gemma said, surprising even herself at the sternness in her voice. "You are not driving in this state. I can't let you do that. Give me the keys."

Maria reflected on what had just been said. She knew what Gemma said made sense. She started to hold the keys out, but her rebellious streak presented itself. How dare everyone around her try and control her, she fumed! Even her friend was doing it now! She snatched her keys back and picked up her bag.

"I'm so happy you and Ava are properly together," she said. She hugged Gemma, who was still stunned by the abrupt change in mood, and walked out the door.

"Wait," Gemma called, following her to the car. The front door had closed behind Maria and by the time she had pushed it open, Maria was already in the car.

Maria pulled off, the car lurching slightly. Gemma's heart was in her mouth. She was worried about her friend. What if she had an accident? She ran back inside and grabbed her own car keys. Barefoot, she jumped into her own car and followed the direction back to town that Maria had taken. The sense of relief she felt when she drove around the back of the restaurant car park and saw

Maria's blue car parked there was palpable. She got out, wincing as her bare feet touched the gravel.

"Gemma!" Marty hurried out. She had seen Maria's car draw up and squeal to a stop, followed by the slam of the car door.

She had turned to go and see what was going on when she had caught sight of a barefoot Gemma.

"Oh, Marty! Hi-" Gemma faltered. She had only wanted to see if Maria had got back safely and was okay. She was slightly in awe of the toppy Marty.

"Anything wrong? Are you okay? Where are your shoes?"

"I-um-no. No-I just..." she stammered, trying to reorganize her thoughts. She certainly did not want to tell Marty that her wife had been drinking and driving.

"Oh, I was just-Maria forgot-no, I forgot..." She was a terrible liar, and her pale cheeks flushed. Marty's eyes narrowed, but she spoke gently.

"Come inside," she said. "Is something troubling you? Is Ava okay?"

"Oh, oh, yes, Ava is..." Her eyes softened "-fine-" Marty smiled in spite of her worry. Clearly things were okay. She put that aside and asked,

"Did you have an argument with Maria? Is Maria okay?"

Gemma paled, the flush now draining from her face. She bit her lip. What could she say?

"I just wanted to make sure Maria got back safely," she said finally.

Marty's eyes narrowed again.

"Is there any reason she would not have gotten back safely?"

"No, no, of course not. She's not drunk...just..." she trailed off, biting her bottom lip again. Why on earth had she said that?

"Were you drinking?" Marty asked the question calmly and

evenly, but in a tone that clearly showed Gemma she would be going nowhere until she answered.

"I-er-no-well, just a few glasses."

Marty kept silent, eyeing her with one eyebrow raised. She could see that Gemma was not tipsy but if she had been drinking it was not wise to drive. Seeing the panic in her, however, she could well imagine that her wife was fairly tipsy.

"Gemma, I am going to phone Ava to see if she can fetch you. Please wait…"

"No," Gemma said, finding her voice. She felt horrified. She wasn't even tipsy. She had drunk two glasses of wine and was fine. The thought of Ava being called panicked her slightly. She did not think her bottom or thighs could take any type of spanking again so soon. She had only wanted to ensure her friend was fine and now Marty was standing in front of her unmoving, even though she was looking at her with understanding compassion.

"I can't let you drink and drive. If Ava cannot fetch you, then I will drive you home." *And after that I will be having a talk with my wife.*

She led Gemma through to the lounge, and taking her phone, called Ava from the kitchen. Her expression was serious and factual as she explained the situation.

Putting her phone back down, she went back to the anxious Gemma and told her Ava would fetch her. She noted the flare of annoyance in Gemma's eyes and grinned. She felt quite sure Ava had her hands full and would even more as time went on.

"How much did Maria drink?" she asked.

"Not too much," Gemma said.

"But you felt the need to follow her?"

"I…um…" Gemma felt terrible. Marty moved to sit next to her. She softened the look in her eyes.

"Gemma, I love Maria and I don't want her in any accidents," Marty said. Gemma blushed.

"I know," she said. "It's just that I felt bad."

"Not as bad as if you did not tell me and something does happen to her in future for drinking and driving." Marty said evenly.

That was true. Maria was edgy and that made her erratic at times.

"I hope she does not get angry with me," Gemma said. "She's just seemed a bit...far away lately. Today when she came over, she was tense...her usual lovely self...but on edge. I wanted to ask her what was wrong but we spoke about me and Ava." She lowered her voice. She wished she had been more insistent.

"Okay," Marty said. "Thank you for telling me. I'm glad she has a friend that cares so much for her wellbeing. How much did she drink?"

"Just-just four glasses of wine." She saw Marty's eyes narrow even further and she gulped. "I mean...maybe...maybe it was only three...but she seemed a bit...I did try to stop her."

"I am sure you did," Marty said. She looked up as she heard the door open. Ava came in, wearing her adventure center gym wear. She did not look impressed to have been called away from work. Gemma gulped. This was not a good first day of '-turning over a new leaf-' as she had agreed to the night before.

"Gemma's fine," Marty said. "Other than the drinking and driving! I'm just going to find out what's up with Maria."

Leaving them alone, she walked out the lounge and started up the stairs to the bedroom. There was no way she was going to let this go.

Marty marched up to their bedroom. Her wife would either be in there or one of the two guest rooms which she occasionally used to do her exercise in. She opened the door calmly despite the anger she felt. Maria was sitting on their bed, pulling off her clothes, obviously about to take a shower. Marty approached her evenly.

"Maria."

"What?"

"Have you been drinking?"

Maria's eyes flashed. She felt totally irritated by the question and pushed any guilt to the back of her mind.

"So what if I was?" she countered. She felt a bit sleepy and her words were more careless than they might normally have been.

Marty looked at her, assessing her state. She was definitely tipsy, not totally drunk, but not in the right state to be reasoned with.

She needed to manage this; first the drinking and driving and later on what was causing this behavior. To have a conversation about those issues now would achieve nothing. Maria was also belligerent and that wasn't something she could easily deal with right now. Tomorrow she would have a serious talk with her.

Making a snap decision on her course of action, she walked over to the drawer and, opening the middle drawer, took out a paddle. It was made of lightweight wood and guaranteed to cause a sharp sting unlike the heavier woods. Maria had clumsily risen to her feet the minute she saw Marty open the middle drawer. That middle drawer was only opened when Marty had decided that some serious discipline was needed.

A host of feelings ran through her. Defiance, upset, anticipation, dread and an intense feeling that she wanted to talk about her feelings with Marty but did not quite know how to. Added to this was the physical feeling that she just wanted to close her eyes and sleep. Sleep however would not come whilst she felt worked up. She was well aware she had driven home after drinking with Gemma. Well, lots of people do it, she thought mutinously.

Marty strode over, the shorthanded paddle in her right hand.

Maria opened her mouth to protest but her reactions were slow, tempered by the alcohol, and she found herself over her wife's lap on the bed. The top half of her body and legs were supported by the mattress and her bottom angled over Marty's upper legs, the tops of her thighs held firmly against the larger, muscled ones of her wife.

"I know you had four glasses of wine and drove. I also know you are not up to talking about it. We will discuss it tomorrow," Marty said.

Maria's top and trousers were already off. Marty pulled her panties down and soundly landed the paddle. It landed with a thud and Maria found her voice. She yelled loudly. It had been a few months since Marty had spanked her with an implement. Generally 'the look' and a firm scolding grounded her. She also usually used her hand. The implements were for serious punishment. Marty did not use any of her implements for pleasure. Sexual pleasure was an intensely personal affair, hot and heady with no need of any disciplinary implement to enhance it.

She shrieked and tried to wriggle off Marty's lap. A strong arm held her securely and the right hand continued landing the paddle with a steady rhythm on the now already heated pink bottom.

It was not pleasurable in any way at all but the consistent stinging thwack seemed to penetrate the emotional turmoil inside her mind and on the tenth spank Marty felt the body over her thighs sag slightly. She was not going to let up though. This had to be something Maria would not forget easily.

Maria was soon uttering small cries, turning to sobs as Marty continued landing the paddle on the tender spots where thigh and bottom met. She was careful not to hold the paddle so as to break the skin or cause welts. She knew that it stung and that Maria would not forget the spanking tomorrow. When she sat her down tomorrow she would be reminded of it when they spoke. More importantly she knew that Maria needed it to allow herself to cry and feel emotional relief.

When the sobs turned to whimpers of release she stopped. She wanted to hug and cuddle her and beg her to tell her what was wrong but she knew Maria was not ready and was too tipsy for a serious discussion. She gently pulled her upright in front of her, holding her by the tops of her arms.

"Babe," she said sternly, "-you will never again drink and drive...or you won't be sitting for a month, not just a day."

Maria looked at her. Her eyes held a hint of tears. Release, yes, but not total letting go, Marty noted.

"I...I'm sorry...I just...just..." she said, unable to form the words but stammering slightly in temporary relief. For the minute she felt cleansed. She was so tired.

Marty sighed. She held her. Forget the shower, she thought.

She put her wife to bed, pulling the duvet over her, noting that her eyes were almost closing in sleep already. She leant down and smoothed the black hair away from her face. The circles under her eyes were pronounced and Marty's heart ached to think of the emotional stress her wife was carrying around.

"Sleep well, sweetheart," she whispered. She kissed her lips gently. Maria reached up.

"Babe, I'm sorry-I'm-sorry. I just can't-talk-I...thank you."

Marty understood her. She understood fully what she was thanking her for and felt grateful that they were so well matched in that regard. She waited until she was sure Maria was asleep and then left the room.

Going back down, she went through to the bar. Her mind was troubled. She loved Maria and needed to help her.

CHAPTER 6

The next morning, Marty woke up first. It was unusual, but not unexpected given Maria's state the night before. She turned and slipped her arms around her wife's body. Unbeknownst to Maria she had arranged that neither of them would work that day. The staff would manage well without them.

She was determined to find out what was bothering Maria. Her mind was working overtime. She decided she would let Maria go for her run and then tell her they were not working that day. If she told her first it would cause anxiety and Maria might not return from her run and get herself worked up as anxiety over whatever was troubling her increased.

Maria stirred. She woke and wiggled back into Marty sighing, a soft, sensual sound that immediately aroused Marty. She fought for self-control. Making love would only cloud the issue at hand. Turning around she kissed Marty lightly.

"You're awake," she said. "Good. That means today you can come for a run-a bit later. Let me get us some coffee first."

"Babe," Marty tried. She sank back against the pillows. Okay, she would wait until they had coffee. Maria returned with two cups, the steam slightly curling upward, the scent rich. It was a good idea. They sipped coffee in silence,

Marty thinking about changing her strategy slightly as Maria had not set off on her run yet. Maria reached out for her phone. Marty saw a name flash up on the screen -'Gemma-'. She tensed. She did not want their friend to warn Maria about last night and have her sense something was up. She saw Maria's body stiffen. Okay, she was going to have to talk to her now.

Maria placed her coffee cup on the bedside table and took Marty's from her surprised hand. As she leant to put it down on Marty's side, her body, still topless from the night before, brushed over Marty's stomach. Her breasts were full and sensuous. Marty tried to stem the desire flooding through her. Maria looked at her, her body still over Marty's, with a naughty and knowing look in her eyes. She sensually and slowly moved her body back, letting her breasts trail over Marty's. Bending, she lowered her lips to her wife's. Marty tried to fight the desire as she picked up what Maria was trying to do. The minx was trying to sidetrack her with sex.

"Babe-" She injected sternness into the endearment. The word was lost in the sensation of warm lips, the faint taste of foamy coffee and a hot, searching, moist tongue. Maria lowered her body, one thigh between Marty's and her center pressed tightly against Marty's left thigh.

Marty bucked upwards, all sense of trying to maintain control gone. Maria's hips lifted and she began to thrust gently and rhythmically. Marty felt her wife's wetness and along with it her sense of increasing loss of physical control. She needed to use this to her advantage, she realized. Maria would definitely get more than she bargained for.

Her hands pulled her wife's body closer and she plundered that teasing mouth, turning them both over so that Maria's body was firmly below hers. Maria's legs opened welcomingly and, without talking, Marty let her lips feverishly touch the smooth skin as she inched lower, straight to the core of her desire.

She looked up, noticing Maria's hands touching her own breasts and for a minute all she wanted to do was watch the extreme arousal that sight gave her. When Maria's eyes met hers, she continued down and, using the fingers of both hands, opened Maria's lower lips, fully exposing the pulsating clitoris that throbbed between them. Maria uttered small whimpers. The cool air inflamed every physical sense and her wife's eyes watching her movements was intensely arousing, even if slightly embarrassing. She had not lost the slight sense of shyness she felt when Marty looked at her intimately, always noticing how wanton she made her feel. When the open mouth descended over that swollen bud she bucked and cupped the blonde head, not knowing whether to try and pull it away or force it closer. The sensation was overwhelming.

"Move your hands," Marty instructed. A sharp spank landed on the fleshy side of her one thigh. Maria jumped, but still hesitated. She knew Marty loved the sense of total control she had in this intimate position. It was a highly vulnerable position Maria was in when she was not touching anything but lying helplessly under the onslaught of those searching lips. She knew Marty would probably tie her hands gently if she did not. The force of the spank had heighted the engorged feeling between her legs. She obediently moved her hands away from the blonde head and stretched her arms above her, knowing that she was not to touch her own body. She was to come helplessly and exquisitely whilst her wife took her. Once she had complied, Marty opened her legs further, listening to Maria's cries of desire as she inserted two of her strong fingers deep inside her.

As soon as Maria had adjusted her body and her fingers had taken up a thrusting motion, Marty lowered her head. Her lips captured the swollen clitoris, tongue licking then nuzzling and sucking. Maria tried to hold on, tried desperately to wait but she came almost immediately. The sensation of the fingers she knew so well deep inside her and the hot, moist mouth capturing her center drew forth an orgasm that had her legs and hips trembling.

Marty rested her head against her wife's pelvis. She loved the taste and scent of her and revelled in the fine tremors that coursed through her limbs in the aftermath of feeling. When they had first met, Maria had been reluctant when it came to oral sex but Marty had patiently and determinedly taught her over time that that was how she enjoyed sex and knew that Maria would as well.

She felt Maria move and knew she was going to touch her. Sometimes other methods of control worked just as well as a spanking, though. She would learn not to try and distract her way out of issues with sex. She firmly curled Maria into her, holding her tightly. Her body throbbed, but she wanted to get through to Maria that she knew something was wrong.

Maria felt frustrated. She felt incomplete. Trying to turn toward Marty, she found the arms were unyielding. She had a great need to touch Marty. She wanted to see her wife come, to watch her ride her hand, to know that she had the power to give her the orgasm that would rip through her. She had never told Marty, but watching Marty come did the same to Maria; her insides curling gently as her muscles contracted alongside her wife's.

She realized that her plan of seducing Marty after she read Gemma's WhatsApp had not worked. When she had read the hastily written words of apology from Gemma, telling her how much she had drunk and how Marty had been worried and was going to talk to her, she had planned to distract her wife. It was an impetuous decision and obviously not going to work. She panicked. How could she tell her what was distressing her?

How did she tell her she was not fully happy? She loved Marty so much. Her breathing quickened and anxiety filled her.

"Babe-let me touch you-please…" Her words were soft.

"You can touch me later," Marty said. Her voice was also soft, but it held that edge of firmness that Maria knew from experience would be hard to break through. "I want to know what's bothering you lately. You have been so tense."

"I have not!" Maria immediately denied. She tried to sit up, but the unyielding arms prevented her.

"No! Lie here by me. Sweetheart, I know something is wrong. Please talk to me."

Tears welled up in Maria's eyes. The feel of her wife's sturdy body was reassuring against her own, but the thought of hurting this amazing woman or telling her she needed more was a feeling laden with guilt.

"There is nothing wrong!" she snapped. "Honestly Marty, when you don't let me touch you back, you make me feel like…I mean, I feel like…like…like a…prostitute!" She regretted the words the minute she uttered them. She did not have to turn to look at Marty's face to know that her eyes would have glinted with anger.

"I'm sorry," she said meekly. "That was uncalled for." Marty inhaled. She was so tempted to give her wife a spanking but she controlled herself. Maria was highly stressed about something.

"Okay, babe, tell me what is going on with you. Something is wrong; it is not like you to be this snappy so often."

"How many times do I have to tell you…nothing…is … wrong-!" Maria had raised her voice, biting out each word. Marty reached to her bedside table. Okay, enough of this; her current approach was definitely not working.

She turned Maria on her tummy on the bed and before Maria knew it a smooth yet hard object landed on each bottom check with a hot, painful intensity. She leapt up, but was prevented from leaving the bed by Marty's arm.

The hair brush Marty held was large and rectangular with a standard length handle. It stung but not enough to bruise. It was an uncomfortable sensation and the punishing pain made Maria gasp and rub her bottom to ease the sting.

"What is wrong?" Marty asked. Maria hesitated and the hair brush landed again. "Ow...fuck!" she shrieked. It now imparted a sting that was crisp and fast as opposed to heavier and slower. She immediately flipped over and sat up. She also knew Marty was holding back as she definitely had spanked her harder previously, but the hairbrush was a hated implement. It was solid and unyielding.

"Um..." she said. Her mind whirled. Marty laid the hair brush down and looked at her. Her heart contracted with love. A slight fear passed through her. Did her wife want to leave her? She mentally squared her shoulders. Whatever it was, she would support her.

"I'm waiting..." She hardened her tone knowing that Maria needed help to voice her thoughts. She saw a flare of anger and then a fleeting look of longing in Maria's eyes. Her shoulders slumped and she lowered her face into her hands, her black bob partly occluding her face.

"Honey, please-" Marty said gently. "Whatever it is, it's okay."

Maria looked up. Her wife's brown eyes were deep and tender, regarding her with compassion, sternness and love.

There was no way she was going to upset this woman, she decided. She sat upright, determination showing in her features. Marty noted the slight change in body language and wondered if Maria was pulling away emotionally. She normally became softer when expressing her feelings.

"I…er…I am…um…unhappy with…"

"Yes?"

"Er-how I look…"

"How you look?!" Marty was surprised. When she first met Maria, she certainly had had a lot of insecurities about her body. She failed to see the beauty in her shape that others saw in her. Over the years though, with Marty's consistency, this had lessened. Maria was perfect for her height and bone structure.

"Yes. I feel too-um-fat, no, I mean-not fat…" she amended hastily, watching Marty's eyes narrow. She knew her wife hated it when she disparaged herself. Marty had a completely different body shape from her but she was comfortable in her own skin. Physical beauty was not something that seemed to enter her world in the same way it did for many people. She saw others as they were and loved and accepted them.

"Your body is perfect, babe," Marty said, slowly wondering what was going on that had caused this old issue to resurface.

"No, it's not," Maria retorted sharply. She felt calmer now that she was off the shaky ground of her real feelings about her current life.

"Watch your tone," Marty said mildly. "I won't have you talking badly about anyone and that means yourself included." She leant nearer.

"Babe, you are beautiful just as you are. There is nothing wrong with you. There is not one thing I would change about you."

"Maybe you would not change anything but I would. I-I need to diet and I know that you stop me. I need to…" she trailed off, her emotions making her voice wobble. This was going so wrong. She certainly did not want a long, intense conversation about something that was basically a lie.

"No. You are not dieting. That is not appropriate." Marty

looked at her. She did not feel this was the real concern. But she had only her wife's words to go on. She ran a hand through her short hair.

"Okay. Look babe-you don't need to diet-you have an ideal figure. But if you feel you need to tone up, well, I can support that. So what about going to gym or-"

"Yes!" Maria agreed immediately. She sighed in relief. They could finally get off this topic and start their day. Besides, she could do with toning up anyway. Marty's next words made her heart sink.

"Right," she said briskly getting off the bed. "In that case I'm going to join you as a member at the adventure center gym and will book Mel as a personal trainer for you."

She walked to the bathroom as if the conversation was finished. She had deliberately chosen Mel knowing that Maria would feel more at ease with someone she had known longer. Ava was also a lot stricter than Mel and she knew Maria would rebel more with Ava than the calm firmness Mel would train her with.

"Oh... um.... no, please. I mean...thanks, that is very thoughtful of you, babe. I don't need a trainer though." And certainly not another top, she thought. A toppy wife was more than enough. A toppy personal trainer, who was also a friend, would be a bit too much. "I can work out by myself." What had she gotten herself into? She groaned softly.

In the bathroom Marty grinned. If this was how her brat wanted to play it, she would go along.

"Nope! If this is what is really worrying you and putting you in such a state, then we will manage it. So you will get trained-by someone we know-and-you'll probably be able to work out with friends which you will enjoy. I will feel relaxed knowing you are not over doing it." She leant forward and turned the shower on.

Maria followed her.

"Babe..." She tried furiously to think of how to get out of the situation. She did not enjoy the gym, preferring jogging for exercise. It felt too organized and limiting. She needed space and freedom to do as she wanted to, she fretted silently.

The water was warm and Marty gently pulled her into the shower, trailing her lips down her neck. Maria was unable to form clear thoughts, let alone continue pleading her case.

"Hmm. I think it's time you touched me like you wanted to," Marty murmured.

CHAPTER 7

Mel's mood was thoughtful as she walked back from work, after a half-day shift. She was meeting Em for a hike. The call from Marty earlier had surprised her. She was glad to be able to help a friend but it seemed odd for Maria to want a personal trainer. She had never seen her in the gym. Maria was well proportioned and slender which was probably due to genetics. Still, everyone could aim for toning and fitness, she mused. They were meeting for drinks later and she'd quiz Marty about it then.

Em was waiting patiently for her on the porch. She had recently become more involved in the amateur photography club, lending her business skills to the management of it. She had originally joined to have an activity to do with Maria and make new friends, but photography did not really interest her, no matter that she had tried hard. Business management, on the other hand, suited her background and personality. Mel was happy to see her so engaged in the community and putting her skills to good use.

"You look well prepared," she remarked, noting Em's hiking boots. They were not going far but it made her feel good to know she was being sensible unlike when she had first met her over two years ago. She smiled at the memories.

They linked hands whilst they walked along the flat road toward the hiking trails.

"Marty asked me to train Maria-at the adventure gym," Mel said.

"Really? I don't think I've ever seen Maria go to a gym," Em said, surprised. "She runs a lot though."

"Yes, I thought it was an odd request. Any idea what's causing it?"

"None. Although Maria has not been herself really, not since just before she broke her wrist anyway. It was as if...as if she... wants, perhaps, needs something-" Em paused, trying to think of how she would describe their friend.

"What do you mean?"

"Well, she has always been a bit...rebellious and needing something that was just hers in her life," Em said. "Unlike me , who is so content to just be your stay-at-home partner."

Mel stopped and gently swatted her.

"You are not 'just' my stay-at-home partner. You are a wonderful talented woman, who is a great homemaker and now business manager of the photography club. It's become much more successful since you joined them. Babe...you are happy, aren't you?" Mel seemed unsure for a minute and it touched Em that Mel was still able to show her vulnerable side to her.

"Yes, of course, I am," she said. "I feel I have found my niche and role here. But Maria...since she broke her wrist over the surfing incident..." Em trailed off, wincing slightly even though the incident was months back. She continued hastily, trying to erase the memory of the sensation of tingling pain in her bottom. Em seldom needed any spanking or discipline ,but when she did it was hard and thorough.

"She seemed slightly preoccupied. I'd say she was unhappy about something as she is generally such an upbeat person-I don't know-" Em continued.

"Hmm..." Mel thought over Emma's words and then Marty's phone call. There was definitely a story behind this.

They released hands as the path neared and she stood back to let Em go in front of her.

"Perhaps you need to speak to her, or I could try and discuss it when we are training," Mel said.

"Perhaps. I'll arrange a lunch date with her and Gemma to see if she'll open up to us," Em said.

"Great," Mel said. She decided to let Marty know that Em and Gemma were worried about Maria. If they were unable to coax out what was worrying Maria, then when their training sessions started she would try and find out what was bothering their quirky friend. It interested her that it was Marty who had phoned for the sessions and not Maria herself.

The two of them walked in silence, absorbing the sights and sounds around them. The trees were thick and green. One would expect a deep silence in such coolness but the sound of birds was distinct and the undergrowth rustled in constant movement reminding them that wildlife was ever present, if seldom seen.

Walking back after a couple of hours, they noticed movement below them. A flash of neon orange trainers moved in time to the muted black color of the leggings and sports top above them. The black bobbed hair was unmistakable.

"That looks like Maria," Mel said. "I thought she only ran in the mornings."

Em nodded. Maria generally helped out with the lunch crowd and set up for the evening opening time. She was heading away from the town toward the longer stretch of woodland that bordered the far end of the lake.

"I might join her," Em said.

Mel debated. "Okay babe. I'll watch until you've safely joined her and then you can walk back together."

Emma wanted to protest that waiting to see if she caught up with Maria was not necessary but knew better. She instead welcomed the caring concern her partner had for her and set off, cutting downward and to the left. Mel watched her until she saw Em was not that far behind Maria and then set off to the right toward the town.

She decided to go and see Marty to better understand what was wanted from the personal training sessions. It would have helped to have spoken to Maria but a good starting point would be with the person who had phoned her.

Em panted. Maria was running faster than her usual jogging stride. Em called out and was surprised when Maria stopped, turning almost guiltily. She had seemed so focused that she had doubted that Maria would hear her.

"Hi honey," she said. "I saw you from above. Can I join you?"

"Of course," Maria said, relaxing. She had felt pulled to see the empty wooden cabins and shops again. Her run was much later due to her 'session' with Marty. She had felt guilty leaving Marty with the lunch crowd but the staff they had was more than capable of managing.

"You normally run much earlier."

"Yeah, I know," she said, not elaborating.

"Honey, Maria…come on! We've been friends for almost three years now. Is anything wrong?"

"Why do people keep asking me that?" Maria snapped, kicking up the dust with her trainer in frustration. Em lifted an eyebrow.

"Maybe because of reactions like that," she said.

Maria laughed.

"I want to show you something," she said.

Em was intrigued. They jogged comfortably together until they came to the clearing along the shore of the far end of the lake. It was ten minutes from town and not an area she often came to. The wooden cabins were quaint in their isolation and still except for the continual sound of bird life. It was tranquil and calm.

"It's a beautiful area," Em said. "I always wondered why the original owners left."

"I think they emigrated or moved to one of the cities. I remember there was talk of one of the children being ill," Maria said. She had walked to one small cabin shop, its sign still hanging outside, lightly bounding up the two wooden stairs to the porch.

"Look," she said, peering through the intact glass door.

Em pressed her face against the glass. The interior was bare but the sunlight shone through a window making dust motes dance like little creatures from another realm and she could easily imagine what it had been like when it was open. Her business mind clicked into action. She turned, surveying the other wooden cabins.

"I was..." Maria stopped. "What do you think...?"

"Yes-?" Emma took her friend's hands ,trying to coax the words from her.

"Honey, what-" Her mind whirled with different scenarios. Was Maria trying to leave Marty and move in here?

"Well-can you see it...as...well, as a studio for...me or us? Our photography and Gemma's art?" Maria blurted it out. Her eyes lit up, even though her words were stammered out. Em watched her, thinking. She could definitely see Gemma's pastels on the walls and Maria's black and white prints and colorful images of the lake. She wondered if these were her own thoughts or if she had been captured by Maria's infectious spirit, as often happened.

"I can," she said slowly.

Maria's shoulder sagged slightly as if relieved by her answer. Her words tripped over themselves as she spoke; how she had felt she needed something-something different, something she was passionate about other than the restaurant.

Em pulled her down beside her on one of the steps and listened. When she finished talking, Maria laid her head against her and Em smiled affectionately, patting her on the top of her head. Her fiery friend had such a vulnerable side.

"It's a fantastic idea," she said.

"Do you really think so?" Maria said. "What if-what if…"

"What if what?"

"Nothing…"

"No…come on…out with it!" Em injected a slight sternness to her tone hoping it would help Maria open up further. Maria responded well to other people taking charge when she was overwhelmed by her feelings. She seemed so nervous about it.

"Well, what if…what if Marty thinks I'm ungrateful or that I want to leave her? For five years we have built up her restaurant together. I know it was fine before I arrived but now it's really flourishing and she has literally shared everything with me."

Em nodded. She could see where Maria's thinking was coming from but she also knew Marty and was able to view both her friends objectively.

"She would be happy that you had your own dreams and needs," she said.

Maria grimaced.

"I don't think so. I was such a mess when she met me. I feel as if I am turning my back on all she has given me."

Em turned, lifting her chin to force her to look into her sincere eyes.

"No, you are not," she said. "You are improving on what she has given you."

Maria fell silent, mulling over Em's words.

"Is this why you have been so unhappy?"

"I have not been unhappy!"

"Well...pensive then," Emma conceded.

"Maybe, but I only saw this yesterday and I felt such a pull toward it.

I was thinking it might attract tourists and townsfolk out this way. It's only a ten-minute walk."

Emma nodded. She could see the area attracting tourists but it had to have something more than one studio to offer them.

A coffee shop and souvenir store would flourish here. There definitely was great potential in this area. She felt excited. Her head spun with business ideas.

"I think it would take some planning. What about involving Gerry? He might have some ideas."

Maria perked up. Gerry was the leader of the town photography club and was very creative with a previous high-flying career behind him. He also had connections with the local municipality. Then she slumped forward.

"I can't. I need to speak to Marty and I just can't. I tried today and have ended up having to have personal training sessions with your Mel."

Emma laughed at her woebegone expression.

"So that's what happened," she said.

"I sort of-had to say I was unhappy about my body."

Emma laughed again.

"Well, you can do with getting some proper exercise training and not overdoing things until you get the courage to speak truthfully to Marty. Mel is good at training but she takes no nonsense."

"I know," Maria said. "I am going to try to cancel."

"I wouldn't do that if I were you. Try it for a month and that way everyone will be happy."

"Except me-no insult to Mel," she said hastily. Em grinned.

"Come on, let's look around some more."

Maria relaxed and they wandered around, discussing various potential ideas. Perhaps other businesses, such as local hotels might want to help revive the area as well, Em mused.

They walked back companionably arm in arm.

"Don't say anything please, not even to Mel...not just yet." Maria said.

"Okay, but how about we include Gemma? She might want to be involved because of her paintings,"

"As long as she keeps it quiet. She's currently in the thrall of her newfound relationship depth. If Ava asks her anything she'll never be able to keep quiet."

Em laughed. She and Mel did not have as deep a domestic discipline relationship as Maria and now obviously Gemma. That suited her fine but she could well understand the pull both of her friends felt toward it with their personality structures.

Maria went back to work determined to carry on as per normal. Her heart dropped slightly when she saw Mel there chatting with Marty.

"Hi babe, we were just talking about you. Good run?"

"Yup," Maria said.

"Has Em gone back home?" Mel asked

Maria nodded.

"I'll see you at the gym tomorrow at 8 a.m. sharp and we'll discuss your goals then."

"Er...about that..." Maria started.

"She'll be there," Marty said, getting up and putting her arm around Maria.

Maria smiled faintly. Great! She really had no option but to go along with this.

Mel laughed inwardly. Maria's face transparently showed her emotions. This idea was certainly not hers. She would enjoy training Maria and in the process hopefully help both her friends.

CHAPTER 8

Maria arrived promptly at the gym and Mel took this as a good sign. They chatted about what Maria was hoping to achieve. As Maria stuttered and stammered something about 'toning up,' it was clear to Mel that she had no real intention of working out.

This was going to be fun to play out, she decided. She suggested they start with a body assessment and fitness test. Maria looked slightly bored but agreed. She waved to someone across the gym and her mouth curved into an attractive smile.

Mel turned to see who Maria had waved at. Charlie was training two women. They were not local, so were most likely tourists hoping to try and get fit during their break. She knew Charlie had water sports on that afternoon and the clients she was training were private and not through the central booking system. She let it go and concentrated on Maria.

Charlie set the two women to complete three sets of pushups alternating with planks and then went over to Maria. The two women had an easy and affectionate bond. They were both naturally flirty, but had not crossed the boundary into an actual sexual act.

"What are you doing here, honey?" she said, eyeing Maria in her usual suggestive manner. "Not that it's not good to see you. I've just never seen you here." Her eyes roved over Maria's Lycra clad body, appreciating her figure. Maria laughed and hugged her.

"It WAS Marty's idea," she said, forgetting that Mel was listening.

"Really?" Mel said, deciding to stir the pot slightly. "I understood from Marty, indeed from you yourself a short while ago that you wanted to get fitter and tone your body."

"Oh yes...er...that's right." Mel caught Charlie's eye and they grinned.

"Well, let's get on with it then," she said.

Charlie smiled and tapped Maria's bottom gently.

"Best get on with it-though don't tone this too much." She let her hand slide over the curved buttock and with a naughty grin sauntered off.

Maria ducked her head shyly. Charlie was an incorrigible flirt. Mel pursed her lips. She was not sure she liked what she was seeing. She might have a word with Charlie if this continued.

If there was any tension between Marty and Maria, she did not want Charlie's suggestiveness making things worse.

Mel weighed and measured Maria's body fat level which was within normal limits. She did a cardio-vascular fitness test which was also good due to Maria's daily running routine. She really could only offer weight training. This would strengthen her muscles and firm her body. It would be harder with Maria as she naturally tended toward a leaner physique with a fine bone structure that would not easily build muscle bulk.

"Maria, honey, what do you really want? A more muscular physique? I'm not sure it would suit you-" She tread carefully not wanting her words to hurt the woman in front of her.

Maria flushed. "Are you saying that-?" She broke off thinking of Marty. She certainly did not want to be more muscular. But she could not think of a way out of this.

"I want to get ripped…just a teeny bit-not bulky." she finished.

"Okay," Mel nodded. Her eyes searched Maria's face. "You would tell me if something was wrong, wouldn't you?" she slipped her arm around her friend's shoulders.

"Yes, yes, of course," Maria snapped, shrugging her off. "Let's get on with it. I wish everyone would stop treating me like there is something wrong."

Mel resisted the temptation to swat her and decided to let her work out her irritation during exercise.

They spent the next hour testing Maria's weight strength and doing a full body workout. Maria's limbs were shaking at the end of the session.

"Good work!" Mel said. She had worked out alongside her and a sheen of sweat covered her skin. Maria had a small smile on her face. Perhaps the combination of workout and praise would do her good, Mel thought.

She made sure to remind Maria why working out daily would not tone but rather break down muscle. Working out three times a week would be best. She suggested Em join them in the next session. It might make Maria more relaxed, she thought. Maria's smile brightened to a grin.

"That would be great," At least it would help ease the boredom of lifting weights and pretending to enjoy it, Maria thought. Mel watched her closely. It would be good for Em as well, she thought. She focused too much on writing and her work with the photography club. Doing some exercise might help ease her headaches as well. Em would see sense and if not, well, she'd help her to.

Maria made her way to the changing room. She felt slightly better but still rebellious and pent up. If only she could chat to Marty without hurting her feelings. It did not occur to her that Marty might understand her needs and not feel hurt.

Charlie lounged against the doorway.

"What are you really doing here?"

"None of your business!" she said, unable to stop the words slipping from her lips. It was so unlike her. "Sorry-just a situation I don't feel I can get out of." Charlie looked at her. Her eyes were generally unreadable but now they shone with compassion and empathy.

"Anything I can help you with?"

"No." Maria said. She exhaled and leant against her friend. Charlie hugged her. For one brief moment Maria relaxed into her, and she automatically lifted her head giving in to the natural attraction she felt for Charlie. Instinctively Charlie leaned down and kissed her. Maria's lips searched Charlie's, her mouth opening, finding release in that chemical sensation.

Mel opened the changing room door. She started and then gave them privacy as they pulled apart. Charlie ran a hand through her hair.

"Sorry," she said, her tone of voice indicating that she really was not. Maria hugged her, knowing Charlie well. She was naturally a very physical person.

"It's okay. It was me as well. You know that I feel, well something...but I-"

"I know," Charlie said. She understood Maria was settled intimately with Marty. Charlie was unable to settle down though, enjoying the intimate company of many women as opposed to one. She had occasionally felt a desire to commit but a part of her knew it was unrealistic. It was the consistent company she craved, as opposed to the romantic liaisons. It was also what had made her feel unsettled recently.

"Are you going to tell Marty?" She felt slightly uneasy. Despite being a dominant woman herself, she fully remembered Marty's firm hand of guidance just a few days back.

"No," Maria said. "She'd understand-I think...but I'm sorry, I don't know what came over me."

"Girl, something is bothering you. We've all seen it."

"Well...yes-less so now though. I spoke to Emma."

"That's good."

Charlie gave her two hard swats that stung. Maria bit her lip. She would not give Charlie the satisfaction of seeing the jolt.

"Sort your mind out," she said. She kissed her chastely on the lips and turned away. Maria ached between her legs as Charlie's lithe form backed off and disappeared through the door. Charlie was so sexy.

Exiting the change room, Charlie's eyes flit straight to her two clients who were roughly her age and were being quite flirty. Charlie was convinced the women were straight but had no qualms about meeting their bisexual curiosity if they seemed up for it.

Mel waited until Maria came out. She met Maria's eyes, her expression serious.

"Either me or you. If it's me I'll be spanking you first and then speaking to Marty." she said. Maria knew immediately what she meant.

"I'll tell her, but it meant nothing...I mean, well it does but-"

"Honey, you are being reckless. Please speak to Marty."

"I spoke to Emma-" Maria said. Mel nodded. That was a good step. She'd find out what was going on. But Maria needed to let Marty know her response to Charlie as well.

Marty will understand, Maria told herself. Her wife was

generally open- minded but she did not really know how she'd react to her actually kissing Charlie. They had agreed to a closed relationship which was something that Maria had requested, even though occasionally she felt the stirrings of desire around other women. She knew Marty's history of having lived with two submissives before she met Maria. Perhaps it would be better to say nothing.

She saw Mel watching and dismissed the thought. Honesty would be best.

CHAPTER 9

Marty went through to the kitchen. Maria was standing at the thigh high counter with a cup of coffee. Her vest top bared most of her shoulders and Marty's body responded with a sexual energy that was part animal instinct, love and attraction for her partner, and partly a form of control to show her she would not tolerate her cheating with others, no matter how innocent it seemed.

Maria had spoken to her the night before about the incident in the gym. She had walked away, not wanting to overreact but think first. She knew that Maria had previously felt attracted to other people, as she herself had, but they had never acted on it. She would not be averse to it, if it was something they spoke about and both agreed to, but not something that happened behind each other's backs.

Maria turned to face her, the words fading on her lips as she saw the sexual hunger and dominance in her wife's eyes. The effect was powerful and erotic. Her nipples contracted, jutting out sharply against the thin cotton vest. Marty strode forward removing the mug from her hand in one smooth movement. She turned back and roughly pulled her wife's skirt up and her panties down. As Marty lifted her onto the counter, Maria automatically wrapped her legs around Marty's body. Placing her hands firmly beneath Maria's buttocks she pulled her closer, forcing her thighs wider than they already were and ensuring that her clitoris was held firmly against her own clothed body. Maria's hands pulled at her jeans, trying to remove the offending material that prevented her from feeling her wife's bare skin against her center.

Marty did not want to lose the control she currently had over her wife, but she stepped back briefly to remove her jeans. She needed to feel the slick wetness of her wife's desire and submission against her lower stomach. She moved back into position and felt Maria thrust against her. She nipped her neck lightly, intentionally grazing the skin and listened with pleasure as Maria yelped in surprise and brief pain. Maria clutched Marty's back, realizing that her wife was taking control in the way she did only when she felt Maria had been completely out of line.

She tried to gain some control by slipping her hands under Marty's T-shirt and bringing her hands around to her breasts. When Marty did not stop her, she grew bolder and pulled the T-shirt over her head. The plain black bra followed, falling to the floor like a silken scarf drifting down in abandonment. As she lowered her mouth down her wife's neck she felt the back of her head grasped and guided to the erect nipple of one breast. Her mouth pulled on the peak, nipping and grazing it with her teeth. Marty stiffened, the sensation running straight through to her clitoris. She wanted to take her wife...and she would, but in her way. She moved Maria's head to the other breast.

"Suck," she said. Her voice had a hard ring to it and Maria glanced up. Marty's eyes were pools of black desire and intent that sent a shiver down Maria's back. She was sure she would feel pleasure but knew it would not take much for Marty to exert a harder pressure bordering on pain. She knew she needed to submit to her wife.

"I am going to fuck you hard," Marty's voice was low in her ear. Maria wanted that but she knew she was walking a fine line. Marty had definitely processed the kiss she had told her about yesterday with Charlie. "Babe-" she tried hesitantly. "I did not-" She did not manage to say anything further, as she felt herself swung off the counter. A hard hand landed on one bottom cheek, inflaming every swollen sense she had. The hand grasped her spanked buttock and the fingers inched toward a very sensitive place.

"I've never entered this side of you." Maria jumped. Those were not words she expected to hear even though she sensed Marty's mood.

"Go to our bedroom!" Maria tried to say something again but catching the look from her wife, she walked toward the door. She swayed her hips slightly, meaning to taunt her. She knew it was wrong to tease her that way but felt she could not move off like a silly chastened housewife. She could feel Marty behind her, the heat and sexual tension radiating off her.

Once on the bed she removed her vest top, leaving her bra on and lay down, her pupils dilating as she watched her wife go to the drawer and fit herself with the strap on. She watched her wife lube it and come toward her. She leant over her.

"Open your legs," Maria's legs opened and she panted. Although she fought against it, the dark desire to be claimed and taken was uncontrollable. Marty leant over her and roughly pulled the material of her bra down, pushing her breasts up and exposing the nipples. The material felt harsh as it caught the swollen peaks. She reached her hands toward Marty, slipping one hand between her legs. Her hand was slapped away and Marty's head descended over the breast; her teeth nipped each aching bud the resultant sting of pain causing a further pool of wetness between her legs. She whimpered, her breath catching. Clutching her wife's back for support, she focused on not surrendering too quickly. Marty pulled back slightly.

"Wider," she instructed, her voice low and husky but firm. Maria opened her legs. She saw Marty grasp the dildo and guide it into her. She braced herself against the anticipated pain as it entered, but her wife had judged her correctly. Her center was wide and wet and easily accommodated the slender dildo. Marty leant forward.

"Open your mouth," she breathed. Marty's tongue invaded Maria's mouth and the sensation of being taken by her wife vaginally and orally overwhelmed her. Her pelvis lifted and strained against her wife as Marty settled into a hard rhythm. Maria knew her wife would not stop until she came and she concentrated on letting the sensations flood her. Her clitoris hit against her wife's mons as she thrust and her nipples grazed against Marty's breasts with force. Her mouth was plundered by the hot, dominant tongue and lips and she felt her inner muscles contracting in orgasm.

"Uh huh...uh huh," her sounds of desire grew louder as she came, arching up and down as the waves of release filled her entire pelvis. She loved the sensation but the total sated desire she felt from her wife's fingers was missing. She also longed for the intense external release of her clitoris being thoroughly taken by Marty.

Marty waited whilst her body shuddered, then gently pulled the dildo out, un-strapping it from her thighs.

She did not give Maria time to fully recover and flipped her onto her stomach. "Kneel!" she commanded. Maria's body immediately leapt to attention again. She felt an intense desire to pleasure her wife though.

"Babe-let me-" she started. She heard the swat before it landed but was unable to move fast enough to avoid it. She immediately obeyed; her buttocks elevated. Marty pushed her shoulders down.

"Stay like that!" She leant over her from the back and, bringing her hands around and underneath Maria's body, caressed her breasts.

Maria cried out. The sensation was intense and she pushed back into her wife. The caressing hands disappeared and she felt a hand massaging her buttock cheeks. The fingers flickered over her anal opening and Maria pulled herself foreword. This was something she was not sure of. Her hips were pulled back.

"Who are you faithful to?"

"I...you..."

"So what was yesterday about?"

"Nothing-" Maria said. "A moment of lust-um-comfort..."

Marty understood her wife. She did not feel that they could not be attracted to other people. But acting on it, without prior agreement and especially in a public place, was completely out of order.

Marty's hand was forcefully caressing Maria's swollen clitoris. "How are you going to remember that?"

"It was not...I mean-" Maria gasped as the fingers left their caressing and started ringing her anus. It felt pleasant and the tension left her body. She did feel vulnerable, though, in the elevated, open position.

"Relax." Marty slapped her buttock. Maria consciously relaxed her muscles. She felt her wife's fingers move and enter into the area that had never before been entered. The pleasure gave way to a painful yet warm sensation. She bucked up.

"Back now," Marty said. Her voice was not harsh. It was unyielding as if she were determined to show Maria just how helpless she was in her wife's love and lust.

Maria's breath caught in her throat, sounding almost like a sob. It was not fearful, just the resultant sensation of completely yielding to another's will. She lowered herself, aware that the sensation was no longer unpleasant but full. One hand slipped back around to her clitoris and she felt her wife's comforting pelvis nestled securely against her buttocks. The finger thrust gently. Marty debated entering two fingers but knew that Maria needed to adjust her mind and body to the first intrusion. She kept the rhythm up until she felt Maria's clitoris swelling and slipping on her fingers as her desire grew until she was gasping and sobbing uncontrollably. Her finger was now sliding easily in and out her anus.

She thrust harder, wanting her to feel pleasure and just enough pain at the same time whilst conquering her. Just as she felt her starting to come, she pulled out and turned Maria onto her back. She straddled her thighs, pinning the sides of her hips.

"Tell me about Charlie," she said. Maria's breath was ragged, she was full of need. "Tell me."

"It was nothing!" she shouted. "I was…I was…I wanted…"

"What?" Marty said. "What?"

"I wanted…Charlie…no….I mean….someone else…No…"

Marty turned and slapped her thigh hard. The sharp smack jolted Maria and tears filled her eyes.

"I wanted…I want to…I want my own career…I want to start… an art studio…I want to leave the restaurant… not leave it…I mean just have my own passion…" She sagged down. Her desire deflated in her confession.

Marty lay down next to her. She pulled her sobbing wife into her arms.

"Honey," she said, her voice soft and relief flooding her. "Is that what this is all about? Why you have been so worried and prickly?"

"Yes..."

"Why didn't you tell me?"

"I couldn't. I thought you might..."

"What?"

"Hate me-"

"Hate you?" Marty blinked in surprise. She repeated the words softly, almost painfully. "Hate you? I could never hate you!"

"Yes you could! For-for wanting something different than you-for wanting something different from everything you have made me a part of..."

"Honey..." Marty struggled for words. Had she made her wife feel beholden to her? She had tried to include her and make her feel part of her life; the main part of which was her restaurant. Perhaps the love she had for her bar and restaurant and the desire she had had to have Maria feel part of this had overshadowed Maria's own career and passions.

"Do you feel you owe me something?" She finally asked.

"No-yes. You helped me turn my life around and you have given me everything-and made a part of everything..." she sobbed.

Marty held her and listened.

"I feel I am being so ungrateful. I should want what you want-"

Marty's thoughts whirled. She felt anguish at the confusion and distress Maria had obviously been in. Her personality would not have helped. Not wanting to hurt others and not being able to vent her thoughts and feelings would have made her torment larger and more unbearable than it needed to be.

"No, no, honey...Perhaps that is what you needed then, but not now. It's good and healthy for you to have your own dreams and passions. I have loved having you with me as we changed the décor and grew the restaurant. I know you enjoyed it whilst that was being done, but there is nothing wrong with you growing beyond that and moving on to something you love or going back to something that you used to enjoy."

"So you don't hate me then?" Maria sat up, her eyelashes wet as she looked at her wife, half relieved and half indignantly.

"No, of course not! Why would I? We need to also concentrate on your dreams and as you never said anything, I had no idea."

"So I wasted all that time worrying-for nothing." Maria sounded almost annoyed and a lot more like her cheeky old self.

Marty grinned.

"We are going to discuss this in-depth but for now I believe you have some chores to do." The sight of Maria's slender body with its full breasts and still wet pubic curls excited her.

Maria smiled sweetly, and pushing her wife back, she trailed her mouth down her breasts and stomach reaching the top of her legs. She kissed and licked the inside of each thigh.

Marty groaned. She guided Maria's head toward her center. Maria debated teasing her wife further but knowing the mood she had been in, wisely decided to follow her lead. Her mouth covered her vulva and she nuzzled deeply. She slipped her tongue inside the entrance of her vagina and felt her wife stiffen. Marty was near to coming. She pulled out and focused on her clitoris, her lips teasing and her tongue continuing to lick, but shying away from the movements she knew would give Marty release. Marty held her head closer.

"Again," she said. Maria gave in and her searching tongue again entered the opening of Marty's vagina. Her one hand held her wife's pelvis, and her other fingers pressed hard against the taut clitoris. She worked her tongue until she felt Marty's body give way and her exhaled breaths signal her climax.

Marty pulled her up to lie on her shoulder. Maria's sated body curled into her wife's sturdy one and she closed her eyes. Marty felt her wife's eyelashes on the area above her breast like butterfly wings as she fell asleep. She cradled the dark head gently, her heart relieved. She should have done this sooner, she thought. After a brief sleep they would tackle this head on.

She left Maria sleeping and went to sit back at the bar where she did her best thinking and work. They would fully discuss what Maria needed and was thinking of doing and achieving. She would help her reach that goal just as Maria had helped her to improve on her dream of creating the success that the restaurant and bar had become.

CHAPTER 10

Looking through the lounge window, Maria smiled in contentment. Three months had passed since the intense release of her feelings and the explanation of her needs to her wife. In that short time so much had changed.

The direction she faced was toward the area of the small cabins. She finally owned one. A small pleasure of excitement passed through her when she thought about it. Even more exciting was that it was not only her that owned one; the town photography club had purchased one and would set up their display there. The club had the town's municipal support as it provided tourist income in the prints the club sold.

It had taken longer than expected although the owners had been easily traced. There had been so many financial and legal hoops to jump through. Maria was grateful for Em's assistance in that regard. She had liaised with the town municipality and their lawyers, for both Maria and the photography club.

The town municipality had had to negotiate the way forward as the area fell under the town's municipal restriction.

That was behind them now and the thrill of seeing her name on the title deeds had lifted her spirits.

There was still a lot to be done for the entire area, but from her own perspective all she had to do was move in and create her own unique space. Her idea seemed to have grown into a project which the whole town wanted to get involved in.

As tourism grew in the regional area, the town community agreed it was a good idea to increase their attractions. Maria knew that some of the smaller hotels were looking toward expanding and were thinking of building new hotels. That would be a few years down the line, however, and she decided not to worry over whether her cabin view would be impacted.

She had to live for the present and strive to achieve what she wanted to.

She had the support of her two close friends daily and Charlie also passed by, teasing and flirting with them. Em and Gemma were heavily involved in the photography club move and Maria had invited Gemma to display her art work alongside her photography.

Although grateful to have been asked, Gemma had seemed reluctant and it had taken a lot of coaxing. Maria had not fully realized how insecure Gemma felt about her work. She had numerous pieces of her own photography but felt a keen interest in artwork. Gemma's pastel landscape scenes captured the eye. She had a few portraits and her talent was undeniable. Gemma was content having her few pieces in the photography club where her work was placed amongst all the other work. That they tended to stand out, not being photographs, went unnoticed by her.

Once Maria had managed to convince her, she entered into the planning with creative thought and enjoyment.

Maria had experienced a few hare-brained moments. The thought of owning a little studio to display her photographs resulted in her photographing everything that moved and quite a lot that did not.

Locals had gotten used to seeing her pop up at various times, snapping them drinking coffee or playing backgammon in the open spaces, the lake shimmering in the background. She had been chased off by a couple of tourists amorously kissing outside the town's small museum. The image of their entwined bodies leaning against the old grey stone work beneath the museum sign had captured her imagination.

One day she had laboriously rowed out to the middle of the lake with Gemma, planning to take photos of the town from the lake. They had got caught in a current and the resulting unsteadiness had Gemma falling overboard. Charlie ended up helping them and she delivered a scolding which ended abruptly when she told Maria to stop being such an idiot and 'pull herself together '. Maria hardly listened to her. This was an area for growth with no limitations and no one was going to tell her otherwise.

A week later she decided they needed to start planning what they wanted to focus on for their opening exhibition. The photography club was also going to exhibit that same day and she wanted something that was a cut above the ordinary. She already had a few photographs up and allowed anyone who wandered around to view them. The exhibition would be the official opening, though.

"You could exhibit us-naked," Charlie said laconically, as she listened to them batting ideas back and forth one day. She was smoking, her eyes half closed in relaxation. It was an attractive pose and Maria's stomach muscles contracted.

Em almost choked on her coffee. Maria immediately jumped up. The idea appealed to her. Her photography was mostly black and white landscapes. Black and white photos of women's bodies would be amazing, especially if surrounded by Gemma's paintings of the same. She bet the photography club would not be doing anything like that.

Gemma blushed. "I'd love to, but..."

"But what?" Maria said.

"Well-it's quite intimate..."

"Gemma! it's art..."

"I know. I mean, would it be okay with..."

"Of course," Maria said. She presumed Marty would be okay with it, but probably only after discussing it. Whether Ava or Mel would be, well that was for Em and Gemma to decide, but she hoped that speaking confidently would allay any concerns they might have.

"I could work from photographs," Gemma suggested. "But how would you get Em in?"

"Leave me out of it, please," Em said. The idea of nude posing did not appeal to her, but she felt intrigued from a business perspective. Nude photos and paintings would certainly appeal to many people. Her foremost concern was what it would feel like for their respective partners to see their nude bodies on display to the public. Although she belonged to the photography club, she was not particularly creative and her interest lay more in managing the club's finances and forging the links between the town municipality and their club. She had gained the support of the municipality once they had started a dedicated shop in the town to sell photographs to tourists. It had been her idea not long after she and Mel had moved to the town. She also enjoyed writing and had recently been freelancing for the town's magazine. In fact, her mind was already composing an article about the exhibition.

As she mulled over the idea, she drowned out her friends; chatter. Mel's birthday was coming up. A nude painting of her and Mel as a personal gift was appealing and she decided to approach

Gemma privately. Perhaps she could get a photograph of Mel and Gemma could use that to add to Em's. It was hard to give Mel something she valued as she was not a materialistic person. This was ideal.

She was brought back to the present by Charlie laughing.

"So, what about it?" Charlie asked. They were all looking at her. Her eyes were sparkling with mischief and daring.

Em hesitated again. She felt too body conscious to be sitting around naked with her friends.

"You all could. I could help by…" Em said

"No! All of us or none of us," Maria said. She jutted her chin out slightly. Charlie laughed. She knew that look well.

Em nodded slowly. She did want to make the exhibition a success for Maria. A good, affectionate friend would do that… surely? She shivered slightly. She was not sure Mel would agree with that thought.

"Guess we'll all be posing then," Gemma said. "I think we should discuss, well, at least mention…"

"No," Maria said decisively. "We'll just do it." Em looked down, taking a deep breath. Okay, she was joining them and she was going to have an intimate painting of her and Mel. A niggling feeling told her Mel would not appreciate her nude body being displayed for the public. Knowing Ava as she did, she did not think she would appreciate Gemma's nude body being displayed either. Best not to think about it too much, she reckoned.

Charlie got up, a wicked grin lighting up her attractive features.

"Sure…let's start now." She opened the buttons of her shirt and smirked as Maria shrieked. Charlie laughed and buttoned up again.

"Tell me the date and time and I'll be here." She sauntered out, rolling her eyes as Ava walked in.

"What are you ladies up to?" she asked, smiling at the noise and excited atmosphere.

"Best ask this lot," Charlie said.

Gemma blushed bright red as she walked up to Ava, giving her a gentle kiss.

"Hi babe," she said. "What are you doing all the way out here?"

"Slow day," Ava said, "so I decided to walk up to meet you. Mel asked me to deliver a message to Em." She turned to the poised blonde-haired woman. "She said she's working late this evening as she has a late personal training session."

Em smiled, but her mind was working overtime. This was the third time in two weeks Mel had messaged to say she was late.

"And she said not to worry about supper." Ava watched her closely as she spoke. Although Emma was mostly sensible and poised, there was vulnerability beneath her confidence. She certainly was not the same as outspoken Maria and shy Gemma whose submissive tendencies showed naturally. She wanted to be sure Em felt okay.

"Thank you, Ava," Em said calmly. "I'll head home."

"Say here with us," Ava said, linking her arm. Em was a stabilizing influence for Gemma and helped her out of her shell. She felt a genuine fondness for her as well as responsible for her safety, as she did for all of her friends.

"No thanks," Em said. "I'm going to walk home, have some alone time if Mel is getting home late." The words flowed easily but Ava could see the unease beneath them.

"No, stay, honey," she said. "You will walk home with us later." The words were gentle yet firm and Em felt relief that the decision was taken from her. Maria came over to hug her, sensitive to her mood.

"I should go," she said. "Marty might want my help."

"No, she won't," Ava said. "She's fine. You ladies continue and I'll rustle up some food." She held up a basket showing she had brought supplies.

Gemma lowered her eyes. She definitely did not want to continue talking about nude paintings, or nude anything for that matter, in front of Ava.

Maria took over the conversation and they continued discussing the layout of the cabin and potential placement of the exhibitions. When Ava returned with food and a locally sourced bottle of red wine, they slipped into easy conversation and the four women enjoyed the afternoon together.

For all her hesitancy, Gemma's mind was working overtime. She could visualize what she wanted to create but needed time to think.

"Next week then," she said. Maria nodded in approval. She might not have nodded such approval if she had known what Gemma was thinking. Maria had already envisioned scenes: black and white nudes with strategic draping of scarves or other such items.

Gemma's mind raced creatively, busy with the paintings she planned. They certainly had no impediments to the use of imagination. The women would be drawn and photographed in their full and splendid nudity.

CHAPTER 11

The week passed in a blur for the women. Maria helped out at the restaurant although it was not needed. Marty welcomed her presence but reminded her that she fully understood she had her studio to get ready. Maria affectionately rubbed the top of her head as she passed.

"Come on, you know you love me being around. Who else would drive you crazy?" In truth, although the situation was working well, Maria still felt a lingering sense of guilt and she wanted to make sure Marty did not tire herself out, which is what she used to do when they first met.

The restaurant and bar were the major part of her life and as her passion was cooking, it was not unusual for Marty to work long hours. Maria worried about not being there to make sure Marty took a break during the day.

Marty hugged her when she voiced her concern, her heart melting with affection for the woman she loved.

"Babe, I'll be fine."

"Well, if you're not, I'll know. Perhaps I'll be taking that wooden spoon to your backside," Maria said, giggling and grabbing the wooden spoon from her hand where they both stood in the restaurant kitchen. Marty was preparing the soup starter for lunch.

"Get off with you," she said. Her heart felt light at seeing Maria happy and the joking affection her wife displayed. It was true; she did love having her around, but it was better seeing Maria happy and energized again.

Maria kept deliberately pushing to the back of her mind any doubt she might have about the upcoming photo shoot. She knew Marty wouldn't forbid her but that it might be best to at least inform her wife of their plans before she displayed their semi nude bodies. And, her inner voice said, the friends showing their naked bodies to each other.

Emma had spent a frustrating week trying to capture a shot of Mel naked. This was not easy as her photography skills were limited. In addition, trying to capture a nude image of her partner without her being aware was difficult. She eventually managed to get two photos. One was of Mel sleeping after a hard day at work, when she had showered and collapsed naked on the bed. She was lying on her back, one leg straight and the other slightly bent. In the second one she was walking naked from the shower, her attention focused on a text she was reading.

Gemma had become totally engrossed in her new project. Her ideas consumed her, and she was unfocused at part-time job at the museum. She spent her waking hours rearranging scenes in her head over and over and when not at work experimenting with various colors in oils and pastels. The women, she decided, would be shown going about their lives doing the work and activities that they loved...but naked.

Ava wondered what was happening to her girlfriend. She was used to Gemma's quietness but the faraway look in her eyes at times concerned her. She enquired if anything was wrong, to which Gemma answered "no" in a dreamy state. It was a dilemma for the dominant Ava who would have loved to have spanked her back to her usual self. However, as Gemma had not really done anything wrong, that would not have been fair.

At work, she asked Mel and Charlie if they had noticed anything unusual with the three friends. Mel said no, but she seemed thoughtful. Emma had been a bit furtive, she thought. Charlie laughed in her usual way.

"You imagine too much," she said. Her statement sounded confident and dismissive. Knowing how close Charlie was to all of them, Ava trusted her.

Charlie was looking forward to the photo session. The tourist season was winding down and she felt bored. Fewer women turned up to the gym and for adventure sports. The nude posing would be a welcome distraction.

She whistled, winked at Ava and Mel and said she had the morning off.

Ava laughed uneasily.

"Sometimes I don't know how to take Charlie," she said to Mel, who had known Charlie longer.

"She's a born flirter and a switch, never serious-but she does seem a bit too relaxed lately." Mel said thoughtfully. Charlie's easy answer had seemed evasive to her.

The group met up at agreed upon time at Maria's cabin studio. She had placed stools in various settings. The women, barring Charlie, felt self-conscious. Maria showed them the scarves and items she had readied to cover their strategic parts, hoping to relieve their understandable discomfort.

Charlie had already removed her clothes and sauntered out

from the back. She had an athletic, toned body and the other three women blushed. Maria swallowed. Charlie was hot. Best to get it done as soon as possible, she thought.

Maria discussed what she wanted and set about photographing. She hoped that her friends could see that, once behind the camera she was professional and dispassionate about their bodies.

"But you won't be in any of the photos," Em said, as Maria gently pushed her back on a stool, and instructed her to lift one foot onto the supporting rung, whilst draping a white scarf across her breasts. The ends of the scarf cleverly hid her pubic area whilst still displaying her hips and inner thighs.

"I will be," she said, "just not right now. I'll use the timer when it's my turn or Gemma can take them."

None of the women had posed before. Charlie was the most natural. Being completely secure in her body and with a photogenic air, she casually lounged in any position Maria asked her to.

Behind the camera Maria was professional and confident, seeing in front of her a subject that she wanted to showcase the beauty of. Her focus helped decrease the shyness of Gemma and Em.

They stopped for a break to try and ease the slight tension of the two women.

As they ate lunch, Maria asked Gemma what she planned to do with her paintings.

Surprisingly Gemma's voice was steady as she spoke.

"Well...For starters I don't want anything in the way. No props, no scarves; nothing, just your beautiful natural selves."

Charlie whistled.

"Wow! Never knew you had it in you, kitten," she said.

Gemma blushed.

"Do you mean fully naked?" Em asked bluntly and with slight shock.

"Yes."

"I can't!"

"Wait," Maria said, worried that Em would back out. "I'm sure Gem does not mean fully...well...exposed, do you?"

"Yes. I want to showcase what you all look like; you're breasts and well-" She stopped blushing. "I mean..."

Maria laughed.

"Give us an idea."

"I mean...one would see your...er...yes..."

Charlie's eyes glinted with humor. It was always the quiet ones.

"...Your...um...lady bits..."

The three women started laughing. Gemma was so sweet and funny trying to get her idea across.

"But not...not distastefully but yes...Plain to see," she finished lamely. "I will take photos and paint from those."

The three women stared at each other. The idea appealed to Maria and Charlie. Em felt it was wrong, but it was seldom that the shy Gemma was this forthcoming with her ideas. Her eyes lit up as if her very essence was on fire. She'd hate to be the one to extinguish that look. Maria saw her hesitation and pounced.

"Right, come then, Gem. Tell us where to stand and what you want us to do."

The woman took their stances as Gemma instructed. It was interesting to see the change in Gemma. She was confident and spoke easily. Her photographs were not like Maria's. It was as if she were looking at them from a completely different angle. Her focus was on letting the story show the strength of them as women from the environment they were in. She planned to use the bodies within the context of what the women liked doing, by painting in the lake, the adventure center as well as showcasing them rowing and hiking.

She knew her friends well and planned to photograph the activities later.

The poses were intensely intimate and open, although the activities were common to each woman.

Charlie had no problem lying on a bench, her tight thighs spread open as she simulated a bench press, her breasts arching upward and her intimate center exposed.

The paintings verged on erotica, however the activities the body engaged in and was surrounded by, would distract the viewer's eye from the bodies sexual elements.

In contrast, Maria's photos would focus on the woman's body itself, starkly in focus, just about decently covered with no distractions around it or in the background.

The door handle of the studio turned and the women leapt up trying to cover themselves, except for Charlie. She sauntered to the door completely naked.

"Don't open it," Maria squeaked. Charlie yanked it open.

"Yes?" she said. The woman on the other side, obviously a tourist judging by the bright red backpack she touted over one shoulder and a leaflet in one hand, colored as she took in the naked woman in front of her.

"Oh, I'm sorry," she said, "I thought this was an art..." Her voice faded away as she lowered her eyes from Charlie's breasts.

"It's a massage parlor," Charlie said laconically. "...And it's not open to the public yet." She closed the door and they heard the woman almost run off. Maria could not help laughing.

"Charlie, that was mean!" she said, half heartedly, scolding her.

"Time to carry on," Gemma said. "The natural light is changing." They responded to her obvious passion for the task and Gemma spent the next few hours continuing to contort their bodies into the poses she wanted.

Once she had exhausted every angle she could think of, they grabbed a bottle of wine from the small kitchenette at the back and sat around the counter discussing the session. Posing was not easy. Gemma had been so matter of fact though, that none of them had felt too embarrassed.

After the wine break Maria took the photos of Gemma, listening carefully to her instructions as to the focus of the shot.

Once they were finished, Maria and Charlie went to the small kitchen to pour some more wine.

Em took the chance to chat privately to Gemma, showing her the amateur photos she had takeN on her phone and asking if she would be able to do a painting from them. She could add Em to the scene from the photos she had taken of her, she suggested.

Blushing, she told her friend that she wanted it for their bedroom for Mel's birthday. Gemma smiled. It was an honor to be asked to do an intimate painting for her friend. Em felt relief when she saw Gemma viewing the photos in a purely professional manner. It helped ease her worry that Mel might not appreciate anyone else seeing her naked body no matter how close their circle of friends was.

Gemma thought the painting Em wanted would be different from what she was intending for Maria's exhibition. The focus would be the intimate and loving scene between her two friends using their nudity as bonding, as opposed to nudity being natural in any setting such as nature or work where the focus was the whole content.

Charlie and Em set off home, arms linked companionably. It was a different scene from the first time the two of them had met when Em had gotten lost on a hike and Charlie had come across her whilst taking a tourist group on a hike.

Maria and Gemma followed later, after discussing their ideas further. Waving goodbye to Gemma as they neared the town entrance, Maria entered the restaurant and bar.

There was an excited hum among the usual locals and a few of the tourists. As she walked through, she heard someone say, "A massage parlor? How interesting. It's not something I thought we'd ever see here. Something we need to try out, if it's true." One of the locals remarked that he had thought the area was for arts and crafts and cafes only. Maria's heart dropped.

"Massage parlor?" she queried, stopping by the table of the tourist who was discussing it.

"Yes, my wife was there earlier. Said there was a naked woman who answered the door. It's called Maria's Studio. Probably a front." Maria paled. She saw the local seated near the tourist turn and looked at her. It was an unoriginal name but the inspiration had not yet come for her to change it and she had needed a name for the deeds. The fact that someone thought it was a massage parlor was definitely not good for her reputation.

"Oh, I don't think so. Massage parlors were not part of the planning for that area," Maria said.

"Don't think so...what?" Marty said behind her.

"Oh, nothing-" Maria felt panicked. This was not what she needed right now.

"There's a-" the guy started again.

Maria pulled her away.

"Oh babe, I wanted to discuss something..."

"Wait a minute, please," Marty said. She did not want the customer to feel neglected. That was also unusual for Maria who was generally very polite to clients. Experience also told her that when Maria tried to get her attention publicly it was often to avoid some error she had made or hide some ill thought through scheme.

Maria slipped out, realizing Marty was not going to budge.

Marty listened to the customer explain about the massage parlor called Maria's Studio. She wanted to laugh and scream at the same time. What had Maria been up to now?

"Your Maria owns that, does she not?" the local at the next table said. "I must say I'm surprised-"

Marty cut him off kindly.

"There is no massage parlor. There has clearly been a misunderstanding."

"But-" the first tourist who had spoken looked disappointed and disbelieving at the same time. "My wife said a naked woman with skin the color of honey and blonde hair answered the door and that the room was packed with naked women." His voice seemed to portray disbelief and jealousy that his wife could describe another woman in

such sensual yet innocent terms.

Marty kept her face straight. She reiterated that it was probably a misunderstanding.

She continued working calmly for the rest of the afternoon. Skin the color of honey and blonde hair was most definitely Charlie. As for the naked women that could only have been Maria, Gemma and Em. As she worked she pondered how to handle it. She was not one to fly off the handle but would certainly deal with the issue that same day.

The first place to start would be with Maria, she decided. She ensured the main meals were ready for the evening and made her way to their home behind the restaurant. It was no surprise that Maria was not there. She might be at a photography class or going for a jog to hide out from Marty as long as she could. She dialed her mobile with no answer as expected. Marty decided to wait until 7 p.m. before contacting Maria again if she was not home. In the meantime she dialed Charlie's number.

Charlie answered promptly and from the laconic drawl in her voice and noise in the background it was clear she was on one of her numerous dates.

"What's up Marty?"

"What do you know about a massage parlor at Maria's studio?"

Charlie laughed.

"Just a bit of fun," she said. "A woman came to the door whilst we were busy and I told her it was a massage parlor."

"It's all over the town," Marty said. "We now have leering men wanting to book for the massage parlor. And what do you mean you were busy? Busy doing what?"

"Well, don't go blaming Maria," Charlie said, totally ignoring the last question. "You know that sometimes you are a bit too hard on her."

Marty ignored the mild chastisement. She knew her wife well and what best suited Maria's temperament. Charlie needed pulling into line.

"There was talk of naked women. Apparently the woman who answered the door had 'skin the color of honey' and was totally in the nude."

Charlie laughed again easily.

"Yeah, that was me. Again...don't blame your wife," she said. "I'm busy, Marty. I can chat to you about it tomorrow if you still feel like being anal and prudish."

Charlie hung up and Marty's palm itched. Charlie might be a switch and mostly lived her life as a top but she was the one person in their group that Marty felt needed a sharp correction in her life's path, more even than her own wife.

The mystery of how the studio had turned into a massage parlor was solved, but she needed to find out why they were naked in the studio. She had no qualms about Maria cheating as she trusted

Maria for all her flirty nature and the obvious attraction between Charlie and Maria. Hell, she herself felt attracted to Charlie!

At 7p.m Maria walked in. She must have been in the town photography club studio that had not yet moved to the new area as she had no yoga mat with her and was not dressed in jogging clothes.

"Been developing some photos," Maria said airily as she walked in. "Hi babe, did the evening meals go well?"

"Yes," Marty said. "Come and sit by me and let's chat about how your studio dream has turned into a massage parlor." She smiled as she said it to show that she trusted Maria but made sure she sat near to her, letting her know that it was definitely a conversation they were going to have.

Maria relaxed. It might be okay; the smile was a good sign. She knew Marty trusted her and vice versa, but she was not sure Marty would like to know that they were planning semi nude photos for public display.

She would definitely not mention Gemma's explicit nude paintings. They certainly had done enough poses for her. She had enjoyed seeing Gemma visualize Em sitting at a desk naked, concentrating on her writing and the way her breasts fell slightly forward as she wrote. It had obviously been difficult for Em, who felt uncomfortable. She had been a bit stiff and Maria had hoped that Gemma would be able to soften her angles in the painting.

She had loved jogging gently around the studio for Gemma to capture the running motion.

When Charlie had bench pressed, Maria had tried not to stare at the full open center of Charlie's pubic area which was completely bare of hair. Her own was more natural. Charlie had winked at her.

Gemma had surprisingly displayed a confidence not seen when Maria had taken her initial photographs. She had placed an easel near a stool and hopped up, imagining herself painting; a mountain, tall and majestic as a backdrop.

Charlie had whistled as Gemma had thrown her head back and lifted one hand as if holding a paintbrush, leaning back slightly, legs parted and her rounded breasts fully exposed as she held one hand back and looked straight toward the camera, a faraway look in her eye. Maria had snapped away, wanting to capture the moment for her. She smiled as she remembered the session.

She was brought back to the present when Marty cleared her throat and tapped her arm gently.

"So...?" she said.

"Well, it's nothing," Maria said airily. "We were taking a few photos. That's basically it."

"Photos that required you to be naked?" Marty patiently clarified.

Maria stopped short. It did sound odd when Marty asked it that way. She decided to tell her the plan; only the photographs though, definitely not Gemma's paintings.

Explaining her vision, her voice faltered. Marty did not look happy.

"They weren't...aren't...nude...my photos, I mean. Well, I suppose they are but only partially because the important bits are covered."

"The important bits?" Marty struggled not to smile. Her wife might be flirty but she struggled to be overtly sexual when talking.

"You know what I mean," Maria said crossly.

"Okay, I get your vision and I appreciate that you are not fully naked in the photos, but babe, did you not think you should have discussed this with me first?"

"Why?" Maria asked. Her tone was slightly belligerent, but only because she felt guilty.

"So that I would know my wife and friends bodies would be displayed in intimate positions publicly before that actually happened?" Marty said.

Maria stopped short, her mouth open at the retort she had been about to make.

Marty was correct. It would have been best to prepare her at least. She would not have prevented it and she did have a right to know her wife's body was going to be on display even if it was covered over the 'important parts'.

She swallowed her cheeky words.

"Yes, babe. I did not think of it that way. I'm sorry." The words were sincerely said and Marty hugged her.

"Okay. Remember for next time and I'm glad I know about it. I'd also like to be the first to see them; along with Ava and Mel of course."

"Sure." Maria smiled, hugging her back. It was understandable. She would like to see any photo of Marty before others did. Her conscience pricked her. But she could not bring herself to say there would be fully naked paintings of them done by Gemma.

"Also," Marty continued, her voice turning from affectionately firm to serious. "I would not want the restaurant to be affected or the adventure center."

"What do you mean?"

"What do you think it would be like for tourists or locals seeing those photos and then seeing the actual person at the restaurant or bar and thinking they have free and easy access to you? What if tourists saw semi naked photos of Charlie and then saw her as a trainer? Do you think the museum would tolerate their part-time assistant's body in nude display no matter how tastefully covered?"

Maria paled. It was an angle she had not thought of. This was an issue, as the town was small, catered for tourists and they all worked at different centers.

She deliberately pushed the disconcerting thoughts to the back of her mind. She felt too relieved that her conversation with Marty had not turned into a spanking. Maria kissed her wife and suggested they watch something on TV before bed.

This was easier said than done as she was unable to concentrate. She tried to stifle the thought that if her wife needed forewarning of semi naked photographs of her body for display she would definitely need warning of totally nude paintings of her and her friends' bodies. In fact, it seemed likely she probably would not allow it.

She could not even think of what management at the adventure center would say about Charlie's body, naked whilst training, flaunted over her studio walls. And-what about Gemma? Certainly the museum she worked part-time at, might not find such nude painting displays of one of their employees acceptable.

Another day's issues, she decided. Besides, surely that was not her problem. Gemma was the one painting the nude images.

She only managed to drift off into an uneasy sleep long after the movie had finished.

CHAPTER 12

———————

Life settled back into routine for everyone, except Gemma, who was still completely out of hers. She lived for, breathed and dreamed about her paintings.

Charlie was her usual self. Marty had gone round to see her. She had listened with exasperation to her friend. What Marty said about jokes damaging reputations made sense. Charlie spoke to both Ava and Mel, so that there were no misunderstandings about the massage parlor incident. She was careful not to mention semi nude photographs or nude paintings. It was not her place to tell Mel and Ava any details.

Charlie certainly had no qualms about the photographs and had told Marty that if the center did not want her, there were plenty of other places who would want her skills. Marty palms had itched, but she had held her tongue, knowing that Charlie was not in the right frame of mind to hear anything further.

Maria continued editing the photos she had taken. She knew there were critiques of photo editing and toyed with the idea of displaying the generic image and the edited one side by side. In the end she decided that as she had planned the focus to be the women's bodies, she would edit them to ensure that the body was forefront but with no editing of the body itself. As the images were in black and white she needed to ensure the emotions such photos could evoke were central to what she envisioned.

She had tried to capture the feeling of beauty that women's bodies evoked in her as she had clicked her shutter, adjusting the light in the cabin and taking the photos in color so she could have better control during the editing process. She had ensured the back ground was soft by adjusting the aperture so that the women's features stood out.

Maria asked Em to come back in as she experimented with different poses. Em had been the shyest of the four women and she needed to capture her in a more natural and relaxed pose. She wanted to portray her for the intelligent and elegant woman she was, and the black and white images she had created so far, clearly picked up her uncomfortable shyness.

It had taken time, but she found Em was far more at ease when alone in the cabin with her. They experimented with different poses and the addition of objects as opposed to scarves.

Maria managed to capture her at the moment when someone knocked on the locked door and they had both laughed, remembering the debacle of the massage parlor. It was spontaneous and portrayed a free and relaxed image of a woman who was strong and happy in her life.

She planned to change the current landscape photos soon in her little gallery for the official opening exhibition. People had trickled in more interested in walking as opposed to actual photography or arts and crafts.

Four more cabins had been occupied and the area was starting to blossom albeit slowly. One was a small café selling snacks and drinks. It had already started to make a profit as everyone who walked to the area stopped there.

Ava continued to monitor Gemma's behavior. She did tend to get that way when she became obsessed about a project she was working on, so Ava cut her a lot of slack. It started to worry her though; the constant faraway look in her eyes and the way she rushed off, not eating, to their spare room to paint.

Em decided to go and see how Gemma's painting of her and Mel was coming along. She knew Gemma worked on Tuesdays, so she walked to the small museum. Gemma was not there and a temp was at the front desk. The young woman shrugged her shoulders when she asked where Gemma was, and turned her attention back to her phone.

Em walked to their cabin, not far from her and Mel's, finding her totally immersed in her paintings. She was delighted to see Em however, and showed her the painting which was almost complete. She had used the one of Mel lying on the bed and had painted Em's body next to hers, one arm curled around Mel's middle. It was intimate and sensual and Em loved it.

She did not love the pale and tired way that Gemma looked though. Gemma brushed her well intentioned concerns aside. She had less than a week to finish the paintings.

That evening Ava decided to lay down some boundaries. She agreed to leave Gemma alone, after obtaining a promise she would finish within a week on whatever project she was working on. It would have been a perfect time for Gemma to explain to Ava, but all that mattered at that moment to her was to continue her work and achieve what she knew she could.

CHAPTER 13

A few days later, the three women meet up again. Em had arranged posters around the town and left some at all the hotels, advertising the display. It was good timing for them, as the other cabins that were occupied had started displaying their products and services. Em had also designed a web site and advertised the little gallery exhibition date on it.

Seeing Maria and Gemma engrossed in the display planning, she decided to go across to the photography club cabin and work on their web site. She knew the club had decided on exhibiting a display of their own, showcasing the area as it had been when there were people living there in the past, how it was when abandoned, and how it was changing now.

In addition, one of the members had done a series of photographs on the original small town and how it looked today, busy with tourists. As she left, Gemma came up to her and handed over a small framed print carefully wrapped.

"Your painting," she said.

Em thanked her, blushing. Maria watched covertly, wondering what it was but not intruding on the moment.

When Em looked at it, her heart skipped a beat. The passion that Gemma had lent to the painting between her and Mel was obvious and raw in its intensity. It touched her deeply. Mel lay on her back as she did in the photo, one leg straight, the other slightly bent. Em lay on her side, her one arm across her pelvis, hand dipping down into the velvet folds. Both women were asleep and the portrayal of her fingers still being deep within her partner's most intimate area was immensely arousing.

Mel still held such attraction for her. She was a one-woman type of person and knew her passion and desire for Mel would last as long as she was alive. If she and Mel ever separated, she would always have that same passion for her, even if it was not reciprocated.

Once Em left, Maria and Gemma stood back, critiquing their work. It had taken them the whole morning to arrange the paintings and photographs and adjust the lighting.

In the end they had interspersed the paintings between the black and white photographs which Maria had initially thought would not look good. However the contrast between the materials used and the way the subjects were displayed was enhanced and forced the eye to focus on each individual image. It was obvious that the women in the photographs were also the women in the paintings.

Maria tried to view the exhibition through Marty's eyes. The photographs were sensual. Okay, they were almost nude, but not quite.

She looked at the paintings and felt amazed by the beauty that Gemma had portrayed in their nude bodies. Her heart thud uncomfortably loud in her ears when she thought of Marty seeing them. She could not imagine that she would totally agree with them.

A wolf whistle behind her made her jump.

"Geez, Charlie," she said, placing a hand on her heart. "Don't creep up like that!"

"Darn, but those are explicit," she said admiringly, hands in her pockets as she looked around. It was one thing posing for a photograph with one's legs apart or one's breasts proudly lifted, quite another to see them in the bold strokes of Gemma's paintings.

"I'm magnificent," she said, a wicked smile curving her lips. Maria laughed.

"You are," she agreed. It was true. Charlie's body was toned with high, full breasts, her shaved pubic area exposing her thick and full labia.

Each woman was exquisite in their own way.

Emma's body showed her larger hips, curved and intensely feminine. Her pubic hair enhanced her femininity, just as Charlie's shaved pubis did hers.

Gemma's self-portrait displayed her larger rounded breasts with pink tipped aureoles fully erect as she sat at her work place desk. She gulped. It was so overtly sexual that she could not imagine Ava reacting calmly to it.

Maria tried not to look at her own painting too long. The reality of preparing Marty to see her wife's totally nude body jogging through the woods, no matter how slender and attractive it looked, was beginning to pierce her conscious mind.

"Excuse me. I-" a measured voice that suddenly stopped mid-sentence, broke into their reveries. Maria shrieked and turned. "Sorry, we're closed-" she started.

"Hullo," Charlie said at the same time. "Come in, look around"

"Charlie...!" Maria scolded her gently.

The woman who had interrupted their thoughts had curly, brunette hair, elegantly pulled back and was clad in brand clothes with sun glasses pushed back on the top of her head. The scent of an exotic perfume hung in the air. Her voice was friendly and warm, as was her smile at the exchange between Maria and Charlie, but it was her eyes that had them staring at her a bit longer than was polite. They were a brilliant green and totally guarded, as if secrets lay behind them and warned the looker not to get too close.

"Sorry," she said. "The door was open and I..." She stopped talking again as her eyes continued to flick around the paintings and photographs.

"Oh!" she said, "...Stunning...just stunning...so..." The words were softly murmured and trailed off again, as if she were talking to herself.

She drew herself up as Charlie went over.

"I'm Charlie," she said, holding out her hand. The woman took it just as Maria said, "Thank you. They are for our opening exhibition display tomorrow. We've not yet finished the arrangement."

Charlie felt the hand in hers. It was not the smooth palm that she had automatically assumed she'd feel. The ridge on the palm was raised but warm. The scar invited Charlie's finger to gently trace it and she had to fight against the impulse as the woman drew her hand back from hers.

"I'm looking for the photography club; apparently there are some amazing scenes of this area."

"It's just opposite this cabin," Maria said, catching the dazed look on Charlie's face. She felt a pang of jealousy. Charlie seemed smitten, bewitched.

"It's cabin number 4," she said. Then, relenting, she added, "Please come to the opening display tomorrow. I'm Maria and this is..."

"Yes I know; Charlie," the woman said. She smiled at Charlie, their eyes at the same height and Charlie felt as if she were looking into a future she was not aware could exist. She blinked; the woman was gone and she did not even know her name.

"What's wrong with you?" Maria asked.

"Nothing." She felt unsettled.

"Charlie," Maria said, leaving the subject of the mysterious woman, "I'm wondering-well, do you think Marty-and Ava and Mel- will be annoyed at this."

Charlie looked at her, hugging her close.

"You know they will be, so you have a decision to make. Go ahead and display your talent and risk your butt, or take the chance of not displaying anything. Personally, I'd go ahead and display. Gemma might be in much more trouble than you though," she said, looking again at their most intimate body parts on show.

The display was undeniably sexy and sensual and would certainly draw people as the word spread, but Charlie had started to feel a tinge of discomfort. There was nothing wrong with it, but a discussion with their three friends might have been better before the public saw it. Maria started sweating; if even Charlie, so laissez faire and carefree about life, had some misgivings, then perhaps this was not a wise idea, no matter how much she felt she wanted to 'grow' as a photographer.

CHAPTER 14

An excited and nervous Maria leapt from the bed. The exhibition was today.

"Babe," Marty murmured groggily.

"Gotta go," Maria said. Marty grabbed her hand.

"I am so proud of you," she said. Maria pulled away.

"Thanks." She turned to go and looked back at her wife lying sleepily on the bed, pride and love evident in her eyes.

At that moment, everything in her relented. It was not fair. She needed to warn her wife. Her desires should not come before respect for her wife.

Making a snap decision, she neared the bed again.

"Marty, I've got something to tell you." Her voice was so hesitant, serious and shaky that Marty sat upright in alarm.

"What's wrong?" Maria closed her eyes. *Gemma, forgive me,* she silently pleaded in her head. Marty clasped her wife's hands. "Just tell me,"

Maria pulled away slightly. She did not want to be trapped in those strong arms.

"Um, well, I just wanted to say that, well, you know I have the exhibition today...you know...of my and Gemma's work?"

"Yes, of course. I'd not miss it for the world."

Maria groaned inwardly. This was going to be hard.

"You could, if you needed to work. I mean-I don't want to drag you away."

"I would never miss it," Marty reiterated. "I am so proud of you."

She looked at Maria's clenched hands and her antenna pinged.

"Babe," she said sternly. "What is it? Come here!"

Maria backed away.

"Well, I just wanted to tell you...so you knew beforehand and were not shocked, that the photos...you know that we are covered over our...private parts right?"

"Yes, I know and I plan to see them before you open today," Marty said.

"Well, they are still a little bit...sensual...and," she hurried on, her words tripping over her tongue making her stammer slightly, "the paintings... well, the paintings aren't...are, I mean...full frontal nudes!" With those words finally said, Maria was out the door.

Marty inhaled sharply simultaneously trying to leap out of the bed. The words were like a glass of cold water in her face.

"Maria!" Marty swore as she tripped on the sheet. The front door slammed.

"That little minx..." She stopped, knowing she could not catch Maria.

She sank back on the bed. She needed to think about what to do. If they were all nude and recognizable this would not be good for her business or the recreation center, nor the small museum where Gemma worked. In addition it would not be good for the women's self-esteem when they had every male ogling them as they walked around town. There had to be some way the exhibition could go ahead but not allow for full nudity.

She leant over and picked up her mobile. Scrolling down her contact list she rang Mel first, knowing that she would take the news better than Ava.

Once she had explained, Mel agreed to go to the recreation center to chat to Ava in person to prepare her and then drive them both over. Agreeing to their plan, Marty dressed hastily and waited for the two women to arrive.

Mel had the day off. She eyed Em as she left, not saying a word about where she was heading. Em was engrossed in her own anxiety about the day and did not notice the firm, determined look on Mel's face.

"Who was on the phone, babe?" Em asked absently.

"Just a friend. I need to pick someone up at the adventure center," Mel said casually. She hoped Em would confide in her, but Em headed off as soon as she could, wanting to ensure Maria and Gemma had everything under control. If she had turned back as she usually did to blow a kiss, she might have seen the thunderous look that passed across Mel's face.

Reading her 'to do' list on her phone, she walked off determinedly. The photography club had decided to have two exhibitions, both in the new cabin and the old small shop in the town center. They would be busy and the amateur photographers were excited. She needed to ensure that things were in order on both sides.

Ava was at work, having left Gemma sleeping, kissing her forehead gently so as not to disturb her. She was surprised to see Mel stride in, her expression serious.

"You aren't on shift today," she said.

"Sit down," Mel said. "I need to talk to you." Ava sat. She did not like the sound of this.

Gemma had woken shortly after the forehead kiss, hazily aware of her partner's sweet lips and an impending excitement of something major happening that day. Opening her eyes, she leapt out of bed and readied herself. She headed off for Maria's studio, her heart beating fast. It was the first time she would display portraits instead of landscapes. She was proud of her work, having poured her talent as well as her admiration and love for her friends into her paintings.

She arrived at the studio flushed with excitement to find a visibly nervous and anxious Maria talking to Em.

"Is everything okay?" She looked at the photos and paintings and her heart swelled with emotion and pride. It was still hours away from opening time. Across the dirt road she could see the photography members arranging their displays, not only inside their cabin but also on the grass verges around it. There was no way they would display theirs outside, Gemma thought. Even she drew the line at that, no matter how proud she felt. She failed to notice that Maria had not yet answered her question.

Charlie popped her head around the studio's front door.

"I can't stay long. I've got to cover Ava's shift. Apparently she got called away for an emergency. Can't say no, now that she's acting manager for the next three months. Sorry to miss this." Noticing the apprehensive and slightly guilty look in Maria's eyes, she walked up to her.

"What's wrong?"

"I...told Marty..."

"Yes...?"

"Well...that the paintings were full nudes!" Maria blurted it out, unable to look at Gemma.

"She already knew about the photographs and that they are not fully nude," Maria finished.

Charlie whistled.

"I'd hate to be you right now," she said.

"Us! You mean us," Em said, turning toward her. "You suggested this and you are one of the full nudes-probably the most overt...." Charlie hugged her, encouraging her to be calm.

"I know. I also know you've done a lot of work, so I say go ahead. I've got to go, I need to relieve Ava." She disappeared quickly.

Maria looked after her. Did her friend seem nervous? The cocky, self-assured Charlie? She shook her head. She needed to focus and get sorted. Now was not the time to think of any potential partner storms brewing. Marty could be managed later. Surely Marty would not...

The thought halted abruptly as she heard a car draw up. That was unusual. Most people ambled over from the town, following the scenic route through the trees. Three car doors slammed. She looked through the window and saw Marty, Mel and Ava walking purposefully toward the studio. If there had been music playing it would have been like a scene from a western, she thought. Three strong women coming for their ladies. Despite the butterflies that immediately started whirring in her stomach, she could not help but admire the attractive scene they made.

Gemma turned to her, her eyes flashing.

"This is my work. Why did you..."

The door opened and all six women fell silent. It felt like a standoff; who would draw their weapon first, Maria wondered.

Marty and Ava had both noticed Charlie slipping off. Marty wanted to haul her back in, but she knew she was covering for Ava. She bet anything that Charlie might have started or at the very least encouraged this.

Marty was the first to draw her words. "Now..." she started, turning to look at Maria. She stopped, noticing how Ava and Mel were staring around the room with dazed looks. Her eyes followed their shocked gazes.

No getting away from it. The exhibition material was stunning. Beautifully and erotically inspiring. The black and white photographs showed the skill and talent of the photographer, making Marty long to touch the almost naked forms of the women portrayed in them. At the same time the thought of someone else wanting to do that touched a raw nerve. A nerve twitched in her lower jaw.

Her eyes were drawn to the paintings and she almost shouted in shock. They were incredible but totally nude. Although no prude, Marty almost blushed at the erotically open pose of Charlie's, her legs splayed suggestively as she bench pressed. Her eyes roved slowly over the naked limbs of her wife in the painting of her jogging through the trees, her breasts pointed and full, begging to be cupped. She averted her eyes from Em and Gemma's nude paintings, trying to respect Ava and Mel.

There was dead silence.

Ava was the first to speak. Her eyes flicked between pride, admiration and shocked stern hardness.

"These photographs and paintings are amazing. Is this what your exhibition to the public is, though?" The words were level, even, measured but it was plain to hear the anger in the tone. Surprisingly it was the shy, hesitant Gemma who answered first.

"Yes."

"They are incredible and I am proud of your talent...and Maria's," Ava continued. "But this is not appropriate nor decent. It is not going ahead. Well, at least not for Gemma's work. I do not want to see my partner's and friends' completely naked bodies open to everyone's prying eyes."

Gemma turned angrily.

"It's my right-" she started.

Seeing the growing tensions, Mel calmly stepped between them.

"It is true that your work is your right. It is also your and friends right to bare your bodies if you choose to. But there is also a right of how those to whom you are committed might feel about this," she said.

"-And our businesses-" Marty added evenly.

The silence that followed was so intense that Maria felt her head would burst with the unbearable guilt of it. Why, oh why had she not thought all this through at the beginning?

"I am displaying my work," Gemma eventually said stubbornly.

"Not this type, you aren't," Ava said. "You can choose other scenes; your landscapes, for example, of which you have plenty. But no-not this." Her voice was firm, her body language unyielding.

Gemma's eyes flashed, her heart beat fast. Part of her knew that the paintings were too open, too erotic for this tourist town, no matter how good they were. But she wanted to feel for once, just once, that she was a success, in her own definition of that word. Anyone could paint a boring old landscape, she thought mutinously.

"I refuse to remove them!" she said.

"Then I will remove them for you," Ava said. "But not before this." She grabbed her partner's arm, turned her around and started spanking her bottom.

The firm hand landed swats that were hard and unrelenting. Gemma gasped with the sting. She supposed she should feel embarrassed, but she did not. Her temper was high and she felt too stubborn to worry about anyone else watching. It was almost as if Ava felt that as she switched hands. The sounds reverberated around the wooden room and Em winced. That was going to be her shortly or later on that evening.

Maria sneaked a look at Marty and Mel. Both looked equally determined, but Marty looked disappointed and angry. Surely she had a right to do with her body as she wanted?

"You do," Marty's voice replied. Maria started. She had obviously said that aloud. "But then you need to accept the consequences for that if it harms our relationship or does not take into account my feelings or those of your friends. If you cannot live within this type of relationship or have respect for my feelings whether in a domestic discipline relationship or not…then you need to think about what you want."

Maria trembled. The words were so simple. Marty had always told her that was how she lived and she knew she would not bend. Her only option would be to alter the exhibition and accept her punishment later or keep the exhibition as it was and lose Marty.

Emma had stood still and silent through all of this. She was aware that Mel had come to stand behind her. That very act of quiet dominance made her legs shake. "I'm sorry," she said, turning to her.

"I know you are and will be even more so later," was Mel's calm reply. She never lost her temper and was consistently even, measured and firm in her approach.

"I'll remove the photos and paintings of me. Maria, I'm sorry." Em turned to her friend, hoping she understood.

Maria nodded, numbly tears stinging her eyes.

"Thank you. I don't want anyone to see you like this, even with your breasts covered by that scarf," Mel said simply. Em understood where she was coming from. She would have felt exactly the same if the situation were reversed. She slowly and carefully started taking the photos and paintings of herself down. Her actions left gaping holes in the displays and Maria felt a brief anger flash at the disarray of her first public event.

Marty addressed Maria.

"I don't mind the photographs," she said "Whilst quite sensual, they are tasteful and cover your intimate parts."

321

"I don't mind them either." Ava said. Em glanced at Mel to see if she had changed her mind. She had not. She swallowed when she thought of the nude painting she had had Gemma do. What would Mel say when she realized she had shown her nude body to Gemma through photos she had not known Em was taking?

Gemma had collapsed onto a chair. She felt outraged and hurt, even though she understood where the three women were coming from. Ava hunkered down beside her.

"You can still display your landscapes," she said. "I will drive you home to get some."

"It's not the same!" Gemma burst out. She was pale and trembling. Lack of sleep and good nutrition for the past few weeks were making her irrational.

"It's not, but that's the deal," Ava said firmly.

Marty watched Maria. She saw the internal struggle. It was unlike her wife, who usually apologized straight away or when she knew she couldn't voice her struggles needed a spanking that would help her do that. Right now, she knew that would not help.

"Whose idea was this?" she asked.

"Does it matter?" Maria asked quietly. She was pleased with her photos, barring those of Em, were to stay, but she felt bad for Gemma.

"Yes," Marty said gazing at the fully splayed open nude painting of Charlie, captured forever in that act of lifting weights. There were others of Charlie as well in various weight lifting poses.

"It was all of ours," Emma said.

"Gemma," she continued, trying to smooth things over, "let's go and fetch some of your landscapes."

"Yes," Maria encouraged. "We'll alter the arrangement; black and white portraits on one side and your landscape paintings on the other."

"No," Gemma said stubbornly. Ava sighed. She stood and pulled Gemma to her feet.

"Right, that's enough. You either choose to display your landscapes or nothing. If you continue this way I will make the choice for you, but not before I take you over my knee right here, right now." The words brooked no argument, the hand on the buckle of her belt subtle but evident in warning.

Gemma wanted to protest but her lover's words made her tingle and squirm and she knew she would obey her. She also knew she was right.

"The landscapes," she muttered sulkily.

"I can't hear you," Ava said sharply. Gemma resisted the temptation to shout her response loudly, but she knew Ava was referring to her attitude. It was so unfair though, she had put her heart and soul into those paintings. She spoke up slightly, making sure to keep her voice even and polite.

"The landscapes...please..." She kept her eyes averted so no one would see the shimmer of tears in them. Ava nodded.

"Good choice!"

"Fucking mean cow..." Gemma muttered softly under her breath as she turned away. Ava heard and chose to ignore it. Gemma never swore. She understood how Gemma felt, but she would not let her committed lover's body be on display in this manner.

Tonight she would use the cane on her lover and it would not turn into an amorous session. In addition, she would set firmer limits with Gemma from now on. She knew that Gemma would accept this as naturally as she would apply it.

"I'll drive you," Emma said. She wanted to get away for a short while to settle her mind, as well as help Gemma. Mel went to stop her but Ava caught her eye. She knew Em would probably help calm Gemma on the drive. Mel nodded, understanding her unspoken words.

"Straight back, please," Mel said to them both.

Once the two subdued women had left, Maria set about altering the photograph displays now that Em's photos had been removed. Ava started taking down the paintings.

Marty and Mel stood together.

"It really is remarkable. They are so talented," Mel said. She was also very proud of Em, whose business skills had played a major part in the cabin set- ups.

"They are," Marty said. "But more remarkable is that we had no idea. I bet this was Charlie's idea."

"I am sure it was. But everyone took it on board willingly enough it seems." Mel wondered if she should have a word with Charlie but something told her Marty or Ava would take care of that.

She felt calm and determined. Em would feel her hand later tonight, possibly the hated rectangle hairbrush. Em would reluctantly accept it. Knowing her partner as she did, she knew she had probably been reticent from the beginning about the project and now felt guilty. Well, she would help relieve her of that guilt without doubt as soon as they were home. Emma never needed much physical discipline; when she did Mel delivered it hard and fast. That worked best for Em. She responded well to the respect that they set for each other.

Marty was worried about Maria. Her normally feisty wife would have wept and wailed and flung her arms out, complaining about injustice. Her slender body would have trembled with passion as she struggled to voice her words, unable to fully verbalize her feelings.

Instead, she had retreated inward just like a few months before when she had been unable to explain about wanting to pursue a different dream in life. She heard Maria's phone ring and saw her take a call. Moving closer she heard her choke out the words,

"I just feel so bad for Gemma. Charlie, it was silly we should not have-" She halted as she saw her wife.

"Is that Charlie?"

Maria nodded.

"Give me the phone,"

Maria held it out reluctantly.

"Charlie, woman, you'd best come over tomorrow early. I need to talk to you." Maria could imagine the response. She watched Marty's eyes narrow as she closed the mobile and handed it back to Maria.

"Honey, I am proud of you, but can you see this was not the right way to go about what you wanted to achieve?" The words were rational and her tone of voice was gentle yet firm.

It was the tone of voice that always made Maria see complete logic but also want to shout with frustration. Her wife was so often right compared to her hasty and ill thought through way of doing things. It made her want to walk into her wife's strong, solid arms, but indignation held her back. Marty might be correct but she wanted to decide what she was showing in her very first exhibition. To be honest she had never envisioned her first display being nudes or even partial nudes for that matter, but the idea had seemed so appealing at the time when Charlie had suggested it.

Thoughts whirled through her mind. Okay, so perhaps she should have been more respectful toward her partner and friends and she knew it would not be nice for Marty or good for her business to have the regulars at the bar tease her over her wife's totally nude body. But still...She almost stamped her foot.

Marty was watching her closely. She had a feeling that this was not an issue that was going to be dealt with as easily as it normally was, with Maria over her lap. Maria had changed her life's direction by following a passion she had. Perhaps she needed more time to figure out what she really needed and wanted.

Maria drew back, counting 'til ten to help steady her temper.

"It's fine!" she snapped, brushing her away, tossing her head in a manner indicating it was anything but fine. If there were not just a few hours to meet the deadline Marty would have spanked her then and there, no matter how much time Maria needed.

"Watch your attitude," she said abruptly. "Now let's get this sorted. Tell us how to help."

Maria swallowed another hot retort and centered herself on re-arranging the photographs minus Em's and visualizing where Gemma's landscapes would go.

As soon as Em and Gemma returned, they all helped carry the landscape paintings into the studio. She had chosen a variety of styles from pastels to oils. Some landscapes depicted early morning misty pictures over the town lake and others captured the fields and mountains, where the sunset rays had turned them to various hues of red, orange and pink. Ava felt immense pride in her girlfriend's talent as she saw each scene being hung.

The six women worked well as a team to meet the opening deadline.

Maria relaxed as she worked and contemplated the displays, moving and shifting stands and eventually placing sections of them along two of the walls. Marty patiently followed her around, carrying stands and setting them down where indicated. There was a lull in the previous angry passions and frustrated emotions; a truce as it were.

Mel hugged Em from behind.

"You've done a great job securing this along with all the work you've done to get these cabins functioning." Emma leant back into her and smiled.

"Don't think that gets you off the hook though!" Mel's words seemed playful but the look in her eyes was anything but.

Emma groaned at the thought of what lay ahead, but she'd give anything to get rid of the guilt she felt.

She planned to give Mel the painting of them soon as they got home so that would be out of the way before her discipline.

Maria watched them with a slight sense of jealousy. They were so easy together. Em might get riled up and into trouble at times, but never to the extent she, Maria, did. Em accepted herself and the way she was, whilst Maria often fought her needs every step of the way. In addition, they seemed so passionately and contentedly in love with each other. Em never eyed Charlie the way Maria eyed her. She loved Marty, but felt drawn to Charlie. It certainly did not help that Charlie also seemed to be attracted to her-and as many other women as possible, she thought wryly. Maria also knew with certainty that Charlie would never be able to meet all her needs, so why she was not able to accept Marty and her discipline right now she did not know.

Marty approached Maria again.

"You have done brilliantly, babe, changing direction like this. I am so proud of you."

Maria glowed from the genuine praise, but a niggling stubborn feeling kept her wary.

"Thank you," she said stiffly.

"We will deal with everything later." Marty said, trying to reassure her that she was there for her, for every incident Maria created or went through.

"No, we won't," Maria whispered suddenly in an outraged tone. "I am...I am...I am not coming home to be spanked just because of…of…naked bodies…which by the way are totally normal and natural! I am…I am…going to stay with Charlie where no one will spank me…and just…love me." This was not strictly true. Charlie had spanked her before, but she definitely would not spank her for this situation. She supported Maria's work and ideas.

Marty straightened her shoulders and looked at her.

"If that is your choice," she finally said. "You know my rules and how I live. I love you Maria, with everything in me, but I have to be true to myself. If you cannot accept a domestic discipline relationship then there is no future for us." Her words were simple and factual with no hesitation or argument about them.

Maria paled. She knew Marty was firm in her lifestyle needs and would never budge. She lived true to herself and had explained that to Maria when they first got together. She also knew that she responded well to their domestic discipline relationship, that it enhanced her life, focused her and made her feel cherished and loved. Right now, however, something in her felt stubborn and she was unable to back down.

"This has to be your decision," Marty continued, taking a step back, her eyes fixed on Maria's face. Her heart felt heavy and dull, as if at any minute it could crack and shatter like a vase full of water that was placed too near the edge of a table.

"I will not force you. I know my needs and I know yours. But you have to do what you feel is right for you."

Marty turned and went over to the side wall, taking a seat in one of the wood backed chairs. It was only a few minutes away from the 4p.m. opening time, and she heard voices of locals and tourists outside milling around. No matter how sad she felt, no matter what happened, she wanted-no-needed to be there to see Maria's achievements hopefully translate into success.

Em and Mel covertly watched the interplay. It was painful.

The studio was not large and they had continued to rearrange the displays, trying not to listen.

"Should we-?" Em began.

"No, babe," Mel said, knowing that Em would want to go and comfort their friends. "Let's wait a few days. They need to sort this out themselves."

Gemma had noticed the tension between Maria and Marty and, for the first time, she felt genuine regret. It was true her passion and fire were evident, but totally naked paintings of people she knew so well, including herself, did not belong out for public display; they were best as intimate images for personal viewing.

Being immensely fond of Maria and having a lot of respect for Marty, she worried about what was happening between them.

She turned with anxious, distressed eyes to Ava.

"Ava, are they...will they..." Ava kissed her.

"Let's hope so, my love. Don't panic now. The exhibition is due to open in a few minutes. Your landscapes are incredible. Let's focus on that and later you can think about how your actions affect others."

Gemma leant into her arms, gratitude and love flooding her. She had been so stupid. How could she forgive herself if a relationship broke up because of her? Ava watched her, knowing what she was thinking. What Gemma had done was wrong, but if Maria and Marty broke up, it would not be because of Gemma's paintings, it would be from something each of them was experiencing or needed in their lives.

Gemma went over to Maria.

"Are you okay?" she asked gently, seeing the sheen of tears in Maria's eyes.

"Yes," Maria said curtly. Gemma ignored the short tone and put her arms around her friend. She felt Maria's body soften in

329

the comforting embrace, her slender shoulders shaking slightly. A small sob escaped into the room. Marty shifted uncomfortably on the chair. She wanted nothing more than to go over but knew that Maria needed to make her own decision on this.

Mel glanced at Marty and thought about what she would want for Em if the situation were reversed.

She walked over to Maria and led her away from the display.

"Hey..." Mel said, lifting her chin with one finger, "Look at me. You have done great work, yes with some misjudgment, but now you need to get your head into gear and focus on making the success that the four of you worked toward a reality."

"I wish Charlie were here to see it."

"She will be. Ava has arranged for coverage during her afternoon break. Besides, Marty and Ava want to chat with her."

Maria sobbed again and Mel's heart contracted with compassion. She held her just as she would have held Emma, rubbing her back and soothing her. Marty looked at her with a heavy heart and made a quiet 'thank you' sign to Mel who thumbed up back.

"Come on, honey," she said. She kissed her forehead. "Go and wash your face. Em, help her." Her kind words and firm manner helped Maria focus. She deliberately avoided eye contact with her wife and allowed Em to lead her to the bathroom at the back. Gemma followed.

The three of them looked at each other. Em smiled first.

"For the record, I'm pleased I did it. But I do think we were wrong. We should have discussed it first. I am never getting into scrapes with you two again!"

"Yes, I agree," Gemma said. Her anger at not displaying the intimate paintings had totally dissipated. The creation of them remained and that was what was important. She would gift the paintings to the women whose bodies she had lovingly displayed in all their natural power and beauty.

330

Maria laughed, for a minute her usual naughty glint back in her eyes.

"I'm happy we did it," she said. "I'm sorry, Gemma. If I had not said anything, your paintings might have been on display...well for a short while at least."

"-And I might not have sat for a month or more! So it's a good thing you did. At least your photos are displayed," Gemma said, comforting her in return.

"Except mine..." Em was secretly relieved. She did not like her body on public display no matter how artfully it had been covered at strategic points.

"Are you alright? You and Marty, I mean?" Gemma asked outright.

"Yes...no...I don't know. I just feel...well, it was my choice and...I don't know." Maria ran a hand through her sleek bob ruffling it, so that the top of her head looked like a fluffy chick.

Her eye shimmered with tears again. She did not understand why she was being so stubborn. At the moment she wanted both the comfort of Marty and Charlie as well as her two best friends.

"I'm not going to go...back..." she carried on. Gemma looked distressed, unconsciously wringing her hands.

"Oh no," she whispered. Em took a look at her friends. Both should be feeling happy and excited for the exhibition, not one looking like she was going to faint and the other about to march out the door. Adopting a bright business tone, she told them to clean up, snap out of it and put a smile on.

She helped Maria smooth her hair and instructed Gemma to wash her face. It was time to start.

As they walked towards the display, Maria felt a sense of achievement. She clasped her friend's hand and leant across to Gemma.

"We did well," she said.

Gemma glowed.

"We did. And none of this would have happened without Em's business sense in the first place." The three women laughed. Em grinned. This was more like it.

Ava opened the champagne bottles and filled the glasses. The tiny bubbles fizzed festively up, almost spilling over the rim of the crystal flutes. Gemma turned on the overhead lamps.

The clink of glasses and warm studio lights against the wooden log walls eased the tension and imparted a cozy and congratulatory atmosphere.

At the stroke of 4 p.m, Maria took a deep breath and opened the small wooden door. Quite a few locals had already turned up. They strolled in chatting and clearly interested in this new extension to their town.

Perhaps they were there only for the advertised champagne, Maria thought anxiously.

Her thoughts were allayed by the overt admiration from tourists. A small group of women asked her if they could photograph the display, which she politely refused.

The astounded looks from locals as they looked at the photographs were quite comical. Overall it was going well and she relaxed when a few of the town's residents went over to speak to both her and Gemma.

Marty was not as relaxed. She clenched her fists when two men stopped by Maria's photo and commented on her legs and the size of her breasts. Struggling to remain calm, she was relieved when Ava slipped across to her. The distraction helped her to maintain her composure.

Ava was not entirely at ease with Gemma's photographs. but as her breasts and genitalia were not fully visible she felt it was acceptable. If Gemma felt the confidence to display her discreetly covered body, she would support that, but nothing further. She sent up a silent prayer that no one commented on Gemma's body as they had on Maria's. Marty would have to hold her back, she thought.

Maria was surprised to receive offers of purchase for the photographs as she had not displayed them for sale. Sales would come later and she did not plan to be known as the photographer who sold erotic or sensual photographs.

She politely refused all offers. The photos would remain a part of her studio until she was ready to part with them. They would be gifted to the women whose bodies she had photographed.

Gemma's landscapes did well with tourists, selling six out of the ten displayed within the first two hours. Her shy, but proud blush was a delight to see. She had already sold a few at the town photography club in the preceding months and was able to judge a fair price.

Charlie turned up at her break time. She had not wanted to come, knowing that everyone was there, and were most likely annoyed with her. Ava, who was currently acting manager, had first asked her to cover her shift that morning, and then phoned to say she had arranged for Jose to cover her afternoon break and she was to come and see the display.

She hung around awkwardly. She felt no remorse for the suggestion of the naked photographs and paintings that had led to all this drama. A movement caught her eye, and the faint scent of an exotic perfume assailed her. Her heart almost missed a beat. She looked up to see the brunette from earlier looking at a pastel landscape of the lake. She walked over.

"Hullo again."

"Where are the nudes?" the curly haired brunette asked without responding to the greeting.

Charlie laughed.

"It seems the artist's partner was not happy."

"We all weren't," an even toned voice interjected. Marty had been standing behind one of the stands. She eyed the woman with interest.

"I'm Marty. Maria is my partner; the photographer," she said by way of explanation.

"She is very skilled. Did she do the paintings as well, the ones that are not here? I'm Isabelle." She held out a hand. Charlie felt a pang of jealousy. The brunette had not introduced herself to Charlie. She could not explain the strange pull she felt toward his woman.

"No. They were painted by the woman who did these landscapes." Marty was not impressed to know that the woman had seen the naked paintings.

"What a pity they were removed," the woman continued. "They were stunning."

She turned to go. As she passed, her arm brushed against Charlie's and she smiled as Charlie jumped at the feeling.

"Bye, Charlie. See you around."

Marty grinned. Finally! Someone who did not fall for Charlie's charms. Was this Charlie's match? Charlie made a move to follow the woman.

"Uh uh, lady, you stay right here," Marty said. "In fact, let's go to the back. I want to talk to you."

Charlie felt annoyed but walked to the back with Marty.

"Was this your idea?" Marty asked her bluntly. Ava and Mel joined them.

"Yup," The word was casual and flippant, but Charlie's natural bravado seemed somewhat diminished facing the three tops. "It's not their fault. I suggested it... blame me."

"Thank you for admitting that," Ava said, "but they all joined in willingly."

"I'll be seeing you tomorrow-early," Marty said. Ava closed her mouth. She had been about to say the same thing. Charlie's actions showed disrespect for the adventure centER she worked for. This was the final straw amid all her flirting with the clients.

"Fine," Charlie snapped. "I deserve that. What did you think of that brunette?" she asked Marty, abruptly changing the subject. Marty laughed. At least Charlie was the same.

Ava watched Gemma. It was good seeing the confidence this exhibition gave her. She might mess things up or make wrong decisions at times but she was talented, beautiful, shy, and attractive, and she loved her. Gemma glanced up to see Ava's adoring gaze and melted. She would accept any type of lifestyle to be with this woman. Her punishment would be no hardship, she felt. Then she gulped as she remembered Ava's cupboard and the implements in it, fully aware that she was not acquainted with them all yet.

At 8p.m they closed the door and the tourists and locals drifted back to town.

Maria and Em ran over to the photography club to see how they had done. The members were all in high spirits and the happy atmosphere relaxed both of them. Reluctantly they walked back to the cabin after congratulating their club colleagues.

"Let's clear up and get home," Emma said.

"No," Maria's voice was strong though she did not feel it. "I feel like being alone here, for a bit."

Em, Mel, Ava and Gemma walked out, feeling that they needed to give Maria and Marty some space. Mel looked back toward Marty. She had a feeling her friend would need someone to lean on soon.

Marty walked over to Maria.

"Honey, I'm so proud of you," she said again. She had said it many times that night but felt a need to keep repeating it for Maria to realize that no matter the errors in judgment, she supported her.

"Thank you," Maria said. She turned away, busying herself tidying up.

"What are you thinking?" Marty asked.

Maria turned sulkily.

"I'm thinking...I'm thinking I will be going to Charlie's tonight...as I said earlier,"

She really wanted to say 'I'm coming home and I accept whatever punishment we both decide on' but the words would not form properly.

She knew Marty would never push her, that she would have to accept her punishment. She also wanted to talk about her feelings, the strange feeling of independence she was having lately and the attraction she felt toward Charlie. Did it all mean she no longer wanted the domestic discipline relationship she had with Marty or was this a combination of a phase of life or growth?

The thoughts flicked through her mind, confusing her. Her heart yearned for the growth and discipline she needed. Why she did not realize at that moment she could have both was not something that she considered.

Marty kept her facial expression neutral and her voice level.

"Okay," she said. "I love you. I accept your decision. If you change your mind, you know where I am. I will not wait forever, though."

She walked to the door and all Maria wanted to do was run after her and fling her arms around her. She could not understand why she was acting this way.

At the door, Marty turned, one hand on the door handle.

"All or nothing," she said softly, "remember..."

Maria remembered clearly. They were the words her wife had

said to her before they committed to each other. She knew Marty needed to be a top and live her life in a way that fulfilled her. In that sense it also fulfilled her but just now, today, tonight, she felt like rebelling.

Wanting to cry, she said, "I remember..."

She turned away. The door closed softly yet firmly. Maria sank to the floor amid the remains of champagne glasses and echoes of admiration and wept.

CHAPTER 15

Charlie was not surprised to find Maria at her door that night. As was common of close friends who share an intimate bond, she understood her in a way that Marty did not always.

She opened the door and her arms. Maria fell into them, inhaling the fresh cologne that Charlie wore. Charlie closed the door with one arm.

"Come in, honey," she said. "Tell me everything."

"I can't," Maria sobbed. "I just want to be hugged. It's all so stupid! I don't even know why I'm like this."

Charlie sighed. She knew full well. Maria had a chemical reaction toward her, she had started a new passion and career in her life and she was growing in her experiences. This was confusing Maria.

Maria loved Marty and Charlie knew that she also loved her, though not in a deep partner way but in the long-lasting bond of friendship, kindled with a spark of chemical attraction. She felt it too, but she knew she was not right for Maria. She was too flirty and unsettled. Maria was also flirty. They would not be well suited as partners. Part-time lovers, yes-but she did not want to betray Marty's friendship, nor confuse Maria further.

Maria lifted her head and before she could stop herself, she kissed Charlie. Charlie kissed her back passionately. Her body betrayed her logical mind at that moment. Everything in her felt like it was on fire. Charlie inhaled raggedly. This was not one of her clients or a casual tourist flirt. This was her friend and she respected her enough to know that she was sad and longing and confused. It was up to her to stop it.

"Sorry," Maria said. Her breathing was fast and Charlie could see her erect nipples beneath her blouse. Her instinct was to rub her thumbs over them. She closed her eyes and rubbed her hand over her face.

"It's okay. I'm sorry for responding-but hell-you don't make it easy-" Charlie said, hugging her. Maria burst into tears again.

Charlie led her to the sofa and gently pulling her friend down with her, she cradled her in her arms, head on her shoulder and shushed her until she fell asleep.

Tomorrow she would manage this, but for now, they both needed to sleep. Quiet fell over the apartment that looked out over the dark lake.

At the end of the road leading out of town Mel was facing Emma in the kitchen. She knew Em would prefer to get everything out the way. That worked best for her.

"Babe-" she started.

"Wait," Em said.

"No!" Mel responded, thinking Em was going to produce some type of excuse, to delay the inevitable. Although Em longed for release she also dreaded it until it actually happened.

"Get over here!"

Em hesitated. She wanted to come clean about the painting,

but did not want to push Mel further.

Before Mel could grab her arm, she spoke hastily.

"I took photos of you...naked ones, without you realizing and asked Gemma to paint the two of us together.... I wanted it to be a surprise, just for us...for...our..." She trailed off. The look in Mel's eyes did not bode well for her bottom.

Mel stood silently, arms folded, digesting this new piece of information. She was not impressed about the covert photo taking. If Em had asked she would not have agreed. On the other hand she understood that her partner was trying to give her a precious gift that depicted their private love. However, the fact that all their friends had seen her partner's totally nude body detracted from the privacy of the painting that Em wanted to surprise her with.

Em turned and went to fetch it.

"Here," she said awkwardly. This was totally not the way she had planned to give this intimate gift. Mel took it slowly. Did she want to see this now or deal with the seemingly endless list of broken trust issues to get through, she pondered.

She decided on the former and carefully unwrapped the package.

The loving intimacy of the portrait demanded admiration, no matter that she felt slightly shocked at seeing her naked body portrayed in it. Gemma had perfectly captured her and Em; their bodies fitting together, their nakedness not crude but skillfully crafted into a symbol of their love.

"It's beautiful," she said truthfully. "Who saw this photograph?"

"Just me and Gemma. I promise." Em said.

"And when did you take the photo? Did you think to ask me about what I felt or just decided that it was okay to disrespect me?"

"It was a few weeks back. I wanted it to be a surprise." Em said. Her breath caught in her throat.

She felt terrible. She and Mel were private people, not prudish but with no need to overtly flaunt their bodies or sexuality.

"I appreciate that, honey," Mel said calmly. "It's a beautiful thought and I love the painting. I don't love the way you got my photo nor do I appreciate you keeping secrets from me, and I don't like you showing your body to others, especially not public displays. This is something you know." The sentence was long, filled with cracked trust.

Em knew this well and knew it was unfair of her to have not even spoken to Mel about this. She herself had not been comfortable. Why, oh why, had she gone along with all that?

"I'm sorry," she said awkwardly. She could not quite look her lover in the eyes. "I truly...really...am." A sudden distressing thought gave her an insecurity she seldom felt. What if Mel felt she could no longer trust her and wanted to break up?

"Good," Mel said, deliberating as she looked at the bowed head in front of her. "Come here."

Em grit her teeth, whilst at the same time breathing a sigh of relief. Mel was obviously prepared to work through this. That realization did not make the reality of what was about to happen any easier. She hated this part even though she knew it would help her feel better. She shook her shoulders slightly, straightened and started to say, "I am not a..."

Mel walked forward. She knew her lover well. Taking her by the arm she pulled her over her lap. She loved the feel of her partner over her firm thighs, loved seeing the vulnerability of her bottom and thighs over them. It was sensual and yet disciplinary. She knew Em did not find it sexual, but rather that it relieved her pent-up feelings. She could definitely make it sexual and knew Em would respond, but tonight was not about that.

Tonight was about reminding her partner of their relationship agreements and that a lack of disrespect for those agreements resulted in consequences.

She lifted the skirt Em was wearing, exposing the pale, creamy buttocks and thighs. Her pink lace bikini panties were thin and sheer. There was no warm up, no soft pats, just a hard hand hitting the soft bottom and sit spots. She contemplated using the hair brush but decided against it. The bottom over her lap would sting even without any implement. She landed twenty spanks on each buttock. That was far more than she normally gave her. Em did not cry but called out, each slap a stinging reminder of how she had disrespected the woman she loved the most in the world.

"Please stop," she begged. Mel ignored her, changing to the back of her thighs which she knew was especially painful for Em. When she finally felt her body sag, she pulled her up.

Em could not look at her.

"I'm sorry," she said softly, her words penitent, her body pliant with relief. It was easy to speak pleasantly when she felt she had paid the price and was forgiven. She knew that Mel understood her and she accepted this punishment that helped to center her. The words flowed easily from her as though all negative emotions had been released and forgiven.

They discussed why she had gone along with it. Certainly, Em assured her, it would not be a reoccurrence. Mel smiled secretly. She doubted that. Em had a way of going through life centered and calm and then going off the rails until she was helped back onto a safer route again. And she would be there to help her back onto that route no matter what it took.

They sat side by side on the small porch, looking up at the brilliant stars painted on the dark night sky.

"I wonder if they will be okay," Em said. She could not stop thinking about Maria and Marty.

"Let's hope so," Mel said. "We need to give them time. Em. Have you noticed anything between Charlie and Maria-as in-attraction?"

"There always has been-and Marty is aware of that," said Em.

"I could never share you," Mel said. It was clear as to what she was thinking.

"I think Maria could easily share-especially her spankings," Em laughed.

"You're probably correct. Marty could as well," Mel mused, "but only with strict boundaries and I don't think Charlie could live like that."

"She's certainly...amorous, but she'd never cope with the discipline Marty would dish out," Em agreed.

Charlie certainly seemed like someone who would manage, even want more than one partner, but she would need to be in charge.

Mel turned to her and kissed her gently.

"Let's forget about them for now. We have the whole night ahead of us."

Em leaned into her. It felt good to have her secrets out and done with.

In a cabin not far from Mel and Emma's, a different scene was being played out.

Ava had used a cane quite thoroughly on Gemma. This had led to tears and lots of remorse. At the end, relenting on her earlier decision, Ava had changed tactics and quietly taken a crop from her cupboard. She had applied it softly to the sore upturned bottom. Gemma had turned in confusion. This felt different. When Ava nudged her thighs apart and gently slipped the looped end between the opened legs Gemma jerked as it touched her sensitive areas. Instantly she felt wet, her clitoris swelling, the stinging of her bottom now intensifying the heat between her legs.

Ava turned her, leaning close to her mouth, her breath hot and heavy.

"How sorry are you?" she said. Her hand grazed Gemma's one breast through her T-shirt and she arched upward. How she could feel this turned on after that cane spanking was beyond her logic. She could only hopelessly give in to the intense pleasurable sensations.

The quick spank to her thigh had her answering.

"Very…" Her reply was soft.

"Good." The word was breathed close to her mouth and she felt Ava's hand slip between her legs with a firmness she had not felt before.

"Wait here and don't move!" Ava said, dragging her hand across her center.

Gemma gulped. She did not think she could move anyway. She felt glued to the spot by a sense of relief and the intense sexual excitement filling her. Lying with her sore exposed bare bottom over a couch back with only her T-shirt on and wetness pooling between her legs was a new and exciting experience.

She closed her eyes. Whatever Ava was going to show her now she would enjoy with a clear conscience.

Marty sat at the restaurant's bar. She had closed up but had left the lights on around the bar. She cradled a beer, her shoulders slightly hunched over the bar top. Anyone seeing her from outside would have thought the pose lonely and sad. If they had seen her face they would have seen hurt but also strength of determination to live true to her nature.

She finished the beer, turned off the lights and sighing slightly, walked through the kitchen and to her home out the back. It was quiet and dark. Maria needed time to make her choice. She would leave her alone and if she decided to permanently move out or make a life with Charlie, she would not stop her. If she chose to be with

Marty then she needed to remain true to their domestic discipline relationship. She would choose to be single before she gave up her ideals of what made her happy and fulfilled in her life.

CHAPTER 16

Charlie was up early the next morning. She had managed to wake Maria at midnight and help her through to the bedroom, where she had undressed her to her underwear and drawn the covers over her before slipping in beside her.

"Spoon me," Maria's weepy voice had said. She had complied, loving the feel of her sweet friend in her arms.

The angle they had fallen asleep in on the couch was awkward and she massaged her neck in the warm shower. She checked on Maria who was still fast asleep, looking adorable scrunched up with just her black hair peeking out. She left a note to remind her she was going over to Marty's and made her way over to the restaurant. Her shift was that afternoon and she needed to see Marty early before Marty started her day.

She went around to the back. The door was unlocked and she went in calling out a greeting. Marty was in the lounge, coffee in hand. She nodded in response.

"Look..." Charlie said awkwardly running a hand through her blonde hair which showed her dark brown roots coming through.

"I should have told you or at least helped Maria make a better decision."

Marty stayed quiet, hearing her out.

"Well...Perhaps I should have not suggested we run a nude exhibition. I know Maria can be suggestible if an idea is daring enough," she admitted.

Marty nodded.

"True," she said. "To both. You should not have suggested it and you should have told me-us." She looked at the door and Charlie was disconcerted to see Mel and Ava coming through it.

"That said they are adults and independently decided to go ahead with it." Marty added.

Charlie felt uncomfortable, as she watched Ava's serious 'acting manager's' face.

"Sit down ladies, I'll pour you some coffee," Marty said. She moved to the small table where the coffee pot sat steaming.

"Look Charlie, everyone looks to you as the flirter, the fun person, but you know how Maria is. Feisty as she is, she follows you...admires you...is attracted to you." Charlie looked down.

Ava spoke up, fixing her with a stern stare. "Your shenanigans did not help the reputation of the center, either," she said. "I don't want people coming in to see the 'hot trainer' whose body is plastered over Maria's studio walls." "Surely that would help business," Charlie quipped. "More people would want to get buff like me-" Her smile did not reach her eyes. She knew exactly what Ava meant.

"...And what about those who are just there for ogling and asking for 'massages'. We are serious business Charlie. If we lose our reputation that puts all our jobs in jeopardy. It's enough that you already flirt with every woman who walks onto the premises."

Charlie leaned forward, elbows on her spread knees. Damn, she felt bad.

347

Ava carried on. "So, I am suspending your employment for two weeks, starting effectively, whilst you think about your actions and decide if you can fully commit, attitude-wise, to the center."

"You can't do that!"

"Yes, I can...and have. Look at your contract."

Charlie leaned back. This was a far worse outcome than she had thought it would be. The thought of not working made her feel uneasy. It was not a financial concern but more so the feeling of what she would do every day. Her work, which was also her passion, gave her a distinct sense of purpose in her life.

Marty sat forward, an angry glint in her eyes. Charlie had done something that had seriously affected her life. She had not known Ava would suspend Charlie and could see the effect this was having on Charlie. It was probably the best approach to shock Charlie into reflecting on her lifestyle.

"I should take that paddle to you again. Look at the mess you are in now," Marty said.

It should have seemed odd, a top threatening to paddle an obvious dyke looking switch, but it did not. Charlie could feel the care and concern in the room.

Mel looked at the tense, distressed faces.

"Charlie, we are worried about you," she said. "You seem to be so determined to never let anyone- other than Maria get really close to you. You live recklessly and with no seriousness to your life in any way." Before she could continue Marty cut in.

"How is Maria?" Marty bit her tongue; she had been determined not to ask.

Charlie's gaze softened.

"A ball of tears, remorse and confusion," she said honestly.

"I know she's attracted to you," Marty said. "-and you to her." The words were not painfully said, but stated as fact. Attraction in life to others was natural and could not be helped. It was the behavior that went with it that was important. She also found Charlie attractive, but would not act on it.

"Yeah, but it's you she totally loves," Charlie said.

"I'm sorry," continued, turning to Ava and Mel. "I regret being so inconsiderate."

"Thank you for acknowledging that," Ava said. "We will review after two weeks and I'll compile a report. It will go in your file. You will need to come in later today to read through it and sign the action plan going forward."

Charlie nodded. She wanted to get out of there. Marty hesitated. She wanted to spank some sense into this attractive woman, but she could see the self-awareness in Charlie and the struggle she was going through. Now was not the time.

"I'm sorry," she said again. Ava nodded.

"Your clients will be taken by Mel for the next two weeks." Mel looked at Charlie. She felt sorry for her and did not blame her. Em was an adult who had made her own choice to follow Charlie's idea. It would be helpful if Charlie were more sensible, though, for all her mostly toppy manner. In the end, however, she held her partner fully responsible for her own actions, irrespective of Charlie's influence.

"Fine," Charlie said. She stood, hands in pockets and walked out. It was unfair, she thought as she wandered along. She moodily kicked a stone. How would she occupy the next two weeks? Other than her work and flirting she had no hobbies. She also knew as much as she loved Maria, she belonged with Marty. She would have to help her friend see this.

Life seemed bleak. What type of person had nothing when their work was not there? She kicked another stone.

"Ouch!" The word was bitten off. "What the-"

Charlie started. She had not seen the woman in front of her. Her heart rate picked up.

"Isabelle! I'm sorry!"

"It's okay," Isabelle said. The curly haired woman looked as attractive as she had been at the studio. She wore her jogging clothes with elegance. Her eyes still held the same wary look although her tone was as usual, light and friendly.

"No, it's not okay," Charlie said. She was about to ask her out for a drink when she stopped. The woman made her feel differently. This was not someone she wanted to buy a drink for, flirt, kiss, end up in bed with, and leave. She also felt instinctively that that was not Isabelle's style.

"I'm sorry," she said again abruptly and turned away.

Isabelle watched her move off, eyes thoughtful. She had been sure the bold, attractive woman with the glowing honey colored skin and piercing green eyes had been about to ask her out. She was glad she had not. She needed to relax more and think about why and how she had ended up here. Charlie definitely interested her though. She watched the athletic form for a few seconds longer and then turned, heading the way she had been going before the stone had hit her leg.

Charlie got back to her apartment to find that Maria was still in bed, the note she had written lying where she had left it, unread. Although she wanted to sit down and wallow in self-pity, her concern for Maria took over.

"Come on, lazy butt," she said.

"Go away," Maria said groggily. "Leave me alone."

Charlie pulled the bed covers back.

"Come on, honey. I am not going to let you lie here getting more depressed. Get in the shower. I'm making you some breakfast."

"No...not hungry," Maria said. She hunkered back down pulling the duvet over her, lips almost pouting. Charlie pulled the covers back and landed what she knew would be a stinging smack to the buttock nearest to her that peeped out from the edge the black panties.

"Ouch!" Maria shrieked. "Stop that. You are not..." she stopped, tears in her eyes.

"Not what...who...?" Charlie said.

"Nothing," Maria said, warily inching away from Charlie. She got up and slouched over to the bathroom. She started crying again.

"Charlie..." she said, turning back. "I don't know what is wrong-what is wrong with me. I love Marty and yet...yet...I mean I even have my own studio now...and Marty and I have a good life...and yet...yet..."

"Yes?" Charlie said patiently.

"I feel attracted to you...and I hate spanking and I like it and I need it and I don't...and..." The tearful words were tailored off.

Charlie sighed.

"Honey, come on. Chill a bit. The attraction people feel for others is not anything to be ashamed of...it's natural. It's what we do with it that matters."

Maria nodded. How could she feel attracted to both Marty and Charlie though? She was not like Charlie or Marty. Was that why she felt so angry? She leaned against Charlie and Charlie kissed her.

"We can satisfy your lust if you want," she said, "because that is what it is." Maria wanted to. She even knew Marty would accept that-if they were all three of them in a relationship. Did she want that? She lifted her head and kissed Charlie savoring the taste of coffee and warmth and something new and unfamiliar. It was delicious and exciting. Charlie groaned as she touched her breasts, the peaks hard tipped. And then Maria drew back.

"You're gorgeous," she said. "I would totally sleep with you. If only we all were together. Maybe we will one day...?"

"Maybe," Charlie said. Maria seemed clearer. "What is going through your head?"

"You...Marty...me...my work... my pride...my sense of loss. I love Marty-and you," she said. "But-I can't live without her and the love and stability she brings to my life."

Charlie kissed her.

"Then you know what you have to do," she said. It was good to see Maria make her mind up. She felt a sense of loss but not a heart wrenching one. Maria would always be her friend. And who knows...maybe one day they'd all be in a different situation or space. She felt an attraction to both Maria and Marty, not that she would ever let on that she felt drawn to the solid and strong Marty. For now, however, there were decisions to be made and her own life to think about.

"Get showered, get dressed, I'm making breakfast and then we are chatting. Later this evening you know what you've got to do." She spanked the buttocks again, this time playfully, and Maria smiled and hived off into the shower.

"Charlie," she called, "where did you go so early?"

"I'll tell you everything in detail when you've dressed and got some food in you," she said, "I've got some other news. I'm suspended."

"Suspended?!" Maria shrieked, sounding a lot more like her usual fiery self. "Tell me all-"she backed out of the shower.

"Shower, you brat!" Charlie said laughing. "We have the whole day to chat."

CHAPTER 17

That evening Charlie watched Maria walk out the door. Her heart ached but she knew it was right. The feisty, sweet Maria belonged with the steady, sensible Marty. They would always be good friends, the spark they had for each other tempered by the deep affectionate bonds of long-lasting friendship.

She sat back down, her thoughts captured by the lively brunette with the lost look in her eyes. Isabelle was mysterious, open and friendly but with secrets. She felt intrigued and attracted, not just to the woman's body and good looks, but to what she felt was behind that façade of sexiness and friendliness.

Linking her hands behind her head, she stretched. Life was good and endless possibilities lay ahead of her, right in this town with her circle of friends who had become her family. She would be there always for both Maria and Marty, just as surely as she knew they would be there for her.

Maria walked slowly across town. She did not contact Marty via WhatsApp to tell her she was coming. There would be no need for words, she knew that. She refused to allow herself to dwell on any thoughts of whether Marty would accept her back or not.

She knew they deeply loved each other. It was up to her to take the step and win Marty's trust again. No amount of love or egocentrism about her work should disrespect her wife's views and stance. She knew the love was there. It was not easy. She was naturally high spirited and although she responded well to discipline given with love and care, it was at times hard to submit to it. Her life overall was smoother, easier and happier with Marty. She missed her arms around her and the love that she would always feel flooding her when with her wife.

As she walked, she thought of her. Her strong, solid Marty; her deep warm brown eyes and her short blonde hair, the way her breasts lay against her chest, the fleshy part of her thighs and the way she trembled when Maria touched her, the small mole on her lower back... Her heart contracted. With each step she felt wetter. She deliberately ignored the weight of what she carried in her hand and the way her bottom cheeks clenched as she thought of Marty and the night ahead. Instead she focused on the feeling of having her wife in control again and gaining her own sense of focus. The thought of that control made her wet and the walk home much easier.

The external lights of the restaurant driveway came into view and a rush of coming home filled her. The moon was high and bathed the gravel of the yard in a silver sheen. She stood at the back door, lifting her hand and hesitating. She briefly allowed the thoughts of doubt to creep forward now. What if Marty had had enough of her? What if she did not want...the thought halted as the door opened before her hand could knock.

The light behind Marty framed her comfortable figure. She looked strong, beautiful and utterly attractive. Her eyes reflected the tiredness Maria felt. She looked at Maria, her gaze level, even, unwavering and...waiting.

Maria looked back, and then dropped her eyes, unable to hold that look, full of passion, love, pain and firmness. It was a gaze she had seen a million times.

Marty stood silently. Her heart beat loudly in her chest, but she stayed unmoving, watching the slender woman before her. She had noticed the slight intake of breath, the unshed tears in the deep blue eyes-almost elf like in the moonlight, the droop of the shoulders. She exhaled mentally. She knew exactly what this meant.

Maria raised her head again.

"I love you," she said simply. She lifted her hand at the same time, giving to Marty the very implement she knew Marty would need to use.

Marty continued looking at her. Her brown eyes softened. She lifted her own hand and, taking the offered paddle, she took her wife's other hand and pulled her gently in through the front door. Her Maria was home and the paddle would be put to good use before their balance was restored.

She hugged her in the doorway, unable to wait. Maria leant into her, a sob caught in her throat. Relief flooded her entire being. Marty pressed her lips against hers and Maria opened her mouth, submitting to the demanding, plundering tongue, allowing herself to be taken and her heart reclaimed. She was home where she belonged and that was all that mattered. Charlie would join them; she knew that as surely as she knew the force of this woman in front of her. The door closed.

Across the road, a woman with curly brunette hair and a secret behind her soft eyes watched them. It was an intensely personal and private scene and she stayed still so as not to disturb the couple she had seen at the exhibition. Her heart thumped wildly watching the obvious display of love, affection and covert dominance and submission. Her pupils dilated with longing. When the door closed, she released the breath she had not known she was holding and walked on softly, her hips swaying slightly and her eyes dreamy.

Unbidden, the thought that she had been led to this little town by fate invaded her mind. The same as it had been when she had first seen the beautiful woman with dyed blonde hair, her dancing green eyes and flirtatious manner. She laughed gently. Fate; who believed in that?

The End
(For Now)

Thank you for reading this book. If you enjoyed it, I would love it if you would leave a review or rating on Amazon.

Leandra Summers Books

The Eternal Love Stories Series: Lesbian Romance

http://www.amazon.com/dp/B085WVJD5T

The Mountain Town Series: Lesbian Spanking Romance

https://www.amazon.com/dp/B08423ZZXV

For the Love of Her: Lesbian Spanking Romance

https://www.amazon.com/dp/B07NYFHJQd

Jo and Jane: A Lesbian Domestic Discipline Romance

http://www.amazon.co.uk/dp/B07DB9H6DK

Emma and Melissa: Lesbian Spanking Romance. The Mountain Town Series Book 1

http://www.amazon.co.uk/dp/B0788SMVJJ

Ava and Gemma: Lesbian Spanking Romance. The Mountain Town Series Book 2

https://www.amazon.com/dp/B0841LQVGX

Marla: A Lesbian Domestic Discipline Romance Trilogy

http://www.amazon.co.uk/dp/B01HIQ8WJY

Emily's Choice: A Lesbian Domestic Discipline Romance

http://www.amazon.co.uk/dp/B07KXZWZ9B

Instagram

leandrasummers_author